THE TEARS OF DESPAIR

The continuing

Give you joy!

Alan Lawrence.

June '20

ALAN LAWRENCE

In the midwinter frosts, when the seas broke o'er the bow,
On the barky sailed, ever fightin' through the low;
Her deck canted over, her gun'ales deep within the froth,
Every man frozen to the bone, chilled in sodden cloth.

The gale growing stronger, her braces groanin' with the strain,
Homeward bound, the deck a misery in the freezin' rain;
The dear Surprise making water, the ship a shattered mess,
The hurricane raging, hell approaching with the darkness.

The yards all struck down, waves everywhere raging white,
The last of daylight fading, despair coming with the night;
The bilge water ever rising, the boats all smashed away,
The sails long shredded, no hope left of seeing the new day.

Ever on we fought, until that fearful night was left behind,
The fears of all subsiding, hopes afresh astir in every mind;
And there in sight at last, distant off the larboard beam,
Blessed Falmouth town! For every man his precious dream.

The pumps a'workin' hard, the Black Rock at last astern,
As we reached the Carrick Roads, the barky made her turn;
The hated wind gone at last, we brought her about,
From hundreds along the quay, came the welcome shouts.

At last our familiar King's Road, no more the terror of the sea,
And so to the boats, every man pulling hard for the quay;
To the anxious arms of mothers, to families and dear friends,
Welcome tears of joy at last, the voyage at its blessed end.

Winter Homecoming
Alan Lawrence

THE TEARS OF DESPAIR
The continuing voyages of HMS SURPRISE

Until when, brave warriors, shall we live under constraints,
Lonely like lions, in the ridges of mountains?
Living in caves, viewing wild tree branches,
Abandoning the world, due to bitter slavery?
Losing brothers, country and parents,
Our friends, our children, and all of our kin?
Better an hour of free life,
Than forty years of slavery and jail.

> ***Rigas Feraios***
> ***Apostle of the Greek revolution***

A tale of the struggle for Greek independence by
ALAN LAWRENCE

Mainsail Voyages Press Ltd, Publishers,
Hartland Forest, Devonshire
www.mainsailvoyagespress.com

THE TEARS OF DESPAIR
The continuing voyages of HMS SURPRISE

This edition is copyright (c) Alan Lawrence 2019. Published by Mainsail Voyages Press Ltd, Hartland Forest, Bideford, Devon, EX39 5RA. Alan Lawrence asserts the right to be identified as the author of this work in accordance with the Copyright, Designs and Patents Act 1988. The reader may note that this book is written by Alan Lawrence. It is not authorised, licensed or endorsed by Patrick O'Brian's family, agent or publishers. There is no association with any of those parties.

ISBN-13   978-0-9576698-8-8

Story text typeset in Times New Roman 11 point.

All rights reserved. No part of this publication may be reproduced, stored in a retrieval system, or transmitted, in any form or by any means, electronic, mechanical, photocopying, recording or otherwise, without the prior permission of the publishers. Specifically, the author and publishers DO NOT consent to the scanning and/or digitalisation of this book in part or in whole by AMAZON or GOOGLE or any of their subsidiaries or associates, nor by any other entity or individual, which this author and publisher consider would be a flagrant breach of the copyright attaching to this book. This book is sold subject to the condition that it will not, by way of trade or otherwise, be lent, re-sold, hired out or otherwise circulated without the publisher's prior consent in any form of binding or cover other than that in which it is published and without a similar condition being imposed on the subsequent purchaser. A CIP catalogue record for this title is available from the British Library.

Cover painting by Ivan Aivazovsky, *with minor graphic modifications applied by the author.*
Cover comments by Eileen Reynolds, London and Larry Finch, New York.
The Reef Knot graphic in this book is courtesy of and copyright (c) United States Power Squadrons 2006

The continuing voyages of HMS SURPRISE

The series:

The Massacre of Innocents   *(first edition 2014,
second edition 2017)*

   Freedom or Death   *(2017)*

was originally published split within the lengthy first editions of the preceding and succeeding titles, both of which have been abridged for the second editions

The Fireships of Gerontas   *(first edition 2016,
second edition 2017)*

   The Aftermath of Devastation   *(2017)*

   Mathew Jelbert   *(2018)*

   The Tears of Despair   *(2019)*

THE TEARS OF DESPAIR
The continuing voyages of HMS SURPRISE
A FOREWORD BY THE AUTHOR

In this sixth book of my series I have continued the story of both actual historical events and the fictional adventures of my characters directly following on from the end of my previous book. However, although this is a series and each book generally follows on from its predecessor, all of them may be enjoyed as standalone tales.

The modern world's greater understanding of "PTSD" (post-traumatic stress disorder) in large degree began during the First World War. It was remarked upon to a greater extent during the Second when the US Army conducted studies in 1944 of its infantry in North West Europe. Of course, medical understanding of the psychological mechanisms in play were little understood until much more recently; however, as long ago as the early nineteenth century, military commanders such as Clausewitz and Napoleon had at least a limited grasp of the susceptibilities of their men to the debilitating effects of observing and experiencing combat losses, both men always keeping the most careful dispositions of their reserves in mind during a battle.

Nineteenth century warfare was characterised by brief battles of one, two or three days duration, and this facilitated the mental recovery of participants during the long periods between exposure to combat. However, the infantryman in the trenches, when wars became greatly more static, had far less opportunity to escape the constant strain of duty, usually under interminable artillery bombardment. Hence it was only these later, more cataclysmic and far lengthier wars which provided the surfeit of evidence with which to grasp that something, little understood, was happening in the minds of men who were exposed to hell on earth. Before this emerging plethora of material there was only a very incomplete picture and the most severely limited comprehension of what might be done to help the soldier who was afflicted; rest alone was helpful but did not 'cure' the patient.

The scale of the effect in terms of the number of combatants afflicted by psychological distress (and lost to their commanders as "effectives") is, even today, little grasped by the public, but it cannot be overstated. For example, in World War Two the U.S.A. lost over half a million men to psychiatric collapse*

The effects on individuals are deep seated, long enduring, and may not present themselves until some considerable time after the traumatic events they are exposed to. Severely afflicted unfortunates in far too many instances decide that they cannot continue with life itself: fifty-eight ex-British Army veterans killed themselves in 2018. In the United States the Veterans Administration estimates that more Vietnam veterans have killed themselves than were lost to death in combat*, a statistic which is truly shocking. Yet in the 21st century, when the causes of these psychological afflictions are so much better understood and more effective treatment is at hand, the military establishment only devotes relative pennies to help the sufferers: a mere twenty-two million pounds in the UK in 2018. This represents 0.006% of the UK's thirty-six billion pounds defence budget.

source: David Grossman & Bruce Siddle, Psychological Effects of Combat. An excellent article which I recommend.

I would like to express my grateful thanks to my helpers with this particular title: Helen Hardin and Caroline Roberts for editing, and my Sally for her support.

At the end of this book is a glossary of contemporary words occurring within the story with which the reader new to the naval historical world may be unfamiliar.

This book is dedicated to all those men and women of all the armed forces of the world who, as a consequence of their devoted service, still struggle with the stress-related mental burdens of it.

'Give you joy, shipmate! Come aboard! Voyage with HMS Surprise! Share her crew's reminiscences in familiar old haunts and revel too in their exciting new adventures. Come aboard! Swiftly now, there is not a moment to be lost!'

Alan Lawrence   *June 2019*

THE TEARS OF DESPAIR
The continuing voyages of HMS SURPRISE
HISTORICAL NOTE

The western Greek town of Messalonghi (variously Missolonghi and Messolonghi) first faced an unsuccessful Ottoman siege in December of 1822; it was followed by another in the months September to November of 1823, the besiegers giving up because of inadequate resupply arrangements for their military forces at the time of the advent of winter. The precursor to this second siege was a bombardment and attempt to capture the island town of Anatolico (modern day Aitolikon) to the north-west of Messolonghi; however, the Turks failed to capture the island.

The town of Messolonghi, it might be argued, was to some degree strategically located: it was situated on the north side of the approach to the Gulf of Patras through which seaborne access was afforded to Nauplia, the temporary wartime capital for the provisional Greek government. In such a location it could always conceivably present the opportunity for Greek nautical brigands to interdict Turk traffic bound for the port of Patras on the south side of the Gulf (in Turk hands). However, Messalonghi's considerable disadvantage was (and still is) that it possesses no deepwater anchorage, it has no port, and the shallow saltwater marshes and lagoons all about the town offer water to a depth of little more than a metre, and that in only the smallest areas.

The narrow access channel (for small boats, typically flat-bottom fishing boats) to the town's beaches from the deeper waters of the Gulf was guarded in 1826 by the outlier island of Vasiladi, which the Greeks had fortified with a disparate collection of artillery pieces. Their eventual escape from that island through the cold shallows was the most desperate affair.

The Turks returned to try for the third time to capture Messalonghi in April 1825, beginning a siege which would endure for a year until the calamitous end in April 1826.

All dates referred to within this book are of the Gregorian calendar.

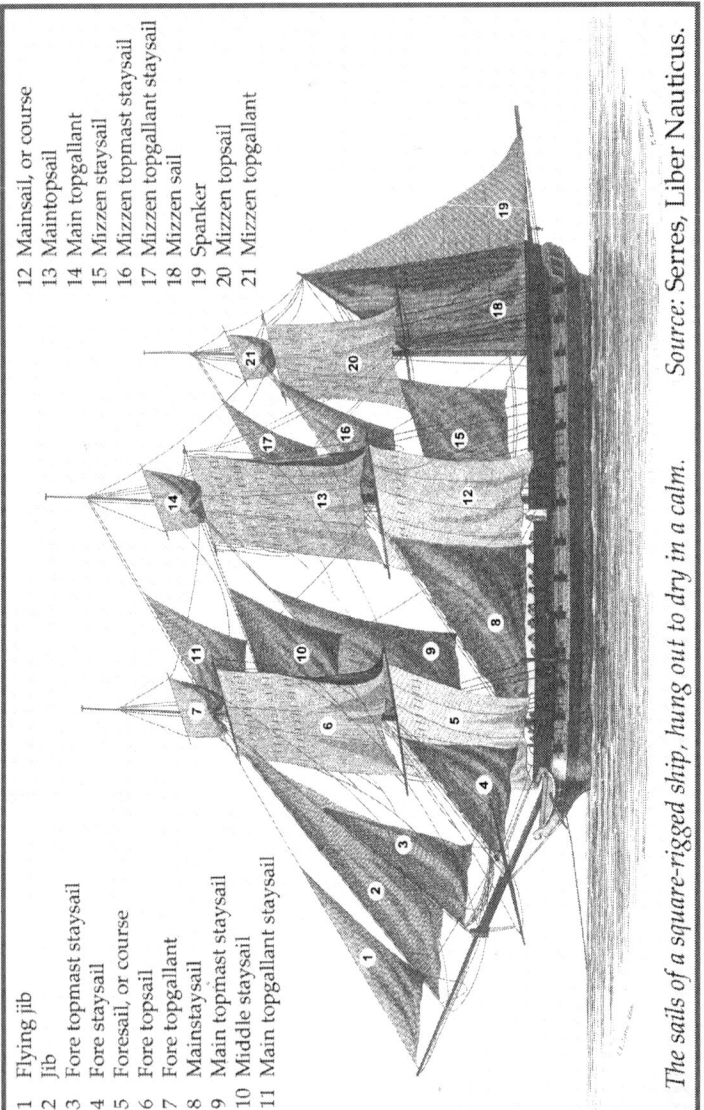

The sails of a square-rigged ship, hung out to dry in a calm. *Source:* Serres, Liber Nauticus.

1. Flying jib
2. Jib
3. Fore topmast staysail
4. Fore staysail
5. Foresail, or course
6. Fore topsail
7. Fore topgallant
8. Mainstaysail
9. Main topmast staysail
10. Middle staysail
11. Main topgallant staysail
12. Mainsail, or course
13. Maintopsail
14. Main topgallant
15. Mizzen staysail
16. Mizzen topmast staysail
17. Mizzen topgallant staysail
18. Mizzen sail
19. Spanker
20. Mizzen topsail
21. Mizzen topgallant

Chapter One

The blinding light, painful to the eyes, was beginning to lose the edge of its earlier, burning intensity, but the fierce, searing ferocity that had been the noon sun, many hours ago, still persisted in the cloudless sky. The air temperature remained baking hot, even so late in the afternoon, a luminescent fire still enduring, radiating from the rapidly sinking, yellow orb. Its debilitating heat severely taxed the weary ship's crew, all standing in silence about the great guns. Without exception, every man exhibited the utmost exhaustion; all were filthy, dog-tired and streaked with sweat which dripped down their grimy faces, an abundance of powder smoke in dirty black rivulets running down bare chests, every man soaked about the waist.

A shattered and debilitated Captain Patrick O'Connor, in command and standing near the helm, stared all around him in grim assessment. The mere few minutes of respite afforded him was the most precious and short interlude in which to take stock. It was the briefest of reprieve from the brutal ferocity of the enemy's attack, the onslaught of several frigates of the Turk fleet, a conflagration which *Surprise* had already endured for many hours. There was yet one more, infinitely painful and anxiety-ridden hour to come before the sunset which O'Connor prayed for, one more hour which he passionately hoped he might still see, sixty more anxious minutes before there was even the slightest prospect of finding sanctuary in the coming cloak of darkness. But that was a very long time indeed, an interminable age, for his cruelly battered ship and his exhausted men in which to continue to hold out, and to his own desperately tired mind it was truly the tallest of orders. He squinted with sore, reddened eyes as he stared in bleak despond at the battle-damaged bulwarks of his ship; he gazed at the scattered detritus of scores of broken timber shards strewn all over his quarterdeck, and he heard only vaguely the vigorous flapping of multiple severed strands of the standing rigging, blowing about in the wind. He glanced up to make a rapid inspection of the mizzen topsail, much rent by long, vertical tears and perforated by a great many holes; but, most demoralising of all, he scrutinised his men, and that every one of them remained hardly able to stand was plain to see. Yet, somehow, they endured, they struggled on, just barely surviving; although he was sure that they too were lingering in similar despair to himself, with infinite determination still hanging on. How, he did not know, for there could be nothing left of their final reserves of energy, every last ounce of it expended, utterly. From where they found the will to fight on, to persevere, he knew not; and he marvelled, for the last vestiges of his own strength were all but finished. He tottered, he swayed, nothing left of vigour to drive his weary muscles; he wavered on shaking legs of jelly, and he clutched the waist rail above the gun deck for support. He wondered again, bleakly, for how much longer his veterans, his shipmates of many years, might yet hold out. It could not be much more than a mere handful of minutes, just a final few; he was sure of that, but he forced himself, with a mighty effort of willpower, to stand bolt upright in case any of his men might perceive his own weak fragility and be set back by sight of his evident and absolute physical exhaustion. With tired, smoke-ringed eyes he turned to gaze aft, and he concluded, with just the tiniest flicker of hope, that *Surprise's* larboard pursuer was a little further astern; not much, perhaps fifty yards more. Was she slowing? With a sickening feeling of rude realisation, his brief flash of optimism ebbed away, was brutally extinguished: the enemy frigate had slowed only because the jagged, rocky shore on the larboard bow was looming ever closer. Still, at least for the moment, she was incapable of firing upon his fleeing, cruelly battered ship, save for perhaps her pair of bow chasers, relatively ineffectual and of small calibre: guns which could hardly make the slightest difference, his ship already so greatly smashed and damaged.

Surprise rolled, nearly indiscernibly, on the slight swell, the wind on her starboard beam pushing her with a leeway drift ever closer to those dangerously near rocks and to ultimate wrecking. The possibility of escape was patently so slim whilst she toiled in the feeble breeze, such as the wind was, to haul off. She had been striving to do so for hours already, her progress interminably slow; seeking to slip away towards the south, in hope of a safety which, Patrick O'Connor himself had reluctantly concluded, she would never make, could never reach, before her second attacker, a powerful forty-four gun frigate on her starboard quarter, closed to finish her off, to pound her to final destruction with those heavy guns she so clearly possessed and which he had studied through his glass. With plentiful water available to her, that Turk ship to starboard was exploiting her windward benefit to creep closer, albeit her own progress was tortoise-like in the weak breeze. Her languid approach was studied by every Surprise, her purpose obvious, as they all stared in bleak assessment of what would be, what must be coming, and in very short order. The heavy guns of the forty-four had been firing for some time at long range, the occasional shot ricocheting over the water to weakly strike *Surprise's* hull with a dull thud or, more often than not, to fall short and sink into the low, rolling waves.

That Turk captain must possess a plentiful supply of powder and shot, thought O'Connor, for of his own he had precious little left of both. Closer, the minutes ticking by whilst the weary Surprises were standing waiting, a resigned and unnatural silence pervaded the decks. All the guns stood loaded and ready; all gun captains awaited the order to fire. O'Connor spat out a congealing, glutinous gob of thick phlegm, bitter with the taste of powder, coppery with the flavour of blood, for he had bitten his tongue a half-hour previously when one of his nearby men had been shot down, a strike from a musket aboard that pursuer to larboard which had since fallen back. He looked all about him once more for a flash of inspiration, for a helpful idea, anything, the least thing; but for the umpteenth time nothing would come to mind, and he sighed. His despairing conclusion was that *Surprise* was entirely at the mercy of the oncoming enemy frigate to starboard; there was not the slightest means of improving the situation, and his morale sank to new depths. With a heavy heart he looked over the rail and down to the gun deck; his officers were all below, standing ready about the great guns: Duncan Macleod, his longstanding friend and First Officer, was in the most dangerous place at the waist guns, the slaughterhouse, as it was known, for midships collected the greatest onslaught of often poorly-aimed enemy shots, fired from the rolling instability of a ship's deck. Lieutenant Pickering was just visible, closer to the foc'sle and commanding the forward division, and Lieutenant Codrington was doubtless aft within the great cabin. There would soon be precious little left within it, save perhaps for bloody bodies and smashed wooden fragments, thought O'Connor, exhaling with another despairing sigh.

He stared to starboard at the Turk frigate. She had approached a little closer in the short minutes whilst he had been thinking. The firing of her guns was now even more immediate upon the senses, distinct, louder. The billowing clouds of her gun smoke were reaching *Surprise*, the recurring strong smell of it being pungent and unpleasant to the nose, and bitter to the taste. The more proximate Turk shot had become sharply perceptible as it whistled overhead or, with breaking, crashing thuds, smashed hard upon the hull. The increased violence and destructive power of the cast iron ball strikes and the consequent vibrations were much more strongly felt than a half-hour ago, reverberating throughout the deck planks of unyielding oak. O'Connor despaired in bleak conclusion: the dreaded final scene had come at long last; the Turk's heavy fusillades were about to be unleashed, and utter catastrophe would be upon his ship and his men in very short order. In a mere few minutes all would be over, the barky would be finished, burning; and his crew, likewise, would all be either dead or drowning. He looked again at the faces of those near shipmates with whom he had sailed for many years, steadfast people who believed in him; was this, after so long together, now the end? Was it really goodbye to his fighting comrades and dear friends? Another near strike from a Turk shot resonated through the deck and his maudlin thoughts were cruelly interrupted.

'FIRE!' The scream of his own command, his desperation audible within it, was followed immediately by the high-pitched crack as the aftmost carronade exploded. Eight feet of searingly bright, orange flame erupted from the short, stubby, black barrel of the smasher, as if akin to the most violent, intemperate flash released from Hell itself. It was followed immediately by the resounding, loud crash as the iron gun smashed back in vicious recoil within its slide against the retaining oak frame. 'FIRE!' Its fellow roared from three yards further forward on the quarterdeck, spitting its flaming, incandescent venom to launch a heavy thirty-two-pound shot at the oncoming enemy frigate. 'FIRE!' Captain Patrick O'Connor could not, by now, hear his own voice. His ears were being violently assaulted and wholly overwhelmed by the ferocious noise of the roaring barrage of fire from the Turk and his own carronades. The third gun, nearest the waist rail, exploded its charge, beginning its own furious attack, the quarterdeck all around suffused with a dense, grey fog of powder smoke, fiery in the lungs, choking. The air he gasped was so much hotter, bitter and poisonous. Simply breathing was becoming an uncomfortable struggle. All three gun crews raced furiously, their men in a frantic hurry, swabbing the barrels with desperate application, manically rushing to load the wetted wads and the fresh powder charges; the iron shot was so heavy that it was only with great difficulty that the weakened men could load it into the steaming mouths of the hot carronades. The air temperature, augmented by the radiating guns and their boiling discharge of noxious fumes, was supercharged with heat, unbearably so. Beyond frantic, O'Connor stared, wild-eyed, all about him; every man on the starboard side of his quarterdeck was striving like a maniac to serve their gun, every one of them bathed in rivers of sweat. The smoke particles of burnt powder speckled their faces with black spots, ingrained itself into grimy skin pores of cheeks smeared by rivulets of lather. Black dust, blotchy and mottled, covered naked torsos. Every man was exerting himself, racing to new heights of frenzy in a furious haste; each one, somehow, from somewhere and with great willpower, had found final vestiges of strength to lift the back-breaking heavy iron balls to reload the carronades. Incoming shot, ever more of it, whistled through the air, its presence felt with a pushing wave of pressure as it ripped close by. One shot smashed into the bulwark to send a flying spray of long and viciously sharp oak splinters showering into the aftmost carronade crew, all four men struck hard; one man was simply hurled across the whole width of the deck, staggering on his legs, helpless; another was flung backwards on his feet to fall over the stern rail of the frigate, utterly powerless to help himself.

With strength he did not know he possessed, O'Connor rushed forward to the waist rail to scream out to the men attending the great guns on the deck below, all still patiently awaiting his order, powder so short. His furious thoughts raced, not a moment to lose! 'FIRE!' As one the starboard battery erupted with a titanic explosion, all the planks of the deck pulsating violently, the frigate in its entirety rolling to larboard as if wrested by a giant hand. He turned about and staggered in his weakness back to the wheel. The larboard gunners, standing by, were reloading that starboard carronade whose crew had all been struck down by flying splinters. 'FIRE!' Jeremiah Prosser, the master, shouted, and the remaining two guns, already reloaded, exploded again to send their metal fury on its way, grape added to the solid shot so as to tear sails and shred the fragile bodies of men. The attacking Turk was noticeably closing in, from eight hundred yards on the starboard quarter when her own firing had opened, to a dangerous two hundred yards on the beam when *Surprise* had, only now, replied; just a cable, only the one, separated the roaring, flaming titans which were the two frigates; violent and agonising death was inexorably approaching in the blazing, raging fury of great guns. 'FIRE!' screamed Prosser again, his filthy face a bright red frenzy despite his tan, a ferocious fury visibly radiating from the blackened, sunken recesses of his wild, manic eyes.

The stricken men of the smashed carronade had been hauled away by their comrades from the other side of the quarterdeck; they themselves were blessed by their own adversary on *Surprise's* larboard quarter falling further back once again. Perhaps that respite was only temporary for, although the approaching rocks of the shore were much closer and very visible in the surging, white wash of breaking waves, clear water beckoned not far beyond the near and obvious danger. At least for the moment that looming danger had deterred that Turk captain from trying to haul closer.

'FIRE!' The middle one of the three carronades exploded once more, and the foul air all about the quarterdeck was immediately recharged with bilious, drifting, hot smoke; suffused with another surge of noxious powder particles, a stinking cloud swirling back all about the helm, a choking miasma of fiery dust which seared hot lungs already struggling with desperate exertion for life-giving air. Every man reacted with more bouts of painful coughing, and rapidly-beating chests were wracked by agonies of burning discomfort. All visibility was nearly totally obscured in the powder fog, and man after man blinked, without the least success, to clear sore red eyes of the smarting, irritating dust spicules; every man was spitting violently to clear the sulphurous, poisonous, choking hot and polluted air from dry mouths and nostrils violently protesting its invasion. Brutal crashes announced another Turk broadside of heavy shot, raging in all along the length of the ship, unmistakeable in the heavy thudding crash and break of strikes, of smashing sounds erupting everywhere as bulwarks, yards and the lower hull itself protested, all resonating with the powerful force of the destructive impacts.

Yet more men were struck down; at the helm, Nancekivell was smashed square in the chest by shot, his body brutally ripped in two as the top of his torso flew through the air to slap against the mizzen boom, his legs a jellied splatter on the mizzen mast; pints of blood were thrown out in a liquid explosion; torn flesh and indescribable gore sprayed every man within three yards. On, yet closer still, came the attacking Turk frigate, the powerful forty-four-gun ship possessing guns of a heavier calibre than *Surprise*. There was just a mere hundred yards of separation remaining between them, only half a cable! Bright flashes of red-orange flame poured from all along her side as a thunderous wave of fiery light, visible even through the grey, near-black, powder-enriched and dense smog of gun smoke, the Turk's heavy solid shot striking *Surprise* instantly, plentiful loud cracking noises audible throughout the unendurable cacophony of great guns firing; men everywhere were grateful for temporary deafness. The deep smashing resonations underfoot were stronger than ever before amidst the higher pitch of the cracking explosions from those nearer carronades still firing on the quarterdeck. The mainmast was struck a glancing blow, a long shard of its dense, hardened spruce splintering and breaking away with a sharp, splitting, tearing noise. Worse, the topmast was simultaneously falling, the stabilising tension gone as its stays were ripped away, the driving force which was the topsail pushing the falling mass forwards. A cascade of heavy yards, a myriad hemp rigging and a mass of torn canvas all came tumbling down to envelop and obstruct the midships gunners.

Heads all about the deck were turning to stare at the unfolding disaster, every seasoned veteran aboard ship immediately sensing the ship's roll further accentuated. Eyes everywhere gazed in horror: the Turk forty-four was no more than fifty yards away, and yet she was still closing! Rising fear was beginning to show and to spread, alarmed faces abounded everywhere about the decks. At *Surprise's* waist her guns had ceased firing whilst men rushed all about the confusion in a furious frenzy to try and clear the debris, abject and general panic looming close. A shocked and despairing Patrick O'Connor looked up to the remaining sails; vastly more numerous small holes were readily apparent to even the most cursory inspection, and the lengthening rents and tears of canvas under strain were much more visible than ever before. He looked forward to his ship's sides: many more flapping ends of the standing rigging had become evident, the tough hemp visibly cut through by the grapeshot which the Turk was, discernibly, now firing. Its shrill, whistling noise was heard and feared by every man; grape: it was fifty or more sizeable pellets of metal which inflicted the most terrible of wounds; larger than a musket ball, just one or two such fragments usually meant an agonising death: the surgeons simply could not cope with the multiple injuries inflicted by it, possessed no remedy for such; the fast-flying hail would rip through vital organs and usually leave the injured man with a swift but painful end. Only a very few were fortunate enough to survive a close strike from grapeshot.

Pat's mind momentarily flashed to a visualisation of what he knew would be a scene of hell below deck; his surgeon and close friend, Doctor Simon Ferguson, was sure to be overwhelmed already, the ferocity of the firing so destructive to his men. He looked about him just as, at the helm, another veteran was smashed away from the wheel: Chegwin, a long-serving shipmate, was struck on his shoulder by solid shot, tearing his arm away, the crushed remnants of the bloody limb flashing by, high in the air, in a shower of gore. Chegwin briefly screamed as he swivelled in a half turn until he crashed to the deck, fresh puddles of blood everywhere about his body.

The noise of the Turk guns, so close, so loud, had become simply unbearable, even to minds long inured to it and ears deafened by it; the close proximity and violence of the cracking explosions and the fear engendered by them could not conceivably be restrained by any deliberate mental effort any longer; shot whooshed by within its own obtrusive and frightening pressure wave, flying close through the air; grape was assaulting the ear and the mind as it declared its dangerous presence by whistling by; every sound of every kind and from every source was grown much louder, the origin of the boom and crack of the firing so very close, so desperately threatening. It was plain to everyone that Pat's ship and men had little time left.

Although *Surprise* had also struck her starboard attacker hard, the Turk captain was plainly an obdurate man, seemingly determined on coming alongside. Perhaps, as many of the Surprises wondered in the desperate seconds between loading guns, he was also intent on boarding? Captain Patrick O'Connor himself dismissed the fleeting idea: the Turk ship would doubtless have many Greek slaves serving her guns, attending her sails; such men would have not the least interest in boarding even as they toiled under the greatest duress to fire upon their own friend.

So close now, the smoke from the two frigates' firing wholly filled the air between them with the densest, the most billowing, great grey clouds of noxious gas, to the extent that the Turk hull could no longer be made out at all; only the ever-rising, deafening noise and her bright gun flashes revealed her nearer proximity. What to do? Pat O'Connor, frantic and beside himself with anxiety and fearful frustration, possessing no idea nor any time left to save his ship, looked about him in stark desperation. Somehow, but only just, he was still managing to suppress his own rising feelings of panic whilst wracking his brain yet again for an answer, anything, any idea at all. A disabled *Surprise* could not open the gap from her attacker; she possessed no sea room to change course, to bear away, for the rocks to larboard were worryingly close, much less than half a cable off the beam. It was also not in his power to alter her sail plan, to slow down, to try to hide on her near adversary's quarter where enemy guns, at least for a brief few minutes of respite, could not register. Neither was it remotely possible to try for another half-knot, to draw ahead and put *Surprise* on her adversary's bow, for her courses were reefed as short as could be, to "fighting canvas", and the maintopsail damage had not yet been cleared away; worse, very little of sound canvas did she possess in her foretop, mizzentop and jibs after suffering a great many tearing rents. He wiped fresh blood spray from his face, salt sweat taking away something of the stinging powder dust from his sore eyes as he blinked, and he surveyed his quarterdeck in something very near to panic: there were only two men remaining standing at the helm. He struggled in the billowing powder smoke to make out any detail of his ship forward of the waist rail; at least he could hear, indistinctly, that those guns nearer the bow were still firing and his quarterdeck carronades nearby continued to be served by his veterans, no man ceasing to swab, load and fire as fast as ever they could. But it was not enough, it would not save them; no, *Surprise* seemingly had no means of escape. His frantic mind raced with considerations of the most desperate measures. What on earth could he do? What was possible? The nearest Turk had closed to no more than twenty-five yards off the starboard beam - just twenty-five yards! Pat's mind raced: the enemy frigate was so close that he could not fathom how their yard tips had not clashed already. It was difficult to be sure of the precise gap remaining between them amidst the fog of gun smoke, but it surely would not be more than a yard or two within a mere few seconds. With another surge of alarming panic, Pat realised that it was conceivable that such close proximity would very likely spark a fire aboard the Turk when *Surprise's* great guns' flames set the receptive resin of her rigging and her dry sails afire, but that was also a prospect for both vessels, and such would surely doom his own ship in the resultant mutual conflagration, for not a man could be spared to fight fire, not that any of them still possessed the least strength to do so. Nothing could he think of to save the situation, and so he reluctantly concluded, because of the perilous risk of fire, that he must take the precaution of drowning the magazines and turning *Surprise* towards her attacker, to force a collision. Such was truly the last throw of the dice, the most desperate measure, for in so doing he must send his remaining men to board the Turk when his ship rolled as close as she could ever be.

'MR REEVE!' Pat shouted with all the voice he still possessed to the only officer near at hand, 'DROWN THE MAGAZINES!' Reeve looked horrified, aghast. A fleeting hesitation of a second or two, the junior lieutenant frozen in horror as the implications registered, and he rushed for the steps in great haste.

The forced collision and boarding was the most last ditch action Pat had ever decided on in all his life at sea; it was also one which was hardly likely to succeed, he realised, for his men were simply shattered, utterly exhausted. Simply standing up was an excruciating trial for them; worse, more Turk vessels were approaching from astern, and they would surely come to the aid of the boarded forty-four; but perhaps the Surprises could hold out just a little longer, a few minutes more, until the sun's weakening light eventually gave out, when the coming of dusk proper and its weak twilight might aid them, for the Turks were never keen to fight at night. No other notion could he think of, *Surprise* was enduring her most endangered moments ever, fighting for her life and that of her men, precious little time remaining to save her, to save his stalwart shipmates. A very few minutes was all that was left to them now. Another carronade gunner was shot down to the deck before his eyes, fresh blood splatter spraying again all over his face, the coppery tang tasting strong on his lips. Ignoring it and the fast-fading strength in his legs, he stumbled forwards a few paces and shouted towards the burly figure helping at the foremost carronade on the quarterdeck, 'DALBY! DALBY!' He looked back once more through the swirling fog of choking, hot smoke to the helm. The great shock smashed into his mind and every fibre of his being with a flood tide of terror: there was no longer a single man left standing at the wheel. All the helmsmen lay dead, dying or injured on the deck. 'DALBY!' He screamed forward in a fresh surge of fear, stark panic for the first time taking its debilitating hold on his frenzied mind; 'DALBY, TO THE WHEEL!' Then came the violence of the collision; CRASH! The Turk frigate had smashed into the side of *Surprise,* rocking the ship violently, the Turk's yard tips overhead and engaged in locked cohesion with *Surprise's* own, and then a Turk ball smashed away much of the wheel itself, a great part of the helm simply disappearing. More shards of deadly wooden splinters exploded from the strike to shower his surviving and frantic carronade crews, another three men being struck down. The master gunner himself was one of them, hurled against the stern rail by a large fragment. Pat, close by, could see blood pouring from several wounds in the gunner's naked chest, his mouth spilling a stream of dark red froth even as he struggled to cough, writhing in pain and fighting to draw breath. Pat, terrified himself now, beheld a scene of unmitigated horror: the shrill, shrieking screams of the injured nearby were registering in his ears even over the explosions of those few of *Surprise's* guns still firing. Abject panic was running riot, consuming him entirely, flooding his mind and body, almost wholly overwhelming all rational thought. He screamed out again as loudly as he could, 'DALBY! MASON! TO THE WHEEL!' More men were needed urgently, nothing was more pressing. Desperate men would surely manage the remnants of the smashed helm, somehow. He felt his final vestiges of strength melting away as his protesting legs gradually gave way beneath him, nothing left of energy to hold his slide towards the deck, and he clutched the mizzenmast for support. His thoughts in a frenzy, he knew full well that he must have more men at the helm and very quickly; a handful at least must come to the broken wheel immediately, and one of his very few officers was needed to lead the last desperate throw, the boarding party; but where were they and how did they fare? He wondered momentarily, his thinking clouding in a fog of racing, conflicting pressures, how his First, Duncan Macleod, was faring. By now many men would surely be killed and wounded below in the ship's waist. He could see unmoving bodies lying on the deck between the guns. His great friend had been tasked with command on the gun deck but had not reported since. Had he been one of those struck down? Was he even still alive? A gust of wind brought swirling gun smoke across the quarterdeck and Pat could see nothing further in the choking powder smog save for the immediate few yards before him. His attention returned to the absolute priority: the wheel must be attended! His final vestiges of strength gone, and sinking to his knees, he waved his arm again most frantically in desperate gesture, 'DALBY! OVER HERE! DALBY! DALBY!'

A sweating and terrified Patrick O'Connor, breathing in great gasps of air, his chest taxing itself with fast, pulsating exertions, turned his head towards a familiar voice breaking through the vivid scene of abject horror all about him. He opened his eyes wide and sat bolt upright in the darkness as he heard the totally confusing and wholly incongruous words once more: 'Wake up, brother; I beg you will wake up!' Simon Ferguson murmured encouragingly from his bedside, pushing Pat gently on his shoulder. 'You are safe! You are here in Falmouth town... *you are safe...* safe at the Royal Hotel. You were dreaming, *a nightmare for sure*; I heard your shouts... *so loud...* from the next room.'

'THANK GOD!' shouted a still half-asleep and horrified Pat, blinking rapidly and wiping his eyes as his peripheral vision registered in the dim light of almost total darkness the image of his friend, Simon Ferguson, crouching low at his bedside and clutching a small candle. He turned his ashen face towards Simon as his breathing began to slow, the frantic pounding of his chest subsiding. 'Thank God...' he exclaimed, still sucking air in great gulps. 'Thank God and all the saints...' he gasped, his voice still loud even as a greater awareness of where he really was began, only slowly, to register with him; 'I was back at Navarino... escaping the bay...' Pat was whispering now, 'Oh my God! Our men serving the carronades... shot down and dying on the quarterdeck before my eyes... *dying...* Jelbert dying... our master gunner himself... and no escape... *there was no escape...*'

For the first time he felt the chilly damp of his sweat-soaked nightshirt, rapidly cooling in the freezing, wintry air of the unheated room. 'Oh, dear God, I was there... in hell again... the thunderous noise... the flames and smoke of the great guns firing... the air choking... I could feel and taste it all again... the barky being smashed... shot and splinters flying everywhere... and our lads... our shipmates... a dozen dead all about me... blood everywhere... *so much blood*. It was so real... *so very real...*'

Monday 12th December 1825   16:00   Royal Hotel, Falmouth

The door from the street had opened for only the briefest of moments when the subdued flames of the coals in the hearth erupted with exceptional vigour in response to the surging, bitterly cold draught flooding in forcefully across the slate flagstones. The fire's flickering, bright orange fingers blazed up to throw at least the semblance of a welcoming warmth throughout the room to greet the new arrival. Captain Patrick O'Connor, his breath steaming as he paused momentarily within the doorway, entered in haste, swiftly closing the door against the prevailing deep chill as unfriendly faces everywhere stared in uncomfortable, silent condemnation. For two seconds his body shook involuntarily, the ambient temperature within the bar making not the least impression after freezing in the glacial air outside, a tribulation which he had endured since the wintry dawn, eight frigid hours ago, the grey, rainy misery seeming like the slowest day of his life.

His numbed, frozen fingers wrestled with painful difficulty with the buttons of his thick sea coat as his thoughts drifted to a recollection of the snow which had, quite exceptionally, fallen in London back in late October. Only a brief instant passed before another unwelcome weather event came to the forefront of his memory: the gales of great ferocity experienced in Falmouth in early November. He shivered again, shaking his whole body and head as if, in so doing, it was possible to cast off the numbing chill, and he frowned as he wondered, gloomily, if the two unusually severe meteorological events, together with the uncomfortable, freezing cold of the day, might presage an enduring frosty winter. With another shudder and a shrug of his shoulders, and after a long sigh, he forced himself to dispel that most dismal of thoughts, and he clapped his unfeeling hands to restart some semblance of circulation and at least the beginnings of a modicum of sensation in his finger tips. He looked up, towards the fireplace, and he paced swiftly towards the glorious attraction of the glowing, fiery coals, glancing all about him to see if his expected friend or anyone else he might recognise might be seated within the deep shadows of the corners of the dimly-lit room. A score of people were taking refuge from the weather and enjoying afternoon tea, several with stronger libations catching his eye, but there was no one present whom he knew and certainly no sign of his friend. He shivered again and began to try once more with his coat buttons, small inklings of feeling returning to his frozen hands.

'Good afternoon, sir,' declared the attentive waiter in bright voice, approaching with a smile, 'Your customary coffee, will it be?'

'If you would be so kind; thank you, Trewin,' whispered Pat, returning the greeting with a vigorous nod as he struggled still with numbed fingers to discard the heavy weight of his coat, with considerable difficulty fighting to remove its leaden burden. The waiter helped him off with it as Pat stood, shaking again violently with cold tremors, for a few more moments until he was finally unencumbered and ready to be seated. 'A pot and *two* cups if you will!' he shouted to the departing Trewin. He shivered again for further long seconds before pulling the chair closer to the fire, its warmth such a blessed relief. A minor feeling of touch in his fingers flagged the start of his trembling release from cold discomfort. Another long sigh and his thoughts drifted back to those of his officers with whom he had spent the frostiest of days; they still remained at the quay for a little while longer, engaged in investigation aboard the new pilot cutter, *Mathew Jelbert*. Pat's men had taken charge of her from the shipyard crew who had brought her from Newham, near Truro, during the morning of the previous day; and all his fellow officers from the frigate *Surprise* were still aboard the cutter, except for his ship's surgeon and dearest friend in all the world,

Simon Ferguson, the man he awaited. Ferguson had devoutly and diligently attended their wounded shipmates of *Surprise* every day for almost four months since they had returned from the war in Greece.

Pat shook off a momentary recollection of his nightmare of hours ago, and he made a determined effort to recall the poignant events of yesterday; it had been probably the most moving occasion of his life, the naming ceremony of the new cutter; the vessel being named in tribute to that most respected of all his former shipmates, the veteran gunner, Mathew Jelbert. He had been killed as the endangered frigate fought to escape the Greek Bay of Navarino whilst being surrounded and fired upon by the invading Turk fleet. For four dreadfully destructive and desperate hours, almost completely becalmed during the afternoon, with scarcely more than the lightest breeze to help the beleaguered frigate, the experience had seemed akin to being in a veritable Sargasso of time itself: time frozen, time which had seemed suspended, whilst all about them the frenzied battle had been unceasing. With no wind to speak of, a fury of shot from many Turk guns had poured in to crush, smash and destroy the stricken barky and her men. Pat shivered involuntarily at the intrusive, vivid and horrible recollection, his spirits plummeting. Survival had truly been a mighty close run thing, miraculous even; only the coming of the night, so soon after Mathew Jelbert's own hand-made incendiary shells had been fired to destroy *Surprise's* nearest attacker, had saved them, but tragically, not the master gunner himself; for he had been struck down by virtually the last shot of the battle, dying on the quarterdeck, coughing a red froth and amidst a torrent of blood spilling from his chest in a despairing Pat's arms, whilst the ship's surgeon, Simon Ferguson, looked on in abject distress. There had been not the least thing that either of them could do to help their stricken shipmate.

Pat forced his mind back to yesterday's important event; the naming ceremony had been an entirely unexpected occasion, the cutter being delivered only on the morning prior to the remembrance service for fallen shipmates, held in Falmouth's Wesleyan Chapel. Both functions had been attended by every man of the frigate's recent crew and also many a shipmate of former voyages, Falmouth's Market Place being crowded with hundreds of veterans and their families, all of whom had gathered to pay their respects to Mathew Jelbert. The gunner had been revered aboard the ship; indeed, he had been loved throughout the town, for he was perceived as the most highly esteemed veteran and the father figure of the ship. His value, his contribution, had been acknowledged by such notable Royal Navy luminaries as local brothers Admirals Edward and Israel Pellew, and also by Admiral James Saumarez, the latter officer attending from his Plymouth command; all three high-ranking officers had been attired for the occasion in ceremonial, full dress uniform, a gesture of respect which had been much appreciated by all present, both crew and families.

There had been many a tear shed throughout the mute crowd of shipmates as the several orators had spoken of Mathew Jelbert, the man. Lieutenant James Mower, in particular, could not conceal his own considerable distress, for he had felt a mutual and deep bond with the gunner, who had nursed him throughout his own long recovery from many wounds, being ever present with kindly words of support and offering close attendance when any demanding physical activity might be required of the young officer. Mower had remained weak for many months after the battle to escape Navarino. All these events, a litany of profound distress, came gushing back as if akin to a flood tide of despair into Pat's troubled mind as he stared, wistfully, into the fire, his mood sinking like the lead line.

'Here you are, Captain O'Connor,' a returning Trewin broke Pat's deep train of thought as he set the coffee tray down, 'Would you care for a morsel to eat... an early supper perhaps?'

'In a short while, if you please; thank you. I await Doctor Ferguson,' replied Pat in distracted voice, a residual anguish in his mind, 'When he arrives... if you will.'

'Of course, sir.'

Without the least hesitation, Pat poured his first cup from the steaming black pot, only a minute passing before he took a large sip with huge satisfaction. Despite the hot, mouth-burning sensation he swallowed it down and he sighed with a profound sense of gratification, setting down the cup, pondering the possibilities for the days before him, several long-standing concerns returning once again to cloud his confused mental horizon.

'There you are!' came the uplifting and loud declaration resonating from near the internal door as a badly-dressed man of small stature and indeterminate age, middle-aged perhaps to the most careful of scrutiny, stepped briskly across the room to swiftly sit in the adjacent chair next to Pat. 'I am come to take coffee with you!' He leaned over to take a deep whiff of the welcoming aroma and smiled broadly, 'Would there be the merest drop of that divine nectar remaining, at all?'

'Simon! Good afternoon to you; of course, 'tis a fresh brew. Allow me to pour you a cup.' Pat's previous face of worry brightened immediately. He poured and passed the coffee, his friend equally enjoying his own first taste of the hot liquid, a larger gulp fast following with evident pleasure.

'Nectar it is!' pronounced Simon with a smile, reciprocated by Pat. Several silent minutes passing with nothing more said by either man, Simon spoke up again in low voice, his concern for his friend plain to hear, 'Forgive me, if you will, but - *please to explain* - for how long have you experienced such nightmares... such violent horrors... as that of last night?'

Pat hesitated, having a reticence about burdening his dear friend with such as no more than a bad dream, or so it seemed in the cold light of day; 'Now and then... when I sleep at all. I venture it was likely the goodly ration of port wine with the cheese last night... I was fast away until... until that dream... so vile and ghastly it was... Will I look to the waiter for a piece of cake?'

'I incline to the view that it was more than a dream,' declared Simon; 'indeed, it was surely a deal worse than any nightmare I can recall myself; that was plain to the weakest intellect. Is it, may I ask, brother, a... *an oft recurring* event?'

'Oh, I am not minded to trammel a friend such as yourself with a dream... a mere dream. Ne'er be so concerned, I doubt you will care to hear of it. Perhaps I should call for a sandwich... to tide us over until supper?'

'For shame, Patrick O'Connor; yes, I am indeed your friend, *your dearest friend*, but - if it is of the slightest help - then you may consider of me in this... *this patently distressing* instance... as a *medical* man, to whom one may say anything, anything at all, the slightest thing, most particularly when your discomfort is so evident.'

'I am a trifle out of sorts, for sure... and I am ashamed it should be so... *so apparent* to the observer,' Pat frowned.

'No shame attaches to such, I do assure you... and I speak with all the conviction I have gathered these many years as a physician. Alas, my dear... Plato - *I dare say you have heard of him?* - would have declared without the least hesitation that your soul is patently *not* in harmony.'

'Plato? My soul?'

'Indeed; he was minded that our soul consists of three parts, these being reason, appetite and spirit. I do not think we need concern ourselves with your appetite... for that is surely untroubled, as is plain to the meanest intelligence; however, let us focus on your spirit.'

'Well... I... I am a trifle low in my spirits, I do admit that, but I endeavour to... to not allow it to show. Note, I do not care to bemoan my lot, to lay it on thick, no. Here, allow me to pour you another coffee.'

'Plato, the great man...' Simon pressed on, determined that he would brook no diversion, 'Plato ventured that our soul is akin to the trio of those three elements... I speak of reason, appetite and spirit... and when all are in harmony, all *three* parts... then so are we; but when all are in conflict, then we are in distress... our mind is troubled.'

'I'm not wholly with you, I confess,' murmured Pat doubtfully.

'Please to think of a coachman, in a degree of difficulty whilst striving to control *two* horses who are out of kilter... One is anxious, flighty, and the other horse is tired, reluctant.'

'I'm sure Plato was a sensible cove... Did he possess a familiarity with horses?'

'Doubtless so,' Simon sighed, 'Please to indulge me: for how long have you been troubled?'

'It is since Navarino... I... I was sure we were dished that black day; I was... I...' Pat halted, unsure of what to report.

'Pray be good enough to continue.'

'I regret to say... I... Yes, it was a dreadful nightmare, and rarely a week passes without something of that infernal ilk besetting me... but, Simon, I don't care to lay it on thick, to harp on about it, puling about my lot; no, I don't.'

'So *it is* something of a frequent malady?'

'Damned frequent... though it don't signify.'

'You will allow me to remark upon that particular statement as a contradiction worthy of Aristotle himself; indeed, Socrates could not have passed it up...'

'For sure they were great men... in the... *the philosophical line*... no doubt,' murmured Pat, most doubtfully.

'... but this is your doctor speaking. Do you suppose I will prescribe a modicum of laudanum to assist your sleeping? I am minded two dozen of drops will serve the purpose very well.'

'I dare say there's a great deal to be said for... for the drops... thank you; but no... no; I do not much care for such as that.' Pat drained his coffee, 'I am of the opinion that, in the weeks ahead, being far away from that hell which was Greece will be the... *the best remedy*.'

'Very well, there is something to be said for that; though - *take note* - I do beg to disagree; indeed, I am not, myself, wholly unaccustomed to such as the malaise which is afflicting you...'

'I am most heartily sorry to hear it.'

'... but I am not inclined - for the moment - to persevere, to argue against my friend's firm convictions, for my own fortitude during these recent times leaves something to be desired, and as for the drops... I do concede that they possess their limitations.'

'Then we will speak no more of drops,' declared Pat emphatically.

Simon nodded, his reluctance to concede plain in his face. 'What, precisely, are your plans for the future, the *immediate* future, brother?' Another broad smile creased the unshaven face as if akin to an encouraging prompt, a reassurance.

'Plans? Of plans, thankfully, for once I have none... Notions... yes, ideas for sure... I am in the way to consider several. Duncan is presently finishing up aboard *Mathew Jelbert*; Pickering, Mower and Codrington too... and, of course, Prosser.' He smiled, a lift from the recollection of his nightmare coming upon him as he considered the new cutter and his shipmates, 'Barton is there... and... Murphy himself is present, cleaning the galley... *bless him*.' The appended fragment of praise was spoken very quietly, as if Pat himself could not quite believe he was saying it.

Simon Ferguson's surprise verged on astonishment, for he had never once in their many years together heard his friend bless or even praise his Irish compatriot and steward, Murphy, another Galwayman, in the slightest. Curses were the more customary order of the day, usually upon the discovery of unexplained shortages in the liquor store or the coffee being reheated, or worse - boiled, to Pat's mind that being the ultimate sin. Simon nodded, 'Ah, yes... I collect the general enthusiasm for the new craft this morning at breakfast... and, indeed, her presence at the Market Strand at Jelbert's funeral; a sloop would she be, at all?'

Pat bit his tongue, a tiny exasperation, no more, felt with his old friend's ever-enduring limitations of knowledge of all things nautical, 'A pilot cutter she is, no sloop; and,' he smiled broadly, 'I am minded she will be an exceedingly swift sailer, even - *I venture* - close to windward and agin the tide.'

'Very good, and those are the most admirable nautical capabilities, no doubt... but what are your *more specific* intentions for this estimable vessel, tell?'

'I am in the mind to take her on a long voyage... the longest, and that is, for sure, a happy prospect; indeed...' Pat's voice was little louder than a whisper, '... Fiddler's Green ain't in it. In fact, we were readying her today for sea.' Pat spoke with his first indication of enthusiasm. 'Admiral Saumarez, after the church service yesterday, proposed a proving trial... and I am in contemplation of taking her to Connemara and back. It is the rare event when I am blessed with the chance to visit Sinéad... rare indeed when I am able to go home...' Pat sighed, '*Home*... I can scarcely believe it... *home*.' The word was repeated very quietly, whispered even, as if the notion was too much to really believe.

'It is the long time since I was in Claddaghduff.' Pat beamed at his friend, 'What about that, eh? *Home*... D'ye care to come with us... with me? We will be shipmates together... *once again*.' The question was uttered with the utmost sincerity, the plaintive lilt very evident in Pat's tone of voice; 'I should greatly like that of all things.'

'I am obliged to you, infinitely obliged, for your invitation; I am so,' Simon smiled, albeit a sad smile, '... and I give you joy of the voyage to that precious sanctuary, but I regret I must demur in favour of the coach.' Seeing his friend's look of disappointment, plain on Pat's face, he added, 'I have paid for my ticket this morning. I have purchased a seat within *The Regulator*, and I am leaving early on the morrow for Exeter, whence I will take the *Royal Mail* to London, and thence for Glasgow. With the blessing... next week... I should fetch up in Oban... and so to goodly Tobermory. I have much delayed my departure these past few months... My conscience has dictated that I look to our wounded shipmates in my care... and, *of course*, to attend the remembrance service yesterday for our old comrade, Jelbert... *but no longer*. No, tomorrow I am away at last... *at long last*; I am leaving for the Isles, for dear Flora; that is to say... *Mrs MacDougall*... and her delightful bairns.'

'Why, it is in my thinking to take Duncan home... to the Isles... *to Lewis*... when we leave Connemara,' Pat's mind raced in exploration of a solution, '... and Mull is no great distance at all from there. Come, Simon, cannot I prevail upon you, eh?' He poured more coffee into both cups.

'Thank you again, brother, that is exceedingly handsome in you, but I must - *I regret* - decline. My attendance in Tobermory is ever more necessary and - *I confess* - I have seen enough of Neptune's watery domain for some time. I have endured the most exacting stringencies of the cockpit for long enough...' Simon sighed, 'It may be that my surgical leanings... though extensive and varied as they have been during these many years and voyages, I grant you... it may be that they are more suited to *terra firma*. Speaking as a medical man - and I only throw out this, the most innocuous of notions - I do incline to the view, from time to time, that perhaps I am no natural mariner...'

'Never in life! What stuff!'

'... and, although I am in dread of the infernal coach for such a long journey, at least I have reserved an inside seat. Hence I am in small hope that I will not freeze... which is sure to be the case were I to perch alongside the coachman; and the additional expenditure, significant as it is, is undoubtedly warranted at this time of year. No, I am away at six o'clock... in the cold twilight before the dawn - *and I dread that particular thought, I do* - for the earliest arrival in London... and the village eventually.' Simon paused as Pat digested his friend's intentions, a minute passing before Simon resumed, 'I am also looking to the fastest possible expedition because my landlord, Salmon, becomes more... *more pressing* by the day in his letters.'

'Your landlord?'

'He has - *alas, the scoundrel* - requested a deal of money for the roof repair... of my home...'

'But surely such is his obligation, not yours?'

'Indeed; but he has, as you may recall, claimed penury... a matter of litigation consuming all his funds. At least now the cost, the money... thankfully, I will anticipate possessing with a deal of relief since your most generous offer of a loan.'

'Gift, Simon; 'twill be a friend's gift, no loan. Pray do not speak of loans between us, of obligations; I beg you will not.'

'A flower upon your head, soul; you are the most generous man, Patrick O'Connor; and I am infinitely blessed to have such a *fidus Achates* as you, I am so.' Simon drank the whole of his cooling coffee in one draught, Pat following, and the two friends sat back in amiable companionship, deep in thought whilst staring at the fire's brightly sparkling, warming flames. Silence endured despite a pervading sense of mutual discomfort persisting even as they both settled with a degree of lingering fatigue, both greatly appreciative of the simple comfort of their chairs and the rare opportunity to relax.

After several minutes more passing with nothing said, Pat looked to his friend, 'I am in the mind to withdraw much of the remainder of my funds deposited at my London bank... and... and before you hand over any money for your roof repair... *before a penny changes hands - am I plain?* - perhaps you might enquire of your landlord the price he would require to sell your house?'

Simon, astonished, simply stared. The hiatus was broken by the entry of Duncan Macleod, Pat and Simon's other long-time close friend and *Surprise's* First Officer. Seeing them seated at the fire, he stepped directly across to the hearth, his body shaking involuntarily as, with difficulty, he peeled off his thick coat to more swiftly gain the warmth of the coals. A nod was all he could immediately manage, his teeth chattering uncontrollably with the severe cold, and he stooped down to warm his hands over the low flames. He turned about, putting his back to the fire as he sensed the presence of the waiter who had speedily followed him across the room, 'Trewin, I will take coffee... and a warming dram, if ye please... Wait! A *brace* would be more welcome, aye.' The waiter hastened away after a sympathetic nod.

Pat vacated the chair nearest the fire, shifting to sit the other side of Simon, and Duncan sat down without a moment lost, pulling his chair closer to the flames and rubbing his hands vigorously to recover a modicum of feeling from frozen insensitivity.

'Is she ready for sea, Duncan?' asked Pat in tentative voice.

'Aye, nae doubt of that; water and provisions to load... and we can be away on the first tide you care to take. She is the finest built of cutters I have ever seen... that she is, for sure... though I dare say her trials may suggest some wee adjustments to her trim... the rake of her mast, the storage of her ballast perhaps... but nothing of the least matter, of the slightest concern; nae, she awaits her crew, a gale and a rough sea to show her at her best.'

Pat and Simon both shuddered, Duncan's mention of the word gale sparking painful memories of a previous return to Falmouth after enduring the longest night of their lives, only narrowly surviving the ferocious hurricane of the previous year. They were both sure that particular nightmare would never be forgotten, not as long as they drew breath. 'Very well,' declared Pat, recovering and brightening, 'then we will begin to stow her stores in the morning and - *will I say it?* - we will look to departing on Wednesday. Now, will we turn our thinking to a bite of supper? I am mortal hungry, horses ain't in it. I am in the way for a grand beefsteak... with roast potatoes... and a good bottle of red - eh? What do you say?'

Tuesday 13th December 1825 06:00   Royal Hotel, Falmouth

The air seemed colder than ever and the horses' breath steamed out in great, expanding clouds under the weak gas lighting, no trace yet of even the faintest glimmer of twilight before the dawn. The team snorted whilst waiting patiently for the coachman's whip of departure, their metal shoes smacking with constant and loud clacking noises on the cobblestones of the street. Simon seemed hesitant to step up into the mail coach and stood at its open door. 'Goodbye brother,' seemed the most inadequate, the most deficient, of farewells even as he uttered the few words to Pat, the friends staring at each other; the unspoken feelings of deep and mutual respect, the rising sense of separation, probably for a very long time, were all too intense to allow for mere words.

Without ado, Pat enveloped him in a tight embrace, holding firm for a long half-minute before releasing his friend and stepping back. He nodded once, swallowed hard, but found he was unable to speak in that moment as he wondered, with bleak uncertainty, whether it might be years before they would meet again, there being little call for naval activity or even officers at all, and so many ships laid up "in ordinary" since the end of the French war. He seized Simon's hand in an iron grip, pumping it for excruciating seconds even as Simon winced, and his brief utterance, all he could find, was spoken with difficulty and an audible tremor, 'Damn me, I will miss you!'

Duncan was more considerate, Simon's hesitation before exposing his slight surgeon's hand to further torture noted; he offered a gentler handshake and an encouraging smile; 'Until we meet in the Isles, auld friend,' were his only words, for he was not a greatly educated man, undemonstrative, and anything more seemed to him to be superfluous, even verging on incongruous.

Simon strived for a smile but failed; a frog in his throat, he mumbled his own farewell, 'May the light shine forever upon you, my dearest friends. Goodbye, and joy be with you both.'

With a degree of difficulty, he tore his gaze away, his eye catching the coachman's anxious face, a picture of impatience. Another try for a weak smile and, with a nod to both his closest friends in all the world, the twin anchors of that which had for so long been his life, Simon clambered up into the coach without further delay. The driver's black countenance glared down, the man becoming increasingly irritable; lost minutes were noted by his seniors, and he did not much care for that. A final wave of Simon's hand from the window, a crack of the whip, and the coach jolted to a brisk start, the horses themselves plainly pleased to be away, swiftly raising a canter which prompted several pedestrians to leap aside as the coach-and-four rapidly disappeared down Market Street. A silent minute more staring into the distance, and Pat and Duncan turned about in the first evidence of the dawn light, no more than a muted glow in the eastern sky, swiftly re-entering the Royal Hotel, both men in grateful anticipation of a welcome and warming breakfast.

'Damn it, Duncan, we will miss that man!' exclaimed Pat, the first words he could manage.

'Aye, for sure. I cannae say I will enjoy life without him, without his company in the cabin.'

Thoughtful minutes passed, both men in sad contemplation of the leaving of their dearest friend and confidant. 'You are sure the cutter is ready for sea?' asked an unsettled Pat eventually, clutching for some small straw of consolation.

'Aye, she is that.'

'Will we leave a trifle earlier than planned?' Pat ventured his idea over the coffee, setting his mind against another cold day in Falmouth; the very thought of home, of dear Claddaghduff, was burning ever more brightly. 'I am wondering whether we might see our way clear to leave this very morning?'

'Aye, I cannae see why not... just the water and stores to take aboard; and, if the wind and tide are with us... if, that is, enough of the lads are ready to join us today... we can be away.'

'Have you asked... that is to say... would you think we will find a crew?'

'Och, I am sure a handful of the lads will be pleased to sail with us.'

'Then I give you joy of our departure... *today!*' declared Pat in loud voice, his dismay at Simon's leaving and his morose mood of recent days lifting a very little.

At eight o'clock and their appetites satiated, Pat and Duncan emerged from the Royal and walked down to the Fish Strand in companionable silence, the pleasurable sensation of anticipation taking root in their minds. In the lingering final minutes of twilight, the sun itself not yet become visible even as its brightening rays illuminated the sky, they gazed out over the harbour to the distant houses of Flushing on the far side, the gas lighting along its quayside still prominent as tiny, yellow beacons. The air, even in the relative calm prevailing, was still insufferably cold. They assessed, automatically, the prevailing westerly wind: weak, little more than a breeze; albeit such, were its direction to endure, would be greatly favourable for a slow, steady departure from the King's Road anchorage; and that was noted by both men with satisfaction. They turned about to walk through Falmouth's streets, the town coming to life all around them as they progressed up the High Street. At the top of the hill, as they began to descend Prince Street, Dunstanville Terrace before them, the sun's emerging brighter radiance of the dawn proper was lighting up all the edifices of the town, low rays of glaring sunlight brightly illuminating all the waters of the harbour, flickering arrows of light and silver reflections everywhere atop the sparkling panorama. They walked on with a brisk pace, their spirits rising with every step, in minutes approaching the Green Bank Quay where the cutter was tied alongside. A half-dozen plainly torpid figures were already standing on her deck, huddled together and talking amongst themselves. They all looked up as Pat and Duncan arrived.

'I wonder, might this truly be our final voyage together, Pat?' murmured Duncan; 'Is it likely that the dear *Surprise* will be paid off?'

'I dare say she might... I have heard nothing from His Lordship, nor indeed even the slightest murmur from Pellew for that matter, and he is a man who generally knows which way the wind is blowing in these parts.'

'So, our likely future is half-pay ashore?'

'Perhaps Saumarez may have better tidings when we return to Devonport after this proving trial; I would like to believe so.'

'But... if *Surprise* herself is not paid off... if she is to re-enter service, would it not likely be to Greece once again; and... and I have long wondered... will you yourself be minded to return to that hellish place, to that desperate conflict? I collect that you said not.'

'It is a... a... that is to say I... I am mired in a quandary, for sure,' Pat's face creased in uncertainty, 'I had not the least intention of returning... after... after we had lost so many shipmates there...' He swallowed hard and sighed deeply, '... but could I really look on from the quay... Could I watch the barky hauling up her cables to go back... with all our lads aboard... *and without me?*' He shook his head in weary resignation, 'I collect it was that same dilemma which brought Simon back from Scotland for our second voyage, and so I ask myself: what will I do? *What will I do,* Duncan, eh? Tell me, for I know not myself; 'tis ever difficult to choose between two blind goats.'

'Two blind goats?'

'Oh, pay that no mind... my grandma and her sage words. For the moment, we are in contemplation of a voyage to sweet Connemara, and so let us dwell no longer on thoughts of Greece... of that terrible place. We truly are going to blessed Connemara, Duncan... *to Connemara... to my home...* and then on to yours, to the Long Isle, and I give you joy of that wonderful notion!'

Climbing aboard, Pat called his men to assemble all about him, 'All hands aft!' Lieutenants Pickering, Codrington and Mower stood alongside the master, Jeremiah Prosser. At his side was also a lad of about fifteen years old who Pat recognised in an instant: it was Jago Jelbert, nephew of Mathew. The youngster had been presented to Pat by Mathew's widow and had spoken only to ask one solitary question: if he might join Pat's crew. Pat had acquiesced, not knowing when, if ever, *Surprise* might return to sea, but he had also been much impressed by the zeal, determination and conviction offered by the young man, particularly as it was so soon after his uncle's death. Indeed, his cousin too had been killed aboard *Surprise* during the previous voyage. Barton, who was Pat's cox'n, and Murphy were the final members of the gathering.

'Gentlemen,' declared Pat, his cheerful feelings rising like the sun, visibly climbing higher in the morning and at least an illusion of warmth accompanying its presence, a bright glare all over the harbour waters to the distant Carrick Roads, 'The proving voyage I have remarked on for tomorrow... well, I am decided that the cutter will depart *today*, for Ireland, and I am in need of a few good men...' Heads everywhere nodded cautiously, low murmurs in affirmative tone reaching Pat's ears. 'She is only a cutter... and... and Mr Macleod is with me... with us; that is to say... there ain't no officer's pay... for I venture the Admiralty will find only a trifle, no more, for just three or four hands... and precious little that will be...' Silence; Pat stared at the familiar faces of men he had sailed and fought with for years. He knew from long experience that not one of them would ever let him down at sea, every man a staunch comrade aboard ship, but in the present situation he wondered whether he was asking too much; it was a hard life, with so little money, for every one of his men, officers too, when they were not serving aboard a rated warship; and an able seaman's pay was small indeed. There was also the matter of being at home, in Falmouth town with their own families. That was surely precious after the hell that had been Greece.

No man ventured to speak for a few seconds until Prosser spoke up in a deep, firm voice, 'Beg pardon, sir, but every man here is minded to stay aboard the cutter.' Pat simply stared, lost for words.

Lieutenant Pickering, in years gone by ever the ship's wit but a man who had been singularly dejected in the final months serving in Greece as casualties mounted, all his good humour seemingly long lost, stepped forward, 'Sir, I care little for the lack of pay...' Every man's face stared with visible, flickering alarm at the lieutenant, '... but I prefer to be at sea...' All present were mindful of Pickering's descent into a deep and evident, indeed unshakeable, depression long before the barky had departed Greece; this was indeed a bleak utterance: what did Pickering mean? The mood of all present sank like a stone before he piped up again in conclusion, 'Yes, I prefer to be at sea... *at sea...* where my dear wife can't press me about it... the lack of funds that is!'

The relief was palpable, the laughter loud, all his friends delighted to see the beginnings of the lieutenant's return to jest, and all congratulated Pickering with smiles, with a pat on the back or a shake of his hand, before all eyes turned once again to their captain. 'Well, gentlemen,' declared a relieved and happy Pat, 'I thank you all, and... and allow me to say... we will all share equally what little money Saumarez cares to pay. I trust that will serve?' The voluble thanks, expressed in loud voice, left no doubt that such would serve to the full satisfaction of all present, and Pat was immensely pleased to see the similar delight in the faces of his officers. 'There is precious little wind...' he declared, heads everywhere gazing all around in survey, '... and so I am minded to leave at High Water, at two bells of the afternoon watch... if, that is, we have all our water and stores aboard. We will have an hour of swift ebb tide with us to reach and carry us past the Black Rock...'

There was a groundswell of murmurs from all present, as if in corroborative welcome of the news. Pat paused briefly to look to each of the faces of all his men. Pleased countenances everywhere, he continued, 'Bearing d'reckly south to the Lizard, near five leagues, I venture we can be sure she will make eight knots on a beam wind; and I am minded we will make our turn, west with a trifle of north, an hour before the sunset when we will see how close to the wind she will stay as we approach Gwennap Head...' Several exclamations and three or four heads were turning to look east, behind Pat. The low-hanging sun full in the faces of his men, hands everywhere were raised to shield eyes from the direct light and the glare of reflections off the water. Pat, his own back to the sun and his good cheer becoming slightly deflated by his men's apparently diminishing interest, pressed on with his briefing in louder voice, 'After we clear the point... AFTER WE CLEAR THE POINT... 'tis then seven leagues of close-hauled sailing before midnight... when we will set up... *we will set up...* FOR THE SCILLIES... WHAT IS THE INFERNAL MATTER?' Pat's temper, his patience long left behind in Greece with his shattered nerves, exploded at last, several of his men muttering ever louder; 'Mr Codrington! Are you listening?'

'Sir, 'tis *Bramble* approaching; 'tis Admiral Saumarez's vessel, his personal Devonport cutter... She is closing to come alongside.'

Pat swung round to see that *Bramble* was swiftly nearing; indeed, she was already slowing and almost alongside already. There was a dramatic turn at her helm, and the oncoming cutter sheered away into the breeze before came the slightest of collision nudge as she lost all way and came to a very demonstrative full stop close alongside. An anxious Lieutenant Hemming, aboard the Devonport cutter, swiftly climbed up on the gunwhale and leaped aboard *Mathew Jelbert* even as his crew held the two vessels apart with oars, *Bramble* allowed to drift a yard off, a slack sail giving her the most minimal momentum and drift, her crew tossing a line which was secured by Barton. Hemming presented a hasty salute to Pat, who stared in mute astonishment that anyone might attempt such a hasty and impetuous manoeuvre with obvious prospects of damage to both vessels, particularly so to the gleaming, new *Mathew Jelbert* in her state of pristine perfection. But he reined back his indignation, Hemming obviously being in some small state of agitation.

The lieutenant stood on no ceremony to deliver his report, 'Sir, I beg pardon for coming alongside in such haste, I do, but I bear the most important communication from Admiral Saumarez.'

Pat, still annoyed but even more flabbergasted and lost for words, simply nodded, another minute passing before he spoke in no more than a whisper, 'Mr Hemming, I will say nothing for the present on the manner of your coming alongside... that I will save for your private ear... Please, let us hear the Admiral's instruction, if you will.'

'Of course, sir; I have it here... written orders. The Admiral himself returned from Falmouth very late yesterday, well after sunset, to find a telegraph from the First Lord awaiting him. After Admiral Saumarez had read it I was ordered to leave

Devonport without the slightest delay... *without the loss of a moment*... save for the writing of his letter to your good self, not even the least time allowed to provision... and here I am. We have crossed the bay with neither food nor even any drop of water.'

'Well, Mr Hemming, that is most extraordinary,' declared Pat, astonished and suitably mollified by such urgency that dictated the absolute absence of provisions, 'And what, pray tell, merited such immediacy?'

'I beg you will read the Admiral's letter, sir,' said Hemming, proffering the important missive.

That all his men were listening closely and staring in similar disbelief was obvious to Pat, and so he opened the folded paper and began to read aloud,

'The Hamoaze, Monday 12th December 1825, 17:00

To Captain Patrick O'Connor, Falmouth

Sir,

You are herewith ordered to attend Lord Melville at the Admiralty at your earliest convenience; your most earliest attendance being necessary; more so, it being of the utmost urgency, the very utmost.'

Pat gasped; what could conceivably merit such extreme terminology, the underlined expression of emphasis being something which he had never, in all his years of service, seen before? He read on, still aloud, totally fascinated,

'In the circumstances, you are instructed to leave immediately, upon receipt of this instruction, aboard the pilot cutter Mathew Jelbert, and you are to proceed without the slightest diversion for any measure whatsoever to the Pool of London whence without the least delay you are requested to attend His Lordship at the earliest moment.

No time can be allowed for the loading of stores or water, save what is directly at hand at the quay.

Whilst I regret I, myself, can offer no explanation for the urgency or purpose of this order, for such is plainly unprecedented, no contrary or prior intentions of any nature can be considered in the present circumstances.

*I am, Sir,
Your obedient servant,
James Saumarez, Admiral'*

Pat looked up to stare at the admiral's emissary; 'On my life, Mr Hemming, this is a rum business!' he exclaimed; 'We are to leave immediately... for the Pool of London...'

'Yes sir, the Admiral's instruction is a near verbatim reproduction of what was received on the telegraph from London, nothing more offered by way of purpose for the order or the urgency of it.'

Pat looked away, 'Mr Pickering, have you begun to load water?'

'Yes sir; in the order of half of what was planned for the passage to Ireland is already aboard.'

'And provisions?'

'Fresh beef, potatoes, eggs and butter, sir... all be stowed.'

'Well, there's coffee aboard!' declared an ebullient Murphy in loud voice, standing near Prosser and listening with ill-concealed curiosity.

'Very well,' Pat, still in subdued disbelief, nodded; 'That will serve us admirably for our brief voyage.' Murmurings were evident from all present at the complete change of plan before Pat spoke up once more, 'Mr Prosser, do we have charts for the Channel and the Thames aboard ship?'

'Aye sir. All of my collection was fetched from home last night, Mr Macleod having mentioned your intentions for Ireland.'

'The compass and sextant?'

'All aboard, sir.'

'Well done; thank you, Mr Prosser. Gentlemen,' Pat raised his voice, 'It seems we are London bound... and with not a moment to be lost...' A minute passed like an age, puzzled faces all around, and Pat scrutinised every one before he continued, 'If anyone does not care to make the voyage, let him step ashore now.' Not a man moved in the slightest. 'Very well, let us get underway without delay; I venture we may struggle against the rising tide, precious little wind to aid us. Mr Hemming, please to communicate our departure to Admiral Saumarez upon your return to Devonport; I dare say you are minded to leave immediately...' Hemming nodded, '... and the admiral will wish to telegraph the news of our departure to London. We are blessed with a westerly, slight that it is, and I hope we will make good time after we escape the Roads and clear the Black Rock. I believe we may likely make the Pool late on Thursday morning - *with a fair wind* - when I will hasten to the Admiralty directly. Until we meet again, Lieutenant, I bid you farewell.'

'And to you, sir; I wish you safe passage.' Pat and Hemming shook hands. The line holding *Bramble* close to *Mathew Jelbert* was hauled closer on Hemming's wave until, when she was once more within a yard, the Lieutenant jumped across the gap, the cutter swiftly diverging; and, with waving arms from all her men, the Devonport crew hauled away, their own vessel shifting slowly on the light westerly towards the Carrick Roads.

'Welcome aboard, Jelbert,' Pat, his attention returning to his own men, smiled at the youngster, a fleeting diversion from his concentration. This day was turning out to be something far different from his intentions and quite the mystery, but he reined in the curiosity of his own thoughts to make a final close inspection of his vessel. 'She is a large cutter, Duncan; why, I venture she may gauge forty tons or even more. I am accustomed, of course, to the Scilly cutters; they are generally smaller. She is also broad of beam... and her high gunwales will serve us well, no doubt...'

'Aye, I fancy she will keep the sea with nae difficulty,' said Duncan with conviction, 'and I dare say she will sail well to windward with short boards.' Prosser, nearby, nodded in sage agreement.

'Lads,' shouted Pat, 'Prepare to cast off!'

Two more frantic minutes of busying about the cutter and Duncan presented himself to Pat, 'Ready to depart, sir.'

'Very well, Mr Macleod,' Pat reverted to a customary minimum of shipboard formality, 'Cast off!'

'Aye aye, sir; Mr Pickering, cast off!'

Pat stared at his crew in mild disbelief: a cutter with fully five commissioned and one non-commissioned officers, the very few hands being only his cox'n, his steward and a boy; he had never experienced anything like it. He wondered how he might write it up in his log or, indeed, whether he would ever write it up at all. He turned his gaze from Prosser, standing with Barton at the helm, to look to his watch. It was five minutes short of nine o'clock as the gap between the deck and the Green Bank quayside began to widen. 'This is a rum affair!' he exclaimed to no one in particular. His roving eyes admired the newly-built cutter: she was sixty-eight feet in length and built of larch on oak frames, a quite beautiful vessel and most pleasing to the eye; indeed, his appreciation seemed to be shared by all his men, for there were pleased faces all about the deck, a general delight evident everywhere, and for that he was most grateful, for it lifted his own fragile spirits a little more from his former doubts and hesitations, all born of a lingering uncertainty. His plans now seemingly decided for him, he allowed himself a smile.

'Eighty-two leagues to London, sir,' declared Prosser, stepping across from the helm. 'I venture it will present not the least difficulty for this vessel, sweet that she is.'

'No doubt, Mr Prosser,' murmured Pat with a rising feeling of contentment, his former concerns falling away as if irrelevant, 'No doubt at all... none.' He nodded as if in confirmation, another smile crossing his face. 'Well, all hands to make sail,' he ordered, looking to the flapping sails, the rising strength of the westerly increasingly declaring itself, 'Let us away and profit by this wind.'

Chapter Two

Wednesday 14th December 1825   09:30 New London Inn, Exeter

A yawning Simon stepped out from the inn with a degree of resigned trepidation about the further journey, the feeling of fatigue weighing heavily upon both his tired mind and his weary body; for he had spent an uncomfortable night after arriving very late the previous evening. Several spokes of one wheel of the coach had broken when encountering a severe pothole whilst crossing Bodmin Moor. Fortunately, the proximity to the *Jamaica Inn* facilitated repair without excessive delay, although he had walked two miles in the cold air to reach the welcome warmth of the hostelry. However, it had been near midnight when he had finally reached Exeter for an exceedingly meagre, cold supper. The solicitous innkeeper, John Clarick, had been preparing to retire himself, but he had offered warming coffee, brandy and very welcome slices of bread, beef cold cuts and fat dripping. Even so, a night of little sleep had followed as Simon had pondered his future. It was one in which - as seemed most likely - he would be far from his close friends and comrades of *Surprise*, and that he found to be a somewhat distressing prospect, countered only to a degree by the pleasing anticipation of his hoped-for life with Mrs MacDougall, with *Flora*, as he preferred to think of her. She was the identical twin of his own deceased wife Agnes, and, since shortly after meeting Flora for the first time exactly one year ago, he had nurtured a rising and passionate hope that marriage might eventuate. However, whilst friendship was certainly assured, for Flora inhabited his own house in Tobermory as his housekeeper, the closer bond which he so keenly sought had remained somewhat uncertain, and that was of deep concern to him. It was therefore with a degree of surprise and pleasure that, standing ready for imminent departure under the portico of the front door, he encountered his childhood friend, Benjamin Peddler; rediscovered of late in Falmouth town, now standing outside and clutching an overnight bag, and plainly intending to board the coach.

'Simon, old friend; it is you!' cried Peddler, letting fall his bag and seizing Simon's hand, a mutually vigorous shake persisting until Simon could endure it no longer, his hand still suffering from Pat's fierce goodbye grip of the previous morning.

'Benjamin, good morning to you!' exclaimed Simon; 'I hope I see you well. Would it be uncivil to ask where you are bound?'

'Why... London it is, and from there I am going home... home to the Isles, to Oban and Tobermory.'

'So am I! I am minded it is truly the blessed day of the year, for sure it is. We will be travelling together. Give you joy, old friend!'

'Of course, it will be a wonderful pleasure to journey in your company and to be in our old home village with you... and perhaps, if you are so inclined, we will revisit our old haunts?'

'Sirs, I beg you will board the coach!' declared the driver with resolute emphasis. Simon and Peddler climbed aboard to sit opposite each other, Simon's mind racing with an intensity he had not felt for some weeks. Peddler, his closest boyhood companion, the dearest friend of his youth, would be with him for many an hour, would be good company for many a day, whilst travelling; and that thought he relished, but he also felt sure that it would present the best opportunity to clarify precisely what had happened on that memorable day in Greece when, as had been believed, the Tsar's gold had been stolen whilst in the possession of Peddler and his associate, Edwin Perkis. The frigate *Surprise* had conveyed half a million pounds in gold bullion to Greece, a treasure sent from Saint Petersburg to Calamata as a loan from the Tsar's own burgeoning Urals' production to his Orthodox religious compatriots. The ingots, disguised as ship's ballast with iron plating in Perkis's factory, had disappeared overnight from the Calamata quay. Peddler and Perkis, entrusted with delivering the gold, had alleged that they themselves had been kidnapped by bandits, only escaping days later and eventually returning to England aboard a merchantman. However, the criminal enterprise had failed; the miscreants, whoever they were, had taken off with real ship's ballast, with *iron* ingots, the plated gold ones remaining untouched, having been redistributed aboard the frigate by the bosun to adjust for the bow being down in the water, the weight of the gold so greatly heavier than iron; indeed, the redistribution had been initiated after Simon's own suggestion. He had no personal knowledge of the gold, the more valuable and far heavier metal being disguised, but had simply assumed that the weight difference was related to the size of the ingots, never having actually seen them himself.

Simon indulged himself with intriguing thoughts of speculation after he had made himself comfortable in his seat; surely the time had, at last, now fortunately come to thoroughly discuss the events, to dispel the cloud of doubt, to dismiss the allegations of dishonesty that had persisted about his old friend? Simon himself clung firmly to the belief that Peddler would never stoop to theft, nor even any disreputable venture for personal gain, for was this not the same person with whom he had played as a boy all about the streets of Tobermory before life had served up their parting of the ways? Was not the man before him that same soul who had shared his every spare hour, who had explored all of Mull with him, in their youth together? Simon could not conceive that his old friend would ever let him down in his estimations of the man by participating in such a thing as the attempted theft. However, his belief was not shared by others in *Surprise*, Pat in particular having little truck with either Peddler or Perkis, and not believing a word of Peddler's explanation for the theft. In fact, Pat had declined Perkis's offer of an early-stage investment in his own, greatly speculative, Connemara gold mine, not trusting the man at all.

'Benjamin, dear friend; with plentiful hours before us, do you care to speak of our months in Greece?' ventured Simon in friendly tone, scrutinising his friend closely. 'Why, there has hardly been an hour to talk about it since we both returned from that stricken, despairing land... and our paths having taken their diverse roads. We are surely blessed with that most delightful prospect of all things, a surfeit of time, in the immediate days ahead...' Did he detect a semblance, a trace perhaps, of reluctance in Peddler's face? '... and here is the opportunity, the moment... to touch upon every matter requiring of... of greater clarity. What do you say?'

Thursday 15th December 1825 11:30   Pool of London

A greatly curious Pat stepped ashore at Billingsgate's Cox's Quay as soon as the mooring lines were cast and tied off, the cutter held close alongside a coal barge. There were no vacant spaces along the whole length of the wharf, nor indeed at any other quay nearby, the capital's waterway being so very busy. He hastened off at a brisk pace, not caring to be accosted by any Customs Officer in attendance at the Legal Quays. Swiftly he walked up to Lower Thames Street where he was fortunate to hail an empty cab passing by. Urging the coachman to make haste with the promise of a silver crown if he could make the Admiralty by noon, Pat rummaged through his pockets for coins with which to pay for his carriage. He heard the occasional whipcrack; indeed, his message of urgency, doubtless much reinforced by his promise of generous remuneration, seemed to have been greatly heeded as the coach sped on with alacrity, jolting wildly over cobbled imperfections and vigorously throwing Pat about, the driver shouting loudly to all pedestrians to 'STAND ASIDE!' whilst offering frequent prolific and abusive curses to all who were slow to do so.

A minute to noon and the driver brought his horses to a halt, climbing down without the loss of a moment to open the carriage door, one hand offered to assist a most uncomfortable Pat, the other keenly awaiting the promised crown. Pat handed it over with a grateful, albeit short, sentence of thanks before rushing off in haste towards the entrance portico, the cab driver deciding he would allow his horses a brief rest, perhaps whilst he himself enjoyed a well-earned nip from his gin flask.

'Captain O'Connor!' exclaimed a very surprised Old Tom with obvious pleasure, the long-serving porter hurrying to the door as Pat entered with great alacrity, in the utmost haste, his breathing visibly fast, his demeanour anxious. Old Tom hurried to take his coat, 'Good morning to you, sir! Do I see you well?'

'Good morning to you, Tom; obliged... yes, I am well, thankee,' gasped a slightly florid Pat in loud voice, much pleased to see an old acquaintance, one who would assuredly offer no frustrating delay at all, '... and it is a pleasure for sure to see you.' Pat pressed on without pause, 'I am summoned from Falmouth - *with the greatest urgency* - by the First Lord, to present myself without delay, *without the least delay*; indeed, there is not a moment to be lost!'

A fleeting look of doubt crossed Old Tom's face, but only for an instant. Though such things simply did not happen at the Admiralty - never in all his years had an officer arrived without appointment and seemingly *demanding* to see the First Lord *immediately* - he was acquainted with Pat of old; indeed, he recalled his first arrival as a junior lieutenant many years ago. In the intervening years they had struck up something of a mutual liking and respect during Pat's attendances ever since. Old Tom therefore knew without the least doubt that the declared urgency must be genuine, and he recovered in an instant. 'Will you take a seat, sir? I will advise Lord Melville of your arrival directly.'

'Thank you, Tom.' Pat, still gathering his wits and his composure, sat down in the small ante-chamber, The Bosun's Chair, as it was called by old custom.

It seemed only a minute before Old Tom returned, Pat's acute anxiety subsiding to something near its more normal, subdued level of recent months; 'Please to follow me, sir, if you will.'

Melville rose from his chair as Pat entered his office, and stepped around his desk to offer Pat his hand, 'It is exceedingly good to see you again, O'Connor, and may I thank you for the swift arrival in response to the unseemly haste with which I have summoned you from Falmouth.'

'Thank you, sir.' Pat could say no more, his mind was seized with curiosity and always awed in the presence of the great man.

'Please, sit down.' The First Lord, to Pat's keen eye, seemed unusually alert, perhaps even on edge. Old Tom returned to deposit a tray with coffee, and left immediately, a grateful nod of thanks offered by Pat.

'You have certainly made good time,' Melville smiled encouragingly, seemingly intent on a welcome with unusually friendly preliminaries to put Pat at ease, 'How did you fare with the new cutter? I understand that she is named after a veteran shipmate of yours... Indeed, was he not one of the hands?'

'Yes sir, Mathew Jelbert it was; he was lost in Greece.'

'I am greatly sorry to hear it,' Melville's words appeared wholly genuine to Pat's ears.

'He was our master gunner... and... and it was thanks to him that we escaped the Bay of Navarino... Without his incendiary shells... without his genius as a gunner...' Pat found himself whispering, a sense of dread returning, and he consciously raised his voice, '*Without him*... I have not the least doubt that we would all have perished... The barky would have been destroyed and every man jack of us all killed...'

A short pause by Melville, who considered the visible and the evidently deeply-felt substance of Pat's report, before resuming in a low voice, 'Such a man deserves to be remembered; indeed, lauded; such a man is worthy of the greatest praise... *and honours*. I applaud you for taking his name for the new cutter... a most commendable thought, O'Connor, estimable, indeed it is. Well done... *well done*.'

'Thank you, sir,' whispered Pat. It was most unusual of Melville to engage in such exchanges, for he was not a man for preliminaries; certainly not with relatively junior officers such as mere captains.

'In fact...' Melville paused for an instant, a change of thinking evident in the inquisitive tone of his voice, 'I presume he has a widow?'

'Yes sir, Mrs Jelbert is herself a remarkable woman; indeed, she has introduced her nephew to me, and... and an enterprising young man he seems to be; he is, in fact, aboard the cutter at this very moment, for he did ask that I take him into my crew.'

'Admirable, admirable indeed!' exclaimed Melville, obviously and genuinely impressed. 'I was thinking just now... *I was thinking*... I am minded that a sum must be found for the aid of Mrs Jelbert, the poor soul. Such a... an *arrangement* is unusual... as you know... and there are - *I regret* - no formal procedures available to me... A great pity it is... However, for deserving people - *and your shipmate, Jelbert, surely was one such* - and for Mrs Jelbert, I venture a modest sum might be found from the... the secret fund; indeed, I am sure it will be. Perhaps you would favour me by conveying mention of such a... *an endowment...* to the worthy widow, O'Connor?'

'I would be delighted to do so. I would be most honoured. Thank you, most kind of you, sir.'

'Very good. Perhaps we might pass a few minutes whilst we enjoy our coffee and before we proceed to the matter of substance which I have called you here to discuss... and speak of an account of your passage aboard the new cutter and, indeed, your opinion of the said vessel?'

'She is all we might hope for, sir, a fine vessel; she will hold closer to the wind than any other I have ever sailed aboard; indeed, we had great need of her abilities in that respect to come up the Thames this morning, the wind not favourable to us.'

'Please, do go on,' prompted Melville gently, enjoying the diversion from his customary, more onerous affairs.

'She found nine knots, nearly ten, sir, on a beam reach coming up from Dover, and that in nothing much more of a wind than a strong breeze, certainly no gale; and before that she made eight knots tiding it up the Channel in the weakest of south-westerlies.' Pat smiled, 'She answers her helm with an immediacy that is a joy to experience... and she boasts a generous freeboard... even in the most violent of turns; she has no weather or lee helm to speak of, certainly none that we could find, and... well, she is a delightful vessel, sir, quite magnificent; and it much pleases me to report such.'

Melville beamed in the presence of Pat's enthusiasm; not that he had followed much of Pat's technical commendation, being no sailor, but the praise was plainly both abundant and heartfelt. He set aside the empty coffee cups and hauled out a whisky bottle with two shot glasses from the drawer behind his desk, quickly pouring two measures. 'Well, O'Connor, you will allow me to offer a toast. I mentioned just now a minor allowance from the secret fund... We will also be drawing on it for a substantially larger sum to pay the yard which has built your new vessel...' Melville repeated with emphasis, 'That is to say, *your* new vessel...'

'*My* new vessel, sir?' Pat gasped, unsure he had heard correctly.'

'I collect that your own vessel, your cutter - *Eleanor* was it - was lost, run down; was she not? Off the coast of Portugal, if my memory serves me, Captain Macleod nearly losing his life; was that not so?'

'Indeed, it was, sir; I have yet to hear his own words of his escape, for it troubles him so greatly to recall it, even now. I heard the account only from one of his men.'

'Well then, it is perfectly equitable that your loss... *in His Majesty's service...* is recompensed. I therefore give you joy of *your* new cutter... and... and I also praise the man of that name... Will you raise your glass with me in a toast... to both the man *and* the vessel? To MATHEW JELBERT!'

Pat gasped, for he could not believe his ears; quickly reacting, he replied, 'To Mathew Jelbert, SIR!' He drank his shot in one, as did Melville. The First Lord offered his hand across the desk, both men experiencing, indeed enjoying, the warming flow of amity and respect which followed through the physical bond, not a word uttered for another minute, each in silent contemplation of the other. 'I owe you a thousand thanks, sir,' mumbled Pat eventually, scarcely believing his good fortune, Melville still exhibiting the broadest of smile.

'And now to more pressing matters, if you will,' declared the First Lord eventually as the clock chimed one o'clock, regaining his customary cool and aloof tone of voice.

'Sir,' Pat, marvelling at his luck, sat back in beatific pleasure, tongue-tied and sure that nothing else that might come to his attention this day could conceivably be anything of a greater shock.

'O'Connor,' declared Melville in little more than a whisper, as if in emphasis of the gravity of his words or, perhaps, in case Old Tom might be outside and listening, 'I have asked you here to undertake a mission which ordinarily would not fall to the Royal Navy; indeed, the gravity, the sensitivity, of the... *the situation...* is such that I could entrust this to few officers... *very few*; and it is also the case that a particularly swift vessel is required... the very fleetest of such, one which will brook no delay due to potentially inclement weather, nor to adverse tides or any other such nautical impediments that might arise...' Pat simply blinked as he strived to digest Melville's incredible words. The First Lord continued, '... and, I believe, from your own account, that your new cutter will serve us admirably... Yes, I am sure she will.'

'Sir? May I ask, what is the nature of this... *this situation?*'

'Of course,' Melville paused momentarily, as if he could not quite believe he was speaking about the subject in hand with such a lowly-rated officer as a ship's captain; 'O'Connor, the Bank of England is... is... desiring of carriage of certain important resources... *substantial ones...* from...' Melville strived to ignore the persistent tapping on the door until, with a sigh of exasperation, he conceded defeat in loud voice, 'YES, TOM, WHAT IS IT?'

'A most urgent missive, sir, delivered but a minute ago,' said the veteran porter at the threshold, plainly agitated. He handed over the letter. Melville tore off the seal with great energy, his exasperation and rising impatience overcoming his usual reserve, scattering the wax fragments across his desk and showering them all over the floor. 'Thank you, Tom; that will be all.' This was spoken very emphatically, the First Lord nodding towards the door as if to reinforce the message. Two minutes passed with Melville utterly engrossed, his face becoming red, redder, his eyes ever wider, until he looked up at last to stare at Pat. His voice reverting to a hesitant whisper, he uttered the astonishing words with the utmost disbelief, 'I was speaking of The Bank of England, O'Connor... *the Bank of England...* Upon my word... *can you believe it?* The Bank is bust!'

Thur. 15th December 1825 13:00   The Feathers, Westminster

Simon Ferguson sat back in relieved relaxation before the roaring fire in the public saloon. The room was busy, filled with patrons from all over the Liberties: well-spoken lawyers from the Royal Courts, from Lincoln's Inn Fields and the Inner Temple; thirsty merchants from Covent Garden, vibrant actors and theatregoers from the Royal Opera and other houses, inquisitive members of the press, voluble politicians and affable ship's captains from far along the Thames, all taking their ease. It was a diverse and happy clientele of many persuasions, for Mrs O'Donnell's reputation for a warm welcome for everyone, and her good food, had spread far and wide, even beyond the Liberties of Westminster and the Savoy; seafarers, in particular, disseminating favourable accounts of a fine hostelry to many a distant port. Simon had staggered into the inn after arriving in London shortly after the dawn, deeply chilled, his extremities numbed after enduring the overnight coach from the West Country, alighting stiff and frozen to manage the uncomfortable final mile to the Feathers on foot. He was a favourite of Mrs O'Donnell, as were his two friends, Duncan Macleod and Patrick O'Connor; indeed, Mrs O'Donnell maintained a bedroom for them, reserved for their occasional visits, although it did double as a store room to ameliorate the expense. Duncan Macleod's two nieces, Sandra and Emma, orphans since a young age, lived and worked at the inn. Upon arrival, some hours before, Simon had enjoyed a gargantuan fried breakfast at Mrs O'Donnell's insistence, and that after the most generous bowl of hot porridge, all washed down with bountiful coffee. Warming pleasurably at the hearth, his deep satiation was such that he was sure he would not eat for the next two days, his sublime comfort so gratifying that he could not readily contemplate stepping out into the frost once again for his reserved seat on the *Express* coach for York, to Carlisle and thence to Glasgow.

'There you are, sorr, and how are you feeling now?' Mrs O'Donnell's voice boomed out even above the loud background noises of a score of animated conversations.

'Exceedingly well fed and watered, Mrs O'Donnell; I thank you for that most gratefully, and...' Simon smiled, 'I do believe that I have finally thawed at last.'

'Will ye be wanting the room, sorr? I will ask the girls to make up the bed.'

'Thank you again, but no; I beg to decline your further hospitality, for I am returning to Scotland... to the Isles and home. My modest house in Tobermory beckons with an appeal - *I confess* - which I have never formerly felt for it; indeed, a more pleasurable prospect cannot be imagined.'

'Oh, I understand, sorr, sure I do... Your feet will ever bring you to where your heart is... 'tis the long road to my own home in the blessed County Clare... and many a day I have the hankering to return, I do... but no, I doubt I ever will; I have been too long here, sorr, at the Feathers; 'tis the world's pity that I will never see the fair Killaloe ever again... No, I fear not.'

Simon smiled again, 'Never is a very long time, my dear Mrs O'Donnell; why, I believe it would give your compatriot, Captain O'Connor, the greatest delight to convey you to Ireland. I believe he is minded to leave Falmouth for that very place only this week... but there is always a next time, no doubt. Will I mention your leanings... indeed, might one say, *your aspirations* to him?'

'Oh no... no; doubtless he will be visiting before many a month has passed... and perhaps I will speak then with him of the notion,' ventured Mrs O'Donnell somewhat doubtfully. 'Now, sorr, is there a particular reason you are in contemplation of your home on this occasion? I beg you will forgive me for asking.'

Simon, in that moment of settled relaxation within the ambience of what was almost another home, in the presence of a sincere and valued friend of many years, Mrs O'Donnell, and in a mood of profound contentment which he had not felt for many a month, confessed, a flush of relief overtaking him, 'Why, yes there is... there is indeed. It is a lovely lady... who has made my acquaintance, so it is...' Simon swallowed, gazed at Mrs O'Donnell's enquiring face, 'I would never have thought it... all these years since I lost my beloved Agnes... I...' Mrs O'Donnell squeezed his shoulder, '... I am... I am minded to ask the lady for her hand.'

'Oh, sorr, that is the most wonderful news. I give you joy of it, I do... Bless you, sorr, bless you!' Mrs O'Donnell, greatly popular and closely watched by her clients, stooped down to seize Simon in her arms and bestowed the tightest of hugs, squeezing him until he could not draw breath, not letting go for a minute whilst showering her delight with words of congratulation upon him, rather loud and joyful words which resounded throughout the saloon and attracted the attention of everyone present, scores of faces turning to stare. 'Marriage! Oh sorr! A wife, a wedding... 'tis a marvel; to be sure it is! Bless you! Bless you, sorr!' The noisy room had by now fallen silent in its entirety, much to Simon's embarrassment, and every patron looked across to the fireside armchair with undisguised curiosity. Mrs O'Donnell finally relented her grip to kiss Simon on his cheek, and then the general applause broke out, a loud eruption of clapping, vigorous and sustained, from all around the room, from everyone within it, all persons present shouting their own congratulations in hearty voice. Mrs O'Donnell beamed and seized Simon again in another hug, bestowing further kisses on both his cheeks, the vigorous clapping everywhere elevated to new heights, continuing even as further loud shouts of enthusiastic endorsement came from all corners of the room.

Thursday 15th December 1825 13:00   The Admiralty, London

Pat stared, stupefied, at Melville; the very idea that the Bank of England, the most respected institution in the land - save perhaps the King - could fail was simply incomprehensible.

The First Lord looked as if he could not believe the notion himself, seconds passing before he rose from his chair. 'Come, O'Connor; we are leaving for that place. Let us away directly.' He stepped briskly round the desk, seized his hat and overcoat from the stand and brushed past a bewildered Old Tom outside the door, shouting out a train of instructions as he hurried down the corridor, the porter rushing to keep up. An astonished Pat hastened along three yards behind. 'Cancel my appointments for the remainder of the day, Tom!' shouted Melville.

'All of them, sir?'

'Yes, yes, all of them!'

'But Admiral Harvey is returned, sir...'

'Do give him my regrets... my apologies...'

'But sir, he was exceedingly angry when you refused to see him in August...'

'No doubt, but I must attend other matters... Please extend my most sincere apologies for any inconvenience to Admiral Harvey.'

Old Tom fell silent, stopped, Melville plainly having no further interest in the subject. The First Lord swiftly exited the door to the courtyard with not another word uttered. Pat whispered to the porter as he passed by, 'It is a matter of state, of the utmost importance... the very utmost.' With that he was outside too and rushing to catch Melville who was already beckoning a cab.

By the time the coach and horses clattered along the cobbles of the Strand, Melville had overcome the shock of the news and endeavoured to further explain to Pat, 'It is my understanding that... consequent to the failure of a prolific number of country banks... there has been a run on the resources of the Bank...'

Pat nodded, uncomfortable recollections of his own bank's near and recent failure coming to mind. He reaffirmed to himself his unspoken intentions of withdrawing the remainder of his money from Pole Thornton at the earliest moment; indeed, he determined to go there himself in the morning.

Melville continued, 'The Bank has... so I was led to believe in the most succinct of notes from the Prime Minister on Monday... has resolved upon a number of actions, ones to which I am not party to, including the import of specie...'

'Specie, sir?'

'Gold, O'Connor, gold; from where I know not; however, that is the essential reason in my summoning you from Falmouth. I had been led to believe that such was being arranged for... for the next few days... and a reliable captain and a suitably swift vessel would be required. Doubtless all will be better explained to us... us souls *of a different persuasion*, as we are... We are no bankers, for sure, eh? All will become clearer when we reach the Bank.'

'No doubt,' mumbled Pat with grave doubts, his heart sinking as he considered the prospects of security or the lack of it for his own meagre funds within a bank so greatly and recently endangered. He decided on offering his own personal and relevant recollections, 'I attended the Bank of England, sir, when I was in London on the first Sunday of this month...'

'What! You have already attended the Bank?' Melville stared in disbelief.

'Yes sir, my own bank had come near to collapse. I was attending Pole Thornton on that prior Saturday morning... with the intention of withdrawing my own small savings, cognisant of the cautious sentiment concerning banks generally and the demise of the Plymouth Dock Bank specifically... My surgeon and friend, Simon Ferguson, had lost all his money on deposit there. However, Mr Thornton demonstrated that my fears in the case of his own bank were unfounded. In fact he asked that I escort him to the bank... *the Bank of England that is*... to collect very substantial funds which were provided to ensure his own bank's stability.'

An astonished Melville offered no comment to this, digesting the story for several minutes until he resumed in warmer voice as St. Paul's was passed on the left, 'O'Connor, whilst we have a very few more minutes, allow me to speak of another matter, one which has sat on my mind these recent weeks with a... a degree of discomfort...' Pat remaining silent, the First Lord resumed, 'I must ask... *enquire* of you... whether... whether you are acquainted with any officers who would be minded to serve... in Greece... if... if called upon to do so.' No immediate reply offered, Melville, sensing Pat's reluctance, continued, 'It is my understanding that the prospects for the Greeks are most substantially diminished... and that their remaining stronghold in western Greece, the town of Messalonghi, is under the severest siege; the Egyptian, Ibrahim, has turned his every attention and all his considerable forces to reducing it, and the inhabitants are once again in dire difficulties, the most dreadful of such...' Melville tailed off to await Pat's reaction.

'Yes, sir; the town lacks a harbour and is surrounded by lagoons of no great depth, and there are high hills on the landward side; as such, replenishment by land will assuredly be blocked by Ibrahim, and the shallows will deny Admiral Miaoulis the ability to land stores from all but the smallest of vessels; indeed, I venture nothing drawing more water than a small boat - *a yawl might serve* - can reach the town's beaches. I much sympathise with the defenders, sir; it is a tenuous location to defend, for sure it is.'

Melville nodded, digesting Pat's analysis. 'The Foreign Secretary has indicated that he is minded to provide such assistance as can be delivered without... without our... our *ostensible* interest becoming recognised by the Ottomans. Doubtless you will recall the need for secrecy when you served there before?'

'Yes, sir,' replied Pat with the utmost brevity and in an utterly noncommittal voice, the First Lord's previous words leaving not the least doubt in his mind where the conversation was leading, and Pat was far from sure it was a place, the physical one that is, to which he ever wanted to return.

Melville, sensing this, resumed in delicate fashion, 'You stated your own sympathy for the Greeks just now, O'Connor; and you are... I have no doubt... you are aware that the refit of *HMS Surprise... your* command, has been completed during these recent weeks? She sits at Devonport, and I have been informed that all her damages have been rectified... and... and she awaits her crew... officers and men... *and a captain.*'

'Indeed, sir; some of my own men are still there at the Dock, aboard her now; my junior lieutenant, William Reeve, is one, and my bosun and carpenter... with a dozen more hands.'

'Have you considered... of... of going back, O'Connor... to Greece?' asked Melville pointedly.

Pat was saved making any reply as the coach halted with a heavy, abrupt jolt outside the Bank, the driver jumping down from his seat and hastening to open the door, his arm outstretched to assist his passengers. Melville pressed coins into his hand and stepped briskly towards the colonnaded portico, a silent and thoughtful Pat a half-step behind; evidently, to his relief, the First Lord's attentions had immediately shifted to more pressing matters.

Melville's presence and his note from the Prime Minister ensured immediate admission by the porter and, together with Pat, he was ushered from the Front Court, through the Garden Court and to the Committee Room at all speed. Pat was still a hasty pace behind and feeling a curious, enduring mélange of bewilderment and astonishment. He felt a rising sense that great forces and influences were at work, and - he felt sure about it - they were surely ones which he had no personal wish to become accustomed to, let alone to participate in.

The Prime Minister, Lord Liverpool, and the Foreign Secretary, George Canning, stood up as Melville entered. Canning and Pat were very distant relatives, second cousins in fact, Canning being of Ulster stock and a man who had ever considered himself to be an Irishman born in London. They shook hands warmly, even as Pat looked at his cousin with some concern, for he did not look well: his face was ashen, his hair greying more than ever and greatly thinning.

Liverpool stared for mere moments before beginning with introductions, 'Melville, may I present Cornelius Buller, the Governor of the Bank, and his deputy, John Richards. You are familiar with the Foreign Secretary, I am sure.' Liverpool ignored Pat, who stood in mute gaze, for he could not believe his eyes: he was actually in the presence of the Prime Minister.

Melville shook hands with all the illumini before turning to Pat, 'Gentlemen, allow me to introduce a most highly-respected officer of the Royal Navy, Captain Patrick O'Connor...'

'Why, it is Mr O'Connor once again!' exclaimed Buller in a voice of great, good humour. It was a moment of pure light relief, for he had recognised Pat as the man who had attended the Bank's bailout meeting for Pole Thornton a few weeks previously, Pat being present as guardian of the huge funds disbursed to the partner of his own bank. On that occasion Pat had dropped his pistol on the floor with a loud clatter, much to his severe embarrassment. 'Do you presently possess your pistols, sir?' remarked Buller, laughing; and his deputy laughed out loud too, to the confusion of all others. Pat smiled, his personal tension easing somewhat. The Governor turned towards a portly figure who had stepped from behind the table; 'May I present Mr Nathan Rothschild, the banker?' he declared.

Rothschild was still a handsome man, Pat thought, even now in his late forties; he was full of face and lips, his hair almost all gone save for the sides of his head. He possessed dark brown eyes, prominent and unblinking, as if studying the persons before him with searching scrutiny.

Melville and Pat shook hands with Rothschild, although no words were offered by any of them. Pat felt slightly uncomfortable, as if he were being evaluated in some fashion.

Buller resumed, 'Mr Rothschild, as you may know, did provide the most substantial... *the most valuable* financial services to His Majesty's Government during the war. He is graciously attending today as... *as it seems conceivable*... that he may be able to assist once again.'

The Prime Minister coughed and called all to order with a brevity founded on his evident discomfort, 'Gentlemen, to business. Please be seated. Mr Buller, if you will...'

All present taking their seats once more, the Governor began to speak again, 'May I begin by thanking you all for attending. Today is surely a moment of extreme danger... for the Bank; indeed, it is for all banks and... and for our nation at large. The country banks, gentlemen, have reached their point of collapse, and the Bank itself has arrived at its own nadir. It is our conviction that on the morrow the Bank will be drained of all its gold coins... every one, the result being that the Bank will have no recourse but to suspend payment.' A collective gasp followed from all visitors present, the Bank's governors alone aware of the extent and imminence of the looming financial catastrophe. 'However, we do possess at hand several resources; we have a final reserve of one hundred thousand sovereigns... which, I regret, will not last the day if such news gets out in the morning. His Majesty's Government has, most helpfully,' he nodded to Liverpool, 'determined to allow the Bank to issue one-pound notes; yet even that is of no immediate help as we must await the printer.' Buller turned to his other side, 'Mr Rothschild and his brother in Paris have pledged the assistance of their banking house in this acute crisis; indeed, this appears at the moment to be our best prospect for avoiding a banking collapse and a national calamity the likes of which the country has never seen.' Buller drank water hastily from his glass and resumed, 'Messrs Rothschild have promised to deliver three hundred thousand pounds in gold coins... and... and if this can be achieved with the utmost celerity... *the very utmost*, only then, gentlemen, do I believe that this will tide us over until we have the printer's delivery and... and we have implemented our one remaining measure... *the last resort available to us*... I have ordered the melting down of all the Bank's bullion reserves into sovereigns.'

The room remained spellbound, nothing like it had anyone ever heard or even imagined before, never in their wildest dreams; the magnitude of the events before them was simply stupefying. Buller resumed, 'The Bank is in hope that the Rothschild gold will reach us exceedingly quickly... We have no more than a very few days, Monday... or Tuesday at the very latest... before - *as I said earlier* - we must suspend payment. In such a case, the City banks will fail, the country banks will swiftly follow... and all commerce in this country will be halted. I need not impress upon you that in such an event...' Buller glanced nervously towards the Prime Minister, '... in such circumstances, the government must fall.'

Liverpool coughed again and drank hastily from his own glass; he turned to Melville, 'Lord Melville, I understand that you have an officer, this gentleman here,' he nodded to Pat, '... who stands ready to travel to France to collect Mr Rothschild's brother's gold? Do you also have a suitably fleet vessel readily at hand?'

Melville nodded and spoke without the least hesitation, 'I do, sir... Captain O'Connor's cutter. She stands ready at... at...' He looked to Pat.

'She stands ready at Billingsgate, sir,' declared Pat, finding his tongue; 'My crew are aboard and can depart immediately upon your command.'

'Captain O'Connor, tell me... I am no sailor...' asked Liverpool, 'Two tons of gold... Your vessel has such a capacity?'

'It surely does, sir.'

'Is it feasible to reach Calais and return by Monday? That is to say... with any prospect of certainty?'

'Of course, sir.' Pat was sure it was not the moment for hesitation or even the slightest equivocation, for the shocked faces of all persons present were staring at him with burning anxiety plain in their eyes, their apprehensive minds hanging on his reply, and everyone was gripped by the most visible consternation. 'In the short winter days before us... that is to say with few daylight hours, the utmost care in navigation will be necessary with a cargo of such value, yet I venture you may be assured of our return before the sunset on Monday.'

'Thank you, Captain,' Liverpool exhaled with relief, albeit he was looking extremely perturbed, nervous even, as were Buller and Richards.

Melville interjected, 'Mr Rothschild, whilst Captain O'Connor's vessel can *and will* leave immediately upon the Prime Minister's instruction, I am mindful of the Governor's words, the need for urgency. How, may I ask, will your House, your brother, receive word of the necessity for such a vast quantity of gold coin? There is nothing like the naval telegraph at hand... *serving France...* and I am minded that days must surely be lost in communicating the instruction... *and indeed its urgency...* to Paris.'

Rothschild spoke for the first time, his voice heavy with a Germanic accent, 'Have no fears of that, sir; my brother stands ready with the gold and will send it immediately to Calais for collection.'

'But sir, Melville pressed, 'How will he know to send it?'

'Pigeons, sir... pigeons; I will despatch several today and...' Rothschild looked to the windows, the end of the day flagged by the fast diminishing light, only a weak dusk radiance remaining as four o'clock chimed, '... and I will despatch several more at the dawn.' A stunned silence followed audible gasps; for several seconds all present digested the fact that the survival of the Bank of England, indeed the future of all of England's banks and the mercantile trade of the entire country, appeared to rest upon pigeons! Rothschild continued as if to try to assuage the very visible doubts upon the faces of his audience, 'It is... *it has been for some time* our method for swift communication. We possess many birds here in London, in Paris and also in Frankfurt, where our older brother resides. Indeed, it has been reported in certain circles... *and I have never remarked upon this to anyone before...* that I was apprised by pigeon of Wellington's victory at Waterloo before any news of it arrived from the continent...' This further astonishing information being absorbed generally, all persons present being dumbfounded and remaining wholly silent, Rothschild continued, '... and... *so the popular story goes...* consequently I was able to take a favourable position in Consols, gentlemen, before the market responded generally...

making an exceedingly large profit.' The eyes of everyone widened in something akin to amazement, and Rothschild concluded with a tantalising smile, 'Well, that is the story!'

Mute stares endured all around the table until Liverpool spoke up at last to conclude the meeting, 'Gentlemen, our course is plain: Mr Rothschild will inform his brother of our intentions... *by pigeon* ... and Captain O'Connor...' The Prime Minister looked towards Pat, 'You will return to your vessel forthwith and depart for Calais *immediately* - possessing of Mr Rothschild's note; and we will hope... *indeed we will expect...* to see your return as soon as possible, and... and Monday would be exceedingly convenient!' No further comment at all followed from anyone; their numbed, blank faces stared in collective disbelief. Liverpool looked momentarily at everyone present in turn before concluding, 'We are now adjourned, gentlemen! Captain O'Connor, I bid you safe passage; good day, sir.'

Outside the Bank, Threadneedle Street illuminated by its gas lighting, Canning paused to speak with Pat, 'Well, have you ever heard the like? Allow me to say, dear cousin... you spoke very well in there. I congratulate you.'

'Thank you, sir.'

'Would that we had the time to pass a convivial few hours together and to enjoy a good supper.'

'I much lament it, sir; indeed, it was in my thinking to attend my own bank in the morning, Pole Thornton that is... to withdraw my own meagre monies. I am minded to help an old friend who is oppressed by his landlord, and - *if such can be arranged* - I am minded that I will provide the cash to buy the house, its necessary repairs being the subject of much distress for my friend; and I do believe that I may possess just sufficient of funds to cover such costs. However, such will have to await my return, next Monday.'

Canning sighed, 'I much regret to tell you that Pole Thornton has closed its doors, and that as recently as *last* Monday. Indeed, a number of banks have failed in the past week; the Bank Governor explained that to me before your arrival with Melville, and I collect he spoke of Pole Thornton with particular emphasis, the Bank having made a large loan to support them.'

'On my life!' Pat gasped, 'I am greatly surprised to hear that! Thornton himself was in receipt of four hundred thousand pounds at the beginning of this month from the Bank! I was there!' He stared into the air for a moment, 'Four hundred thousand pounds! Can you believe it? I cannot conceive of such a sum... 'tis a fortune us humble mortals may only dream of... and... *and he's closed the doors!* How can such be?' He sighed, a deep exhalation of resignation, of despair; 'These are black times, for sure they are.'

'I beg you will allow me to offer you such assistance... *such monies*... as may be necessary,' offered Canning, placing his hand on Pat's arm, 'We are family.' His words were spoken in a voice of utter sincerity, reiterated with emphasis, *'We are family,* dear cousin, and I am... I am not... entirely without funds.'

Pat seized and shook his hand, 'Thank you; you are very good, sir... and I am most grateful... *cousin*, I am so; 'tis a matter to consider most carefully, but... if I am to make Calais and return before Monday... *and may Saint Patrick bless us with both tide and wind...* I must leave such matters in abeyance and be away to my cutter directly.'

'Then I beg you will afford me an evening of your company upon your return?' declared Canning earnestly, 'Farewell and God speed!' Pat nodded and hastened away, rushing across the street to bear down Lombard Street as fast as he could go without breaking into a trot, his mind awhirl with racing thoughts of his mission, of its urgency, of what he would or could tell his men, if anything; he could hardly believe it; what a rum affair it was!

Thursday 15th December 1825 19:15   The Bull and Mouth Inn

A chilled Simon sat inside the gloomy darkness of the Royal Mail coach in a mood of mixed feelings as it pulled out from the courtyard of the inn into St. Martin's Le Grand. He pondered briefly taking a small sip of Irish whiskey from his flask, gifted by Mrs O'Donnell, but decided against it, and he settled back in his seat. With a sigh he endeavoured to reconcile himself to the exceedingly long journey north. He hoped, with all his heart, to reach Carlisle without delay in the late evening hours of Friday, when, all being well, he would take a swift supper before the onward journey to Glasgow. The coach timetable suggested - and it would surely be with considerable good fortune, Simon thought - that he would arrive there at five o'clock of Saturday morning, well before the late hour of the winter dawn, when he would rest there for the day. Oban would be his journey for Sunday. Oban! He would be almost home! He revelled momentarily in the delightful frisson of pleasure that came to him as the image of Flora filled his mind. How very much he hoped that developments at home would turn out to be as he so greatly wished. From Oban there was only the short passage to Tobermory, to his house, to his friends, to Flora. He basked in that delightful train of thought and he decided that he would take a sip of his whiskey after all; yes; and perhaps it was time to indulge his curiosity once again and rekindle his personal investigation into the mystifying events in Greece, only the slowest of progress made thus far and curtailed on arrival in London. He turned to his side, smiled and spoke to his companion, 'Peddler, you would not care for a sip of Killaloe whiskey, I suppose?' A cautious nod and he passed the flask. 'Now where were we, old friend? Our time in Greece, yes; you were about to tell me yesterday... just as we arrived in London... of your capture... with the... the...' A hasty recollection of the secret nature of the valuable cargo and Simon bit his tongue while four other passengers looked on with unconcealed interest, '... *the merchandise*... That is to say... *as you thought it to be.*'

Friday 16th December 1825 07:30   Cox's Quay, Billingsgate

Pat, immersed in deep despondent thought, all his money evidently lost with the closure of his bank, paced up and down *Mathew Jelbert's* deck, shivering in the cold air as he awaited the first faint glimmer of morning light. During the previous evening he had, after only the briefest of evaluations, abandoned all intentions of an earlier departure, the few remaining hours of the afternoon passing all too quickly. It had been a day of incredibly shocking events, and he could scarcely believe that he had attended the meeting at the Bank, one so critical to the interests of the state. On his return to the cutter, the afternoon's dismal overcast had presented a gloomy forerunner to the coming dusk, only the final weak vestiges of light still persisting in the gloaming, but without the least glimmer of moonlight under a dense, low cloud blanket. A faint illumination of the general Thames river course had lingered still in the evening, offering diffuse, rippling reflections on the flowing river surface from the glow of bankside street lamps, a yellow aura afforded by the new gas lighting. Pat had pondered whether such poor light made it practicable, indeed even feasible, to depart. However, he had concluded, without a great deal of indecision, that little or no meaningful progress would be made during the night in such moribund weather conditions, a chill easterly wind making up his mind for him. His announcement that a warming supper must be enjoyed before a good night's sleep and the earliest departure at the dawn had been well received by his shipmates. A most cordial and garrulous conversation followed for several hours, the rather unexpected excursion to France something of a mystery, the reason for which Pat would not reveal. He had discussed the passage to Calais at length with Duncan and Prosser before settling into the tiny cabin with all his officers to share a convivial supper of Murphy's stewed beef and boiled potatoes, the meal generously washed down with a half-dozen bottles of red wine of doubtful quality, purchased at great expense from a nearby merchant brig awaiting the next day's Customs inspection. Rest, for much of the night, had eluded him; thoughts of his bank's demise, all his money lost, and his inability to help Simon all being matters preying heavy on his mind, the severe cold also not conducive to sleep.

A new day and a wintry morning, and a tired Pat stared up and down the somnolent river. There was a small degree of early activity on vessels of all kinds and sizes tied alongside the quays; evidently the customarily dense water traffic was similarly awaiting the imminent dawn. The events of yesterday had been utterly astonishing; even now he believed he must pinch himself to believe them. Although his own modest bank deposits were lost to him, incredibly, the Bank of England itself was also about to run out of money! His thoughts drifted back to the forecasts described in the meeting at the Bank; yes, it surely would mean a run on the banks such as had never been seen before; that was certain once the news leaked out, as it surely would. His own monetary loss paled into an uncomfortable insignificance in comparison. His mind drifted to other issues: what did the future hold for him and his shipmates? Would they ever go to sea again? He recalled that *HMS Surprise* had been repaired since several weeks, as Melville had remarked; all her many and varied damages inflicted in Greece had been remedied at Plymouth Dock, or *Devonport* as he reminded himself that he must now refer to the navy's south-west port. He recalled Melville's final question, one left hanging, unanswered, Pat unable to answer in his discomfort, in his disinclination to settle upon the idea that he would return to the hell that was Greece. He pondered all these unknowns and several others, uncomfortable in both mind and body as he waited impatiently for the first inklings of the dawn proper. He stared down the river; in the gaslight he could see water steaming off the water's surface as a wispy grey blanket. He shivered: the air temperature was barely above freezing. At least the sky was beginning to lighten, solid black relenting slightly to the darkest of grey, the tiny variation discernible just above the Tower as Pat gazed in searching scrutiny to the east, one eye as ever for the wind. It had changed overnight and was now a moderate westerly which he much welcomed, for such would suit their purpose admirably.

'Well, sorr, 'ere be your old coat,' Murphy emerged from below to attend his captain, 'and a right proper wool scarf. Now put 'em on afore you catch your death!'

Pat nodded his thanks and looked around once more, momentarily assessing each of his shipmates in turn, all of them standing on the deck and keenly awaiting his order. They were generally of a slightly older age than perhaps the great mass of men of the Royal Navy, and that was also true of all of the crew of *HMS Surprise* generally; indeed, many of them had served with Pat aboard *HMS Tenedos* before that. Some of those men, with whom he was so familiar, he had met for the first time ever aboard his own first command, the gun-brig *Starling* in Portsmouth. He gazed again in rekindled assessment of the weather all about him; the air of the river was palpably clammy, tiny water droplets coalescing amidst the stubble on all his men's unshaven faces. He turned his head, stared to the east once more, the light noticeably brighter in just a few minutes. He wondered if the Rothschild pigeons might fly over even as he looked up; they would surely be faster than the cutter, of that he had no doubt. Did the Bank of England's survival really depend on pigeons? Pigeons! He could not resist a smile. No, the Bank depended *on him*, on Patrick O'Connor, and - of course - a swift passage to Calais, but not really on pigeons. Would that gargantuan sum of gold really be handed over to him, a lowly sea captain? All such notions seemed utterly inconceivable, absurd and far beyond belief as he shivered again in the cold air. What had the world come to? 'Mr Macleod, we will depart,' he declared eventually with a resigned nod of his head. With luck and a fair, brisk wind the cutter might make the most unobtrusive entry to Calais, nearly forty leagues away, sometime on Saturday.

Friday 16th December 1825   08:15   Tickhill, Yorkshire

After hours of dozing in near freezing discomfort, the woollen rug provided to him having fallen on the coach floor, Simon awoke with a start as the coach jolted uncomfortably to a halt outside the Red Lion Inn on Castle Gate. As the creaking door was opened by the driver, the stuffy fug of the air inside the coach, noxious to the nose, was refreshed by the freezing winter draught, for once very welcome to the occupants. 'There is a stop here for fifteen minutes for breakfast, gentlemen... and not a minute longer - *if you please* - before we will away at all speed with fresh horses. If you care to alight now for your comfort and perhaps a morsel of breakfast... the innkeeper and postmaster, Mr George Binge, awaits your pleasure.'

'And a binge will be most timely,' murmured a hungry and thirsty Simon to himself, stepping down from the coach without delay, most anxious indeed to indulge his several needs and comforts. The dawn sun was coming up but the street remained in shadow save for the expanse of the Market Place, a little ahead of the coach. He hastened inside the inn. An attractive elderly lady behind the servery smiled in friendly fashion as he entered. Simon scrutinised her momentarily, 'My dear, perhaps you might be so kind as to indicate the location of the head?' A look of confusion being the only response, Simon resumed with only the slightest inflection of self-satisfaction, 'Forgive me, it is a nautical term of we mariners, and we are a trifle given to jargon; I beg your pardon, I mean the privvy.'

'Just through that door, sir,' she pointed, 'and would you care for breakfast?' but Simon was gone before the slightest delay might bring embarrassment.

Five minutes later he emerged to speak once more with the woman, 'Might I ask... would you be the good proprietor's wife... Mrs Binge?'

'No sir, I am the breakfast cook; Caroline Johnson at your service. Would you care for hot tea or coffee? Would you be hungry at all?'

'Hungry can be the most inadequate of adjectives, my dear; and it does not come close to describing my... my present state; indeed, *famished* might answer tolerably well. I aspire to a full breakfast, the fullest... bacon, eggs, sausages... a fried tomato or two would be most delectable... blood pudding perhaps, and with all the customary accompaniments that the house can manage... toasted bread, butter and the like, if you please.'

'I regret, sir, that there is no time for that, none at all. The coach will leave without you while I am still cooking it.' His grave dismay was plain to see on Simon's face, and Mrs Johnson spoke up in consoling voice, 'If you will, sir, if you care for hot food, I have prepared a plentiful supply of bacon sandwiches... *that most precious standby...* during these past few minutes, which you may eat directly.'

'Mrs Johnson, you are the treasure of the world, you are so,' Simon beamed. 'That will serve admirably... you have my most grateful thanks. Would you also have the kindness of a pot of coffee?' He turned back to his friend, 'Peddler, do you care for a sandwich?' Sitting by themselves at the fireside and munching with serious intent, Simon seized the moment, 'Benjamin, before I fell asleep shortly after departing Baldock, you were about to tell me of the theft in Calamata of the Tsar's gol... *valuable cargo* - as you believed it to be in that hour. Captain O'Connor's officer, young Mr Mower, vouched that the... *the cargo* had been delivered to the quay and offloaded from *Surprise's* tender, the ... the *smaller* vessel... *Eleanor*. Indeed, I collect his sense of apprehension as he reiterated the tale of leaving it in your custody... with Perkis of course. If it is not disagreeable to you, I should very much like to hear your account of the event. Most particularly, is it the case that you declined the proffered escort of Mower's own men... or am I much astray?'

'That is the truth of the sad matter, old friend; I much regret to say it, even now. Perkis and I had no wish to draw attention to the... *the consignment* as we awaited the morning... whilst we passed the night there on that bleak quay. We felt sure that guards all about us would signal the presence of something of extraordinary value. We were, of course, in anxious anticipation of Prince Mavrocordato's arrival... during that evening; we hoped to see him... or at least his note with due authority for the release of the gold within a very short time... a few hours perhaps and no longer. Yet the night passed without the least communication from the Prince, and we became increasingly in fear of every passer-by, scores of the most doubtful brigands wandering along the quay and staring with undisguised curiosity at us and our charge.'

'You were aware of the value... the exceedingly *great* value of the... *the gold?*' Simon whispered the sensitive word and only after casting a glance all around the room to ascertain that all the other passengers were absent, perhaps relieving themselves or having returned to the coach. 'Half a million pounds it was... *half a million!* The Dear knows... I can scarcely comprehend a sum of such magnitude.'

'Indeed, Mr Perkis himself had most closely supervised the plating of the ingots with iron at his manufactory in Exeter, it was one occasion when I was present.'

'GENTLEMEN!' the coach driver bawled from the door, 'We are departing in ONE minute only, ONE MINUTE! Please to re-embark if you will... and without the slightest delay!'

'Here you are, my dear...' Simon rose and hailed Mrs Johnson, '... a silver sixpence for the sandwiches and an honest threepence for yourself. Oh, is that a surplus sandwich there?'

'Yes sir, the last one and unsold. Would you care to take it? There is nothing more to pay.'

'Most generous of you,' and without the loss of a moment Simon seized it, wrapped it quickly within his somewhat grubby handkerchief and stuffed it into his coat pocket. 'Thank you kindly, Mrs Johnson, and I bid you goodbye.'

Friday 16th December 1825   15:30   off Margate, Kent

The cold air was bitter, the chill north-westerly wind seemingly uninfluenced by dense layers of wool as it bit fiercely through every stitch of clothing that Duncan was wearing. He stood in frigid discomfort next to the cutter's helm, Barton at the wheel and Prosser standing at his side. An hour previously Murphy had emerged from the galley with hot coffee for all on deck, but that small gesture to comfort had long faded with the descent of the sun in the cutter's wake. The steward's suggestion that the occasion surely merited an early and extra issue of the shipboard rum, although disregarded at the time, tantalisingly, still hung in the freezing air and in the thoughts of everyone on deck who had heard it. Indeed, it was in the thinking of all who had not as the steward had emphatically reiterated it to all below, Pat's own reply being a mute, noncommittal stare. Progress had been slower than he had anticipated, the moderate westerly wind fading to a weak breeze in the late morning, the tiny vessel making only as far as the north Kent coast. Astern, the winter sun, low all day, was sinking fast, hovering abaft as if suspended on some heavenly cord just above the horizon; and in its diminished radiance tiny white sparkling crests lingered on the ripples stretching a mile or more in the cutter's placid wake.

In the cabin Pat spoke to his steward, 'Murphy, I am decided we will overnight in the Margate harbour. We will take supper ashore. It is yet a half-hour away, and so I am minded that you will issue the grog now... and please to make it half and half. I am going on deck.'

'D'reckly sorr,' Murphy grinned in satisfaction and hastened to do so.

'Gentlemen,' declared Pat, arriving at the helm, 'It is in my thinking that... our mission being of such... *such importance*... to certain significant officials of state...' Pat reminded himself that his men knew nothing of the purpose of the mission, '... I am minded that it would be ill-considered to venture into the vicinity and undoubted hazards of the Goodwins in the coming darkness... little moon do we have to aid us, and so we will haul into Margate and continue at dawn.' Relieved faces and nods all round followed; perhaps precious warmth might be found ashore; certainly, welcome refreshment would be, both hot food and warming drink.

Duncan spoke in quiet voice to his friend as they were enjoying their own grog ration minutes later in the cabin, everyone else save Murphy having remained on deck to prepare for making port, 'On the matter of returning to Greece... I will admit that I have had my own hesitations.' A mute Pat simply staring, he continued, 'It was the massacre of helpless Turks... on the quay in Hydra... in June... The brutal images are so greatly vivid in my mind... in my dreams... *so real.* I regret I have not spoken of it with you before... but I could not bring myself to inflict such upon you; I am not... *not unaware* that... that you have yourself been similarly afflicted.' Duncan did not care to mention that Pat's shouts during his nightmares had been much remarked upon within the barky. He swallowed a deep draught of his grog and resumed with obvious hesitancy, 'Admiral Canaris himself was with me... but the Greek mob would listen neither to him nor to the island Primates... or to anyone else. Canaris appealed to the mob to halt the killing... to no avail.' Duncan turned to Murphy, 'I would be obliged for a trifle more of the grog, if you will.' The steward, who had been eavesdropping with great interest, nodded and hastened away to fetch it. 'Later that evening, and *Eleanor* still moored at the very same quay, there was blood everywhere... and scores of bodies floating in the harbour... I... I could not endure the vivid recollection of the terrible event... and.... and I threw up my supper over the side. In that moment I resolved never... *never* to return. I confess I have been plagued by nightmares about... about those poor souls... women and children included... ever since... The images of the dying and the sounds of the screaming haunt my nights... and sleep proper is oft denied me; indeed, I awake in... *in something of a panic...* on the very verge of screaming myself.'

'Duncan, old friend,' the shocking story of the massacre of Turkish innocents had horrified Pat on hearing it the first time from others whilst in Greece, but at least - *thankfully* - he had not witnessed it himself, and he could scarcely imagine the extent of shock and horror which patently continued to afflict his dear friend and First; 'I am mightily set back to hear your tale, I am so.' Other horrific events which Pat had seen at close hand, more than two dozen of his ship's crew killed in battle, were bad enough, but at least the casualties were combatants and not utterly helpless civilians, *not children*. Such deaths as he had witnessed aboard the barky, amidst the roaring, flaming violence of the great guns, were to be expected; and whilst they often came to his mind and coloured his own sleep, at least it was seldom that they awakened him in such vivid and horrific distress as appeared to be afflicting Duncan. He wracked his brain for something to say, anything, *anything at all*, the least thing which might help his old friend, but eventually, and feeling entirely out of his depth, he could only mumble in a weak voice, 'I am most heartily sorry to hear of your personal distress. Have you spoken to Simon about your nightmares?'

Friday 16th December 1825 16:00 Catterick Bridge, N. Yorks.

Sunset was a few miles behind them and the coach rolled on with fresh horses in the dusk twilight as Simon continued talking in low voice to Peddler. It had been a long day on the road and a somewhat tedious one. His entreaties to Peddler to reveal greater detail of the theft of the supposed gold, as it was thought to be, and the kidnapping of Peddler and Perkis by the Greek brigands in Calamata, had not been significantly fruitful. His boyhood friend had appeared to conceal nothing in his replies, but neither had any greater revelations been added, to the extent that Simon's rising, mild frustration had prompted him to rein back his questions. Indeed, in his own thinking he considered it impolite to persevere further. All subsequent conversation had settled on their mutual recollections of childhood and youth, of long summer days spent together in Tobermory and the wider island of Mull, and, aided by the whiskey flask, the ambience in the coach had gradually warmed as they found the delightful frisson of pleasure in nostalgia, a contentment and satisfaction gained in re-establishing a mutual connection, one founded on those all-important years of growing up as close-knit young friends.

The other four passengers had striven for an escape into sleep from the cold of the grey winter day, and seemingly they were all dozing and had been for an hour or more already. Simon resolved to capitalise on the cordiality gained with Peddler and to return to the mystery of the great theft that never was; he leaned forward in his seat and whispered, 'The gold... *the real gold that is...* had previously been redistributed within the ship, the bosun being exceedingly unhappy about... the ... I believe he referred to her trim... yes, her trim; I collect he said that she was down at the front of the vessel... *the bow*... Such a plethora of maritime technical terms we seafarers are obliged to recall... and, indeed, it was my own suggestion that he shift a number of the ingots further back... *aft*... in the bilges... or perhaps it was the hold? So you see, dear Benjamin,' Simon laughed out loud for the first time during the tedious journey, several passengers stirring, '... you see, the brigands made off with only *iron* ingots!' An excited exclamation, 'YES, only with IRON!' and another, louder laugh, all weary eyes in the coach opening wide to stare. 'So, old friend, it was actually myself that you have to thank for saving you from losing the gold! What about that? What do you say to that, eh?'

Peddler had no words of reply and simply sat in shocked disbelief for the next five minutes whilst the attention of the other four coach passengers were fixed firmly upon Simon, all of them now awakened and keenly re-invigorated by his laughter.

The coach clattered on its way over the bridge across the Swale as the last residues of dusk light, filtering through the low cloud cover, faded away to leave the road and countryside only dimly illuminated by the weak light of the waxing moon.

Chapter Three

Friday 16th December 1825 16:30 *Margate quay*

Pat's men having tied the cutter alongside, all drifted off to explore the harbourside hostelries of the town, seeking a welcoming inn for seafarers and a hot meal. He had himself remained behind, writing in the tiny cabin below deck in the flickering, yellow glow of the solitary Argand lamp. Duncan too had held back from going ashore, although his claim of staying aboard to adjust the mooring lines with the rise and fall of the tide had not entirely been believed by anyone, for all had seen him together with Pat, emerging on deck in a plainly difficult conversation as the cutter had approached the harbour, and all had presumed that the two friends were minded to continue speaking in the privacy of the absence of all others. Before disembarking, Murphy had brewed a fresh pot of hot coffee, but that was all long gone, and the cold was rising to increasingly chill the feet and legs of an uncomfortable Pat.

Another cold half-hour passed, and Duncan, after looking to the mooring lines as the tide changed, resolved to go below to seek a little warmth and perhaps to speak once again with his friend. He descended slowly from the deck, an air of hesitancy in his step. Pat looked up, a feeling of curiosity settling upon him as a silent Duncan approached, 'We are a miserable pair, to be sure,' Pat spoke first, offering a weak smile; 'I was thinking that we would by now have been in Claddaghduff, warming at the flames of a peat fire and enjoying a generous whiskey... but no, I regret it ain't to be.'

Duncan nodded and sat down at his side on the bench. To Pat's eyes his friend plainly remained troubled, for his voice was halting, an anxiety within it as he spoke up, 'We were speaking earlier of Greece, Pat... I will say that I remain undecided myself... whether to return, if ever I am asked.'

'I understand, I do so, and Simon for sure does not care to consider of returning; indeed, let us hope that his intended proposal of marriage falls on fertile ground... and that he finds the contentment at home which he greatly deserves... the precious relief from that which we all saw in Greece. Such horrors... they haunt us all, for sure... even now... and I am myself oft greatly troubled in my sleep, I am.'

'Aye,' Duncan nodded as if in reluctant confirmation. 'He mentioned your offer to buy his house for him. That is most generous of you. In fact, I collect he was much pleased that he would be able to speak of it with his intended... *with Mrs MacDougall*; and he hoped that such might conceivably aid his marriage proposal. It is a concern for the ladies... *security*.'

'Oh yes, it is that... but, I regret to say, I find myself without funds... my bank has failed. Those stocks I had thought to be worthwhile investments in the new south American republics are also - *so I have been told during these recent months* - utterly worthless, and the modest sum I have in canal stocks has long declined in value since the coming of the steam engine and the railways. Hence, I am without a penny, Duncan, all thrown out; *I am flat broke.* As the old song goes,

> *I've got sixpence; jolly, jolly sixpence;*
> *I've got sixpence to last me all my life.*
> *I've got twopence to spend and twopence to lend,*
> *And twopence to send home to my wife...*

except that I no longer possess tuppence, nor even a penny piece of my own money, only that which Melville has provided for this short voyage.'

'I regret to hear it, but surely there are enduring positive prospects back in Connemara? I speak of your gold mine.'

'Oh that... sure, but it is early days and I do not care to count my eggs before they hatch, no. We have only the trial shaft excavated, but no gold has been found as yet. On the other hand, that speculator - *Perkis* - has offered to buy a substantial share, forty percent for himself and a further twenty percent to be bought and held by his crony, Peddler. I provided Perkis with the report of Thomas Weaver, the great mining engineer, who has visited and who has assured me that it is the exact same rock - *granite* - as the Ballinvalley river in Wicklow where gold has been found.' Pat sighed, 'I had hoped for another three months or so at least... to set things in train before weighing Perkis's offer, but such is not to be - *alas* - and so I have reached a decision... as we tided it down the Thames. I have just now been writing a letter to Perkis... to accept his offer. I see I have but little choice if I am still to help Simon in the manner I promised him... to buy his house.'

Duncan simply stared, feeling that the matter was not one he could usefully comment on, and so he returned to the earlier subject, 'And if we are asked to return to Greece... how do you feel about that yourself?'

'Oh, much the same as you... and Simon; that is to say, I am greatly uncertain, exceedingly doubtful. Indeed, the recollection of our former times in that grim place fills me with despair.'

Duncan nodded, 'Well, that is for the future. For the present I am fair clemmed, as hungry as a horse. Will we go ashore for an hour? I have looked to the lines, and we are at the beginning of slack water.'

'Yes, let's do that. A beefsteak and a glass of ale will serve admirably... and we may hope it will lift the spirits.'

Saturday 17th December 1825   05:00   Tontine Hotel, Glasgow

A sore Simon clambered with stiff difficulty down from the coach, immensely pleased and relieved that the substance of his long journey was completed, at least the greater part and all of the coach travel. He had noted with interest and small consolation that the substantial discomforts of his former long and arduous road travel to the north had been alleviated somewhat by two remedies: MacAdam's vastly improved road surfaces of recent years, an exceedingly welcome development; and the most innocuous, the mildest, dose of laudanum from his secret cache, imbibed with great reluctance whilst no one was looking, the ever-present recollection of his addiction of many years previously being highly disconcerting as he replaced the bottle in his bag. Much of his whiskey remained, little of that had been touched. However, the cramped coach cabin had offered no creature comforts whatsoever, save for the warmth exuded by closely packed travelling companions, a sociable fug never entirely dissipating, whether at the top of the day or in the cold, black depths of the night, for the windows were never opened as they had rattled along between the numerous brief stops mandated every fifteen miles or so in order to change the horses. The flimsiest of fleeting small meals had been purchased and swiftly eaten at roadside inns, a rare cup of tea or coffee enjoyed sparingly, all passengers mindful of the cold coach to follow. The six weary travellers had also learned to re-embark in great haste before the driver urged the horses to speed away. In the freezing chill of the dark Glasgow street, Simon assisted Peddler down from the door and the step before turning about. He yawned and offered his tip of a half-crown to the coach driver, a restrained nod being the most ungrateful reply as he clutched the silver, much to Simon's irritation, for he himself possessed the most parsimonious appreciation of funds, particularly small ones which were all he ever possessed. 'I trust you will have a care with that half-crown,' he declared to the driver in loud irritation, 'Seven more and you shall possess a full pound!' Turning away in small disgust, Simon gave sixpence to the guard, and he staggered across the street towards the coffee house, the shackles of cramped discomfort falling away only slightly and his leg stiffness easing just a very little. His heartfelt feelings of good cheer, by contrast, soared, for he had nearly reached his destination; he was *almost* home, much closer to his beloved Tobermory, almost home to the love of his life - *his long deceased wife excepted* - almost home to a new family, to two bairns who revered him, twins who made their respect and admiration perfectly plain. The sudden intense rush of well-being, the charge of highly emotional feeling, the awareness of the imminence of his homecoming, all overtook him in that moment, the thoughts releasing a feeling which was utterly profound and wholly overwhelming. In that instant he saw clearly that the new family which was before him in Tobermory was fundamental to his future contentment; indeed, the surging sensation of that firm realisation was sublime, and he rejoiced as he entered the hotel, wiping away a flood of streaming tears from his eyes and cheeks, his heart and mind, indeed all his feelings, wholly suffused by a powerful meld of deep relief and warm happiness.

Saturday 17th December 1825 15:00 Bassin du Paradis, Calais

Slack water in the basin and his cutter tied alongside amongst a score of fishing boats, an anxious Pat awaited the turn of the tide. He had cautiously delayed the entry of *Mathew Jelbert* to coincide with the approach of highwater, for he knew perfectly well that the basin dried out nearly completely at low tide, and if the cutter was not underway within the hour then it would be at least six long hours or more entirely wasted before she might next depart, for she would be left marooned upon a bed of sand. The local French fishermen, having unloaded their catches, were mending their nets; they watched with curiosity and great interest the delay in loading the obviously monstrously heavy wooden cases from the quayside wagon. The Englishmen handling them were sweating profusely despite the freezing air temperature, and they had visibly been in considerable difficulty even before they had been halted by the French Customs officer. The more inquisitive of the fishermen pressed questions upon the taciturn wagon driver who had arrived only a half-hour ago and who had failed to hold off the determined inspector. The official had espied the cutter despite Pat's best efforts to hide her amongst the fishing boats. That the wagon driver, Michel Desmarets, and his companion were in difficulty with the curious and determined bureaucrat was very apparent as their excited conversation became increasingly heated and ever louder. The eight sturdy draught horses rested, still panting and sweating, their nostrils steaming in the cold air. The greater part of their heavy load of one hundred heavy boxes, each of fifty-five pounds in weight, remained aboard the wagon. Not above a quarter of the cargo had as yet been shifted to the cutter, and Pat pondered with rising anxiety whether his men could load all of the boxes in time to catch the ebb tide. Lacking all save the most elementary grasp of French, he had left things to the Frenchman, Frédérick Charrier, who had accompanied the wagon from Paris. He was the representative of James Rothschild, head of the French branch of the family. Yet the man was plainly in some difficulty, the Customs inspector pressing him hard, to the visible interest and audible amusement of the fishermen, their own tasks finished for the day.

Pat stared at the seawater surface; slack water was gone, the tide was evidently on the ebb; such was increasingly plain to see. Just one more hour and his cutter might not escape the harbour, particularly so with her heavy load to be, all two tons and more of it. He looked anxiously to the continuing discussion; the inspector appeared satisfied at long last, was putting away a purse within his pocket; a smile was finally offered, a wave of his hand, and he turned about and marched away.

'Allons-y, mon capitaine!' shouted Charrier in friendly fashion, though plainly similarly concerned himself and waving his arm vigorously, 'Dépêchez-vous, s'il vous plait!'

After an effusive wave of acknowledgment from Pat, his officers and men rushed to begin embarking the heavy boxes once more, manhandling them one at a time across the quay from the wagon and over the gunwhale of the cutter and to the deck with great difficulty, the great weight an onerous burden. Young Jelbert - a most willing volunteer - moved to carry them below, a very reluctant Murphy assisting him. Five minutes passed for Pat in agonising calculation: progress was slow, far too slow for comfort. He realised that the cutter would never be ready in time to escape on the ebb tide; as things looked, it would necessitate a night in Calais. Well, there was less than an hour of daylight, so perhaps that was for the best. He groaned and threw off his own heavy sea coat, and moved to assist his men; an hour of severe toil would be so much the better to get warm again.

Sunday 18th December 1825   9a.m.   Tontine Hotel, Glasgow

From his bed Simon had watched the tiny glimmers of dawn light around the edges of the closed heavy curtains; he was blessed with an exceptionally pleasurable sense of rare relaxation. He was unmoving save for a stretch of the arms and a turn of his head as he heard the occasional sounds of guests moving along the corridor outside his room. He wondered whether he should hasten to breakfast before it might be all gone, and then he reminded himself that he was not at sea, thankfully, and such things simply did not happen on civilised Glasgow's firm, dry land. He yawned and settled back within his bed, contemplating what he might usefully do all day. His intended vessel, *The Highland Chieftain*, did not depart Glasgow until Monday morning. He would have preferred a coach, but such was not available, the road to Oban was barely suited to drovers with their animals, and he most certainly could not contemplate the rigours of a horse. With a sigh of dismay, he reconciled himself to the necessity for a reluctant return to sea, albeit a brief one. Basking in the relaxing and benevolent feeling of indolence, he allowed his mind to wander, to revisit past occasions on which he had travelled between the Isles and Glasgow. At least he would not be exposed to severe seas and certainly not to the barrage of sound which was the great guns firing, with all the distress that such noise inflicted upon his mind. He sighed deeply: who would be a mariner, even one on civilian vessels? For the moment, he put such depressing recollections firmly out of mind, for the present luxury of time in the premier city of western Scotland was certainly not to be overlooked, the rare occurrence that it had been for such a long time. He relished the thought that he had fully twenty-four hours at his disposal, time in which to do whatever he himself might choose; there were no orders to come, nothing to expect, no patients to attend, nor the least danger of shot, shell and splinter to intrude upon his blessed relaxation. He yawned once again and turned over, intending another hour of sleep; such blissful pleasures were simply never afforded him at sea, and he revelled in the delightful sensation. He would be home on the morrow, home; the beatific thought was simply divine, so much so that he could hardly believe it. Perhaps in an hour he might find Peddler and take a late breakfast with his friend; yes, and wash it down with several pints of hot, black coffee; and a newspaper too would doubtless also be at hand. He allowed his thoughts to drift to pleasurable anticipation of meeting Mrs MacDougall and her two bonny daughters once again, and he settled back with a yawn into the warmer folds of his sheets and pillows, wallowing in the sublime and unusual tranquillity.

Monday 19th December 1825   16:00   River Thames, London

Mathew Jelbert, in the fading of the light and the diminished wind, toiled slowly up the Thames after a long day of sailing from Margate, the Surprises catching a final glimpse of the sun ahead as it finally blinked out its goodbye from the south end of London Bridge, its weak rays putting the bridge into black silhouette as the cutter closed on the Custom House quay. Already the street gas lamps all along the river were lit to succeed the short duration and diffused light of the gloaming, which offered its bleak introduction to the expected freezing temperatures of the imminent night, an increasingly frosty chill having settled upon Pat and his men as they had passed the Tower to starboard twenty minutes earlier. The exceptional cold was a fruit of the easterly wind; however, it had also been a blessing, had much assisted their progress, and they were also favoured by an incoming tide. Pat was grateful for these smallest of nature's mercies and much relieved that there was no rainfall to inflict its depressing, wet misery to all standing on the cutter's deck. At last their voyage was nigh on ended, the Custom House quay was near, just the toss of the lines ahead, all way coming off the cutter, her men standing by at prow and stern. The Bank of England would be saved when it opened for business on the morrow, Pat reminded himself. That strange thought gave Pat a momentary frisson of satisfaction mixed with relief: he had not let the Governor or the Prime Minister down. All the cutter's men had long realised the wooden boxes' contents, for nothing else so compact could conceivably be so immensely heavy, as they recalled from the bullion previously transported to Greece aboard *HMS Surprise,* treasure which had been disguised as ballast ingots. Ribald jest had been enjoyed about the present cargo of gold coins for many hours. The impoverished Falmouth hands - at least for another few minutes - possessed hundreds of thousands of pounds, which was a fortune far beyond the wildest dreams of all aboard, although the fervent mind of Murphy could imagine a very great fortune indeed. Arms still ached from the loading of one hundred of the small wooden boxes; backs and legs were stiff and weary from distributing the gold about the cutter so as to spread the weight of the great load, and the thoughts of all aboard were already in dread of the prospect of unloading the crates.

Gradually the scarcely moving cutter inched closer until she came alongside the quay, when the lines were thrown fore and aft, and the vessel was tied up alongside; it was plain that plentiful space had been cleared ready for her arrival. All aboard breathed a sigh of relief when they perceived the welcoming party of a dozen stout fellows standing ready with two wagons, a dozen constables of the Marine Police Force also in attendance. The vital mission to save the Bank of England from disaster was thankfully completed, and in the time that Pat had promised. An anxious Pat finally allowed himself to concede defeat to the tidal wave of exhaustion and palpable relief rapidly spreading throughout his body, all his stressed leg muscles in particular releasing their final vestiges of nervous energy and succumbing to an uncontrollable shaking. In that moment his legs were no longer capable of holding him up, and he very visibly slumped to sit at the side of the wheel. A worried Murphy quickly hastened to his aid.

Tuesday 20th Dec. 1825   09:00   *The Admiralty*

'Come in, come in!' Melville's voice boomed out as Pat entered his office, 'Please, take a seat. Coffee, Tom, for both of us - *black and strong if you will*... Thank you!' The porter gone, the office door closed, Melville spoke up again in warm voice, 'Well, O'Connor, may I offer my congratulations? You have saved the Bank of England! Well done! Well done indeed!'

'Thank you, sir,' a relieved Pat was more softly spoken.

'Though I doubt that it will count for anything when our navy budget is determined for next year,' murmured Melville with less enthusiasm. 'How did your new vessel... *the cutter*... fare?'

'Splendid, sir; it pleases me to say. She performed most admirably, holding close to the wind when called upon to do so when navigating the buoys and the sweeping curves of the Thames...' Pat smiled, a thin smile. 'The river from the quays to Greenwich is particularly challenging... so many vessels in such confined waters.'

'I am sure,' replied Melville, though in truth his interest was fast waning; 'Ahh, here is our coffee. Thank you, Tom,' he declared as the porter deposited the tray. 'Now to other matters.' The First Lord's voice shifted to a more businesslike tone, having decided that sufficient pleasantries and such social courtesies as he could manage had been extended. 'O'Connor...'

Pat's heart sank immediately, he was sure he knew what he was about to be asked. He gratefully accepted the coffee and took a sip, immediately considering whether to set down the cup and saucer upon the desk before Melville might see the slightest of tremors in his hand, 'Sir?'

'The Prime Minister, the Foreign Secretary and I dined together on Sunday. News had been received that very morning from Russia... The Tsar has died.'

Pat's hand shook and his cup rattled: this was not what he had expected to hear; indeed, he was astonished to be told; his life was seemingly changing in more ways than one. First, poverty appeared to be beckoning after the loss of all his financial assets; second, he had reluctantly decided to sell a majority share in his last great financial hope - his gold mine; third, he had been entrusted to save the Bank of England by conveying gold coins from France - from the greatest financier of the era; and now he seemingly enjoyed the confidence of the leading statesmen of the country. His mind reeled. He considered that it really was too much for the humble seafarer from Connemara that he considered himself to be.

Melville, despite Pat's mute and bewildered stare, pressed on, 'Lord Strangford, our ambassador in Saint Petersburg... communicated the news to London. In his missive he suggests that the succession may lead to some form of civil conflict... perhaps even war... In Russia the deceased Tsar had *two* brothers... and, conceivably, they might now compete for the Imperial throne... such is the rumour... and there is, too, a degree of discontent within elements of the army. However, what *has* become clear is that Alexander, before he died, had resolved upon war with Turkey...' Pat's mind whirled with information he did not care to possess let alone consider, as Melville pressed on, 'Madame Lieven, the wife of the Russian ambassador to the Court of St. James's, a woman who shared the Tsar's closest confidence, had remarked in October to... *to your own cousin...*'

Melville uttered the words with an audible degree of disbelief, perhaps not wholly accepting that this lowly sea captain before him could be so well connected, 'She had remarked to your cousin, the Foreign Secretary, that the Tsar had concluded that England had no regard for the interests of Russia's Orthodox Christian brethren in Greece. Perhaps, and I venture we will never know, that was a contributory influence in his making of that exceedingly substantial loan of gold to the Greeks? We did not, O'Connor, make great show of your own commendable efforts with the Royal Navy's frigate... no, we did not.' Melville lowered his voice, 'Indeed, the Prime Minister had hoped such activity would remain entirely a secret, for His Majesty's Government has not the slightest wish to offend the Porte, preferring to maintain good relations with the Ottomans.'

Pat groaned inwardly, recalling the Turkish frigates firing for hours upon his ship as *Surprise* strived to escape the Bay of Navarino. It would hardly promote good relations if the true identity of *HMS Surprise* were to be made plain, but perhaps the reality was already known within the corridors of power of the Ottoman empire.

The First Lord continued, 'Furthermore, the Foreign Secretary has despatched a new emissary, *also his cousin,* Stratford Canning, to replace Strangford in Constantinople, and with instructions to seek negotiations to bring the war to an end.'

Pat nodded, he was striving to take in things which were so far removed from his life, as it had always been beforehand as a simple mariner, albeit captain of the frigate which had already served, covertly, to aid Greek interests. He wondered whether the fact that the Foreign Secretary was a relative was significant in this matter, the great officers of state speaking so candidly to him, a most lowly ranking captain on the list of the Royal Navy. Perhaps, he wondered, they did not realise that Canning and himself were only the most distant of cousins, twice removed. Indeed, they had seen very little, almost nothing, of each other for a very long time until this year.

'The Foreign Secretary,' Melville continued, '*your cousin*, is most unhappy with Strangford's proposals to Madame Lieven. Seemingly Strangford had sought to bring both France and

Austria into a coalition with England with the intention of... of facilitating the Russians entering the war against the Ottomans...' The First Lord halted, as if he could not himself quite believe that he was uttering such words, or perhaps he had simply noted Pat's disinterest. He concluded in a voice of weary resignation, 'But we are merely the maritime servants of the King, officers of the Royal Navy, eh, O'Connor? We are certainly no politicians!'

Pat managed a cautious nod; he knew that Melville was certainly no sailor; indeed, he doubted that the First Lord had ever been to sea, although he had been First Lord for twelve years or more. He was actually a lawyer. Where was Melville going with this? Pat could find no words at all nor any notion of what to say in such high political matters which, he admitted to himself, he neither understood nor had any interest in.

Melville resumed once more, 'Canning has asked me whether an English fleet... off the Morea... would be sufficiently powerful to intercede... *to block* the Ottoman fleet from making further invasions... to prevent troop landings.'

Pat's face revealed his feelings of inadequacy; his jaw sagged, his eyes stared, unblinking, his mouth wide open. Melville looked at him in close scrutiny, evaluating the man before him. 'Perhaps we will take a restorative, a wee dram, eh?' he said. Without waiting for any answer, he reached round behind his chair to the filing cabinet, extracting the whisky bottle and two tumblers. He poured two exceedingly generous measures and raised his glass, 'O'Connor, allow me to raise a toast... To your future! To you!'

'Thank you, sir,' Pat mumbled, endeavouring with difficulty to overcome his own many and varied uncertainties about his future, but he strived to present a smile, and he took the smallest of sips, hoping that the First Lord would not notice his hesitancy, and he set his glass down.

'I was informed, at dinner on Sunday by both the Prime Minister and the Foreign Secretary...' Melville resumed, '... that His Majesty's Government wishes to make a further substantive indication to the Russians... to Madame Lieven in the first instance, in the hope that she will similarly gain the ear and confidence of the new Tsar - *whichever of the brothers it may be*

- to demonstrate England's commitment to furthering Greek interests in this war, to assist the Greek aspirations for freedom and independence...'

Here it comes again, thought Pat, the particularly distressing subject that he had no inclination to hear anything more about.

'*HMS Surprise* is... that is to say... the Prime Minister himself has decided... she is being sent to Greece once again,' Melville paused once more, the better for the implicit message to sink in. 'However, on this occasion it is to be considered more akin to a *humanitarian* mission, one which Stratford Canning, our ambassador in Constantinople, can more easily explain if pressed by an angry Porte. *Surprise* is to take provisions to the besieged and blockaded town of Messalonghi. Ibrahim's army surrounds the town on land whilst the Turk and Egyptian navies control all its approach waters and the Gulf of Patras. Greek resupply has therefore been exceedingly precarious and intermittent for some time, and the wretched inhabitants are starving; so say our sources... including Captain Hamilton of *HMS Cambrian*. I collect you have long been familiar with those parts... since delivering Lord Byron?' Pat nodded cautiously and drained his whisky, setting down the glass, but he still did not speak. 'O'Connor, you are the long-established captain of *HMS Surprise* and the man who is most accustomed to all elements and conditions in those particular waters...' Still nothing forthcoming from Pat, Melville pressed on, 'I can tell you that the Prime Minister has informed me that he is much impressed with both your prior service there and, indeed, with your confidence and reliability in fetching the French gold; so much so that he has himself pressed me to ask of you... to ask... *if* you would return... to Greece.' The briefest of pauses in Melville's flow of words followed before he concluded in little more than a whisper, his attempt at formality quite failing him, 'Will you take command of your frigate, *HMS Surprise*, once more, O'Connor?' The plea was spoken with an accompanying intense stare, which added to Pat's feeling of discomfort; 'Will you take her back to Greece?' Melville reiterated. A few more seconds passed with Pat still silent, and the First Lord pressed again in more plaintive voice, 'Will you?'

Tuesday 20th December   1825   12:00   Tobermory, Mull

Sublime joy flooded throughout Simon's very being as he climbed up the long ladder from the fishing boat to gain the windswept quay at Tobermory, the low tide presenting him with a daunting number of slimy rungs and a considerable degree of difficulty. Several times he struggled to avoid letting slip his weighty seabag into the waves of grey water crashing against the sea wall just below. At last atop the quay and ignoring the stiff breeze, he turned around and kneeled down to help his companion, Peddler, haul himself up the final few rungs until, all their exertions over, he stared with relief and huge pleasure along the great curve of the harbour, all his thoughts suffused with the blossoming realisation, the keen awareness, that he was really, at long last, at home. The warmest, the most palpable sense of anticipation, of joy, was rising up to overcome him such that it rendered him incapable of the slightest thing save for his immediate thought: the registration within his mind that he had returned, and before him was a homecoming. He had arrived at the village where he had grown up, to the place of his boyhood days; and the feeling simply overwhelmed him, far more so than he had ever expected. For five more cold and windswept minutes he simply stood stock-still, gazing all about him, paying no mind to the cold, westerly wind and the wetting drizzle, utterly oblivious to Peddler's gentle suggestions that they move on to gain shelter. Eventually, the seeping awareness of discomfort bringing him down to earth, a chilling sensation of damp about his collar, Simon shook off his abject fascination in studying all the familiar sights and nodded to his companion. Picking up their bags, they set off slowly towards Simon's house, the formerly great weight of the seabag no longer any burden at all. He nodded in passing to a few familiar and inquisitive faces whom he vaguely recollected from many years ago, from before his long years at sea; he offered a beatific smile to all he encountered as he paced, one slow step after another, along the quay, relishing the feeling that each stride was akin to walking on air, savouring every delightful moment, squeezing the last drop of pleasure from it. He was home at last, ashore in the place of his youth, in the village where he had met and married his beloved Agnes, in that precious sanctuary where he hoped his proposal to marry again might be accepted by Flora, her twin sister. Mrs MacDougall was not far away, his emotions were on fire, a cherished flame of hope was burning within him; the next Mrs Ferguson - *at least he hoped she would become so* - was very near, and so close to his fast-beating heart!

Tuesday 20th Dec. 1825   19:00   Downing Street, Westminster

'So you see... ' declared Canning from his fireside armchair where he sat alongside Pat, whose own interest was fading, '... it is an exceedingly difficult situation... Were we to enter a congress with Russia and Austria, one such as Metternich has been pressing for since October *last year...* and which the Tsar ... *the deceased Tsar that is...* so greatly aspired to... it will, frankly... never bring Turkey and Greece to any mutually acceptable settlement; no, neither belligerent is likely to accept any rulings declared in Saint Petersburg... never in life. Hence I am minded that it is not in England's interest to be represented there.'

Pat blinked, sipped his whisky and wondered whether his cousin expected him to speak on a matter which was so far removed from his own world that he felt he really could not; he nodded without the least expression, eventually offering the meekest of replies, 'On that matter, sir, alas, my opinion would be about as valuable as a Brummagem farthing.'

Canning blinked and smiled, 'Oh, you are too modest by far, and I would never think that of you, I assure you. However, I did send my cousin... *my other cousin*, Stratford Canning, to Saint Petersburg last year to observe developments there... but the Tsar now having died... *doubtless that will complicate matters*... and Metternich not best pleased by England's refusal to participate in the congress sought by the Tsar... well, we are all at sea, if you will forgive the phrase. I venture the Chancellor... Metternich... is still in hope that our participation would stay Russia's hand, and that is to the advantage of Austria... whilst the Tsar was - *doubtless* - minded that a congress of the ilk that he proposed would have, ultimately, mandated military force against Turkey... *Russian* military force.'

Pat's mind was utterly befuddled, the political machinations of great states completely beyond his grasp. 'I am, sir, a humble man of Connemara, a mere devotee of the sea, a... a mariner; certainly I am a man more customarily at home on the oceans; my life, sir, is entirely that of a ship's captain in His Majesty's service, and I confess I know nothing of such matters of state that you speak of... and likely never will.'

If Canning had heard Pat's interjection, he affected not to notice, continuing in full flow, 'Russia and Austria... both are freed from Bonaparte's yoke these ten years... and what do they care to do? Austria covets expansion into the Balkans... and doubtless too has aspirations for those neighbouring Romanian provinces which are now - *thanks to the Greek war* - plainly the most tenuous of possessions of the Ottoman Empire, whilst Russia too desires greater influence in that very same place... and this whilst Russian armies are already fighting today in the Caucasus and in Persia! As if she did not have enough wars ongoing! Can you credit it, the Tsar - *the last one, that is* - was also minded to invade Turkey!' Canning, his momentary excitement seemingly spent, paused as his servant entered to deposit a tray with coffee.

It was the most welcome of sights as far as Pat was concerned, and he seized the moment to venture a tentative few words, 'I understood that, when I was in Greece, sir, the Greeks themselves were grateful for the interest of their Orthodox co-religionists, the Russians; indeed, some of them looked to the possibility of Capodistrias becoming national leader, he having departed the Tsar's service, having left Russia to live in Switzerland; yet I heard nothing at all spoken of Austria... from any source during my time there.'

'Russia and Austria... Those two great powers will never reconcile themselves to their widely differing aspirations and when, *ultimately,* they fail to do so - *and it becomes public knowledge* - then I fancy England will be influential with both Greek and Turk belligerents as mediator. But enough of such matters, eh? I am sure you have heard enough of such things...'

Pat nodded emphatically and Canning paused for reflection whilst pouring the coffee. He passed a cup to Pat and resumed, 'I collect a brief poem of mine; it was written an age ago, but might well describe our circumstances... *the prospects for the continent...* as they are today,

> *And oh! if again the rude whirlwind should rise,*
> *The dawnings of peace should fresh darkness deform,*
> *The regrets of the good and the fears of the wise*
> *Shall turn to the Pilot that weathered the Storm.'*

Pat, although he had scant leanings towards poetry, managed a smile; he had hoped for some considerable time that he might find safer ground on which to tread, to speak, some subject of which he had at least a modicum of knowledge and interest, and he spoke up quickly before Canning could return to politics, 'I venture, sir, that you would enjoy the company of one of my officers, Lieutenant Mower; he is a most proficient poet.'

'A poet, eh? Doubtless he is a wonderful companion to have aboard ship. One day perhaps... *one day...* when the world is at peace, when the House permits of my absence without the furore rising from the benches... I will indeed hope to meet him.' Canning smiled, 'A quiet day, eh? We can but dream... *oh, we can but dream.* May I count on you to introduce us, cousin?'

'Most certainly, sir...'

'In the meantime, and coming back to the matter of our immediate interest, to Greece and its parlous situation, I assuredly will not countenance any indication of support for Russian intervention by military force to effect a resolution of the Greek war; for how can this government express hopes of success to our own people, hopes which we do not feel? To do so, to mislead the public, as is ever the sad wont of some of the Members in the House, is the conduct of charlatans; I condemn them wholeheartedly, most particularly those who endeavour to gull the people with fanciful notions, with claims that the most detailed and complex of political arrangements might simply be wished for and they will appear! Shame on them!'

The servant re-emerged with brandy which he quickly set down upon the table, no words exchanged, leaving on Canning's curt nod. As his cousin filled their glasses Pat plucked up the courage to speak on matters which he would never allow to cross his table when in the great cabin, for political speculation was not a subject he much cared for, 'Does Greece's cause merit England's assistance, sir, for her own *exceedingly limited* military prowess will hardly serve to deliver her independence, to bring her freedom?'

'No, we must consider the state of the world as it is, not as we fancy it ought to be,' Canning spoke emphatically; 'It is a monumental dilemma... Let us not seek to hide from our own eyes...the real, the imminent and awful... danger which threatens us were we to side with either party in this conflict... It is but ten years since we saw off one tyrant after twelve long years of war... which near brought old England - *and Scotland* - to bankruptcy. The choice for Greece, for its future, is not in our power... No, we are too far removed... for which I maintain we should be thankful, and all about little Greece are great powers with *greater* designs... I speak of Turkey, Russia and Austria. And yet, as moral people, we have... we have no refuge in littleness, in standing aside; we must maintain ourselves for what we are, a people holding to principles, or else we must cease to have a political existence worth preserving. For that reason, I am minded that we must do *something* for poor Greece.'

Pat's mind had seethed within a cauldron of confusion all day, his discomfort persisting since he had hesitated to answer Melville's question definitively at the conclusion of their morning meeting. His painful prevarication had left both men exceedingly uncomfortable, and their farewell handshake had been, in reality, the most tortuous gesture of dissatisfaction. He struggled to consolidate the various strands of equivocation and incertitude pressing hard upon his mind as he wondered if his cousin was also about to speak on the one matter which was of such mental anguish to him; it certainly seemed that way; he sighed inwardly and he despaired.

Canning, observing Pat's dismay, which was plain in his face, spoke as carefully and as gently as ever he might, 'Dear cousin, do not think for one moment that I am unaware of the injury and distress inflicted upon every member of your valiant crew... *including yourself*... Brave men all. I applaud every one of you.'

'Thank you, you are very good, sir.'

The briefest of hiatus followed, Canning waiting to see if Pat spoke further; he did not. 'I have spoken with Lord Melville about your service... of your fortitude in the face of a deal of tribulations... of the many deaths and injuries which your men... *your shipmates...* suffered whilst fighting in Greece. The toll that it has undoubtedly taken upon you all has been reported to Melville from Falmouth... from Plymouth - *from Devonport* - by Admirals Pellew and Saumarez; indeed, I understand that those senior officers attended the remembrance service in Falmouth for your men...' Pat's mind flooded immediately with discomforting memories, and he could offer only the merest nod as Canning continued, 'Is it the case that Melville has gifted a vessel to you... which has been named after one of your fallen comrades?'

'It is true, sir,' Pat whispered all the words he could manage; he could feel his temperature rising, his breathing accelerating as deeply distressing recollections surged into his mind, vivid memories of painful events and the bitter anguish associated with them came into his thinking in a tidal wave of despond. He became dimly aware of his face colouring, of tears forming in his eyes, and he could say no more.

Canning, his cousin's difficulties perfectly plain to see, spoke very quietly, 'Did you yourself choose the vessel's name?'

'I did, sir,' whispered Pat.

'Why, that is the most admirable gesture I believe I have ever heard. I commend you with all my heart, I do!' Pat's anguish, increasingly visible despite his best efforts to conceal a rising tide of emotional distress, could not be obscured, and Canning quickly determined it best to press on with all speed; he continued, 'I am at a stand. It is incumbent upon me as Foreign Secretary to demonstrate that England is not a passive and disinterested spectator in this continuing Greek catastrophe, yet it is also incumbent upon me to do nothing - *nothing* - which the Porte can remonstrate about with unequivocal certainty; in short, we must refrain from anything - *the slightest thing* - which the Sultan might consider inimical to Ottoman interests, particularly so as he has undoubtedly been apprised of your own ship's interventions earlier this year and last.'

'Then... what... what can you do, sir?' Pat struggled with his quietly spoken words, which did not go unnoticed by Canning.

'I am in receipt of reports that the western Greek town of Messalonghi, besieged for a very long time, is perilously close to falling to Ibrahim's troops. Precious little re-supply can be effected for the defenders, who are hungry and deficient in both powder and shot; indeed, they cannot long endure without swift deliveries of the most urgent necessities. Furthermore, they lack all medical assistance and food provisions. In my own thinking, I have therefore devised the stratagem which I believe will best serve the interests of Greece, its defenders of Messalonghi most particularly, and of England... and with a semblance of credible denial afforded to us in the event of complaint by the Porte.' Canning halted; he scrutinised his cousin carefully.

Pat gathered his composure, Melville's earlier and very similar explanation returning to mind; it was plainly the same matter as that to which Canning also referred. He offered his reply with something of a sinking feeling, 'The town, sir, has no port; all supplies must be delivered by the most modestly-sized vessels... schooners must hold off the town whilst the smallest of cutters and such like carry stores to the beach.'

'Your new vessel is... is a small one, is it not, a cutter?'

'Yes sir, but she can carry only the most modest quantities of cargo... The French gold, heavy indeed, was perhaps near its limit, a few tons and no more. That will hardly serve to assist the Messalonghi defenders for very long... No, that don't answer.'

'Indeed, but a larger vessel, a frigate perhaps... such as *HMS Surprise*... What if such a *substantive* vessel were to convey the supplies to a closer proximity, from whence the cutter and other small vessels... boats, barges and suchlike... could offload to the shore? Perhaps with such measures England is able to render meaningful relief and support?' Canning did not pause for interruption, 'I am minded that assistance - *humanitarian assistance* - must be the essence of our presence in those disputed waters. Only as such can it be declared to any Ottoman enquiry that it is a mission of mercy, one which *overtly* contemplates no political purpose; it will be an undertaking which His Majesty's Government may robustly defend if the presence of an English ship in Greek waters is challenged by the Porte. It is patently not - as we will declare if our ambassador in Constantinople is challenged - *not* the slightest act of war, no indeed.'

Pat's mind whirred with considerations of how an English frigate - *his frigate* - might act if hailed by Ottoman vessels in such a particularly hot theatre of war, both Turk and Egyptian warships present in considerable numbers; indeed, *Surprise* had been identified already as a combatant when she had fled the Bay of Navarino, aiding the escape of the Greek politician Mavrocordato after the fall of the island of Sphacteria. Four hours of hell had been endured in a beleaguered bombardment from several Turk vessels whilst the frigate was mired without wind, and such was the subject of his nightmares. He was thinking aloud, '*Surprise* would be obliged to anchor some distance from the shore whilst her cutter and small boats ferried to and fro for some time. Were she to be challenged by several Turk warships - frigates and brigs they have a'plenty - then I venture she would be driven off, the cutter and its men left ashore for who knows how long. That, sir, is the difficulty I foresee.' Canning nodded cautiously as Pat continued, 'You said that it would be a humanitarian mission, one which you could deny was a warlike act; is then the frigate to fly Royal Navy colours?'

'No, I think not,' Canning shook his head; 'It is not for the Royal Navy to *ostensibly* deliver supplies of any kind to combatants in a foreign war. No, I doubt that would ring true to Ottoman ears... if your ship was flagged as *His Majesty's Ship Surprise*. I venture it will be far more credible were your vessel to be an instrument of such as the London Greek Committee; in effect an armed merchant ship... and with papers to vouch that.'

Pat said nothing more in reply, the Foreign Secretary had omitted to reflect upon the fact that *Surprise* had previously fought against Turk warships when last there; was it really conceivable that the Turks would ignore that history when inspecting her papers? He was inclined to think it most unlikely.

Canning continued, 'Dear cousin, I understand that a return to Greece after the painful experiences of prior service there is not something which any sane person would rush to embrace, certainly not; however, the Prime Minister is *himself* decided: *HMS Surprise is* being sent back to Greece *and* at the earliest moment. The instruction has been given to the First Lord, who has not the slightest latitude in the matter, save to favour you with the choice of returning in command or... *or not...* as you yourself may decide.'

Pat sighed, an audible sigh: the painful choice which he had long sought to shut out of his mind was finally before him and there really was no time remaining to consider further. At the forefront of his thoughts was the plain fact that the frigate would undoubtedly depart Devonport with many, likely most, of her crew being Falmouth men - his men, men who looked to him to safeguard them, men who were confident in their duty and assured that he would always look to their safety when they were serving under him. Yes, doubtless there were many other Royal Navy captains, both current and former ones - Cochrane came to mind - who were perfectly capable and who would be prepared to take the barky under their command, but what would his men, *his shipmates*, feel about him if he declined; and, perhaps most important of all, how would he feel himself? Would he be letting his men down? Could he really stand on the quay at Falmouth and watch the barky depart without him? It was a recurring dilemma, one which frequently returned to him in his sleep and often too in his waking hours; it was a matter which was never less than difficult to consider whenever it came into his thoughts, and that was too often to ever escape from the distress which it had caused him for many hours.

Canning, sensing the moment of decision was upon his cousin, tactfully kept his silence and poured more brandy. He passed the glass to Pat with an encouraging nod.

'You speak very well, sir,' Pat sighed, a sinking feeling in his heart, 'for I could not... *could never* countenance my brave lads of Falmouth town departing without me, never in life.'

Thursday 22nd December 1825 01:30 off Portland Bill

The waxing moon, nearly full, cast its bright radiance, illuminating the gently rolling, grey sea surface for miles, the moderate sea state presenting a comfortable passage for Pat's veterans, although the weak wind made for exceedingly slow progress. Off the starboard beam, the twin Portland lights, prominent in a sky almost wholly bereft of cloud, shone like tiny, bright stars, the only relief against the black backcloth of the promontory's heights. For several hours the two sentinels had lingered on the same bearing, the cutter seemingly stationary for an age as wind conflicted with tidal current. So very slowly *Mathew Jelbert* plugged on, her long tack appearing to the men aboard to be never ending, everyone awaiting the turn of the familiar strong tide when better progress might be made.

Forward of the mast, Pat stood with Duncan on deck, a few yards away from all other ears, sleep eluding both men. 'My mind is made up,' declared Pat eventually in little more than a whisper, 'I am going back... back to Greece. *Surprise* is ordered to convey munitions, foodstuffs and medical supplies to Messalonghi. The town is close to falling to Ibrahim.'

'You are really going back to that place?' Duncan turned his head to stare at his friend, his own doubts on the same matter flooding his mind to the exclusion of all else in an instant of profound alarm and distress. For a minute he was assaulted by the most vile, sickening feeling of discomfort within his stomach, his mind churning with anxiety, until the sensation of despair gradually settled back, eased a little. For another two minutes he remained incapable of speech until, his thoughts coalescing to that conclusion he had thought he would never reach, he found his voice, 'Then I too will be returning, I will stand by you... with our lads.'

A long exhalation from Pat, a few moments passing before he spoke, 'Thank you, Duncan; thank you, old friend, but I beg you will not feel obliged to do so.'

'Obliged? Obliged!' Duncan's emotions ran high in his momentous decision, and came out in his voice, 'To whom of all people am I - *and you* - to feel obliged? We have surely done our spell in that... that vile place!' A brief pause for reflection. 'We have spoken on this business, we have shared our hesitations... our concerns... and it is no small matter... but you know that. Yet you have undoubtedly acted - *decided* - because of your own feelings of obligation, for no sane man would *choose* to return of his own will.' Duncan's voice, excited and a little loud in the stress of the subject matter, deflated as all faces near the helm turned to stare with keen interest. 'Obligation... 'tis the heaviest of burdens.'

'I confess it is, yes... for I had no wish to see Greece again, to be back in that... in that particular hell.'

'Hell... aye, I am minded it was surely that. I resolved never to go back... *never*... after the horrors I witnessed on Hydra, the massacre of innocents, the blood... running in a stream of red rivulets across the quay from the scores dying there... bloody corpses... men, women and children all killed... *murdered*... defenceless within the mob.'

'I doubt they will be the last... *poor souls.*'

'That's sure,' Duncan groaned, 'and when, may I ask, is *Surprise* to depart?'

'As soon as she has watered and loaded those provisions the Storekeeper-General has been ordered by the First Lord to make available. I venture Saumarez in Devonport will already have been given his instructions by telegraph. There is a deal of urgency about this matter, not the least time for delay, so said Melville. The Prime Minister himself is behind this.'

Duncan shrugged and sighed, 'Do not feel obliged, you say... well, I do... I am... I am obliged - *I say this with a heavy heart* - I *feel* obliged... to you, to Mower, to Pickering... to Codrington... and, look over there... to men such as Jelbert. Doubtless many others will... will feel so.'

'You speak with that conviction which could never be doubted, but there are many of our lads who have lost their tiemates, their closest shipmates, these two years gone. I venture there may be a deal of hands who may not be minded to return, officers too. Look about you... look there to Mower. Did any man ever suffer as many wounds as he did and survive? I think not. He is the luckiest man of the world... to be attended by Simon Ferguson. I doubt any other surgeon would have saved his life. Will Mower be returning? Does Mower feel obliged? I wonder, will I find a crew in these coming few days before the barky must depart?'

'Allow me to say this, if you will. It is that terrible word again: *obligation*; but that is why you yourself have decided to return, is it not?'

Pat affected to not hear the question and he continued, 'Look to Pickering, the great humourist of the fleet; yet I have never heard a joke from him all year - *until last week...* when we were in contemplation of our voyage to Connemara, all thoughts of Greece cast overboard. See there: Codrington, Prosser, Barton and... and Murphy,' the last name was spoken with the slightest of hesitation. 'Will they feel obliged to return, Duncan... *to return to hell?* Will they?'

'Unless I am very much astray, I venture not a man, not a one, will shirk from joining with his shipmates again aboard the barky. I believe you know... *in your heart...* that is likely the case. Have you spoken of this with anyone else?'

'No, not a word have I said; I... I will speak to all our shipmates after breakfast... in the full light of day.'

Thursday 22nd December 1825 10:00   Tobermory, Mull

'It was the glorious welcome of the world,' Simon enthused to Peddler as they strolled along the quay, 'No hesitation, not the least, from Mrs MacDougall and a hug before my feet had crossed the threshold, and then the bairns... joy in their eyes, smiles on their faces... Both the dear lassies kissed my cheeks. Why, I venture I am the luckiest man alive, eh? Am I not?'

'I give you joy of your homecoming, old friend, I do.'

'I have been cast down into the deepest unhappiness for all the years since losing my beloved Agnes,' Simon's face clouded, 'and the anguish, it pains me to say, never relents, not in the slightest.' He stopped and turned to Peddler, 'I never believed that I might find happiness again with any another woman... I collect the moment... so vivid... the shock of meeting Flora - *you collect she is Agnes's sister* - for the first time. It was more than I thought my heart could stand.'

'I feel for you, I do.'

'For three weeks after the shock of that day I could find sleep only with the aid of laudanum... and...' Simon's voice was reduced to a whisper, '... and it is not a remedy I care to embark upon lightly, for... once... in a dark place... in the months after losing my wife... I became addicted to it.'

Peddler nodded, 'I am concerned to hear it.' He could find no further words, neither did he care to interrupt Simon whilst he continued his confession as they resumed walking.

'I am no *Adonis*... I have few illusions of such ilk - *actually none whatsoever* - but to find a woman who is the twin of my wife, to discover such... and then to share a mutual and... and growing bond of... of comfort and - *will I say it - love*... is... is a treasure beyond my mortal dreams in these recent years.'

'I am fully persuaded of it, and I am in envy of your happiness, dear Simon, I am.'

'It is in my thinking... that is to say... I... I am in contemplation of... of marriage. But I am getting ahead of myself; indeed, I have not yet asked the question of the lady herself, but... dear Benjamin... *my oldest friend*... perhaps you would consider of being my best man? That is if... in the unlikely event... she were minded to accept my proposal.'

'Most certainly,' Peddler beamed, 'It would be an honour.'

'I venture here, home in blessed Tobermory, on the isle, in this place where *we* - you and I - both grew up... Do you remember those days of our youth? Here is where I can serve the people of Mull and the near isles, precious little chance of a medical man to help them, save they go to Glasgow; and many, indeed most, can ill afford to do so.'

'Are you not in contemplation of returning to your ship, to *HMS Surprise*? And were you asked to do so, what of your friends there... are you not inclined to join them?'

'Why, of that matter, I regret I cannot speak. In fact there is a deal of uncertainty about whether that vessel will ever sail again; she was considerably damaged when we were in Greece, when we escaped the wretched bay... Navarino. A near catastrophe it was... and the most frightening hours in life that I can recall.'

'Speaking of your shipmates... will you remain in contact with Captain O'Connor?'

'Doubtless, yes; the mail these days is a service one cannot fault, deliveries thrice a week, and less than a week for a letter from Falmouth to arrive here, in this remote place; that is indeed remarkable.'

'I was asked by Edwin Perkis if I had heard anything more of his offer to purchase a share in Captain O'Connor's mineral venture in Ireland... his gold mine, in distant Galway... in Connemara. I breach no confidence, I am sure, in recounting this to you, for I have heard nothing more of it.'

'Neither have I. However, what I can add... and I do believe I may speak without fear of incurring Captain O'Connor's wrath for the slightest breach of confidence, is his concern that were he to accept Mr Perkis's offer - I believe your associate indicated he wished to buy forty percent on the basis that you yourself also purchased twenty percent - he, O'Connor, wished to be assured that no other individual possessed a majority share... a controlling interest... perhaps leaving him wholly bereft of influence... without the least control in the venture.'

'Indeed, that was the very basis upon which Edwin Perkis understood the matter rested, but he has heard no more.'

'I cannot speak for O'Connor in this matter, obviously; but might I beg the favour of your own thoughts here? Tell me, old friend: is it the case that your own *permanent* tenure of twenty percent of the mine shares would be assured? That is to say, would you conceive of any situation where you might be minded to sell your shares to Perkis... in contravention of O'Connor's understanding?'

'Of course not, dear Simon; on that you have my word, my word as the longstanding old friend that I am. No, O'Connor need have no anxieties of that nature, none whatsoever. How many years have we known each other, you and I? Did we not grow up together, the closest of friends? Did you not call my own mother, Mary, aunt? I give you my word of honour on the matter.'

'Very well; if O'Connor ventures any enquiry to me - which is doubtful, I must say - as to my own opinion on that most personal and so very significant attribute of such a transaction - then I do believe, dear Benjamin, that I may vouch for your good intentions.'

Thursday 22nd December   1825   11:00   off Start Point

'Gentlemen, lads,' declared Pat, his breakfast of porridge long consumed, his uncomfortable thoughts coalescing to a resolute conviction, 'Gather round, over here... closer if you will. Please to stand as near the helm as can be. There is one matter on which I care to speak to you all.' Barton and Prosser, on duty at the helm, pressed closer to it to make space as Codrington, Pickering and Mower closely encroached. Murphy and Jelbert stood to one side, Duncan on the other. 'We have been engaged in a rum business, as you know... fetching gold from France...' Smiles resulted all round, '... but the time has come when... when we must look to our more customary duties. That is to say... the barky is being readied for service once more... for a... a return to Greece...'

The resulting silence was unbroken save for the familiar sound of the circling gulls, the wash of the bow wave along the hull and the creak of the rigging, and Pat stared at the shocked faces before him. Not a word was uttered by anyone present. 'Now, I know that is... *is not*...,' Pat resumed in a voice which did not project confidence, '... it... it ain't the place we might choose to go, no... but the First Lord has ordered *Surprise* to... to ship all kinds of stores to the... to the besieged town of Messalonghi... to that infernal place where we took Lord Byron... where the great man died.'

The silence endured. Glum faces radiated dismay. The bow dipped and a white wave showered up and aft, the substance of it falling short of the helm and all persons standing there but spattering everyone with a wet spray which all ignored. 'I will tell you all now straight... I am going... that is to say... like it or not... *I am going back*. I am decided that the barky will sail when all is stowed aboard in... in a very few days, likely the day after Christmas. Today we are heading for Devonport, *not Falmouth*. I am minded we will be there in a few hours, at sunset or thereabouts. *Mathew Jelbert* will go on to Falmouth on the morrow, Mr Mower in command, to fetch more men to make up enough of a crew to at least sail *Surprise* to Falmouth. In the meantime, the Dock hands will load the stores for Greece and for the voyage. When all is aboard, the barky will depart and call at

Falmouth to make up a full crew. You may care to consider... before we reach Devonport... you may care to decide... to decide if ye wish to join with me aboard the barky once more.' The silence persisted still, not the slightest murmur from anyone, blank faces mute in stunned surprise. Pat pressed on, taking a different tack, 'Allow me to say this: it has been a privilege to serve with every one of you before, and it will be an honour to do so again. Thank you.' Bereft of further words and believing it for the best that his men should be left to debate the astounding news without his presence, Pat stepped down to the cabin below deck, Murphy and Duncan in close attendance. 'Will you look to the coffee, Murphy?' asked Pat tentatively, as if he did not care to impose the least burden on any of his men who had been the recipient of the sobering news of his intentions. The steward shifted to the galley, offering not a word, not even the whispered grumble of his normal demeanour, which left Pat wondering what his fellow Galwayman had made of the announcement. All of a sudden, he felt a surge of brotherly familiarity with his compatriot, a rush of greater appreciation for a man who he generally much took for granted; indeed, Murphy possessed no social skills whatsoever and offered few as a seaman. Even his cooking, limited that it was, fell a long way short of a full house. However, for many years Murphy had been Pat's constant companion, probably more so even than his close and longstanding friends, Simon and Duncan; for Murphy was present for every meal, served his every drink and attended to Pat's clothing. Indeed, he insisted that was washed far more frequently than Pat believed desirable let alone necessary. Even his steward's known fond predilection for the liquor store was something with which Pat had long ago come to terms, and he realised that he could not, for the first time, take for granted that his steward would decide to accompany any return to Greece, *to Hell*. In that flash of revelation, Pat understood how greatly important Murphy was to him. He called across to the galley, 'Murphy! Bear a hand there, I am minded we will have an issue of grog to set us up for a cold spell before dinner. Everyone will doubtless go ashore in Devonport later, and there will be no need for a grog issue then.'

A smile from the steward and he hastened to comply, a few minutes only passing before he set down the jug and glass tumblers on the table. 'Begging your honour's pardon... well, if it pleases 'ee, sorr, I will be a'staying aboard the barky.'

Pat stood up from his chair, seized his steward's hand in a vice-like grip and, for a silent second or two, shook it hard. Blinking rapidly, the sense of gratitude seizing his every fibre, he could only manage to whisper his heartfelt reply, 'I am mightily pleased to hear it... more than I can ever say; thank you... *thank you... shipmate.*'

Chapter Four

Thursday 22nd December 1825 14:00 Tobermory, Mull

The pleasing aroma of cooking vegetables, wafting from the cauldron suspended over the flames of the wood fire, filled the room of Simon's tiny house. A soup of barley, oats, kale, beans and peas was simmering gently, whilst in the oven the tray of potatoes slowly browned and crisped. 'I regret there is no meat nor even any fish for dinner today,' declared Flora with the smallest shade of hesitancy, as if this might present a crushing disappointment to the man she revered. 'There is nothing of significance in this particular day or date, and so I am minded to conserve what little of foodstuffs we presently possess, the sausages most particularly, for eating on Christmas Day.'

'It is of no matter, my dear,' declared Simon with a smile, for nothing short of the house on fire could conceivably diminish his pleasure in being in his own home and with the woman he adored.

It was precisely the scene he had oft imagined when aboard ship; indeed, that very thought had helped to sustain him in some of the vilest, the most horrendous of hours attending his duties in the cockpit, many a bloody casualty brought anew to his table. For a fleeting instant he imagined the putrescent stench that he had become accustomed to below deck in the aftermath of devastation of bloody battle, his mind recoiling even as it flooded with the brutal perception of the familiar, coppery scent of blood and gore. He visualised the many horrific sights that had been presented before him, scores of desperately wounded casualties brought before his tired eyes. He recalled his arms and fingers left utterly weary after many operations, one immediately after another in an unrelenting stream, until his hands were beginning to shake, even as his stricken shipmates were hovering between life and death, only his skill and the knife to determine which result it would be.

The burden of surgical responsibility under the utmost duress was one he had long shouldered, but there was an end to everything, a finite limit to all things under the sun; and, he reminded himself, that candle which burned twice as bright would burn for only half as long. Had he himself been that bright candle? He asked that very question once more, wondered about the answer for the hundredth time; for he could not, in his heart or mind, contemplate a return to the fierce heat, to the dripping humidity and the vile stink of his shipboard world during battle, nor indeed could he contemplate the many months afterwards tending wounded men. With a heavy despair that he could not shake, he resolved that he could never again face the despairing cries, the shrill screams or the desperate anguish of the wounded and the dying when only mere moments were available to him to save distressed shipmates, the most badly wounded of whom had mere frenzied seconds remaining to them whilst he decided what might, what could or could not be done, and then to do it very quickly: to cut through flesh and bone with the saw, and to tie off bleeding blood vessels. He shuddered, the acid sensation of bile rising in his throat.

With desperate determination he forced his mind, his thinking, out of that recurring nightmare which had plagued his every day for a long time: the aftermath of a particularly bloody battle off the island of Samos, and he fought to return to the present, to the sanctuary which was his home. He looked at the two girls at the table, wholly absorbed in playing Mower's new grand chess game, *strategic chess* as his friend had described it, for it offered more than one board, far more pieces being engaged even on the single board, and the greater tableau in its larger forms necessitating a team of players on each side.

It was with relief that he felt the tangible reassurance of the present coming back to him, his racing mind was slowing once more, the frightening and momentary recollection of his shipboard experience was fading. It was with a profound sense of solace that he reminded himself that, here in the Isles, there was a world without such devastating catastrophe and, his heartbeat subsiding, that was immensely comforting to him as the distressing surge of panic in his mind abated. He rose from his chair to speak with Rhona and Annag with something of a rising sense of relief.

Thursday 22nd December 1825 16:00   Plymouth Sound

Mathew Jelbert passed Saint Nicholas Island to starboard on a beam reach, the prevailing weak south-westerly a godsend as the cutter approached the Narrows, Mutton Cove directly ahead, Wilderness Point in black shadow to larboard. To starboard the stonework of the blockhouse of Devil's Point was brilliantly illuminated by the final bright and radiant vestiges of the low winter sun, hanging just a whisker above Mount Edgecumbe. There were few minutes remaining before the sunset and the light was poor, the air temperature severely cold, freezing. All aboard the cutter were shivering even though they were diligently wrapped in every stitch of clothing they possessed. 'The Mutton Cove wall, if you will,' said Pat to Prosser, his teeth chattering, his whole body chilled. 'Near the steps. It is the closest anchorage to Government House, and there is no time to lose walking through the Yard to the gate.' Two minutes passed and Prosser ordered the turn as the sun blinked out in bleak farewell, all dwindling and feeble illusions of warmth sinking with it. The cutter came as close to the wind as she could sail without losing all momentum, and she crept on, much slower now in the perceived calm of the weak dusk light, one cable more, until at last Prosser brought the cutter round once again. The fading breeze was square at her stern as she slowly closed on the Mutton Cove sea wall, barely more than drifting in the tidal slackwater, her sail limp. The extensive sands of Millbrook stretched out to larboard, exposed in the low tide. Jago Jelbert was on the lead line and the youngster, as keen as ever in his enthusiasm, was shouting out the diminishing depth.

'Most handsomely done, Mr Prosser,' declared Pat with satisfaction as they drifted towards the steps, 'Thankee.' Jelbert threw the mooring line to waiting hands, and within moments the cutter was tied alongside. Everyone bar Jelbert clambered up to the quay, the young newcomer left aboard to tend the lines when the tide began to come in. 'Gentlemen,' declared Pat to his officers, 'I am away at all speed to the admiral's office at Government House. It is my intention to join you all for supper before seven o'clock. Mr Prosser has suggested we attend the *Crown and Column* public house in Ker Street. I will find you there.' With that he raced away as fast as ever he could manage to walk.

Thursday 22nd December 1825 16:30   Tobermory, Mull

'My dear Flora,' murmured Simon, 'we were speaking of the landlord, Salmon, before my old friend Peddler arrived this morning. You were about to tell me something of the oppressive vulture, but I confess I did not care to speak of it until the bairns went out.'

'It is a rumour in the village, no more...'

'Please, go on.'

'The Sheriff in Oban has been requested by the Sheriff of Stornoway to investigate Salmon.'

'Stornoway? What, may I ask, has distant Lewis isle to do with Oban, with Salmon?'

'Salmon has sold an Oban fishing boat, and the buyer has made claim that the hull, when revealed out of the water, was rotten, much money required to remedy the disrepair.'

'Well, sad to say, I venture it is yet another example of man's greed and that old principle, *caveat emptor*.'

'What is that... *caveat*?'

'Buyer beware.'

'It is said that Salmon is now pressed for money, that he has engaged an Edinburgh lawyer.'

'An Edinburgh lawyer!' Simon gasped, 'Is the man made of money? There is no surer method known to man desirous of becoming a pauper! Perhaps that is why I have been receiving the most ascerbic letters from him this year when the rent has been late.'

'He was here in the village last week and came to the house.'

'Why ever was that? I collect that the rent is paid up to date, nothing owed, not a sou!'

'He spoke of the very considerable cost of the necessary roof repair...' Flora spoke in a most apprehensive voice. 'He said that he could ill afford it at the present time.'

'That is of no moment, my dear; my friend, O'Connor, has pledged a sufficiency of funds to effect that.'

'Salmon said he had decided to sell the house... to raise capital. He did not speak of the Sheriff. That is merely a rumour.'

'Why the rogue has said nothing of that ilk to me, of selling the house, in his letters!'

'It is a worry... and I have been in fear that the lassies and I will be homeless once more, cast out of this house... out of our home... the bairns and I... *and you*. Will we? You and I... are we to be separated? It was my dearest hope that you were here, at home in Tobermory... and no longer in danger, no longer exposed to... to battle... to bloodshed and death. I am much affrighted.' With that a distraught Flora began to silently cry. Simon, much dismayed by her distress, seized her within his arms.

Thur. 22nd Dec. 1825 17:00   Government House, Mount Wise.

The porter re-entered the waiting room and beckoned Pat into the office of Admiral Saumarez. He was sitting not behind his desk but close by the fireside, a recognition of the enduring cold temperature. He set aside the document he had been reading and rose to greet Pat with the most cordial and welcoming of handshakes, 'O'Connor, welcome! It is a grand pleasure to see you again.'

'Thank you, sir, and indeed it is so to see you. I will ever be reminded of your kind courtesy to me on that black day when I feared that Macleod and his men had been lost. Your words were most assuredly a great comfort on that occasion.'

Saumarez smiled, 'Oh, we must never make the worst of matters, for they are rarely that, if ever. Please, take a seat. Let us endeavour to hold Jack Frost at bay.' The admiral gingerly placed another log on the flames. The servant re-emerged with a tray with whisky, pouring two generous measures on Saumarez's nod and smile before departing. 'I understand that you are aware that *Surprise* is being readied for sea?'

'Indeed, sir.'

'I have been ordered by yesterday's telegraph to provision her with all the customary stores for departure, and also the most plentiful load she will carry of shot and powder; furthermore, she is to be provided with all the medical provisions at hand here in my Devonport stores!'

'For a humanitarian... a relief mission... for Messalonghi...'

'Quite so, and by order of the Prime Minister himself, not the least moment to be lost. She is to sail not later than Monday. The powers that be are not greatly minded to consider from where we might find her crew, her officers and... *and her captain.*' The admiral's last point was left hanging in the air, his question implicit.

Pat nodded, 'I have accepted command, sir; my officers too are all with me, and my cutter is sailing at first light for Falmouth to fetch a sufficiency of men to take her there... where... where we are minded that a full crew will assuredly come aboard.' Pat spoke the words without quite the measure of confidence he strived to convey.

'That is good news, O'Connor, and I commend you, I do; indeed, I commend all your men who have signalled that they will serve again, for I collect the very great deal of strain you and your men endured upon your last return from Greece, the loss of your schooner being particularly distressing. Thankfully your First and... *and almost all* the others of his crew survived.'

'My First, sir... and my surgeon... they are the greatest friends I have; indeed, we all... we all were afflicted by the... the considerable... *the very considerable...*' Pat could add no more, his emotions were rising, and he drained his whisky.

Saumarez rang a tiny bell and the steward returned, 'I collect Captain O'Connor is partial to coffee - *strong, black coffee* - if you will, and perhaps a tad more of whisky will serve us both well; there is a deal of matters to discuss. Thank you, Simmons.'

'Very good, sir,' the steward hastened away.

'My dear O'Connor, we will set aside for the moment the matter of victualling your ship. I have already set a body of men working to effect that, to rig new sails and the like. No, allow me to touch on one other matter. Here, atop this hill, in clement weather, I oft spare a few minutes each day to step out, to gaze across the waters of the Hamoaze, to look across the Sound. I see ships of all flags coming and going; I speak with many of their captains; I hear stories... from many sources, from many vessels, both Royal Navy and merchant ships... all calling here to water, to resupply. For the most part my visitors recount generalities, sometimes the most vague of tales... and oft embellished with plentiful imagination, and - *I confess* - such as that I customarily endeavour to discard; but on occasions I hear from officers in whom I have the utmost confidence, upon whom I place my complete reliance in the veracity of their words; Captain Hamilton of the *Cambrian* is one such officer. From him I did hear of the regrettable, the barbaric, events on the harbourside at Hydra; I speak of the massacre of captive Turk civilians.'

Pat swallowed hard, a fruitless attempt to lubricate a dry throat as Saumarez continued, 'Captain Hamilton spoke of the very obvious distress inflicted upon your First, Macleod, a most credible witness, from whom he himself heard the story. I must assume that you yourself, and indeed all of your officers and men, are familiar with events of that nature.'

'Indeed we are, sir, and it is the trial of the world to hear of another such, for we are ever minded that they are true; neither side gives quarter to the other... and civilians are to be accorded nothing, no assurances are ever given for their safety... and the massacre of innocents is quite the norm, I regret to say.'

A silent minute passed before Saumarez resumed, 'I have served in many a bloody engagement... and I have seen many men killed aboard those ships in which I have served... and commanded. Indeed, there have been *extensive* battles... *bloody battles*... in which I have fought... the Saintes, Cape Saint Vincent... the Nile, Gibraltar... but those were matters between ships of war, with never a civilian present... Tell me, O'Connor - and I ask you this *not as Admiral,* I speak now *not* as your superior officer, *but as one mortal human being to another* - why would you care to return... and how can you bring yourself to go back... to... to such *hell?* From where and how do you find the resolution... *the courage* to do so?'

Thursday 22nd December   1825   18:00   Tobermory, Mull

The fire still burned with vigour in the hearth, the warm room filled with the sweetly aromatic scent of pine woodsmoke, and

Simon sipped cautiously at a similarly smoky but delicious Islay pot-distilled whisky, its malted barley origins the foundation of the most palatable of flavours. It was a present from Flora's brother-in-law. The modest supper of bread and cheese was long finished, and the girls - much excited by Simon's presence - had gone to bed an hour before their customary hour but in irrepressible good humour, not the least notice taken of Flora's suggestions of an hour before that they should retire, and only her pressed insistence eventually carried the day.

'My dear Flora,' Simon began in tentative, nervous hesitancy. He refreshed his glass, wracked his brain for a suitable introduction to his thoughts, ones he had rehearsed over and over within the darkness of his tiny cabin aboard *Surprise*, but to his frustration and chagrin his refined oratorical conclusions simply would not come. The moment which he had contemplated for many months, for all of the evening, had surely arrived, but it had wrought a fear and many questions within him: was it really the right time? Would Flora be receptive? Would the disquieting concerns relating to his landlord, which had so obviously upset Flora, override the calm, the tranquillity, that he believed to be the essential prerequisite to mention that so very important subject which had preoccupied his own thoughts for so long? He drained his glass, refused Flora's refill, and he grasped her hand. 'I am with child to speak of a particular matter with you, I am so.'

Flora's face registered the red flush of alarm, Simon regretting his choice of words in an instant. 'It is nothing to be affrighted by, have no worries of that, my lov... my dear.' He squeezed her hand. 'No, my very close friend, Patrick O'Connor, as you may collect, has pledged funds to buy the house from Salmon; indeed, he has promised a sufficiency to also repair the roof, and so we are assured... *we are assured*, you and I... and the bairns... of staying within this home; we are guaranteed of being together... within *our* home.'

Flora's cheeks were streaked with the beginnings of tears, 'I am greatly sensible of your kindness,' and then came the unfettered crying, not the slightest ability to hold her feelings of the most profound relief in check, the tension within her perfectly plain to Simon, her clenched grip upon his hands being squeezed ever tighter.

He spoke again very softly, his words a whisper, 'It is... it has been... has been in my thinking for a considerable time... That is to say, my dear... and I hope with all my heart that this will not be the end of all our discourse... I beg you will allow me to say that my thoughts for you are... are ever more so in... in the personal line, *the very personal*... more so than the... the friendship... *the solely platonic line*; I... *I love you*. I love you very much indeed... more than I can say.'

From Flora, her face pressed into Simon's chest, the sobbing erupted, loud and utterly unconstrained, severe physical tremulations seizing all her body in wave after wave of cathartic release, a flood tide of uncontrollable emotion erupting.

Friday 23rd December 1825   08:30   Mutton Cove, Plymouth

A night of plentiful food and drink at the *Crown and Column*, a hasty breakfast consumed, and the Surprises hastened to Mutton Cove and the cutter, young Jelbert in solitary attendance. 'Godspeed, Mr Codrington, and safe passage,' declared Pat, shaking his lieutenant's hand, the last one to board. On her deck Barton and Jelbert raised arms in farewell; Pickering, on the quay, cast off the line, and the Tamar current, just past slackwater, gradually pulled *Mathew Jelbert* away from the wall, her taut sails in the south-westerly immediately hauling her away. The gap opening, she rapidly picked up speed, bearing for the Narrows. Standing on the quay in the weak dawn light, Pat squinted and shielded his eyes as he stared into the low winter sunrise, watching with Duncan, Prosser, Pickering, Mower and Murphy until the cutter cleared the Narrows and entered the Sound, her form diminishing within the grey drizzle of the sleety rain, the miserable grey overburden of low cloud streaks partially obscuring the visible blue of the higher sky. Slowly the cutter grew smaller until she was no more than a dwindling and indistinct speck, eventually disappearing beyond the headland as she turned away to the south.

Pat, with something of a heavy heart, nodded to his shipmates, 'Let us away, gentlemen; onwards and to the barky.'

It was with mixed feelings that he paced up the few yards of the slope to gain the James Street entrance gate in the wall. The marine guards admitted him on sight of Saumarez's pass without delay, a gesture of respect offered with their emphatic salute, for Pat was known of old to many of the garrison; indeed, a thousand men all along the quay wall had cheered *HMS Surprise's* previous departure for Greece. Ten minutes of walking inside the South Yard, past the mast pond and to the basin, revealed *Surprise* in all her restored glory, all her yards hoisted, all her sails clewed up, her rigging state one of such pristine perfection that every man simply stared in wonder; no longer was she the greatly battered, damaged frigate which had limped home in such dreadful disrepair from the brutal savaging of her narrow escape from Navarino; nor did she exhibit any vestige of all the subsequent temporary repairs, which had reduced her carpenter and sailmaker to professional despair. All along her side the freshly painted, immaculate and wide yellow band, which Nelson himself had favoured, was more prominent than ever. Passing from bow to stern and through all the gun ports, it looked simply magnificent. The barky, the dear *Surprise* as she was known to every man of her crew and many more throughout the service, was very visibly once more in perfect fettle, and it gladdened the hearts and minds of all five of the arrivals who beheld her in stunned inspection, in near disbelief.

From the deck atop the boarding ramp a familiar figure waved vigorously in greeting before rushing down to the quay; Reeve was plainly greatly pleased to see his captain and colleagues. He arrived in tongue-tied exuberance, shaking hands vigorously with everyone, even Murphy, 'Welcome sir, welcome back... 'tis good to see you all returned!'

'Mr Reeve, I hope I see you in fine fettle!' exclaimed Pat, his own feelings that all would assuredly be well filling his mind, the frigate never allowed entirely out of the corner of his gaze even as, ostensibly, he looked to his junior officer.

'Mighty fine, sir, thank you.'

'Will we go aboard? Mr Reeve, if you will, please to lead the way,' Pat waved his arm towards the ramp. All followed Reeve with a spring in their step, the previously apprehensive mood of indecision of everyone diminishing generally as they climbed up to stand on the gun deck before the coach, where they paused to look about them once more. Stretching away for'ard the great guns were lined up as if on parade: *Devil's Tongue, Heaven's Gate* and *Bill Stevens*, all the way to *Venom*, the most for'ard gun on the larboard side; and on the starboard side *In Your Eye, Revenge* and *Blood 'n' Guts*, the three nearmost guns, positively gleamed in pristine black. All were freshly painted and displayed no traces of rust as they sat on carriages which, to Pat's memory, had plainly been refurbished and renovated to varying degrees, none of them exhibiting their former traces of being struck or smashed by Turk shot.

'Upon my word,' exclaimed Pat, 'she hardly seems the same ship!' He mounted the steps to reach the quarterdeck, hastening aft to the wheel - the scene of his nightmares - where he turned about to stare at the carronades, the 'smashers' as they were known; he looked to the replacement timbers of the formerly shattered and repaired bulwarks, recalling with the most vivid intensity of painful memory the gap where the Turk shot had smashed through the timbers to shower lethal wooden splinters all across the quarterdeck. One of these had been fatal to Mathew Jelbert, and the gunner had died in Pat's grasp. The recollection of that brutal event was usually the horrific climax of his nightmares. In an instant there was a lump in a very dry throat and Pat's heart turned over, the bile rising. Thankfully the repair left no visible reminder of the distressing gore and blood he had beheld on that most savage, the most greatly distressing, of all days. A long exhale escaped his lips, a small tear escaped his eye, his heart rate accelerated, and he swallowed hard before turning about to look at his friends; plainly they too were in a similar degree of difficulty in that painful moment of recollection, and his stomach in that chilling instant turned over.

Saturday 24th December 1825 11:00   Tobermory, Mull

Simon sat at the small table near the fire, consuming his porridge, a pot of coffee suspended over the edge of the glowing embers. The usual aroma of the room's woodsmoke melded with the glorious scent of the coffee; both were a delightful backcloth to his enduring sense of satisfaction. Flora's upset of the previous evening had thwarted his first endeavours to broach the subject of marriage whilst he comforted her, and for that he was disappointed. However, her physical demonstration of relief, of gratitude, even joy, on his news that their home was safe, that the landlord would never have the opportunity to evict them before a sale of Simon's house, that they would remain living there together, was exceedingly welcome; indeed, he found it reassuring, the warmth of her embrace for the remainder of the evening very much more so. He placed another log on the fire, sat back and sipped his coffee. He wondered whether it might be too soon to broach the subject of matrimony when Flora returned from the quay with the promised fresh fish for a meal which he had keenly anticipated all morning. Perhaps his general sense of well-being, fostered by the day being Christmas Eve, would help his cause. The door creaked and Flora entered, her warm smile offered before she passed through to deposit the fish in the cold of the pantry, returning within moments.

'Welcome back, my dear,' Simon rose from his chair. His embrace - much to his delight - was most cordially received, and his prospects for that subject which was very much weighing upon his mind appeared to be blossoming. Summoning up his courage, and mindful that the lassies were absent, he resolved to seize the moment and speak of his aspirations.

'Here is a letter for you...' declared Flora before he could do so, her words spoken with the tiniest hint of anxiety, '... which arrived today. The postmaster hailed me as I walked by with the fish. Were you expecting it?' Flora's tone of voice carried an audible hesitancy which did not pass Simon's notice.

'Not at all; however, it is conceivably from O'Connor, and - *I am only speculating, of course* - perhaps he is writing of the intended house purchase.' Simon sat down, enjoyed another sip of his coffee, and with a degree of curiosity he opened the letter and began to read,

London   Thursday 15th December 1825
Dear Simon,
I hope my letter finds you well and that you have found that

comfort and satisfaction which I recall you much looked forward to securing and enjoying at home on Mull.

It has been something of a tumultuous time these past few weeks. Indeed, the voyage I had myself anticipated with great satisfaction - home to Connemara and Sinéad - did not eventuate. Rather, I was tasked by men of great influence in London - and I will say no more of them - to fetch a certain cargo from France, from Calais, and to bring it to London. Previously, I had been informed by my cousin, Canning, of the insolvency of my own bank, and that after I had been assured of its survival with the receipt of considerable funds from the Bank of England, which I had seen with my own eyes. The conclusion of this regrettable matter is that I am broke! Can you believe it? I can hardly do so myself!

Simon's heart sank, seemingly the security of his home was now to be denied him. How could he possibly speak of this with Flora? Her distress would surely know no bounds. Thankfully she was in the kitchen and oblivious of his own minor panic, which he thought must show plain in his face. He turned the page and read on in haste,

Consequent to the above, and mindful of the necessity for fulfilling my promise to you of - will I say - not inconsiderable funds, I have written to Perkis with my acceptance of his offer to purchase a substantial share in my Claddaghduff gold mine, and similarly there is a letter sent to your friend Peddler, who I believe is on Mull at the present time, for I have also accepted his own indicated interest in the venture.

It may be some weeks before the funds they have promised in order to purchase their shareholdings reaches my advocate in London, when I will be able to make available to you a plentiful sufficiency for your requirements at home on Mull. I trust that the delay will not be too great an inconvenience. Please rest assured that I am in no doubt that Sinéad will be wholly with me in this matter. As my grandmother oft said, "Better the tatties next year than the whiskey this week when considering of the last shilling".

The unfamiliar idiom was as immediately inexplicable as many others which Simon had oft heard from his dear friend, but nevertheless his spirits soared from the depths of despond: the disaster he had immediately anticipated after the opening page was not about to beset him! He did not need to speak of the matter with Flora after all! It was with a feeling of huge relief that he looked at the next page and continued to read.

London   Wednesday 21st December 1825

I must tell you, old friend, of one other event. The First Lord has asked me to take command of HMS Surprise once again. The Prime Minister, no less, has ordered the barky to return to Greece in order to convey supplies to the besieged defenders of Messalonghi. The town is, by all accounts, close to falling to Ibrahim's bombardment and blockade. Quite how we ourselves will be able to safely and surely deliver the promised supplies is a trifle unclear to me - a great Turk fleet harboured so close by in Patras. Yes, I am myself exceedingly surprised to report that I am returning to Greece, once more in command of our ship.

"Our ship", the words struck a powerful chord. Simon read on,

I had believed that I could never again face the tumultuous strain of that infernal place, but somehow - I know not how - I have found the courage and made my pledge to do so. I am leaving aboard the new cutter, Mathew Jelbert, this morning for Devonport. The First Lord assures me that Surprise is there in fine fettle, her refitting all completed. I anticipate that as early as next week she will depart for Greece. My present concern is to find sufficient Falmouth men who will care to join together with me again after the dreadful losses of past times in Greek waters; indeed, all such thoughts - I am sure you will forgive me for saying so - bring on a cold wave of despair in my mind. I will speak of these matters with all my officers when we are en route for Devonport aboard the cutter. I am in great haste this morning to reach the Billingsgate Quay, and hence I have no time to write more at the moment.

Please accept my warmest wishes for your well-being together with all your intended new family members, and I assure you that I will write again when there is further news.

Your dearest friend,
Patrick O'Connor

Simon's mind reeled and, for the second time reading the letter, he felt sick in the pit of his stomach; Patrick O'Connor truly was his dearest friend in all the world and he was returning to the bloody conflict which was Greece. Within seconds came the realisation that Duncan Macleod would assuredly accompany Pat O'Connor. Not for one instant could he conceive that Duncan would demur from supporting his own dear friend; no, he most certainly would not. Macleod too would certainly be returning. What to do? His mind was plunged into a frantic and confusing turmoil of conflicting thoughts and raging emotions. What on earth should he do? What of Flora? How would she react to the news? What of the bairns who had so warmly welcomed his return? What of the landlord, Salmon, and his intentions of selling the house? How could he resolve that with Pat so far away, communications from Greece taking an age? Most significant of all in his slowly coalescing thoughts, how could he not support his close friends and valued shipmates? It was likely, indeed it was almost certain, that men would be once more wounded and severely injured; men he had known and served with for many years would be cast into great pain, when they would be in great fear and - he cursed inwardly - in danger of death. True, Michael Marston likely would be there, and he was undoubtedly a competent surgeon, but he was one man, and one man alone would struggle with an insufferable burden in any battle of even the slightest significance. How, therefore, could he himself continue to live - *safe and secure* - in Tobermory when so many people who were dear to him might, and likely would, be fighting for their lives in distant Greece, wounded and dying in that wretched place? His breathing accelerated and he thought for a few seconds that he might vomit. He drained his coffee to wash down the bile rising in his throat and he silently despaired.

Sunday 25th December 1825 13:00 HMS Surprise   Devonport

The cabin stove was plainly doing all it could, the coals stacked to full capacity by Murphy, the cast iron positively radiating warmth to where Pat had shifted his chair, as close as it could possibly be. Notwithstanding this he was cold; the night had been freezing, and he had lain awake for much of it within his cot, fully clothed and huddled under many blankets but never feeling warm at any time during the wintry ordeal. Uncomfortable in mind as well as in body, he had listened to the fierce wind whistling through the rigging, the canvas bundles of the sails flapping and slapping against their yards in the strong gusts despite being all clewed up as tight as tight could be. Greece was ever in his thoughts. Sinéad would not yet know he was returning, was going back to hell; his letter to distant Connemara would not yet have arrived. He fretted about how his wife, dear Sinéad, would react. She would be dismayed and distressed, of that he was sure, but he hoped that she might understand his reasoning, as best as he had managed to describe it within his letter. Doubtless Simon, the learned man that he was, would have written a better one. He sighed. He drank the last of his coffee as he pondered over the number of men Mower might return with aboard the cutter, which was expected to return before the sun went down over Cremyll. It would certainly not be much of a Christmas Day for all those making the wild and windswept voyage from Falmouth, but at least - a small and doubtful mercy - the south-westerly gale would ensure the swiftest of passages. His thoughts returned to more immediate matters; his steward was expected within minutes, for Pat was joining his small cadre of shipmates for dinner in the closest possible proximity to the warmth of the much larger and hotter galley stove. At least Wilkins, his ever loyal cook who had served with him aboard *Tenedos* before *Surprise*, was present and so the repast, whatever Wilkins had managed to find, would be edible, likely even tasty; at least Pat hoped so, for he found precious little else to look forward to in that moment of profound personal disquiet.

'Ah, Murphy, there you are. Did Mr Laithwaite attend this morning? We will take a few brace of his wine to our dinner.'

'Well, to be sure he did, sorr,' a broad smile from Murphy, 'and a plentiful supply is stowed in the liquor store.'

'Very good; rouse out... *rouse out a dozen* for the table, the Portuguese with the red seal... and look to my private stores to see if you can find any remnant of the walnuts... and MURPHY!' Pat shouted as his steward had just exited the cabin, Murphy's shrewish face returning to peer around the door. 'Please to bring my shoes out from the coach, thank you. I will be away to the table in just a minute or two, after I visit my quarter-gallery.'

'Oh no, sorr; not dressed in them working clothes... no, never in life; you mayn't grace the table in them dirty old rags... beg pardon, sorr.'

'Very well,' Pat frowned, 'Look to what betters may remain in my sea chest.'

Murphy hastened out, returning ten minutes later and possessing a quite triumphant air. 'Well, 'ere be your clean vestments, sorr,' he declared with heavy emphasis, laying them over the back of Pat's chair but, surprisingly, not hurrying away towards the treasure trove which was the liquor store. A silent minute passed, Pat's thoughts remaining elsewhere, and then came the loudest of coughs as Murphy rehung the clothes over the chair in exaggerated demonstration.

'Very well,' Pat sighed with reluctant resignation, nodding to his steward who remained stock still, for he never relinquished the cabin until Pat had commenced to discard his working attire for the freshly pressed dress uniform which Murphy, perhaps having none of his own, gloried in seeing.

Ten more minutes passed and Pat arrived at the galley in all his finery; all his officers who had arrived aboard *Mathew Jelbert* were also dressed as best they could be, and all were engaged in vigorous discussion with William Reeve, who had stayed with *Surprise* during her refit. The master, Jeremiah Prosser, was likewise talking with great animation with the carpenter. Stuart Tizard had served with Pat aboard the frigate for many years; indeed, Pat remembered him since he had himself first joined *Surprise*. He stepped closer to the jovial gathering, 'Mr Tizard, you are still here I see!'

'Aye, sir. I will always be here. You may count on that.' It was an old tradition within the Royal Navy that the ship's carpenter never transferred to any other ship, even if every other man of the crew had departed for vessels afresh.

Pat's attention shifted to the dozen men who had remained aboard with Reeve and the non-commissioned officers. They were, variously, the junior carpenters and men who had some degree of experience as shipwrights. 'Lads, I trust I see you well?' Broad smiles appeared all round and a surge of warm replies followed, contentment being the general message. All clutched a tankard of grog, and this - for so it appeared to Pat as his eyes shifted across many happy faces - was far from their first liquid indulgence of this festive day. That was obvious to his gaze. He shook hands with the first man, the captain of the maintop, 'Williams, I hope I see you in fine fettle... all a-tanto?'

'Never better; thankee, sir.'

'I take that very well... good man.' Pat spoke to the next man, 'How are you, Pascoe?'

'Glad to be aboard the barky again, sir.'

Pat nodded, silently marvelling at the evident good morale of those two of his veterans; 'And how do you fare, Tamblyn?' he said to the next, 'Tolerably spry, I trust?'

'Mighty fine, sir; thankee.'

'Will I ask... you are a family man, if my recall serves me... are you minded to stay with us... we are sailing to Falmouth on the morrow and thence to Greece and... and - *I do not greatly care to say it* - bloody battle might well be our lot once more?'

'Sure, but I am a'staying, sir... and my wife is much pleased, so she is.'

'Very good; that greatly contents me to hear it. You have my best thanks.' Pat smiled and shifted to speak with the next man, and so on, passing by all of the others in turn after a few words with each one, incrementally taking to heart their obvious good cheer such that he was buoyed up himself by the time he reached the head of the table where Murphy passed him his glass of wine, plentifully filled. 'Mr Sampays,' Pat spoke to the bosun, a Portuguese and another longstanding shipmate, 'the lads are in high good spirits.'

'Aye, sir; that they are for sure. It is ever the warm welcome they find here in the town, and the barky being tied at the quay they have made the most of that.'

'I am sure they have. Alongside and a few shillings in the pocket... why, 'tis a sailor's dream come true, eh?'

'Aye, sir; that it is. All of the lads have been working with the men of Devonport for many weeks now, and - *so it is said* - they are usually to be found when off-duty telling the tales of *Surprise's* time in the Greek war, and - *doubtless it is the case* - much exaggerated and glorified in the telling.' The bosun laughed out loud.

Pat managed a small smile, 'Come now, I am sure they speak of such small tales as would hardly raise an eyebrow.'

Sampays continued, 'Why, such stories that the men speak of ever impress the local lads, for they have never heard anything of such ilk, at least not since Boney was finally sorted out and the Yankees had been put in *their* place, for that is how they see things. So, sir, our lads be most popular men... much liked to be seen with in the streets and alehouses of Devonport, and so they never lack for ale. Duty here while we have been in the refit has turned out very nice indeed!' Another loud laugh erupted from the bosun, echoed by several men nearby who had been listening intently to his tale.

Even Pat laughed this time, a little fillip of good cheer coming upon him. He turned to face the bulk of his tiny assembly, set down his wine glass upon the table and raised both his arms in the air, heads everywhere turning towards him, the hubbub of many small conversations dying away to silence. The wind, less fierce than during the night, continued to blow through the rigging, gusts tearing at the netting hanging above the gundeck. The familiar background sounds of creaks, cracks and slaps were still very audible in the expectant air of a score of men waiting for, indeed hanging on, Pat's words. 'Lads, will you join me in the toast? Will you raise your glasses? I give you... ABSENT FRIENDS!'

'ABSENT FRIENDS!' The roar of the reply to the Royal Navy's traditional Sunday toast could not have been louder had a hundred more men been present. At that, everyone took their places around the lash-up of the temporary, large and lengthy table, officers and men together, Murphy and Freeman hastening to refill grog tankards and wine glasses.

The most vigorous and sociable banter, all officers' privileges of rank much subdued and near wholly discarded, with many fond recollections of old days aboard *Tenedos* before *Surprise,* flowed loudly across the table for a jovial half-hour until Pat, drumming his fist upon the table, caught everyone's attention, when he began to carve the first of the turkeys presented by the cook. The square, wooden plates were passed along from hand to hand, Pat pausing in brief assessment as the steaming treasure was handed over to each man. 'Mr Tizard, wait! Allow me to cut you another slice, the starboard side of your plate looks a trifle out of ballast!' A great burst of laughter erupted all around the table. 'Murphy!' Pat shouted up over the re-emerging babble of voices, 'Please to pass round the gravy... handsomely does it... thankee... and Murphy, take your fingers out of the boat!' The steward glared and shifted further away, moving along to the far end of the table. 'Mr Macleod, will I help you to a little more of the dark meat?' said Pat. Everyone being served at last, the table set to with determination to feast upon very full plates, digestion aided and watered by the most generous flow of grog and wine. Occasional jests were offered, usually at Murphy's expense and always followed with an accompanying loud round of ribald laughter, as they gorged with contentment, a glorious happiness having settled upon them all.

Sunday 25th December 1825   16:00   *Tobermory, Mull*

Simon had tried hard throughout the Christmas Day meal to maintain a composure suited to the festive occasion at the dinner table; indeed, as far as the two girls were concerned, he had succeeded, but not so in the case of Flora. The turkey remnants having been carried away to the pantry and the youngsters gone out to call on friends, Flora spoke with evident anxiety, adding to Simon's burning angst. Her entirely innocuous words were little louder than a whisper but the unspoken meaning being of such unsettling effect upon Simon's equilibrium, 'I pray that the dinner found favour with you?'

'The dinner? Why of course, my dear... most certainly it did; it was... it was exceptional, so it was.' Simon's mind jarred: that moment which he had dreaded had come and it could be deferred no longer. Yet he stalled, his thoughts racing, 'Oh, assuredly so... excellent, nothing less. May I say I enjoyed it immensely... the... the turkey was cooked to perfection... yes indeed... and the roast potatoes... why, they were a marvel...' Recognising that his words were plainly falling on exceedingly stony ground, upon the deafest of ears, Flora's silent stare a mute inquisition which screamed out for answers, more than any words might ever do, Simon halted. He took a sip of his wine very slowly, his mind a turmoil of incomplete conclusion and a whirlwind of confusion.

'I beg you will forgive me for speaking of matters which...' Flora spoke in the most anxious of tone, '... which I can hold back no longer... but... that is to say... I.... I... will I speak of it?'

'Please... we are kin... that is to say we are friends, close friends... *the closest*.' Simon moved to hold her close. 'Let us share our thoughts without reservation, without holding back... I beg you will.'

'Very well, it is the year since we met... We... *the bairns and I*... we were an imposition upon the family of my brother-in-law and... and our longer stay in their tiny cottage was... was far from certain... and now I... *we* have found a welcome within your kindly... *your home*; indeed, we have found a sanctuary... within your warm-hearted embrace... yet I feel... in these recent days... a... a holding back. It is clear to me that you are set back with a worry... with something of considerable concern to you; that is perfectly plain.' A disconcerted Simon remaining mute but offering a cautious nod in reply, Flora continued, her voice descending to a whisper, the inflection of anxiety plain within it, '... and I am myself in fear of your concerns...'

'There is nothing to fear in the least,' Simon spoke at last in a soft voice, his own words as gentle, as soothing, as ever he could make them.

'We are... the bairns and I... we are all most grateful for your benevolence... for your generosity. Allow to me say... *and this is my heart speaking*... we, all of us are... that is to say... you have saved us...' Flora began to cry, '... *You have saved me*...'

'No, my dear,' a deep breath from Simon, 'No... the truth of the matter is... the truth is... *and I believe I know this to be the case*... is that it is *you* who has saved *me*.' He seized Flora in his arms, 'Yes, there has long been one vile matter on my own mind, and you will forgive me for exhibiting it so... without speaking of it with you, but... whilst at sea...' Simon struggled for his own words, 'Whilst at sea... all of us aboard the vessel experienced black days... the most horrible events... and... and I have not spoken of such matters to anyone before... *never.* There were moments... hours, many of them during such times... the bleakest of spells when... when it pleased me to think of... of you... and the bairns too, here at home... in my home, *our home*, in... in this sanctuary which is our village, *blessed Tobermory*. It was after the second battle to defend Samos island from Turk invasion... I was...' A long, long exhalation and Simon fought to hold his rising emotions in check, 'I was... mortally cast down in the aftermath of the battle, so many of my shipmates... *so many friends*... struck down. I was greatly set back... so much so that I found myself unable to shake the deep despond which followed... and I found myself living in a cold despair. For months afterwards... in the night... I could not sleep. I awoke in my cot, trying to escape the nightmares... thinking of the cockpit... that foul and dark corner below deck... with dying men on my table who... *who I was unable to save*,' Simon paused, found himself in difficulty, searching for words which would not easily come. A tearful Flora seized his hands as he resumed, '... and then I would go out... go upstairs... to take a solitary turn upon the deck... during many a night... to find a quiet place, a deserted locus, a sanctuary... often to spend hours at... at the side of the ship... to stare out into the darkness, the rolling waves my only audience... to find... to sit in solitude... where no one might espy my bleak distress... to be in a place where I could think... ever wondering... could I have done more for those men whom we had lost, wounded shipmates that I... I could not save? And in the black... *the blackest* of moments... when the tears of despair were flowing down my cheeks... unceasing tears for many an hour... I found relief when I looked forward to... to coming home... home to dear Tobermory... *home to you...* to the bairns...

and those precious thoughts, my love... *those most precious of all thoughts...* saved me, *more than ever I can say.*'

Quiet tears flowed from Flora's eyes as her body was wracked by gentle tremors, the stream of tears bridging the close touch of Simon's face to flow down his cheeks, the salt tang reaching his lips. No words came from her in her distress, and with time seemingly suspended in the profound moment, Simon's hesitant words came at long last, 'Listen child, I beg you will allow me to speak of two further matters with you.' A sharp intake of breath by Flora and apprehension was writ large across her face once more as she pulled back to stare at him, but Simon pressed on whilst his nerve still held, 'For the first, it is, as you say, a full year that we have been acquainted... Do you recall that day when we met... on the quay?' Flora nodded cautiously. 'It was, I think, the most momentous day for me... I... I... that is to say...' As Simon paused, a fresh wave of anxiety flooded Flora's very being, which he could not fail to notice; fresh tears streamed down her cheeks in a rekindled and enduring flood tide of emotion, Simon's personal revelations not entirely quashing her deep-seated fear of rejection. Summoning his courage, Simon took a deep breath, 'Flora... my... *my precious*... would you... that is to say, will you... will you marry me?'

Sunday 25th December 1825 16:30 HMS Surprise   Devonport

Pat and the Surprises lingered at the table in the weak light of the gloaming, the sun not long having gone down. The lights in the South Yard and of wider Devonport flickered as tiny pinpricks in the deepening darkness, and across the Hamoaze all was black. The stewards still busied around the table with plentiful grog and more wine. It was a greatly relaxed gathering, a rare and precious sociable ambience. The yellow glow from the suspended Argand lamps illuminated a scene of gastronomic satiation and gentle inebriation, the four turkeys all consumed. Even the ship's cat, rather fat after weeks in the relative plenty which was Devonport, had indulged to great excess on the most generous of meaty fragments cast upon the deck, and now lay curled up, adjacent to the galley stove, which was a magnet embracing everyone within the reach of its warmth. It was maintained with frequent coal injections by Freeman, and no one cared to shift away, Pat himself having not the least inclination to return to the gloom of his cold cabin and the bleak, uninviting cot.

Over the table the conversation flowed without let or hindrance, albeit rather more slowly than earlier. All the officers as well as the hands were gloriously gorged with the plentiful food and the generous surfeit of drink, none paying any mind to the odd comment which might have, in more usual circumstances, attracted mild rebuke, even laughing at every joke, including those which were certainly fairly near the mark of the Royal Navy's conventions in the presence of officers. Veterans' tales of the old days, long gone, aboard *Tenedos* before *Surprise,* were a substantial element of the discussion; but, perhaps subconsciously, the subject of more recent times in Greece was never mentioned, much less the imminent return. All daunting apprehensions, such as those Pat himself harboured, were kept firmly out of the jovial exchanges, if not entirely out of mind, as time slipped by in the deeply satisfying haze of digestive fulfilment and cordial banter until, from the south end of the Yard, came loud shouts, hails and a rumbustious clamour, alerting the Surprises to dozens of men approaching, all as yet indistinct in the darkness. The Surprises leaped up to the side to stare in the direction of the loudly boisterous gang. Three minutes more and they could be discerned in shape if not in detail, at least thirty men, their shouting ever louder; another minute passed and identifiable figures began to climb the ramp to the deck, a very happy Mower leading the charge. Pat too had shifted to see what the commotion was, and he stood at the top of the ramp, glorious relief and blessed joy the pleasurable meld of feelings infusing his mind as he realised it was the essential crew that he had been hoping to find. Many more of his Falmouth veterans were present amongst them. They were returning to his ship, *to their ship*, to the barky, to their home at sea. With a huge smile on his face he extended his hand and shouted in loud voice, 'Welcome aboard, Mr Mower! Welcome back, lads; a grand welcome to you all! Happy Christmas!'

Sunday 25th December 1825   16:30   *Tobermory, Mull*

Simon held Flora tightly within his arms, both entwined around her slight figure, her head upon his shoulder. Each gripped the other with a fierce determination in the most desperate embrace. Minutes passing, Simon whispered in her ear, 'My dear, will I speak of the second matter, one sitting ill upon my mind? Please, let us be seated.' Wiping her eyes, Flora returned to her chair by the fireside, the logs valiantly throwing a beatific warmth to the room despite the enduring freezing temperatures outside which held the rest of the house in frigid discomfort. 'The letter which I received yesterday from my dear friend, O'Connor...' Simon paused as he saw the anxiety flooding back into Flora's face. 'Be assured that it remains his intention to provide the funds to me with which I will buy the house from Salmon...' Flora nodded, her eyes open wider than ever. 'However, that is not the... *the principal* significance of his letter... much to my regret; no, he writes of more immediate events, ones which - *I confess* - neither he nor I greatly cared to contemplate.' Her face a picture of dismay, Flora possessing the intelligence to perceive the essence of that which Simon was plainly struggling to enunciate, he pressed on, 'It pains me to say this... it does so, and I have struggled with... with some difficulty with the matter since reading the letter yesterday... I will say... *I must say...* that my mind is made up; my conscience obliges me to return, to join my shipmates, my dear friends, aboard our vessel, for she is to leave for Greece in the days - *the immediate days* - of this week. Indeed, it is conceivable that *Surprise* may already have departed. In which event I will board the first packet for the Ionians from Falmouth. I am returning, my love, to Greece.' Simon offered his handkerchief, the refreshed beginnings of Flora's silent tears becoming visible. 'It is not something that I ever wished to contemplate again after... after the last time, but those men... *my friends...* may... *likely will* face difficulties of... of that nature such that I myself am best able to serve them in the time of their most dire distress... and I cannot contemplate them enduring for even a moment such a... *a tribulation* without I am there... I beg you will forgive me, my dearest, but... I must be there to help them. Why, I venture I could not live with myself were I to remain here when they will likely be in peril; no, never in life.'

Monday 26th December 1825 08:00 HMS Surprise   Devonport

HMS *Surprise*, her lines cast off, her topsail yards braced to catch the northerly wind, and her hull pushed in the grip of the Tamar current, shifted a little way from the quay in the weak illumination of the pre-dawn twilight. There was not yet the least sign of the sun itself in the eastern skies above Plymouth. Two score of hands attended the braces, and those dozen men who had remained aboard during the refit stared with mixed feelings at the near-deserted wall of the South Yard, only a very few men present and looking on.

'You have command, Mr Prosser,' declared Pat emphatically, shivering in the extreme cold. It had been a disturbed night of broken sleep, not the least warmth and precious little comfort in his small cot. Staring all about him, Pat beheld a scene of such total contrast to the frigate's last departure; this time there were no great crowds of cheering shipwrights, no farewells from long-established friends within the Devonport community, and no goodbye from Admiral Saumarez. The difference on this occasion, the atmosphere of quietude, was most disconcerting to all on deck.

'Helm hard over,' pronounced the master in firm voice to Barton at the wheel, and *Surprise* began to widen her divergence from the quay.

Half a dozen hands, all veterans, the elders of the Surprises, remained behind to attend *Mathew Jelbert*, every man watching the departing frigate in fascination. Lieutenant Mower too remained behind, standing amongst them. Slowly all waved their arms in farewell. The silence on both the quay and the ship registered with everyone. It was downright uncomfortable to all. The sense of separation of one shipmate from another was most unsettling, even a little unnerving. This seemed, to every man - looking all about him to his fellows - wholly endemic to all; the cheerful feelings of companionship of the previous day and the ebullient evening had ceded to a stark awareness that the barky really was returning to duty, the Surprises were voyaging towards that far place where, in earlier times, prized friends, tiemates even, had been lost. What would happen this time? What did the future hold for them? Would they themselves be coming back? It was with these troubling forebodings that the men aboard *Surprise* settled to their tasks, to the routines of seamanship, of ship handling. Such work was something of a rock of activity upon which to allow their anxieties to settle, to be held in check, and they set to their familiar duties with determination, few words spoken as they worked.

'I dare say... when Mower follows on... after the Yard has installed the chasers which Saumarez has promised...' declared Pat, breaking a general and thoughtful silence, all his officers standing around him on the deck near the helm. '... I venture the cutter, being faster, may likely catch up with us afore we reach Cephalonia.' No reply came from any source, all present failing to rise to the intended distraction, glum stares abounding on every face.

Surprise, gaining the centre of the channel, sailed on, gathering momentum. A turn hard over to larboard, another to starboard within a few minutes, two short boards, and she cleared the Narrows, the rising sun fine on the larboard bow and bright in everyone's eyes.

'At least we are blessed with a dry morning and a moderate sea!' Pat tried again to spark a break from the depressing silence on his quarterdeck. Heads everywhere turned to look upwards, the grey, overhanging cloudy presence in the far western skies an obvious portent of what would likely come later.

Prosser turned to Pat, 'Mr Mower has sent messengers all about Falmouth town to pass the news that the barky is sailing today, sir, and that we will need plentiful men for the morrow.'

'Very good; I hope we may find a hundred and more awaiting us...' murmured a thoughtful Pat, '... and let us hope too that we are favoured by these benevolent conditions all day.'

Saint Nicholas's Island was soon abeam and the frigate passed close by one of Whidby's Bovisand barges, bringing granite to the western extremity of the breakwater, repairs ongoing, the construction much damaged and diminished by that same hurricane assault of the previous year which had almost destroyed *Surprise* herself. At last she gained the open water beyond the breakwater, her fore and main courses were let fall, their yards braced, and the frigate rapidly gained speed. All her crew, officers and men alike, marvelled at her prowess; the replaced mizzenmast and oak yards, and the strong, fresh canvas of her sails propelled her in the freshening north-westerly wind to ten knots with conspicuous ease; her clean hull, free of weed, was canted far over to larboard as the sails took up the strain, the new hemp rigging creaking loud under the load. The Surprises were working hard, constantly heaving on the braces to maintain the tension as the new hemp stretched, all previous concerns cast aside in the familiar attentions and labour of ship handling.

'She is truly a delight to sail!' Pat persevered in loud voice to all on the quarterdeck; he was gratified to see nods and smiles replacing the previous faces of bleak apprehension. 'It is the strange day, Duncan,' he murmured, 'Here we are, the barky as good as new, but... I confess... I never felt less so myself.'

'Aye, I cannae disagree with ye there. I am nae looking forward to seeing the... that infernal place again.'

'... and I am in hope that our part will truly remain the humanitarian one... but I have my grave doubts about that.'

'Aye, I dinnae see the Turk welcoming us back.'

'No indeed.' Pat paused in thought. 'When I was a young laddie the fox was never welcome at the chicken coop in Claddaghduff. My grandma would sit me down with a pile of rocks to throw if ever I saw one.'

'And did ye?'

'I never saw the fox, no... not in the broad daylight, but the O'Malley brothers... neighbours... oft tried to steal a hen... and the rascallions - *they were so* - never worried about my stones.'

'So, did you hold them off, keep them away?'

'Sure I did,' Pat noticed he held the attention of the quarterdeck, all his officers and the helmsmen listening most attentively; 'I gave them a broadside... of the sow's dung!' Pat himself, Duncan and everyone else present all laughed out loud. 'With my catapult!' Louder laughs all round. 'Ten shots in a minute, that served them out! And that is what we will endeavour to do if the Turk arrives. I am in hope that Timmins will be with us as master gunner, and a score or more of his Greek Fire shot will serve us well again... if... if it is called for.'

'Aye, that was surely our saviour at Navarino, no doubt of that. D'ye know if Marston will be with us... to serve in the cockpit? Or even Jason perhaps?'

'No, I'm very sorry to say, I do not.' A thoughtful pause, 'It is the black day when Simon will not be with us. I am much set back by that, I am so.' That particular point brought all mirth to an abrupt end, a sense of despond registering with all present before all settled back to pass the time in private contemplation.

Noon, and Gribbin Head on the starboard beam as Pat took the sighting, 'How are we doing, Mr Prosser?'

'I fancy we may likely fetch home to Falmouth before the sunset,' declared the master with amiable satisfaction.

'That would please me mightily,' said Pat, nodding his head, his mood recovering a very little, 'I am in the way for a fine beefsteak at the Royal Hotel.'

'I beg ye will attend the Chapel first, sir. Mr Mower did assure me that there will be a hundred men and more awaiting us there, to hear ye speak... of Greece and our voyage particularly.'

'Of course, the Chapel first it is.'

Surprise ploughed on, the skies darkening, in sharp contrast to the morning, and a strong rain squall blew up as Dalby rang three bells of the afternoon watch. Although the cold wind was noticeably shifting to the north-west, Dodman Point was coming up on the starboard beam and confidence was rising generally in the master's prediction of reaching the intended anchorage near the town in the final minutes of daylight.

'At anchor in Falmouth harbour tonight... or the wide waters of the Roads for us? What say ye, Mr Prosser?' Duncan spoke up.

'Aye, sir; I think ye can be assured of stepping ashore... the Kings Road it will be. The tide is with us, if not the wind... *that* is not greatly helpful.'

The afternoon progressing, daylight was noticeably fading as seven bells rang out and *Surprise* passed close by Zone Point to starboard. The sun hung very low in the darkening, grey skies over the Lizard, the light much more diffuse in the gentle rainfall which had persisted for an hour or more; nothing much of a sunset was to be expected and the twilight would surely be a dim one.

'All hands on deck!' bawled Duncan. Dalby rang the bell with vigour. The command was hardly necessary as only Wilkins, Murphy and Freeman remained below, sheltering from the weather; every other man was standing ready to make the turn to pass the Black Rock, all aware that the north-westerly was very much *not* a helpful wind but a considerable hindrance.

Prosser, standing near the helm, shouted out his commands, all echoed by the lieutenants at the waist calling out down the length of the ship, men everywhere attending the braces with alacrity. It was a difficult and dangerous manoeuvre to bring the frigate into and through the wind with so little sea room on her lee side. Eventually *Surprise* made her turn, all her yards swiftly hauled round, the men heaving frantically on the braces as she slowed, slowed more, and then she passed the Black Rock to larboard, close-hauled on her north-easterly tack into the wide expanse of the Carrick Roads. It reminded Pat momentarily of the return after the hurricane of a year ago, a greatly damaged and sinking *Surprise* barely making home, and with just enough wind to make her final tack towards the Kings Road anchorage in the safety and protection of the harbour, seven feet of water sitting heavy in the hold and the pumps failing to hold back its rise. He reminded himself, with a degree of relief, that this was not the case today. His men were not exhausted but demonstrating their extreme skill and competence, and the bilges were dry, the pumps sucking; the yards were new and not the shattered, repaired timbers of last year. He was quite content to leave the master in command at the helm, no seafarer knew these waters better. Within moments Prosser had brought her round once more, *Surprise* turning again through the wind, her course settling at a little south of west and the barky sailing as close to the wind as she could; it was the final furlong, or so it seemed to Pat. A quarter-mile more and Prosser ordered the braces slackened, and *Surprise* slowed to a stop, all her canvas flapping as the hands climbed aloft to clew up. Her anchors were let go as the sun, greatly more obscured by denser cloud, finally dropped below the hill behind the town, the waterfront falling into the dark grey shadow of twilight. Pat, his thoughts in difficulty within an intolerable mixture of contrasting feelings, stared towards the Customs House Quay, on which, despite the steady rain falling and the dying of the light, he could make out several hundred waiting spectators, all braving the cold and unpleasant weather, many people waving in welcome. The barky, the dear *Surprise*, had returned once more to her home port, to Falmouth town, but in that moment, Pat, still thinking of his missing friend, felt something of a chilling surge of melancholia.

Chapter Five

Saturday 31st December 1825 15:30   Falmouth

A frozen, immobile and exhausted Simon was carefully helped down from the coach by the guard and driver, for he was utterly incapable of movement; indeed, he felt bruised upon every inch of his body after four days of jolting coach travel on the firmest of seats and with barely the shortest of breaks. He had rested for a few hours and no more between his several journeys to reach Falmouth at best speed, and consequently he struggled, with considerable difficulty, to stand as the driver at his arm assisted him with all due care into the Royal Hotel whilst the guard retrieved his seabag from the coach roof. 'Thank you, friend,' whispered Simon, gratefully settling into a fireside chair, no feeling left in his legs or feet whatsoever and his back aching with a fiery pain.

'From whence have you travelled, sir?' came the anxious waiter's solicitous enquiry, recognising Simon.

'Glasgow... I departed on Tuesday... in haste...' the words came in a low whisper through chattering teeth, 'the Isles before that... a steamer from Oban.'

A sharp intake of breath, 'So many days on the coach... 'tis a trial for sure, and in this cold winter weather! Why you must be mortally cast down, quite worn out.'

'Indeed,' Simon again could manage no more than a gasped reply.

'Do you care for refreshment... anything at all?'

'Strong hot coffee would be the glorious treasure of the world... if you please... and perhaps the merest trifle of brandy.'

'D'reckly, sir.'

Simon was already sleeping when Trewin returned five minutes later, the tray deposited and the most cautious of enquiries whispered to awaken him. Blinking his tired eyes, he nodded his thanks, two minutes more passing as he engaged in tentative stretching of tired, aching muscles before hesitantly sipping the coffee with a shaking hand and very slowly, all the time struggling to remain awake, the fire's flames beginning to return the smallest awareness of sensation to his numbed legs, but still nothing of his toes could he move or even feel at all. Fifteen minutes slipped by, the coffee all consumed, and his voice returning, Simon called to the passing waiter, 'Trewin, be so good as to tell me... My ship... *HMS Surprise*... Has that fine vessel... *my friends*... Have they departed?'

'Why, yes sir; she sailed on Wednesday.'

'Oh dear, then I am too late,' Simon sighed and frowned, a wash of disappointment coursing through him, his heart sinking.

'The gossip in the town, sir, says she is returning to Greece. There was a meeting on Monday evening in the Chapel, after the vessel arrived; two hundred Falmouth men and more attended Captain O'Connor. He spoke for an hour and longer about his purpose, the ship carrying supplies to... to a particular town in Greece which is - *and this is only what I heard yesterday from the chambermaid, she is married to one of the veterans of that fine vessel* - it is... *the town*... it is under siege. The people there are starving, and Captain O'Connor's ship is taking food to them. *Surprise* was anchored here all of Tuesday, and many Falmouth men signed up, went aboard... and she departed at sun up on Wednesday.'

'Would you have any cognisance of the packet timetable for Corfu, the next sailing date?'

'I do, sir. The packet captains all frequent this inn, and I am entirely acquainted with their customs and schedules.'

'The next departure would be... tell?'

'For the Mediterranean, sir, it is always the first Friday of the month; that would be next Friday, January the sixth.'

Saturday 31st December 1825   18:00   off La Coruña

'God is with us, sir, I venture,' declared a smiling Michael Marston, the chaplain, to a discernibly glum Pat, all of *Surprise's* officers standing on the quarterdeck and wrapped in thick sea coats against the cold. The sun was finally slipping away in distant farewell in the west on the starboard bow just as Dalby rang four bells of the first dog watch, and all present stood staring towards the far glow in the sky, an orange effervescence lingering above the final sliver of bright yellow on the horizon. The barky was rolling gently on the long swell, the muted twilight very much a calming, slowing influence upon everyone, all conversation near the helm falling away to a contemplative silence. With four days of gloriously untroubled - although greatly sedate - sailing with only a weak wind on their larboard quarter, only the slowest of progress had been made; but every man aboard was beginning to feel at home once more, back at sea and settling into the familiar routine of the ship. However, Pat himself was striving to come to terms with the absence of his dearest friend, Simon, but with only limited success; for the cabin, in the evenings, exhibited a discernible vacancy, with nothing of the cordial and generally jovial banter that they generally enjoyed. His meals, oft eaten alone, were a time of particular disappointment.

'She is sailing well, for sure,' said Pat cautiously, 'Nothing of weed on her hull, her sails all new... and the hemp of the rigging is the best I have ever seen. Plainly nothing of expense has been spared, and I ain't seen that before; no, never in life. Yes, I think someone is most certainly with us. Melville himself has vouched for her refit, and the Yard's coffers have been opened wide, not the least doubt of that.' He smiled a brief, wan smile, unconvincing, which left Marston slightly perturbed.

'If this finds the slightest interest with you, sir,' Marston persevered, 'I am in the way for an attempt upon a particular piece of music; that is to say, if you care to bring out your 'cello... Would you be minded to play... for an hour after supper perhaps?'

Pat turned towards Marston, recognising his benevolent purpose, 'Thank you... most kind, I would like that of all things.' Pat stared intently at his ship's chaplain for a few more seconds, recalling another instance, one which seemed to be lost in a distant past, when Simon had been absent, captured by the Turks; Marston had been extremely supportive in those bleak days. 'I beg you will consider taking supper with me in an hour; we will partake of a relaxing glass or two. I am minded that Mr Laithwaite's best red wine, a particular favourite of mine... from those lands over there...' Pat pointed to the far distant larboard horizon where a low ribbon of grey, no more, was vaguely perceptible beyond the miles of water, '... from the Peninsula, his Portuguese wine in particular, is of quite inestimable quality.'

'Splendid! Then I will fetch my violin and join you with pleasure...' Marston smiled, '... and with great anticipation.'

An hour later, Duncan remaining on watch, Murphy hastened to serve supper in the dim lamplight of the great cabin as soon as Pat sat down with Marston. Pat's personal malaise, his troubling discontent, was, unbeknown to him, widely recognised within the ship, and so his personal cook had excelled himself. Despite the beef loaded in Falmouth still being fresh, Wilkins had opted for not the smallest chance of dissatisfaction, Jemmy Ducks had been requested to slaughter a brace of his birds. Murphy deposited the tray with triumphant relish as his captain approached the table, looking on with enquiry, with rising and evident pleasure.

'This is a magnificent supper,' declared Pat, sniffing the divine scent arising as his steward lifted the lid before cheerfully attending to the cutlery; 'Why, I was expecting the cheeseboard, biscuit and nothing more.'

'Well, 'tis New Year's Eve, sorr... and Wilkins is in the way for something special for your Honour's table.'

'My compliments and best thanks to him, Murphy, if you will.'

'I trust you will allow me a moment to say grace, sir,' said Marston as they made themselves comfortable; 'A brief one, before we begin.'

'Most certainly, please do.'

Marston nodded, 'Dear Lord, for food that stays our hunger, for rest that brings us ease, for homes where memories linger, we give our thanks to you for these.'

'Thank you, Mr Marston... *Michael,* most admirably said,' declared a softly spoken Pat; 'And now, let us not stand further on ceremony,' this said louder and with relish, Pat visibly cheered. 'Allow me to cut you a leg and a breast to begin with,' he declared, staring at the brace of roasted chickens, liberally coated with salt and pepper. The first cut revealed that they were filled with a plentifully overflowing suet stuffing, enriched with diced ham and chicken liver, the divine scent revealing it was mixed and cooked with an unsparing flavouring of fresh thyme, with sage and parsley leaves. The poultry was accompanied by roasted potatoes and a rich, glutinous, red wine gravy which, when Pat poured, stuck to the birds, to the plates and the serving spoon with immovable tenacity.

'My word, Murphy; this is the most splendid supper ... Be a good fellow and light along the wine, I have promised Mr Marston a drop of the famous Portuguese.'

'Well, it's coming along d'reckly,' declared Murphy in pleased voice, for once seemingly in a rare state of satisfaction, his captain's delight noted.

Later, the food much enjoyed and everything eaten up, the second bottle of wine almost wholly depleted, Pat sat back in much improved humour, savouring his coffee, whilst he talked with his guest. Only the one, the very same subject was still sitting ill on his mind, 'How do you find things, Michael? Tell me, how do you find yourself... the barky at sea once more and bound for Greece, that infernal place?'

'Sir, even despite all the tribulations we have endured, it pleases me of all things to be here with our shipmates... officers and men alike; for here, aboard this ship, is my place... I could not contemplate otherwise. That is the truth of it... and that is despite every hesitation sitting ill with me.'

'I take that very well, very well indeed; thank you.' Despite his words the lines of worry still lingered about Pat's face.

'If I might be permitted the most minor remark, sir,' ventured Marston before Pat could change the subject, 'Doctor Ferguson being absent... I am entirely at ease to contemplate serving in the cockpit... and Abel Jason is a most admirable helper if... if we are called upon to attend any of our men who may... may be requiring of... of our assistance.'

'I never doubted that for a moment,' exclaimed Pat with emphasis, 'but I am heartily relieved to hear it all the same. I am greatly sorry that Doctor Ferguson ain't sailing with us. He had no notion that we were returning to Greece when he set off for Scotland... and neither, allow me to say, did I. It was an uncommon mighty shock...'

'I am fully persuaded of it, sir.'

'I have myself, I confess, been cast down a trifle in my... in my heart since... since Navarino and our escape from that place...' Pat's face fell and his voice was reduced to a whisper. 'It was a horrible day.... I thought we were dished, I did so; and that has weighed heavy in my thoughts for many a month... it has been the stuff of the most horrible nightmares.'

'I'm sure that is so for all of us, sir... to... to varying degrees. However, we will keep our confidence in the fellowship of our shipmates... and we will hold firm to our faith in our Lord; and standing all square together I have not the least doubt that we will get by, that all will be well with us.'

'You are a capital shipmate, Michael Marston,' declared Pat, 'and - *allow me to say this* - it is an honour to serve with you, it is so.'

'Thank you, it is very good of you to say so, sir; but I am the same in mind and spirit as all hands who are serving with us in this fine vessel. I am no better than any other man aboard, and in that I make no exception.'

Pat, his eyes shifting towards a returning Murphy as the door creaked on its hinges, did wonder for a fleeting moment about that last point; 'I am humbled by your fine words, I am,' he mumbled.

'Well, 'ere be the port, sorr, if your honour cares for a tint,' declared the steward, entering after listening intently behind the coach door for some time.

It was a welcome lift to the gloomy ambience of reflection as far as Pat was concerned. 'Thank you kindly, Murphy, and might there be a prospect of some more coffee in about half an hour?' He turned back to Marston, 'Will we look to the music? What is it you are minded to play?'

'It is a work written by Luigi Paganini. The great man himself knew of my own interest in his sonata when we were in Genoa in 'twenty-three to visit Lord Byron. I recall his playing... out there on the deck that day... It was simply magnificent, and I will never forget it.'

'Nor will I,' murmured Pat, wholly in accord; 'We will never hear its like again, I'm sure of that.'

'I most certainly concur with you there, sir. I had mentioned to him our devotion to playing within the cabin and also the particular occasion when Mr Mower had first joined us with his guitar to make a quartet, it is an instrument much favoured by Signor Paganini. He gifted me the transcription of this particular composition - *it is as yet unfinished, a draft, no more* - remarking that it was a variation on his original and written in 'C' for a trio of viola, 'cello and guitar.'

'How, then, would you propose we play it?' Pat stared doubtfully at the paper with a degree of scrutiny, 'We have no guitar, and - Ferguson absent - neither do we possess a viola.'

Marston nodded, 'I will endeavour to take the part of the viola with my violin. Perhaps we may make something of a preliminary attempt upon the structure of the piece, akin to an exploration of sorts, no more, and... and I venture that we will see this as *preparatory to...* to Mr Mower and Doctor Ferguson accompanying us at a later date. I have no doubt they will both grace us with their presence in this cabin in the future... and I am minded that the piece may be played as a quartet.'

'A capital notion!' Pat brightened, 'Please, will you give the note.'

Sunday 1st January 1826   10:30   Royal Hotel, Falmouth

After a leisurely late rising and a hearty breakfast, a tired, greatly aching and fretting Simon resolved to walk to the Packet Office to enquire of the prospects for passage on the next departure for the Mediterranean. Ambling along Market Street in the bright, cold morning, he was utterly unaware of passers-by, his thoughts wholly focused upon the departure of *Surprise;* for the ship being at sea without him was a greatly worrying concern which had kept him awake for much of the night, having to leave Flora compounding his anxieties. He pondered for how long his shipmates might be in potential mortal danger until he might catch up to join them, and he realised with a sinking heart that he would be several weeks at best behind *Surprise*, for the packets were slow indeed in comparison and they called at several ports en route, such that he might not reach Corfu in the Ionians until, as was the norm, forty-four days or even longer. His head down, his thoughts preoccupying him, he bumped into a stout, old gentleman walking towards him. He stumbled sideways and, failing to recover his balance, his legs still stiff and unyielding, he fell upon his chest on the unforgiving, hard cobblestones in complete disarray. He rolled over with the momentum of his fall and slowly sat up, panting hard, rubbing his ribs and striving to gather his violently expelled breath as he stared at the gazing pedestrian with whom he had collided. Fortunately, his careless inattention was immediately forgiven as the man recognised him as the surgeon who had attended his wounded son for many months. He helped Simon to his feet, dusting off his old jacket, one so shabby it hardly merited such solicitous attention. 'Thank you, friend,' declared Simon, tottering in unsteady fashion before gathering his balance, 'I do most humbly beg your forgiveness.'

'That is unnecessary, I do assure you, Doctor Ferguson. It is *I* who will take this opportunity to thank *you*... again, for you saved my son's leg... Jack Colenso, starboard gunner aboard the barky... He serves *The Nailer*... aboard *Surprise*. I am Arthur Colenso, a veteran of *Tenedos*; and I am at your service, sir. May I assist you... with the slightest thing?'

'That is most kind, Mr Colenso, I am obliged to you. I am looking to find the Packet Office; I am told it is a little way further along this street.'

'Please, allow me to escort you. It is but a few yards more.'

'If you will, thank you kindly. How is your son, pray tell?'

'Why, he left aboard the barky... on Wednesday, sir.'

'He was prepared to return...' Simon stared in fascination, '... and that after his severe wound... nearly losing his leg? He was minded to go back to that vile conflict which is Greece?'

'Most certainly, sir,' Colenso paused for only the briefest reflection, 'and so would I - that is to say, were I ten years the younger - for your captain's former ship, sir... *Tenedos*... was my home for many a year, and I have not the least doubt that my son, Jack, is similarly minded in his thinking of *Surprise*; indeed, sir, he said so.' A speechless Simon simply stood and stared at Colenso until the old man prompted, 'Are you sufficiently recovered... and will we cut along now, sir?'

During five more minutes walking, Simon's mind filled with a racing turmoil of thoughts, digesting the significance of the decision of young Jack Colenso to return to the hell which was Greece. A wave of his hand from Colenso and they turned left into Bell's Court.

'Good morning, sirs,' declared the clerk without excessive enthusiasm or, indeed, without any at all, barely lifting his head.

'Good morning to you,' replied Simon, sensing the clerk's indifference. Perhaps he did not care to work on the first day of the new year or, Simon's close scrutiny suggested, perhaps he had enjoyed a particularly festive New Year's Eve, even a drunken one, for his eyes were reddened and his demeanour was tired and sour. 'I require passage on the next packet to the Ionians, if you please.'

A tiny nod of confirmation and the clerk leafed through a large folder, 'You are most fortunate, there is one cabin remaining vacant.'

'Splendid, I am heartily pleased to hear it.'

'That will be thirty-six pounds, sir.'

'I beg your pardon!' exclaimed Simon, for he could not believe his ears. 'Come now, do you indulge my good temper? Do you jest? That is pecuniary oppression in the extreme... thirty-six pounds! Why, how can an honest man afford such an excessive tariff?'

The clerk frowned, stared more closely at Simon's attire and looked to his threadbare coat, muddied from his fall. 'Perhaps you might care to consider steerage class?' he offered in condescending voice as if by way of grudging concession, 'for that would cost a deal less.'

Simon, still shocked, responded after the briefest re-assessment, 'How much, pray tell, will that cost?'

'Twenty pounds,' declared the clerk with an air of finality, almost of triumph.

Simon's heart sank as he peered closely into his purse, 'I regret... I am dismayed, but I possess only twelve pounds and three shillings; I am all thrown out...'

'Come, sir!' interjected Arthur Colenso in condemnatory voice to the clerk, 'Here is a great man, a particular friend of this town; why, he has saved the lives and limbs of plenty of Falmouth's sons, including my own... and you speak to him without due attention. I will not have it, sir! Have a care before you find yourself called out... before you face a pistol perhaps! Indeed, I possess of a brace. Do you hear me?'

'I humbly beg your pardon, gentlemen, both of you,' declared the clerk, suitably admonished, 'However, space aboard the packets, that to Lisbon and Malta particularly, is at a premium... in high demand... quite exceptional it is... and, I beg to say, I have no discretion in the matter of the tariffs, not the least... none whatsoever.'

The clerk's brutally disappointing declaration left Simon cold, for he possessed no more money in all the world than that which his purse exhibited. He had left the remainder of his meagre resources with Flora, and that was a mere ten pounds. He left the premises, accompanied by Colenso, in a mood of the deepest despond. *Insufficient funds*: it was a blunt, bleak statement and one he had oft encountered in his life, customarily in letters from his bank manager. He possessed no means to book passage at a time of the utmost urgency, and he seethed with a cold despair.

Colenso spoke up, 'I regret, sir, I possess but little money myself, much less than the sum you require, even for steerage. If I had more, it would be yours, I do assure you.'

'Thank you, it is most kind of you to say so,' mumbled Simon, only half listening and mortally cast down.

'Sir, there is one notion which comes to my mind, if you care to hear of it?' Colenso stared with transparent goodwill.

'Of what do you speak, Mr Colenso?' said Simon in tired voice, looking to his companion with small but rising interest, searching for the slightest of straws in his desperate predicament.

'Sir, the packets depart from the Green Bank quay; indeed, that place, Selley's Green Bank Hotel, is frequented by many of the packets' officers.' Colenso continued in hopeful tone, 'I venture a number of captains will likely be there now, this very moment... and conceivably too the officers of the Mediterranean packet. Perhaps, with your considerable sea time, with your professional skills and experience, conceivably they might engage your services?' A pause, a mute Simon looking exceedingly doubtful, still visibly dismayed, and Colenso spoke up once again in positive voice, 'There is nothing to be lost.'

'There is something in what you say,' murmured Simon, exceedingly wearily, but failing to dispel his considerable doubt; for he was aware that Falmouth operated a strict policy for the packet doctors, a waiting list and rota both in existence for service which was a far more attractive option than unemployment, the navy being so greatly reduced. 'I will walk up to that place,' he replied quietly, 'Thank you, Mr Colenso; I am infinitely obliged to you, sir... infinitely obliged.'

Farewells and handshakes exchanged with the kindest of good wishes, a demoralised Simon trudged on, passing by Killigrew Street when he started up the hill which was the High Street, his legs, still stiff from his days within the mail coaches, protesting every step. Reaching the minor summit with a degree of relief, for his bruised chest was sore to the touch and his breathing painful, he paused momentarily for air and respite, and he looked out across the water towards Flushing. The bright morning endured, the weather was dry, the day sunny. His gaze returning to the distant Green Bank Hotel, his legs aching interminably, he contented himself that his destination was comfortably less than a quarter mile away. In that moment his eyes caught sight of a small vessel tied against the pier adjacent to the hotel; it seemed vaguely familiar for a few searching seconds, a single-masted vessel. It was certainly a cutter, that he recollected, a vague memory of Pat's ridicule coming to mind. He stopped so that his stare might be more precise: could it be? Still uncertain, he pressed on, walking faster and faster at every step until he was near running down the Prince Street slope, his legs no longer the smallest concern, his weariness and aches quite forgotten. Could it be? It might! On he rushed, ever quicker, gasping for breath. His hopes were fast rising with every step. He blinked frantically, his eyes still heavy with sleep; yes, it really was *Mathew Jelbert*, and she was still here! She was still here in Falmouth! He sensed that his heart rate had doubled; there would surely be a number of his shipmates attending her, there must be!

On he rushed, along Dunstanville Terrace. He was running now, faster with every step but struggling as he found himself painfully short of breath; he really had bruised his chest badly in his fall. He blessed the gentle downhill slope, despite which he was struggling to keep up the pace, his burning lungs gasping for air even as his spirits were soaring higher. He reached the Green Bank Hotel, coughing and spitting, his strength utterly expended, not the least energy left. He was completely shattered by the time he halted with huge relief, completely winded and bent over, gasping frantically for air while, anxiously, he scrutinised the men atop the cutter's deck.

Yes! It was James Mower, his friend and patient of old! The man he had saved when struck down with three damaging canister shot strikes, the most seriously wounded casualty he had ever saved, several pints of his blood lost and the surgeon's table flooded with it. It had been a close run thing, for Mower's body temperature, despite the fierce heat, had started to cool; so much so that no one looking on in the horrific moments of Simon's inspection believed that Mower could possibly survive. Simon shuddered briefly at the horrible recollection and wrested his thinking back to the present: Lieutenant James Mower was here before him! An exalted Simon rejoiced within every fibre of his being! It was several more minutes, his burning lungs still gasping for air, before he had recovered his breath sufficiently to be able to shout weakly across to the cutter, 'Mr Mower!' Simon raised and waved his arm over his head. He blessed Arthur Colenso five times with the most prolific good wishes, a flood tide of relief engulfing him as Mower turned to see him; the widest, the most delighted, smile Simon had ever seen was broad on the Lieutenant's face as he waved back with evident great pleasure, his own joy plain for all his shipmates to see.

Sunday 1st January 1826   Noon   off north-west Portugal

'Did you know, Duncan, I was thinking just now of absent friends, Simon and Mower particularly,' declared Pat as he prepared to take the sighting, 'In fact Mower's shanty comes to mind... Let me see, how did it go? It was sung a plentiful number of times on the deck by the lads... indeed, I dare say we might consider that it was adopted as the ship's anthem, and something of it comes to me now,

The barky's fixed, all a-tanto,
Falmouth's men all set to go;
The wind set fair, and off we go,
Prizes sure, when we will crow;
Black Rock ahead, off the bow,
Back to sea, the tide a'flow;
Way oh, way oh,
Gale wind astern,
and what a blow.'

'Aye, a grand song it is, but I dinnae care to hear anything of a gale myself; I am reminded of the last time I was here in these waters... aye... and the loss of *Eleanor*. I nearly drowned that dreadful day... and we lost Jenkin and Teague, both good men. Thankfully we are blessed to see no fog today, for that was the making of the disaster.'

'Are we *all set to go*, old friend? There's a deal of happy souls aboard the barky... no doubt of that, but I... that is to say, how do you fare yourself?'

'Oh, as well as can be. I have no hankering to fight the Turk again, and I am in hope that we will be able to deliver these supplies to Messalonghi and leave that place without firing the guns... but... but I have great doubts about that.'

'To be sure, it is a plan easily concocted in the safe havens of London, and - *I have seen it with my own eyes* - they have precious little notion of the sea, of the close interest of Johnny Turk in every vessel in those waters; doubtless we will make his acquaintance again when our presence is reported there. I have been thinking of that region, most particularly the shallow lagoons which lie on every bearing about the town. Within those waters are many small islands, scarcely bigger than a Connemara man's holding, a few acres or less. The possession of those islands is the key, for were the Turk to hold them... then, for sure, our way to the town will be barred, even for the boats. Indeed, I am in fear of a Turk capture of those very islands whilst we are there ashore, when our way *out of the town* will become closed to us.'

'Aye, let us hope it will not be so,' said Duncan with a weary and heartfelt sigh, nothing of any personal reserve left to him when thinking of such things.

'You did not care to join Marston and I in the cabin after your watch last night?' asked Pat, resolving to change the subject. 'We greatly enjoyed making our attempt upon another of Paganini's marvels, a splendid evening it was.'

'I was sorely tempted, but unfortunately I no longer possess a whistle. So... *I confess*... I enjoyed a generous dram of whisky, which Murphy ain't yet found, and I retired early to my cot.'

Sunday 1st January 1826   17:30   Falmouth

Simon and Mower walked along a dark and dimly lit Market Street, deep in a conversation founded in their mutual admiration. Mower's recovery from his many wounds was Simon's crowning achievement as a surgeon. The lieutenant had been struck hard with multiple canister shot wounds in his arms, legs and chest. Whilst lying wounded on the deck he had lost a copious amount of blood, and that alone had brought him near to death, only a few minutes of life left to him before Pat, with Clumsy Dalby, had carried him below to the cockpit and directly onto the surgeon's table, all witnesses aghast at the lieutenant's dreadfully wounded state.

There had been not a single man aboard who had believed in the slightest that Mower's life could be saved, but Simon had managed it, somehow. He had worked with desperate, frantic application in the dimly-lit cockpit for an hour with the most intense and skilful surgical concentration, to the extent of burning his eyebrows in the flickering, close candlelight as he sweated over his patient whilst probing delicately to find the penetrating, devastating shot, and then sewing up the many wounds with an infinitely gentle care even as his own fingers began to tremor with fatigue.

Not a religious man, Simon had uttered a hundred silent prayers in his mind as he had diligently worked, refusing to admit defeat amongst the lieutenant's severe and shocking blood loss, Mower only a mere whisker away from catastrophic organ failure and death. At the end of the operation Simon had been in huge distress himself, his cheeks smeared red by bloody hands as he strived to staunch a prolific flow of tears, his emotions on fire in joyful relief that he had managed to save his youthful shipmate's life.

It had been many more months of the most attentive nursing before Mower had recovered the mere beginnings of his health and strength, his return to full fitness still some way from complete. Simon had rejoiced ever since in this walking, talking human reminder of why he did his distressing job in the most foul, dangerous and inhospitable circumstances for any surgeon; and the two had inevitably become the closest of friends. Mower, for his part, adored and revered his saviour; no one knew better than he that what Simon had accomplished had been a miracle, and no minor one at that. Mower understood that very well as, for a long time afterwards, he had struggled in his dire pain and distress, persevering to hold firm to his morale, to keep his enthusiasm and resolution up, even as he could neither walk nor use one arm for months. Left ashore at Cephalonia, he had been nursed by the wives of Pat and Duncan until able to resume a severely incapacitated existence for many more months.

'Allow me to say that you are looking well, Mr Mower,' remarked Simon happily.

'Thank you, sir; all thanks to you.'

Simon smiled, but said no more; it was a conversation oft repeated between the two of them, Simon's denials of particular surgical excellence never carrying the smallest weight with the lieutenant. 'You are minded that Mrs Jelbert will be at home?'

'Oh yes, sir; the Sunday service in the Chapel, which she always attends, will be finished, and I venture she will be preparing her supper. I promised to call upon her before we sail at dawn on the morrow. It was only yesterday that we brought the bow chasers aboard the cutter, her stores and water loaded just this morning. We will be away at first light.'

'I collect that you attended her upon our last return from Greece... when her husband Mathew was struck down?'

'Indeed, I brought the sad tidings... Yes, I called to comfort her in her distress, as best I could. I stayed with her all that first night... I collect neither of us slept for even a minute... and I called upon her every day for the next month... and every Sunday since then. She is a remarkable woman, and exhibits great fortitude, both her husband and her son killed aboard the barky.'

'Indeed; she is a fine lady. I am reminded of my own visit, all those months ago; she is a courageous soul, I make no doubt about it.'

'And now her nephew has joined the crew, young Jago; he left with the barky last Wednesday. I fancy the captain has taken a shine to him.'

Striding along at the best pace Simon could manage, they passed the Customs House and turned right to walk up the steep Hull's Lane and so to the small Hull's Cottage, set back to the right behind a low wall and a tiny front garden.

'Please, do come in,' said the softly spoken, fragile, small lady, ushering in her visitors with the utmost courtesy. 'Mr Mower, how nice to see you... and Doctor Ferguson; good evening, sir. Will you come into the parlour?' They sat in the small front sitting room, a modest coal fire throwing out its welcoming warmth to relieve the severe chill of outside. 'Would you care for tea, Doctor Ferguson, a scone perhaps?'

'That would be exceedingly welcome, my dear; indeed, I am partial to a pastry at teatime,' Simon smiled, delighted to see that Mrs Jelbert did not appear to be in the slightest downcast; and that, he was minded to think, was the measure of a truly exceptional soul.

Mrs Jelbert departed for the kitchen, returning a few minutes later with the teapot and cups. 'The scones are baking, nearly done,' she declared with a smile, pouring the tea, 'A minute or two longer, no more.'

'How do you fare, Mrs Jelbert?' asked Simon. 'Are you keeping well, *keeping warm*, the winter so infernally - *excuse me* - so *exceptionally* cold?'

'I am fine, sir; my friends, the good people of the Chapel, call upon me every day; indeed, they customarily bring small gifts... a bag of flour or potatoes and suchlike... a bucket of coal or firewood sometimes... to help me... in their kindness.'

'I am greatly pleased to hear it,' said Simon with heartfelt emphasis. A squeaky creak, and he and Mower looked up as the kitchen door opened. A lad of no more than five or six years old entered bearing the plate of scones, a delectable aroma of fresh-baked pastry carried along with them which teased Simon's nose. 'And who is this young man, may I ask?' He smiled at the boy who seemed nervous as he approached the chairs.

'Sir, this is my grandson, John; though he is known by all as Jack. His father, my son Annan, was a gunner aboard *Surprise*, after his father, Mathew, before him. He has attended the Chapel with me today, his mother being sick.'

Simon's heart turned over in the most violent of movements, a rush of blood flowing to his head, acidic bile rising into his throat as he recalled the final moments of both Annan Jelbert and Mathew Jelbert. Indeed, he had rushed to attend the younger man when he had been struck down serving his gun in the great cabin; sadly, there had been not the least prospect of helping him, his wounds being so severe. Annan Jelbert had then died in his friends' arms, Simon frantically trying to staunch the blood loss until his heart had stopped. Mathew Jelbert, Annan's father and the ship's master gunner, had died in similar circumstances, but on the quarterdeck at the end of the battle to escape the great bay of Navarino, *Surprise* pursued by several Turk frigates and greatly damaged. Both deaths had been the most horrific of scenes, ones which Simon did not care to consciously recall, but they were, without doubt, events he was certain he would never in his life forget. He nodded weakly, striving for the appropriate words, which would not come, and he hoped that his discomfort did not show to Mrs Jelbert or the boy.

'Did you meet with my father, sir?' young Jack spoke up from beside Simon's chair with surprising resolve.

Simon began blinking rapidly, the rising surge of distress was overcoming him, overwhelming his senses, as involuntary and vivid images flooded his mind. He reached into his inside pocket for his handkerchief, and as he did so a pennywhistle fell out and to the floor. It was a most welcome distraction with which to conceal his bleak feelings of anguish. He quickly leaned over to pick it up. 'Here, young man,' Simon offered the whistle to the boy, who did not move in the least; he seemed still to be greatly shy.

'Go on, Jack; the good Doctor Ferguson is handing you a fine gift,' urged Mrs Jelbert, smiling encouragingly even as Simon's extreme discomfort registered with her.

'Here take it,' prompted Simon in gentle voice, a striking idea coming to mind, 'May it please you to keep it as a memento of your father. It was his own. Yes, I knew him well.' Silence; Simon wondered if he had erred, and then Jack stepped forward towards him and very tentatively, gingerly, put his hand on the whistle. Simon nodded and smiled encouragingly, 'Your father was a fine man and a most valued shipmate, he was so.' Jack looked with evident interest at the whistle, but was still unmoving. 'Here, please... it is yours,' whispered Simon, swallowing hard and beginning to feel even more overcome in that moment, fighting to constrain his bubbling distress from showing to the boy; 'Take it... I beg you will.'

Jack hesitantly grasped the whistle, his hand closing around it, and he carefully withdrew it from Simon's hand. He stared at it with obvious fascination for a long, silent minute, everyone present most passionately willing him well, nothing more said by anyone. The room was still, save for the crackling of the coal on the fire, and another minute passed whilst Jack stared intently at Simon, as if weighing up the man, before making his softly-spoken enquiry, 'Is my father never coming home?'

Mrs Jelbert gasped; she was instantly and wholly overwhelmed, silent tears beginning to streak her face. She moved from her chair to lift up and embrace the boy in her arms, hugging him tight. No reply, not a word, was forthcoming from anyone; all present were simply stunned, speechless, incapable of even a solitary word.

The uncomfortable silence enduring, and making the unwelcome answer plain to young Jack, he broke free of his grandma's arms and wriggled from her lap to stand, staring, his eyes wide, before Simon, his next words almost inaudible, barely more than a whisper, 'Has he gone to Heaven?'

It was too much for Mrs Jelbert, uncontrollable waves of desperately painful emotion surged throughout her very being, and she cried, audibly, her sobs loud, her small and fragile body shaking in abject distress. Mower leaped up from his chair to hold her, to whisper gentle consolation into her ear and to offer such reassurances as he could.

Young Jack, somehow and miraculously, had held firm his own composure, but he was swept up by Simon and held close in his arms, seated on Simon's knee. The most painful of minutes for all passed as the distraught surgeon, blinking frantically to clear away the beginnings of his own tears, gathered his precious words of comfort, 'Yes, yes Jack... your father has gone to Heaven... and that is a better place... where he has many friends... He is there with plentiful shipmates... comrades of ours, all of them; be assured of that.'

Several more minutes passed in the most bleak and distressing ambience until Mrs Jelbert could gather her composure once more and pour the tea. Young Jack continued to demonstrate the most remarkable fortitude as he remained held within Simon's arms, his interest divided between studying Simon and examining the pennywhistle. Time passed slowly as the adults sipped their tea, all eyes on Jack as the tray of scones - a welcome diversion - was passed round, and everyone took one. Simon and Mower, in particular, were most grateful for them, the tiny diversion that they were, albeit it was only the most feeble pretence of a normality which they did not feel in the least. They ate with cautious nibbles and in silence whilst they contemplated whether and when they should excuse themselves. However, the appropriate time to suggest departure never presented itself, never became obvious to the visitors, and it was ultimately Mrs Jelbert herself who came to the moment first and with the remark that it was time for her to return Jack to his mother and so to his bed.

As Mower and Simon were standing at the front door, Simon's hand found his purse. He took out the remaining eleven pounds within it and he pressed them into Mrs Jelbert's unwilling hand, closing her fingers around the notes, 'Here, my dear; this will assist you in the difficult times to come, and perhaps you will allow young Jack's mother to share it with you?'

'Thank you, sir, with all my heart,' Mrs Jelbert eventually conceded, no choice allowed in Simon's enduring steely grip, his face one of determination, for he had at last recovered from his own acute distress.

'Here, young man,' Simon declared as young Jack released his grip on Simon's arm, 'I beg you will save these three shillings for only the wisest of expenditures.'

The boy stared, marvelling at unimaginable wealth. 'I hope I may see you again, sir,' he piped up in surprisingly resolute voice.

'You will surely see me again, Jack, have no doubt of that,' said Simon, a prolific and cathartic wash of relief flooding his entire mind and all his heart; 'I will be pleased if you will consider that we are now friends.' The boy nodded, but could find no further words.

Later, as Simon and Mower walked back along the cobbles of Market Street in the darkness, deep in personal reflection, the candles and lamps of small houses offering weak glimmers of light to illuminate their path, Mower looked to his friend, 'You gifted all your money to them, that was most generous of you.'

'Oh, I have settled my account at the Royal, as we are departing in the morning, and such modest funds as remain to me would serve no purpose once I am within Neptune's briny realm on the morrow; and I could scarcely credit my conscience to keep it, Mrs Jelbert so greatly in need. No, I trust it will help them, for they have lost their dearest people in all the world. I confess I was most deeply moved by the boy, such a brave soul, and so young.' Simon sighed, 'Would that I was still as steadfast myself. There, I have said it now.'

'I am wholly of your way of thinking. These months of visiting Mrs Jelbert... There were many a time when I could not find any words...' More contemplative minutes passed as they walked on in silence, until Mower spoke up again, 'The pennywhistle... I cannot collect Annan Jelbert ever possessing one, or am I much astray?'

'Oh, it actually belonged to Macleod. He gifted it to me as a memento of our playing in the cabin as I prepared to depart the ship... and with no practical means to convey my viola to Tobermory aboard the coach, I believed I might find a modicum of solitary pleasure in the smaller instrument... and so it has been in my possession since. I confess I have made but little progress with it, and it had been my intention to return it to Macleod.'

'The lad was best pleased.'

'Indeed, and I dare say I will confess my gift to the boy when I again make the acquaintance of Macleod. Young Jack now possesses a memento... which he will treasure as something to recall his father, and I dearly hope that will help him in the troubles which doubtless lie ahead for him; and for that small mercy I believe we might all be thankful.'

Tuesday 10th Jan. 1826 08:00 Surprise, approaching Gibraltar

'Mr Pickering!' declared Pat, stepping up to his quarterdeck to take the early morning air before his breakfast, 'I trust I see you well this fine morning?' Only a cautious nod was returned by the tired lieutenant, coming to the end of his watch as Dalby rang out eight bells, and Pat, perceiving Pickering's air of fatigue, spoke again in quieter voice, 'Tom, I collect your morale has been low for many a month... I regret we have not spoken of it. I remarked that you have been signally cast down since we left Greece... or, I venture, even before then.'

'I am well, sir, thank you,' the lieutenant hesitated. Sensing Pat waiting for him to say more, he reluctantly resumed, 'I doubt there was a man aboard who was not best pleased to quit that place... *I surely was.*'

'I will say I feel much the same...' Pat nodded, 'but let us cling to a trifle of optimism for this voyage; after all, we are not tasked with more than the delivery of our cargo.'

'I hold to the view that the man who is an optimist after forty, sir, knows too little.'

'Well, I confess I am, myself, forty-four, so perhaps I do indeed - *even now* - know too little,' declared Pat with the slightest of smiles and trying to keep the exchange buoyant. 'I have oft thought that in the matter of many and various subjects, usually when I am speaking with Doctor Ferguson on the classics or such as the philosophies. That man is an encyclopedia of all subjects, save, perhaps, for all matters relating to the barky, where he has not the least notion of which side is the starboard...'

'He is, sir, most assuredly the ultimate nonpareil of knowledge,' offered the lieutenant, nodding sagely.

'I am not acquainted with the term *nonpareil*...' said Pat, thoughtfully, 'Doubtless it is a foreign word, but no doubt too it is a very good thing... and how old would you be, Tom?'

'Thirty-five, sir.'

'Then all is well with you, eh? You, at least, may hold to a goodly measure of optimism without fear of ridicule!'

'Thank you, sir,' Pickering smiled at last, 'I will endeavour to do so.'

'Anything to report?'

'It has been the quietest of nights, nothing in the least to remark upon, nor anything from Mr Codrington in the middle watch before me. This enduring absence of strong wind is something of a small blessing, the hands having not the least difficulty with the sail handling.'

'If it is a blessing then it is certainly well disguised.' Pat looked to the sails; to his eyes they were plainly under not the least of load. 'This feeble wind is no help to us, 'tis a week and more since we raised more than seven knots.'

'Greater expedition, sir, and striving for it, is most surely a commendable virtue,' said Pickering with a broad grin, appreciating his captain's interest in him, 'but for myself I incline to taking things as they come; it is a deal more... *restful.*'

Pat laughed, 'I venture you are coming round to your old self, eh? And what are your further thoughts on this venture... our return to foreign parts... to Greece, tell?'

'Oh, I have seen enough of that place, sir,' Pickering paused for reflection, '... and I am reconciled that the only foreign places of any interest which lie ahead for me are heaven and hell, and I possess not the slightest notion of which one I will be going to... but I venture Greece is nearer the latter.'

Pat sighed, the good cheer he had strived for in recent days swiftly evaporating in the cold reminder of realities. In a more sober tone he spoke up, 'I am reminded of Mr Marston's words of recent days, when we have enjoyed pleasant hours of music together in the cabin after supper; indeed, after taking a tint or two and our playing finished, we have touched upon our very purpose in this voyage... this mission of mercy... I speak of our carrying of supplies to Greece. Marston declared, and I urge you to hold firm to his words in the weeks ahead - for I myself will doubtless endeavour to do so... He said... *"We must find our courage anew, and we will surely find it; have no doubt, for it is not the absence of fear but our overcoming of it."* Look to your shipmates,' Pat patted Pickering on his shoulder, 'Look to your friends, Tom; I most certainly intend to do so myself!'

'It is good advice, sir,' murmured Pickering, 'Thank you for your kind solicitations. I believe you may count on me.'

'Very good, and you may count on me; indeed, I venture you may count upon all your shipmates aboard the barky, for we are blessed to serve with such men as these be. Ah, I see Mr Macleod is arrived to stand his watch. Would you care to take breakfast with me? I think the sausages are holding up... will be edible for another day or two... if you do not greatly mind the taint of age.'

Pickering nodded doubtfully, 'Most kind, sir.'

Fri. 13th Jan.1826 13:00 Mathew Jelbert   off Cape St. Vincent

With Mr Reeve on duty and all the hands on deck, Simon sat in the cabin with Mower. The two were enjoying a quiet hour before dinner whilst sipping coffee and playing a variant of chess, a game of Mower's invention, a much-enlarged board of fourteen squares on all sides and with two full sets of pieces for each player, save for there being no second king or queen. Mower had claimed that it was a game which introduced a greater element of chance and, as such, was less cerebral, each position much more exposed to error in the prolific expanse of the board, and therefore greatly more pleasurable to play. An error usually lead to swift calamity and the loss of the game. It also served as entertainment for more than two players because an infinite number of boards, in theory, could be conjoined, and pieces were also allowed to migrate from one board to the adjacent one, were players minded to donate their piece to aid a fellow team player of black or white, as may be.

'I commend you for this invention, Mr Mower,' declared Simon, pondering his next move, 'for it has brought many a jovial hour to the captain's table in the great cabin; indeed, I would scarcely have imagined O'Connor could become engrossed with it, for he never before paid the least mind to chess... the regular form that is. There!' Simon's leftmost pawn was withdrawn one square, as Mower's rules also permitted. 'How are your healed wounds? Do they trouble you in the least during these past weeks?'

'Not so that I heed them, sir; yes, they ache; and, the muscles being severed, it is even now something of a trial to shift anything heavy or to stand for the duration of my watch, but I beg you will say nothing of this to Captain O'Connor.'

'You are speaking to me in this matter as patient to doctor... and your words are for my private ear alone. Please, continue.'

'Thank you, sir. I will say that, as each month passes, I feel the stronger for it; why, when I was carried ashore at Falmouth after the... *the hurricane*... I was doubtful that I would ever have the strength to go back to sea, to gain my place again in the barky.'

'Then I commend you most sincerely, for you are here, at sea once more and sailing to join our dear *Surprise*... I do most sincerely wish that we do reach that inestimable vessel before...' Simon gulped, '... before I might be needed to serve our shipmates.' A momentary recollection of old Arthur Colenso's words came to Simon's mind, 'And although the prospects, on occasion, might seem to be dark, I am reminded that we are returning to be reunited with those many dear and valued friends whom we possess aboard that gallant ship. Do you suppose we might yet catch up with them... at all?'

'I venture we have every prospect of catching her, sir, for the cutter is a swifter vessel, even in these weak winds, for she will stay much closer to any headwind than the barky when we are called upon to make long tacks.'

'No doubt, and...' Simon frowned, '... and I have heard the principles of seamanship forever from O'Connor's own lips, of course; however, I confess it is the rare event when they come to mind with that necessary clarity required for a perfect understanding; after all, I have never considered myself to be a great navigator; no, never in life... far from it.'

'This wind the last week is nothing worth speaking of, and it will surely slow the barky such that I am minded we will gain a knot or even more on her... indeed, we may likely overhaul her before she fetches Cephalonia.'

'I am heartily glad to hear it,' Simon frowned and resolved to concentrate harder as Mower's knight took his retreated pawn.

Saturday 21st Jan. 1826 14:30   Surprise   passing Sardinia

A hungry but cheerful Pat sat down in the great cabin with Duncan Macleod and Abel Jason, the purser, his guests for an imminent dinner. Jason had, in the years during the Napoleonic wars, served as an Admiralty messenger, and as such he had possessed a well-informed understanding of the political and military standings of all parties in that long war against the tyrant; indeed, he did so in respect of the belligerents in the Greek war. Doubtless, Pat thought, it was a lingering residue of all those former years, the latter years in the struggle against the dictator, when his service had evolved such that he had become an Admiralty intelligence agent. During an uneventful forenoon watch, spent in reflective thought on his quarterdeck and carrying into the afternoon watch, he had considered setting aside his personal disinclination towards speaking of anything remotely political at his table so as to ask Jason what he knew of the present Greek situation. Time was marching on, Pat reminded himself as he looked across his table to his guests, for the familiar routines and slow progress of the voyage had brought about a settled ambience throughout the ship; although to Pat's mind this was more than a little frustrating given the expressions of urgency he had heard in London.

The Mediterranean had followed its Atlantic cousin in being as settled as Pat had ever experienced it, even the passage through the Strait of Gibraltar had been as uneventful as any he could remember; indeed, he had been grateful that nothing of the customary easterly Levanter of the winter had been blowing to further brake their already ponderous progress. During the long hours on his quarterdeck, it had seemed as if time itself had slowed, and consequently Pat looked forward with exceptional appetite to his meals, his dinner most particularly; it had become the highlight of his day. During every morning after breakfast he had toured his ship in inspection, never finding the slightest thing at fault to remark on, for all was in excellent physical condition after the refit, and his veterans were, most evidently, pleased to be aboard and sailing once again. After the noon sighting, he had lingered on his quarterdeck before eventually retiring to his cabin at four bells of the afternoon watch, Wilkins striving to oblige him with an exceptional offering for his dinner; that Pat's demeanour remained unsettled was still patently obvious to all his crew.

'Mr Jason,' declared Pat, 'I have been considering our likely reception in the Gulf of Patras. We are not sent there, on this occasion, as a combatant; well, that was what they said.' Something in Pat's tone suggested that he did not entirely believe that. 'We do know something, of course, of the Turk fleet and their Egyptian vassals' ships... as we found to our cost at Navarino...'

'Indeed, sir,' murmured Jason noncommittally, wondering where his captain was leading. Many years beforehand, during Pat's South Atlantic command, Jason had served as purser aboard *Tenedos* until she had paid off in Chatham. However, he had been fortunate, his considerable linguistic abilities had brought employment with the Admiralty for several years afterwards, and that had led to his present position as aide in that respect for Pat's mission. He was appointed officially as the titular purser, albeit his less-official talents had already proved helpful on *Surprise's* prior voyages to Greece. A man of nearly sixty, quite short, he possessed a good head of pale grey hair, almost white; and he was always immaculately shaven and plainly dressed. A most intelligent man, he had also been willing to assist the surgeons when they had been at the point of being overwhelmed during the battles to defend Samos. In so doing he had earned the undying respect of all aboard the frigate, Pat and Simon most particularly.

'What do you know of the state of the siege of Messalonghi?' asked Pat.

'As you will doubtless recall, sir, the Turk general, Mehmed, has besieged the town since the Spring of last year. He has been unsuccessful only thanks to Admiral Miaoulis breaking through the Ottoman navy blockade and delivering supplies by sea, but also because of Mehmed's want of cannon and shot with which to bombard the town walls.'

'What, pray tell, do we know of the Turk land forces?'

'In the summer of last year, the Turk put to work thousands of Greek slaves to build an earth mound outside the walls, upon which they could better site their guns and from which they could bombard the town; in so doing they forced the defenders out of their Franklin battery. In August the Greeks tunnelled under the mound and blew it up with a mine. Indeed, they have enjoyed similar successes with more mines, to the extent of exploding a great one under the Turk camp. Hence a stasis has resulted, the Turks making gains with daily bombardment and the defenders being able to repair any breaches in the town walls, as the Turk may inflict, by working overnight. However, the Sultan, tiring of his general's inability to bring the siege to an end, has called once again upon Egypt to aid his cause, and for several weeks French sources in Cairo have been reported as speaking of Ibrahim, the son of Mohammed Ali the Great, who is preparing to cross the Gulf of Corinth after his successes in the Morea. He possesses a goodly number of artillery pieces and plentiful shot with which to join the siege. It would seem, sir, that the forces ranged against the Greeks have never been greater... and their prospects, it must be feared, do not look propitious in the least.'

'No indeed, they don't, yet we are expected to preserve them.' Pat's frame of mind in recent times was always fragile, or so it seemed to him, and his mood deflated in an instant. He sighed audibly before resuming in gloomy voice, 'One ship, one cargo, one gift horse... with foodstuffs to deliver for the mouths of a whole town... perhaps enough for only a very few weeks. No, their prospects don't signify... they are caught between a Devilish rock and the deep blue sea.'

'Admiral Miaoulis must surely be their best chance,' interjected Duncan. 'If he can continue to fetch in at least a trifle of essential supplies then perhaps they still possess some small hope to save the town?'

'There's a great deal to be said for Miaoulis, the exceptional man that he is,' admitted Pat, 'but the Turk fleet is provisioned at Patras, no more than five leagues distant, or two hours of sailing with even a modest wind, whilst the Greek must return to Hydra, fully *two days* at sea. I venture that alone might dish the Greeks.'

'Then it is for Miaoulis to deliver faster than the town can consume,' declared Duncan, striving for something of good cheer, his captain so plainly pessimistic.

'There are ten thousand mouths to feed, and the admiral must evade the sea blockade... whatever the weather,' remarked Pat in quiet voice, his face of resignation betraying his fears for the defenders of Messalonghi.

'The Turk is also not without his difficulties, with so many men of his army to provision; and in winter that is no easy feat,' offered Jason, striving to haul the table's conclusion up out of the evident pit of gloom.

Thursday 26th Jan. 1826   Mathew Jelbert   Sicily on the bow

Another game of strategic chess was underway, for such had become the norm, the routine, as one uneventful day followed another, and Mower poured the wine before returning to his study of the board, the game in its advanced stage. Simon was facing a further defeat, the surgeon considering his position with infinite caution, ultimately settling upon an innocuous shift of that one of his four knights which was obstructing his foremost castle's free passage. Mower responded by immediately taking a pawn, exposed by the shift of the knight. Simon frowned before looking to Mower, 'We have touched in prior days upon your *physical* recovery, and it pleases me that it is progressing well, but how are you in your *spirits*, tell?'

'Greatly the better, thank you; why, since I had but little choice when laid up in my cot other than to think, I spent a deal of time musing on my wounds... and on my salvation... for that was your doing, Doctor Ferguson.'

'Please, let us not speak further of my most modest contribution, Mr Mower; I beg you will not.' Simon, distracted, advanced his castle eight squares in a flight of the most reckless adventure.

'Very well, sir. I also devoted many an hour to my poetry and, if I am not to speak of your surgery upon my wounds, then please allow me to read that one of my poems which was inspired by your good self - *and*,' Mower raised his voice and his hand as if to fend off any potential interruption, 'and, also, by the most diligent care of my shipmates, for I could barely shift about the ship without assistance; indeed, Mathew Jelbert became the rock in my life in every hour I was aboard... and he was so when we fetched home to Falmouth. Why, I doubt I could have considered ever returning to the barky, sir, without the good intentions of that man...' Mower's voice sank to a whisper, '... and I greatly miss him.'

'As do we all, Mr Mower. He will be long remembered, no doubt. Well, at least today is a timely date for recalling another great man, and a suitable instance for a poem... for it is Rabbie Burn's Day. Allow me to share with you the rather miniscule residue I still possess of a fine Islay malt. It has been travelling with me for some considerable time.' Simon poured two small measures into the empty wine glasses, his tiny bottle coming up dry. 'That is that. I venture we will not sing Auld Lang Syne nor do I expect sight of the customary haggis on this... *this much reduced* occasion, and so we must content ourselves with a wee toast to the great man. Please to raise your glass to the immortal memory of Rabbie Burns!'

'Rabbie Burns!' echoed Mower.

Both tiny shots were drunk as one, the glasses set down most emphatically. 'Now to your creation, Mr Mower. Pray read your poem.'

Mower leafed through a small bundle of papers, extracting the one he sought, 'Here it is, sir.' He took a sip of his wine and stared at the paper as if considering a chess move.

'Please to continue.'

Mower coughed to clear his throat, looked for a long few seconds at Simon in undisguised admiration, and began to read,

'I have long travelled along life's turbulent road,
Treading that tiring path for many hard years;
My spirits, sometimes, under the darkest of cloud,
All my thoughts oft awash with doubts and fears.

Ever onwards, my eyes wide open and always searching,
Through troubling spells, for life's distant destination;
Thoughts at times a wild confusion, and ever wondering,
When and where would I reach that unknown location?

Yet for every faltering mile along the windswept way,
Striving to find purpose before the obscure and distant end,
Holding firm to perseverance and fortitude each new day,
I was ever grateful for the company of my dearest friends.

Finding courage, enduring strife and - at times - despair,
On occasions my lost friends, near and dear, left behind;
Fond memories of them recalled within private prayer,
Whilst savouring brief, precious moments of peace of mind.

And when the way before me seemed bleak and black,
When my strength and energy was near its final end,
Ebbing on time's fast flowing current, with no way back,
Ever at my side, I always counted on my dearest friends.

Now life's oceans are all sailed, its tempestuous rivers crossed,
And standing strong with my dear, cherished companions,
We hold to that fortitude with which we were blessed,
Whilst still we seek the answers to life's great questions.'

Simon nodded, 'You remark very well upon our distressing times in Greece, that is perfectly plain. It is the case that we all, *and I include myself, I do... we all* looked to our dearest friends to help us in those blackest of vile hours. The rhyme is quite splendid; indeed, it is moving... the most meritorious of stanzas. I commend you most heartedly, Mr Mower.'

'Thank you, sir.' The lieutenant's queen swept diagonally for almost the full width of the board to take Simon's castle. 'Check!'

Tue. 31st Jan. 1826 16:00   Surprise   approaching Cephalonia

The afternoon was drifting lazily towards the sunset as *Surprise* closed on Cape Akrotiri, the coast a prominent black ribbon fine on the larboard bow despite the enduring haze of the late afternoon. There was no more than a few hours of light remaining until the frigate would arrive at the island's principal port. The proximity to the island had brought near every man aboard ship upon deck, scores standing on the foc'sle, dozens of men staring with rapt interest all along the waist, a score and more excited veterans encroaching on the quarterdeck; all of them looking forward very much to the arrival in Argostoli, a place with which they were all familiar, where they had spent many an entertaining hour, and one which they could see for themselves was now not a deal of time away. Pat himself did not mind the jovial buzz of conversation in his close presence, nor the encroaching and noisy jostling of a dozen men who plainly were not on duty and coming ever closer to the helm. No, he did not mind it in the least, for the recent weeks had been languorous and uneventful, the exceptional lack of wind long persisting, such that the entire passage had been exceedingly slow. It had resulted in an unhurried daily tempo gradually, nearly imperceptibly settling in the mind of every man. Whilst there had also been something of a sense of resignation, of inevitability, a feeling of what would be would be becoming common to all, it had somehow and seamlessly mixed with the slow normality, with the pleasurable and familiar routine of the ship as every man attended his duties. However, the exceptional cocktail of feelings had not displaced the customary, settled sense of order and regularity within both officers and hands as they attended their duties; and Pat, for one, was most grateful for that. Indeed, he had adjusted to what, in more exacting times, he would personally have condemned as sloth, taking advantage of the rare surplus of time to speak with as many of his shipmates as possible and frequently appearing in surprising places at all times about the ship, always offering a few warm but enquiring words in every case whilst soliciting the feelings of each of his men.

Now so close to Greece, albeit within the sanctuary of the Ionians, the possible return to imminent conflict had begun to loosen the grip of placidity, to unsettle the thoughts of every man, including Pat. For some weeks, he had sought but failed to find the moment to speak with one particular person aboard, outside of the routine changes of watch on his quarterdeck, and that man was Lieutenant William Codrington. Ordinarily Codrington was a sociable man; indeed, Pat had oft thought that he had seemed anxious to be reassured of his continuing place aboard the barky; not that anyone, least of all Pat, had ever intimated otherwise. However, Codrington had increasingly removed himself from the social intercourse of the ship; why was not known; such enquiries were considered inappropriate, even rude. In the cabin, in times gone by, Pat and Simon had speculated about the lieutenant's early life, for little was known of it before he had joined Pat's crew as an exceptionally young midshipman aboard the brig-sloop *Starling* in Portsmouth in the year 'three. He was reputed to be perpetually in a degree of financial difficulty, seemingly so because of his reported indulgences at the Mayfair gambling tables. There were other stories, of course, to be heard about him aboard ship: some said that he had been born in the West Indies, that he had fled the islands and its frequent yellow fever with his mother a few years after his birth, that his mother had actually been a mulatto of great beauty and his father a titled estate owner. Of such things Codrington never spoke but, as was plain to all, and it did seem to corroborate the rumours, he was relatively dark of complexion; not such as might be described as swarthy but just the merest of permanent tint to his skin, which certainly bestowed upon him the admirable image of rude good health. Indeed the Lieutenant was most rarely to be seen in any way indisposed in the least; so much so that Simon had remarked to the young lieutenant that he did not appear to greatly care to attend the sick bay, and was there any particular reason for such seeming reticence? No answer was ever forthcoming. Pat liked him very much, for he was also reliable, diligent and extraordinarily well-liked by the hands; however, he rarely appeared at the cabin table unless it was with a gathering of the whole of the officer complement of the ship, and so he remained something of a mystery, an enigma, to his colleagues.

'Mr Codrington,' Pat announced himself to his officer, deep in thought at the rail, 'I will stand by you, if I may.'

'I should be very happy, sir.'

To Pat's eye Codrington did not look greatly happy. 'A few hours, I doubt it will be longer, and we will drop our anchor in Argostoli, eh? What d'ye say to that?'

'I will be particularly pleased, sir, to see the place again. I possess fond memories of the town and its people.'

Pat knew that many more of his crew certainly also had fond memories, some of the younger members most particularly; for many of them "fond" might be considered to be something of a not inconsiderable understatement. He waited, but nothing further was forthcoming from the lieutenant. A minute more and he tried again in the most encouraging voice he could manage, 'I doubt we will be there long... a day or two to water... to call upon the authorities. I will do the civil and attend the Governor... to gather what information we may find upon the situation. Colonel Napier may be at hand, and then 'tis off to Messalonghi for us, to carry our stores to that long-suffering town.'

'I collect the plentiful shallow waters all about that place, sir, the lagoons, plentiful islets abounding everywhere... It is no place for a frigate... I beg pardon, sir.'

'No indeed, it will assuredly be a perilous place, and so we will rely on *Mathew Jelbert* to escort our boats to the island of Vasiladi, which guards the approach to Messalonghi, from where they will continue to convey all the many and varied supplies we possess to the town. You doubtless remarked that we carry more boats than usual since leaving Falmouth?'

'Why of course, sir.'

'Admiral Saumarez at the Dock seized all the smallest of boats that he could find immediately at hand, all those that are shallow draught - no more than two feet nine inches - and which are best suited to the lagoons about Messalonghi. All possess a mast and sail, but none are longer than eighteen feet; and so it will require plentiful deliveries to take all our stores to the beach... and that is a concern for sure.'

'Sir, I am greatly aware that the boats have not any shred of protection if fired upon... if... if the Turk has captured any of the lagoon islets...'

'It may be...' declared Pat in an emphatic voice of certainty, much dismayed to find echoes of his own fundamental doubts in Codrington's mind, 'It may be that we will make our deliveries during the night.' Codrington looking no more convinced than before, Pat sighed, his tone deflating, 'I confess, the older I am the less I think of capers of such ilk.'

Time drifted by as the frigate pressed on, sailing large at a sedate six knots in the feeble south-westerly *sirocco*, an hour passing in general contentment as all aboard considered their arrival, until Cape Akrotiri was visible on the larboard beam at last, the small islet of Vardiani on the starboard bow. 'DECK THERE!' came the shout from the maintop watchman, 'SAIL! SAIL ASTERN!' Heads everywhere turned to look aft, Pat and Codrington shifting to the stern rail, but nothing was visible from the deck.

'I venture we possess but an hour until sunset,' declared Pat, his attention wandering away from his lieutenant and towards the master. 'I fancy we may step ashore not long after that. Perhaps another half-hour and the twilight may see us drop anchor. What do you say to that, Mr Prosser, eh?'

The Cornishman exuded his customary confidence in all matters of navigation, exhibiting a broad smile on his ruddy, weatherbeaten face as he replied, 'Why, I think you may count on that, sir.'

'Very good. Ah, Murphy, there you are. Be so good as to light along to the galley for some coffee. I fancy I will keep my quarterdeck until we are anchored. Mr Codrington,' Pat tried again to engage with his lieutenant, 'do you care for a cup?'

'That would be most kind, sir.'

'Two cups, Murphy, if you will.'

The southeast point of the peninsula was passed, and Barton, on the master's instruction, hauled on the wheel to bring *Surprise* round to a near northerly course as she entered the Gulf of Argostoli. From the deck the low sun was lost behind the hillside, the coast to larboard falling into black shadow, the hilltop of the Argostoli peninsula to starboard remaining brightly illuminated; it would be a good sunset, thought Pat.

Murphy returned with the coffee, and Pat rejoiced in the familiar taste as he sipped slowly, minutes slipping by, everyone on the quarterdeck casting glances astern for a glimpse of the reported sail. 'Will I go to the top, sir, with a glass?' murmured Codrington eventually, breaking a long silence and his curiosity rising, his coffee finished.

'By all means, if you will; here, please to take my glass,' Pat smiled and handed over his telescope.

Barton brought the helm over a point as *Surprise* began her final turn to sail around the cape and so to the shelter of the harbour. The sun finally blinked out above the Paliki peninsula, nothing further of its rays upon the island coast anywhere; but the muted dusk twilight remained clear, a heavy ambience about it, an air of expectation general to all. The evening was tranquil, with no wind of any strength as the frigate plodded on in the gently benevolent south-westerly, a comfortable sense of imminent arrival settling upon all aboard. Fifteen more minutes and the master ordered her final turn, a sweeping one to the southeast and so into the harbour proper, the town of Argostoli becoming visible for the first time in the diminishing weak glow of the dusk. An electric, orange phosphorescence hung in the air to the west above Paliki, the final holdout of lingering warmth in the day. Enthusiasm abounded everywhere on deck, for the town was akin to a home from home, many friends possessed there by a great number of the crew's veterans.

An excited Codrington reappeared in ebullient mood, 'Sir, I venture... the sail... it is *Mathew Jelbert*; the cutter is astern, Mr Mower has caught up with us!'

Pat's could find no words in that instant. His spirits soared: this was the most welcome of news. The distant sail was now visible from the quarterdeck, and Pat stared with fixation through his telescope for long minutes, the cutter no more than two miles astern. *Surprise* shifted further to the south, into the inlet, the following sail no longer visible behind the Argostoli hillside and peninsula.

Five more minutes slipped by and Duncan ordered the braces slackened, the frigate's slow progress coming to a gradual halt some two hundred yards off the quay in calm water. 'Let go fore and aft!' he bawled, the splash of the anchors following immediately. The eyes of everyone stared across to the town where several hundred spectators had gathered to watch, the welcoming multitude thronging all along the quay, the crowd still discernible in the fast fading light of the gloaming. The topmen of the crew hastened to clew up the sails, other hands strained to haul four of the boats over the side and into the water. Every man anticipated going ashore, and four boats, as far as they were concerned, were much better than the customary two.

The boats all lowered and tied alongside, a settled darkness came at long last, not the least twilight remaining; all was black except for the lights of the town, an inviting beacon of infinite appeal to the Surprises. Pat gave the order to permit the first parties to go ashore, hugely exuberant men settling on the boats' thwarts in noisy celebration, scant notice taken of the lieutenants' cautions against drink, or at least against excessive quantities of it. Jubilant cries and shouts abounded as the men pulled on the oars.

Another half-hour and the crew much thinned, the approaching *Mathew Jelbert* came up infinitely slowly alongside the frigate, the final few of the Surprises aboard tying her to the boarding ladder. From his quarterdeck Pat watched the cutter's men scrambling to climb up and through the open gun port. He blinked, he stared with difficulty in the exceedingly poor light, his eyes wide open and struggling to be sure in the dim yellow cast of the solitary Argand lamp hanging from the main yard on the deck above the ship's ladder: could it be? Was it? The figure's stature and gait were very familiar; indeed, they were unmistakeable! His heart seemingly missed a beat as he concluded that it really was Simon Ferguson coming across the gun deck and so to the steps, a fleeting further miniscule fraction of a second passing until Pat felt the tidal wave of joy flooding his rapidly beating heart, pounding like a drum. He rushed across and grasped his dearest friend in all the world in both his arms as soon as Simon stepped up and on to the quarterdeck.

Chapter Six

Wednesday 1st February 1826   10:00   Surprise   Argostoli

The bright, clear, wintry sun shone down on the quay with an intangible benevolence, much appreciated by the frigate's men as they toiled to load the heavy water butts aboard the boats. There was, as anyone who paused soon observed, no substantive warmth in the morning, but all the hard-working Surprises were grateful for the lack of rainfall as they laboured to move the weighty, wooden barrels. It was plain to Codrington, supervising, that many a man was suffering from the previous night's alcohol; not that anyone, least of all Pat, minded in the least. Shipboard life had long ceased to resemble those severely regulated days of the Royal Navy of many years ago and, he sighed, it had been something of a tedious voyage, an exceptionally slow one, and consequently nothing of the slightest challenge for the *Surprise* veterans who had taken all in their stride, handling the frigate with the utmost ease, their enthusiasm and pleasure in being aboard ship once more rising exponentially as they had closed on Cephalonia.

Pat himself had rarely, if ever, been in a better mood for many a month. The Argand lamp in the great cabin had burned well into the early hours as Pat and Duncan had welcomed Simon back to the barky in an utterly joyous ambience of reunion, all the other officers attending the cabin celebrations for an hour, or even longer in many a case, to offer their own warm and cordial welcome to the returnee. A general fillip to morale was noted throughout the ship, for Simon was perceived by all the men as their esteemed shipmate, their surgeon, the man who assuredly would heal them were they to become wounded, the man who had saved lives no other surgeon could possibly have preserved, and they all, without exception, rejoiced in his return.

Many a man now labouring with difficulty to shift the great burden of the casks had also sought out familiar acquaintances within the town; indeed, some rekindled old friendships had been the closest possible acquaintance. A positive flow of plenty of local Greek ouzo, retsina and even raki had plainly been consumed in the process - the Surprises were not greatly particular - and all such liquid pleasures surpassed by far the appeal of the ship's four-water grog. At least, Codrington reminded himself, every man had returned aboard, for no absentees had been reported at all, not one, and there was a general ambience of quiet satisfaction throughout the ship.

In the great cabin Pat sat at his table with Simon and Duncan, the three friends in fine good humour, a splendid breakfast consumed and Murphy waiting upon them with a prolific coffee flow. 'If it is not disagreeable to you I would much like to hear your understanding of our more immediate purpose,' declared Simon to Pat in tentative enquiry after the food was all gone; 'Be so kind as to describe your intentions.'

'Why it's time to *shake a leg*,' Pat's own good humour was not to be soured in the least by any inconvenient enquiries. 'You are to consider that we have our cargo to deliver.'

'Are we to be hurried away so soon from this congenial locus?' said Simon, the mildest hint of sinking feelings in his voice.

'We cannot sit here... *fiddling while Rome burns*... while Messalonghi burns... or starves.' Pat managed a small smile.

'Will we depart this very day? Could we not stay a trifle longer... would you think?'

'I am minded to make sail while the sun shines, ha ha! What do you say to that, Simon, eh? *Make sail while the sun shines*!'

'I might remark on the futility of *casting pearls before swine*... and I might also add, with a deal of caution implied, *look before you leap.*'

Duncan laughed aloud and Pat's smile vanished instantly, a reluctant return to earth coming upon him. 'Why, I will go ashore after the table is all cleared up. Murphy, will you look to my uniform, I am minded to call on the Resident, Colonel Napier, to do the civil.'

'D'reckly, sorr.' Murphy, in good cheer himself, began to seize up the tableware.

'Do you care to accompany me,' asked Pat, looking to his friends. 'Napier is, as you may collect, a friend of Greece, and he will possess a very good notion of what is happening in these parts since we were last here.'

Several hours later, the sun already embarked upon its descent through the sky, Napier had not been located at his official residence, which was deserted except for a servant who had no knowledge of his whereabouts. Pat with Duncan and Simon returned to the harbour, where a few of the Surprises were still lingering at the quayside; the freshwater loading had just been completed. A waiting Codrington greeted them as they prepared to board the barge, 'Sir, there is a Greek gentleman come aboard,' announced the lieutenant, 'He is awaiting you on deck. You are familiar with him, Captain Zouvelekis it is.'

Pat nodded. He was indeed acquainted with the Greek. Zouvelekis was a well-respected merchant ship captain who hailed from the sacked island of Kasos. He had joined *Surprise* during the battles to defend Samos, serving as Admiral Miaoulis's liaison officer, subsequently joining the admiral himself when *Surprise* had departed Greece. If anyone knew the latest developments in the war at sea then he surely would.

Warm handshakes and friendly greetings ensued all round upon boarding, for Zouvelekis was well liked, and the four retired to the cabin. Abel Jason and Michael Marston hastened to join the meeting on Pat's call; Jason was a most competent speaker of the Greek language. Murphy darted behind them to wait outside the cabin door with his ear keenly attentive. 'A decent bottle of wine, Murphy, for our guest!' Pat's voice boomed out, 'and doubtless Captain Zouvelekis, Mr Jason and Mr Marston will join us for dinner.'

'Well, it's a'coming up, sorr.'

The Greek nodded, smiled, and all took their seats about the table. 'We possess considerable supplies for Messalonghi, Captain Zouvelekis,' declared Pat, 'both food and medicine.' He hesitated to mention the great stores of powder and shot which filled the hold. 'Will you tell us of the situation about that place? Where is Admiral Miaoulis?'

'All Greek vessels are... are away...' Zouvelekis hesitated, 'Neither the Hydriots nor - *particularly* - the Spezziots will sail again to bring relief without payment in advance, sir... I regret to say... but there was a public meeting earlier this month in Nauplia to raise funds, one which I attended before coming here.'

'Do go on, please.'

'Professor Gennadios - *he is a much esteemed patriot and founder of a school in Nauplia* - he addressed the crowd in the square there; he threw his purse upon the ground, five hundred and more people looking on; and with a degree of passion he made his declaration, which I well recall. He said, *"That is my all, all I possess. I give it freely to my country as I would to my child, and I will do so with all of my salary for all of this year."*'

'Noble words,' murmured Simon.

Zouvelekis nodded and continued, 'A silent crowd was greatly moved... many reduced to tears, and then more voices were heard offering money. The rich amongst the multitude were shamed by his words and, although they were - so it seemed to me - unwilling, they came forward and, despite the heckling and the jeers of those of the gathering who were less fortunate, they did pledge something of their own funds. So you see, Captain O'Connor, after that assembly, supplies were forthcoming in Nauplia... when Miaoulis with twenty-two sail then set off with purchased stores aboard his ships... and all his men paid.'

'When was that?' asked Pat, everyone at the table fascinated.

'The admiral last resupplied the town on that Saturday of eleven days ago, the twenty-first of January, landing provisions on the islet of Vasiladi... to the salute of the town's batteries. However, that was before the combined Turk and Egyptian fleet drove him away on the next day... in the tempest of the twenty-second. On the twenty-third no vessel could keep the sea in a mountainous fury of white wavetops, and all vessels withdrew to whatever sanctuary could be found. A week later there was a battle at sea... and it pleases me to report that the Admiral triumphed, the Ottomans retiring to Patras. The Hydriot, Admiral Sakhtouri, then landed further supplies, and a Turk corvette of twenty-six guns, which had grounded, was burned. Since then all Greek vessels, now some twenty-seven in number including three Spetziots and four Psariots, have been kept away by the constant Turk patrols, never less than a squadron at sea and always with two or three heavy frigates - *forty-four-gun ships* - and ever accompanied by at least a half-dozen brigs, often more.'

'Where is Miaoulis now, Captain Zouvelekis?' asked Pat.

'I believe that Admiral Miaoulis, now that his crew's funds are all expended, has returned to Hydra to seek further provisions for the town. I am, myself, here in Cephalonia to see if I can find fishermen with their small vessels willing to carry fresh supplies across the lagoons when Miaoulis returns, and perhaps to do so at night when the Turk patrols might be avoided.'

'I doubt the Ionian authorities will tolerate that, Captain, if they get wind of it,' Pat spoke very softly, '... and that is despite the personal leanings of Napier who - *it is no secret* - has a kindly affinity for Greek interests. However, if word reaches the Governor of all the Ionians in Corfu, General Frederick Adam - *a most military-minded man* - then there will be a deal of trouble to pay; the islands' quarantine is sacrosanct because of the danger of infections, of diseases, plagues, all prevailing on the mainland, and any fisherman carrying merchandise to and returning from... *from over there...* will be locked up and his vessel confiscated. Why, our own venture is wholly unofficial... and not one word of our purpose must reach Corfu.'

Zouvelekis nodded and continued in low voice, 'Admiral Miaoulis is most concerned, sir; the town is reported to be bereft of powder... and shot, and food is scant... scarce indeed. The corn and bread are everywhere finished, and people have been eating dogs, cats, donkeys, even such mice as may be caught... and precious few of any kind of animal remains there now. For the present the only food is seaweed from the lagoons... and any crabs that may be trapped. The bombardment, although presently halted, was such that all the fish have fled, yes indeed... and people are boiling and eating salt cedar...'

'What is that, tell?' Simon interrupted, the botanist within him alerted.

'It is a kind of tamarisk bush which is native to the coast, but it is painful to the bowels...'

'I dare say it is,' Simon frowned, his thoughts racing, his medical mind alarmed.

'... and it brings all who eat it to a form of madness which lasts for several days.' The Greek, in obvious dismay, continued his sad litany of deprivation, 'Water is poor, brackish... the cisterns are polluted by corpses...'

'Dear God!' exclaimed Marston, shocked. A mute and stunned Simon simply stared in bleak dismay.

'... and only the most limited potable supplies are available to the fortunate few; that is to say... those with influence.'

'Dear God indeed,' whispered Simon who could no longer contain his own consternation.

Zouvelekis nodded and continued, 'Consequently there are many, the sick and the aged most particularly, who are ill, suffering from sicknesses of the stomach, of the digestion. But there are no medicines, none at all, nothing... save for vinegar for the bowels. Scurvy begins to present itself as pain in the joints and there are reports of smallpox. There are a few Greek doctors and several European surgeons in the town, and these are to be found at the smallest of hospitals, an establishment founded by a Swiss, Jacob Meyer. Their medications consist only of herbs and a little opium. A wounded man has precious little chance of the slightest help. Wounds are cleaned with olive oil and raki, and dressed with an ointment made from egg whites.'

'Egg whites? Egg whites!' exclaimed Simon, increasingly horrified. 'And the number of sick, pray tell?' he asked, great anxiety plain in his voice.

'Hundreds, perhaps they number in the thousands,' declared Zouvelekis quietly and in the bleakest of tones. 'Fever too is also rife, for the lagoons are the perfect home for insects of all varieties.'

'The falling damps,' murmured Simon, an apprehensive air about him, 'the evil vapours, the vile miasmas and, indeed, the swamp fever. Doubtless all sources of such afflictions abound there... about the lagoons.' All attention in the cabin switching to him, every face aghast in dismay, Simon continued, 'For myself, I collect that Lancisi proposed that mosquitoes were the cause of such fevers... and that was fully a hundred years ago.' He nodded, 'I have ever been convinced that he was in the right of things. Are mosquitoes present in Messalonghi and its lagoons in winter, Captain Zouvelekis?'

'Most certainly they are, sir; the lagoons are infested with them... they are present in the greatest numbers.'

'Oh dear, that could scarcely be less helpful to the poor inhabitants.'

'Hell and death!' cried Pat, sighing. The sobering and daunting immediacies of his task were coming home to haunt him, to prey again upon his disturbed mind, and he had been in Greek waters for less than a day. 'Murphy! Murphy there!' he shouted, 'Please to send for Mr Codrington.'

The lieutenant appeared within minutes, 'Sir?'

'Mr Codrington, you are to take six men in every one of our boats - *every one of them* - to the quay, where you are to seek out every cask, barrel and butt you may find from every merchant along the waterfront - *every one, do you hear?* - and all of the near town premises. Please to explain that we are intending to take drinking water to Messalonghi, for there is none in that place for the sick, the aged or the children. People are dying there for want of water. Fill every barrel you may find and bring it aboard. I am minded that we will depart at first light.'

'Yes sir, and if the merchants require payment?'

'Then you are to tell them that they will be rewarded in Heaven, for we presently possess no funds, not a penny, for such recompense as they might wish for on earth... and this is not the moment to stand upon such customary trifles. You are to make that clear to them. Give not the slightest heed to any objection, none! Brook not the least withholding! Am I plain?'

'Very good, sir.'

'Mr Codrington!' Pat shouted as his lieutenant exited the cabin door, 'Please to take Mr Jacob with you; he exhibits the most persuasive of tongue, and a Greek one too, so it is!'

'Aye aye, sir.'

'That is exceedingly handsome in you, sir,' declared Marston, impressed and relieved.

Pat nodded, swallowed hard, dismay seizing hold upon his every thought. He collected a chart from his desk, 'Captain Zouvelekis, will we speak now of the military position of the Turks... their forces all about Messalonghi. Do they possess any artillery pieces which can threaten the beach, endanger the delivery of supplies? Please to show me on this chart where they are situated.'

'Here, sir, is my own plan of the town and its situation.' Zouvelekis unrolled upon the table a crude, hand-drawn canvas map. 'As may be seen, the town is bordered to the west and south by the shallow waters of the lagoons; to the north and east the town defensive wall is an earth mound with an exterior moat. The garrison is helped by two score of guns of many calibres around the wall, whilst the besiegers at present possess few. However, since Admiral Miaoulis engaged the Ottoman fleet, Ibrahim has halted his efforts to take the town. It is believed that he awaits twenty-five artillery pieces which, so our spies report, have been embarked aboard barges at Crioneri beach and are yet to be brought up to the besiegers' lines.'

'Crioneri beach?'

'Here it is,' Zouvelekis put his finger on Pat's chart, 'It is the location of the smallest of towns, Parga; the whole is hardly more than the beach opposite Corfu. Conceivably the guns may be those formerly used against the deposed monster, Ali Pasha, in Iannina to the north-east. They are expected to reach Ibrahim in a very few weeks time when, as seems likely, the bombardment will resume.'

Pat stared at his chart for a moment before looking up, 'It is two years since we brought Lord Byron to Messalonghi...' He gazed all about his table at expectant faces, 'Two years on... and in that time we have lost many of our people. I do not care to lose more, and so we must have the most careful of plans. It is not my intention to engage with Turk or Egyptian vessels... Indeed, I pray that we do not bring the great guns to action... for our instruction is only... *only* to deliver the supplies we are carrying. If the Ottoman fleet does appear... then we must flee. We are but one ship and it will serve no purpose to be destroyed... as we so nearly were at Navarino.' Pat looked all about him, his audience plainly filled with apprehension but fascinated. 'We know that the Turk does not greatly care to sail after dusk, and so we must look to these long winter nights to carry out our task. The waters of the lagoons, as we know very well, are shallow... exceedingly so, as is the solitary channel to approach Messalonghi; it will not admit the barky, far from it. Hence *Surprise* must stand off some way, and I venture that will be a mile and a half south of the channel's guardian isle of Vasiladi. *Mathew Jelbert* will approach Vasiladi to alert the garrison there to our intentions, and the cutter will escort our boats between *Surprise* and that island, whence they will take the only channel to the town.' Pat looked all about him; the palpable sense of unease was visible upon every mute face. 'The boats,' he continued, 'when unescorted by *Mathew Jelbert*, will remain within the shallow waters of the lagoons, where no significant Turk vessel of any draught may venture for fear of grounding. Yes, it will require many a trip to convey all the plentiful provisions presently within the barky's hold, but we have the night hours in which to do so. Does anyone have any questions?'

'It is in my thinking to go ashore with the medical supplies,' declared Simon in a flat tone which was intended to show he would brook no refusal.

'It is also in my thinking to do so,' Marston spoke up in as strong a voice as anyone had ever heard him use outside of his church sermons, much to the surprise of everyone present. An astonished Pat, many concerns racing within his own thoughts, simply stared at his chaplain.

'And mine,' echoed Jason, his eyes firmly fixed upon Pat in mute challenge.

Pat, recognising the determination of his colleagues, sighed. He reminded himself that this was no normal situation, at least not officially, not that any of his crew had ever raised that particular point. He allowed his apprehension to relent and from somewhere he forced a smile, 'Have a care, gentlemen, I would not wish you to provoke a mutiny aboard this vessel.' The tense atmosphere relaxed. 'Very well,' said Pat, 'when the barky arrives off Vasiladi, Mr Macleod will take command of *Mathew Jelbert...* Mr Reeve will also remain aboard the cutter at all times. Mr Pickering with six men will accompany Doctor Ferguson, Mr Marston and Mr Jason... to maintain a close escort on land and to unload the boats.' Pat smiled, 'Mr Codrington and Mr Mower will endeavour, with myself, to keep the barky afloat... out of any Turk reach... but, take note, all of you... *you will strive to be mindful of this...* your time ashore must be short. We are delivering relief supplies... and, let it be said, munitions too... but we are not the defenders of the town, nor can we be, one solitary frigate that we are.'

A grim but reluctant satisfaction permeated the cabin after Pat's proclamation, but from near the door Murphy looked on with deep disbelief and a profound dismay writ large upon his face; he knew that not a single man aboard would care to countenance Simon going ashore into a besieged fortress under frequent bombardment from Turk guns, a place also stricken by various diseases. Simon's return to the ship had been extremely well received and morale throughout the lower deck had soared on the news of him returning aboard the cutter, but this latest news would certainly not be taken at all well.

Later, the evening passing with all thoughts of the morrow consciously set aside, at least as much as they could be, and the toasted cheese all eaten up, indeed relished, Pat and Simon sat in the cabin nursing the second bottle of a particularly delicious red wine, a deep satisfaction found in their mutual company. Not the least feeling of obligation weighed upon them to spark discussion of any particular subject, the benevolent influence of the wine delivering a genial contentment, and both men frequently paused for long spells of reflection until, ten minutes passing in silence, Simon asked tentatively, 'Would you care to play a marvel for the strings which Marston has introduced me to? It was written by the master, Paganini, and gifted to Marston.' No reply was forthcoming so Simon persisted, 'Will I send Murphy to invite Marston to join us?'

'Oh, that,' Pat looked up at last, 'I confess I have made my own attempts upon that wondrous piece with Marston. Indeed I have. But I have not mastered it yet; no, far from it. It is infernally complicated, and I am presently not in the way for the playing of anything with the least difficulty.' Pat sighed, 'No, I could not. I confess my mind these days seems oft adrift... it is akin to my thoughts being afloat... on a receding tide, but...' Pat halted, for Simon's face was registering not only his professional curiosity but also his personal feelings of disappointment, '... but perhaps we will play one of our old favourites, eh? Just the two of us. Allow me to suggest Johann Pachelbel's Canon in D; what do you say to that?'

'A most admirable suggestion,' Simon smiled, nodding.

Without further ado, Pat fetched his 'cello and Simon's viola from where they were stowed under the seating at the stern gallery. A minute or two of tuning and Murphy, alerted by the strings, entered to clear the supper remnants, returning unbidden with the coffee. Pat nodded his thanks.

'Are you ready, brother?' Pat paused, his bow hovering above the strings. 'Very well, I will begin.' For ten seconds the cabin filled with the mellow, low notes of the solo 'cello, each one seemingly holding time itself in abeyance, the bow seizing upon the string and lingering for almost a second for every note, teasing the ears with the deliberate approach to play at the slowest possible speed, but in so doing generating an atmospheric infusion of the most haunting ambience. Simon stared, open-mouthed, at his friend: never before had Pat's touch on the instrument seemed so passionate, so heartfelt, a masterfully rich, full sound and in so short a time, merely seconds. Simon was seized by the feeling that he must live up to the wonderful playing of his friend, and he touched upon the strings of his viola with an intense concentration, the higher notes delivering a powerful reinforcement of the intensity of delivery of the simple yet sublime composition. Pat smiled, allowed the power of his playing to diminish slightly, his 'cello to become the background, a deeper rhythmical sound, whilst the viola seized the lead, nearly overpowering the 'cello's foundation until Simon shaded back just a very little, maintaining his viola at the forefront with those rising and falling fluctuations conceived by the composer, the combination of the two instruments delivering the most beautiful, soaring harmonies.

From outside the cabin, a fascinated Murphy peeked around the door. Whilst he was accustomed to the frequent playing within the cabin by a varying group of musicians, most usually it was simply Pat and Simon enjoying a light-hearted pleasure. However, he sensed that before him something different was taking place. He could not, within his uneducated limitations, describe what it was, even to himself, but he was by no means without intelligence, and his ears, long accustomed to the strings - whether good, bad or indifferent - registered that the musicians, on this occasion, were striving for something special. Perhaps the separation of the two friends had brought about a yearning to get back once again that which both had feared was lost, that which they had believed was gone for ever. Whether or not, Murphy, who was no great fan of classical pieces, recognised that before him was a musical reflection of spirit, and a most intensive one. From somewhere, somehow, he dimly conceived that it could only be the sounds of two men's passionate belief in their friendship, and their music represented a profound symbol of their wish never to lose it. For six minutes Murphy was utterly immobile; for six minutes Simon was gripped with an intensity he had never formerly found in his playing; for six minutes Pat consciously allowed his friend to dictate the piece, studiously holding back and moderating the rich, mellow undercurrents of his 'cello to avoid transcending the higher viola's domination. Fascinated, he studied his friend in occasional, fleeting glances. Simon's entire face was a picture of absolute concentration, much sweat upon his brow despite the cold air in the cabin. The end came too soon, both men realising that perhaps they had achieved something as near to perfection as ever they might find in their playing. They stared at each other and, without further ado, they set down their instruments and stood up from their chairs; in their silence a moving and profound realisation was registering upon them both. Simon offered Pat his hand, 'Very finely played, brother. I have never heard the like from you before in all these years.'

'Oh, the older the fiddle the sweeter the tune.' Pat's words were softly spoken, little more than a mumble. He disregarded the outstretched hand and simply seized his friend in a fierce embrace for several seconds, ultimately standing back. 'Thank you, thank you... for coming back...' he whispered, overcome, 'Thank you for returning to the barky... to the cabin, a thousand thanks.'

Murphy, standing on the door threshold, stepped in, his face radiating a smile of an intensity such that a surprised Pat had never seen the likes of before, and without a word the steward burst into loud applause, clapping vigorously.

Thursday 2nd February 1826   07:30   Surprise   Argostoli

Pat stood on his quarterdeck in the pre-dawn twilight as the increasingly bright glow spread above the hills to the east. He stared all about him, many more than the complement of the morning watch were already on deck. There was a general air of expectancy hovering about all of them, tangible, plain to see in the short movements of his people, all conversations little more than murmurings. The mute faces of those standing near the helm, waiting in silent anticipation, were speaking unuttered volumes. Doubtless, he thought, every man was of much the same mind as himself; the barky and all her crew, officers and men alike, were returning to the real prospect of danger, to the likelihood of bloodshed and potential death. All of which certainly sat ill on Pat's mind. He supposed it was likely to be so with every one of his shipmates, all of whom had long become his friends as well as being his brothers-in-arms, for they had all long ceased to be simply his crew. No, they were certainly not merely his ship's crew, that was very much the thinking of a far distant past, long gone; now all was different, and he did not care to lose more men - *his men* - in a cause which, whilst he had great sympathy for it, was not one in which the Royal Navy cared to fly its colours. *Surprise* was reduced to skulking in the shadows, sailing in the darkness, in the black of the night, like some disreputable privateer or, worse, a despicable pirate ship, and that combination of circumstances and prospects sat most uncomfortably on his mind. He paced forward to the waist rail and stared down to the gun deck where a hundred water barrels and more were lashed tightly along the centre line as best they could be secured. It was not a sight he cared to countenance, not least because they would be an obstruction and hindrance to his men, were they called upon to serve the great guns; but so much weight, carried so high above the waterline, was most exceedingly unwelcome. Lord knows what it would do, he shuddered, were the wind and weather to be greatly adverse; but to stow all below was impossible, for the hold was filled to capacity with supplies of all kinds: foodstuffs, munitions and medical supplies. God help them were they to encounter a Turk warship, for they possessed more powder below than even the Devonport hoy had ever carried, and a fire in the hold would send them all to Kingdom Come in very short order. He strived to put such horrific possibilities out of his mind and he stepped back to the stern rail where he looked down once more upon the eight boats tied to the barky on short lines. They would be towed when the barky departed, no longer the least space for them aboard his overweight ship since all the water butts had been loaded. He frowned again; he was sure that his ship was several feet deeper in the water. This was certainly a rum business, nothing like it had he ever done before: delivering munitions to a rebellious Greek town which had been, for much more than a year, fighting for freedom against the Ottoman oppressors. What had his life and navy career come to? Could he ever contemplate returning to his few sodden acres of impoverished, bleak and windswept croft in remote Connemara which was his real home? Indeed, could it really still be considered to be his home, after so many more of his adult years had been spent at sea than ever spent ashore? What would such life be like, were he to return to his croft? Was there really anything for him to do there? Sure, he could feed the fowl and the pigs, cut some turf from the bog for the peat fires of next year, and he might plant the seed potatoes. But was that really the life to be for Patrick O'Connor? Who, indeed, was Patrick O'Connor these days? Did he know himself any more? And what on earth, he wondered, did his wife, Sinéad, think of him? The recent few years of absence had placed a great strain upon their relationship, and what of his children, whom he so rarely saw? Sighing deeply, he determined to set aside such difficult mental enquiries, which he found greatly unsettling, and he looked all about him in a more mundane assessment of the weather. It was cool, but nothing of note; it was certainly not like a Connemara winter in January. No, there was not the least prospect of a frost; indeed, the air was heavy and there was surely some chance, perhaps even a likelihood, of rain, but maybe that was all to the good? After the reported severe storms of a week ago the Turks might not be greatly enthusiastic about putting to sea with the least haste.

'A penny for your thoughts, brother,' the softly spoken enquiry came from Simon, stepping to stand alongside Pat at the rail.

'Eh? Oh... I was in contemplation of... of the... the weather, *yes, the weather*... as we approach the mainland... the Gulf of Patras.'

'Is there some particular signification to the weather?' said Simon, considerable doubt in his voice, 'I am no naval strategist.'

'Oh, for sure there is...' Pat halted, stared at his friend.

'Patrick O'Connor, please do not endeavour to gull me with vagaries, with conventions, with mere megrims which are best suited to a simpleton. I am minded that there is something of note which is troubling you, I remarked it when you said that you were not greatly in the way for music last night... before we set to with our attempt upon Pachelbel's marvel. Furthermore, I did not care to mention it then, but - *take note* - despite the undoubted excellence of your playing... and it surely was so... I believed your 'cello may have been slightly out of tune... the C string perhaps?'

'Out of tune? No, it didn't signify.' Simon's cold stare persevering, Pat took refuge in mirth, 'I am got onto dangerous ground, for sure.' A frosty glare being the only response from his friend, Pat decided upon a final try to skate over things, 'Never be so concerned.'

'If you value candour... amongst your closest of friends most particularly, if it is not disagreeable to you... then will you be so kind as to elaborate on your worriment, your apprehension.'

Pat conceded, decided he would say just a little, the least possible, about his wearisome feelings, but nothing of his anxieties about the future, which seemed so personal, 'I am very sensible of your concerns, never doubt that for a moment... and... and *yes*... I doubt I will ever forget the loss of our shipmates when we were last here, a little ways south along the coast... when we escaped the Bay of Navarino. I would not care to see anything of that ilk ever again, never in life. It is a considerable worry.'

'Will you do me a kindness? I should rather you endeavour to embrace fortitude, for there are a deal of men aboard this ship - *and I include myself, I do* - whose spirits can only be described as fragile *at best*. Why, I myself am oft reminded of one particular day of horror... it was the last of the Samos battles... I was entirely destroyed by the burden... downstairs, the flow of bloody bodies across my table... dozens... *scores* of wounded men, many arms and legs lost... and...' Simon's voice dropped to a whisper, '... and several dying before my eyes... until the time came when I was unable to continue... That is... that is until - *you will doubtless collect the moment* - I spoke with you *here*, here in this very place, here in this locus of many deaths.' Simon sighed, drew a deep breath, the recollection sitting most painfully with him, 'My reserve, my abilities... all were shot through that day... Nothing left of strength in the slightest did I possess, steady nerves were gone... no, nothing at all remained to me, and no longer could I continue... the blood, the gore... I do not care to dwell upon it; I was sick, sick to the pit of my stomach.' Simon swallowed hard, recalling that particularly vivid and abhorrent memory which he did not care for. 'For these next days... and weeks perhaps, allow me to tell you this, Pat... *I will need you...* and many more aboard this gallant vessel will be looking to you when - let me say *if* - such black hours come upon us once again. That is why I have returned, that is the only reason I am here; I care not for serving longer in this vile and bloody conflict. I am no great Philhellene. Here is a place for Greeks and... *and idealists*, and I do not consider myself to be one. Last year I found happiness in Tobermory, that feeling which has eluded me for many a year. I have remarked before... that I found there a woman I love, and I am here with a deal of reluctance, and - *yes* - I am myself much affrighted; nor can I set aside my feelings of despair for our prospects, even as I strive to find the necessary courage to persevere. Many others of our shipmates are similarly so inclined - *let me tell you* - but they will not speak of it with you. We - *all of us* - we look to you... *to you.*' Simon paused to see a shocked Pat's reaction. 'I beg you will forgive me for speaking with such candour, brother.'

'It is I who will beg your forgiveness,' a stunned Pat whispered, 'Perhaps we should have spoken more of our concerns before now... in Falmouth perhaps or... or last night. For sure, my mind was never entirely settled... before we set to with our music, the joy that it was, for there are some concerns I can never shake. As to the string being out of tune, well, doubtless you were in the right of it there.'

'Ready to depart, sir,' declared Codrington in loud voice, appearing at the helm; 'The stowing party is standing ready below in the cable tier.'

'Very good, Mr Codrington,' Pat's attention was jolted to the present, to the immediacies of departure, but he turned back to Simon, 'I will endeavour to do my best, and thank you for your words, old friend.'

The sun had risen to show the tiniest bright peek over the hills during Pat's musings and his conversation with Simon. His eyes returning to the preparations for departure, he looked all about him once more; the tempo of movement of his men was noticeably picking up. Those men on duty at the end of the morning watch had gathered at the braces, at the foc'sle, at the capstans, the bars already fitted in place to turn them. In fact, all the men of his crew were on deck, not merely the duty watch. He became aware of the assembly of his officers standing all about him, all save Mower standing at the foc'sle and Reeve aboard the cutter; he noted the general readiness to be away, to get on with matters. He sighed inwardly, Simon's words coming again to mind, and he consciously strived hard to exude confidence in his voice, 'Take us out, Mr Codrington, if you will.'

'Aye aye, sir,' Codrington nodded. 'All hands, prepare to make sail!' he shouted loud. 'Mr Prosser, hands aloft.'

'Lay aloft!' shouted Prosser, and men everywhere about the deck hastened up the rigging to the yards. 'Bring to the messenger!' he bawled out, and a minute later, 'Man the bars!'

Surprise was anchored starboard side towards the town quay, five cables off, and all her crew could feel the gentle north-easterly breeze, the *grego*, acting upon her larboard side. Prosser estimated the wind at six knots, which seemed ideal to aid the frigate's departure, blowing fine on her larboard quarter.

'Breast the capstan!' shouted Prosser.

'Up anchor!' ordered Codrington.

'Up anchor!' Prosser echoed at the top of his voice.

'Heave and a-weigh!' cried Codrington.

Beer struck up a simple rhythm upon his fiddle, and the cable began to be wound in on the capstan, the sound of eighty men's customary and restrained shouts now general. Slowly the men ran the cable in just fast enough for the tierers present to easily keep up. 'Up and down!' came the loud cries from several hands at the bow.

'Up and down, sir!' shouted Mower from the foc's'le.

'Thick and dry for weighing!' shouted Codrington.

The topmen, in the meantime, waited patiently out on the yards where they had cast off the gaskets. Without the lines holding them furled to the yards the sails drooped in bulky bundles, held up by the men who gathered up the canvas close to their chests, waiting. The tierers were stowing the last of the cable and the best bower had just appeared above the surface, hauled up from the water depths and dripping mud.

'Standby aloft! Let fall!' bawled Codrington at the top of his voice. *Peep-peep, peep-peep* sounded from the bosun's whistle, echoed from his mates.

'Ready about!' commanded Codrington.

'Let fall! Sheet home! Sheet home! Hoist away!' Prosser shouted. The topmen, standing ready, let fall their bundles of canvas, the topsails; down they tumbled, unfurling, flapping in the breeze, men already hauling on the braces. *Surprise* was swiftly shifting, the *grego* visibly acting upon her sails and hull; she was bearing south towards the distant De Bosset's bridge, discernibly picking up momentum for her necessary turn towards the town so as to come full about to sail north-west. She would likely come round only very gradually and it would be a tight turn with only the least of sea room for manoeuvre, whilst the helmsmen would be afforded precious little feel until she gathered way with greater speed.

'Hard a-lee!' shouted Codrington to the two helmsmen, both working hard at the wheel.

Surprise now began her turn, the bow coming round to starboard as she gained momentum, her topsails pushing her round only a little faster, the main and mizzen still flapping until their braces were also hauled tight, when she came further round and they filled to give her progress a much needed boost.

'Helm up!' cried Codrington when her bow at last faced the town. For the first time she was beginning to be driven forward with noticeable speed, and that itself was more than a little daunting with the lack of water before her, the quay directly ahead and merely two hundred yards off the bow. The wind now blowing on her starboard quarter and all her sails filled, she was being pushed faster, the rudder kept hard over, the ship coming round more and more until she was fully turned about. The town and quay were, thankfully - all minds on the quarterdeck much relieved - on the larboard beam. It was not a manoeuvre that Pat had ever relished when departing Argostoli with anything of north in the wind.

'Helm amidships!' shouted Codrington. The north-east wind giving her little save for a worrying leeway, and the frigate holding as close to the wind as she would ever manage, all on deck anxiously watched the nearing promontory tip close to larboard with a degree of anxiety; precious little speed did the frigate possess to be sure of clearing it with her lee drift. A snail might be faster, thought Pat, holding in check his own concern. On the town quay two hundred and more locals vigorously waved farewell. The deck crew completed their heaving-in of the final few yards of the cable and the anchor was catted. Within five more minutes *Surprise* passed by the final rocky yards of the promontory and the broken water's edge to larboard, still shifting barely imperceptibly, but finally clear of all peril. All on the quarterdeck breathed a collective sigh of relief. Barton, on the helm, unbidden, allowed her bow to slip off the wind, a little more of westing being greatly more favourable to her. Pat noticed but said nothing; Barton was unrivalled in his task, and all aboard knew it very well.

Pat spoke up at last, audible satisfaction in his voice, 'Bring her round, Mr Codrington; due south, south to the sea!'

Noon, and *Surprise - Mathew Jelbert* a half-mile astern - was approaching the strait between Cephalonia and Zante; she was making the slowest of progress with a weakening wind on her larboard beam. Pat took the sighting as Codrington ordered her turn to the east and the frigate came round as close to the north-east wind as she would hold, all on the quarterdeck realising that many a long tack was the sure and tedious future for the afternoon. Not that anyone much minded, for it would be immeasurably preferable to close on Messolonghi in the darkness, for such would defer any sighting and recognition of the ship by Turk observers, whether on the hills surrounding the town, at sea, or on the cape and coast on the south side of the

Gulf. Perhaps news of her arrival in contested waters would be significantly delayed in distant Patras port, some thirteen miles further away and where the Turk fleet was based. Pat was mindful that it was the last quarter of the waning moon, which would also be ideal for his purposes: less light for any watching Turks but probably just sufficient illumination to send boats safely with supplies through the shallow waters of the outlying lagoon as *Surprise* stood off in deeper water near the island of Vasiladi. And, if the north-east wind endured, the situation would be more favourable for a swift departure were the Turk navy to appear. He scratched in his memory for any other factors which might be helpful, however small, and he reminded himself of the barky's clean hull, all weed scraped off her copper plating in the Plymouth Yard dry dock. Yes, the barky would surely be faster than any Turk ship, and that too was a consoling thought to cling to in his already rising anxieties, for - try as he might - he could not wholly dispel them. He stared all about him, looked to his men, to his officers, a general air of professional confidence exhibited by all standing about the quarterdeck as he stepped away from the wheel. He descended to the gun deck, unhurriedly pacing along the length of it, and he climbed up to the foc'sle, a nod here and a brief word there to many a man looking to him as he passed by, ostensibly inspecting, and always in his thoughts the necessity to present an image of his own self-assurance. Simon's words stuck uncomfortably in his mind, akin to an itch which he could not scratch. He turned about, slowly descended the foc'sle steps to the gun deck once again and he walked aft in deep concentration but always nodding to small clusters of his veterans in passing; he smiled towards several who he considered old friends of the lower deck.

His mind was fogged with the looming dangers of being at anchor off Messalonghi, in the Turk's near presence, but as he turned his head to greet Bosanko, an old *Tenedos* shipmate, his stomach turned over as he caught sight of Jago Jelbert. The young newcomer was being taught the procedures of loading the great guns by the captain of *Mighty Fine*, Pascoe. In a sickening, brief instant he recalled once again the funeral of Jelbert's great uncle, Mathew, who had been killed as the barky escaped the confines of the great Bay of Navarino. Pat's eyes clouded, he felt them beginning to water as clear and painful memories of Jelbert's burial at sea the day after the action came flooding back; nearly every man aboard had openly and unashamedly wept floods as the body of the master gunner went over the side. Rarely a day had passed since that blackest of days without feelings of despond weighing heavily upon Pat's mind. Indeed, Mathew Jelbert's own son, Annan, had also been killed a year before his father whilst serving a gun within the great cabin. Pat's mind raced; Mathew Jelbert's nephew, Jago, must be protected as best as could be and at all costs, but what to do? He stepped forward cautiously, a lump in his throat, 'I hope I see you well, Pascoe?'

'Aye, sir; very well, thankee.'

Pat nodded, 'If we do find ourselves engaged... against the Turk... young Jelbert here is *not* to serve at the guns. I am minded he will start his service... he will start *below*, in the powder magazine... for that is... is...' Pat did not want to utter the words on his mind - *the safest place* - but he searched for some explanation even as the gunner, staring intently at Pat's confusion, realised perfectly his captain's conundrum.

''tis where the first step begins, sir, for the gun!' declared Pascoe in loud voice.

'Yes... precisely so!' a relieved Pat smiled, 'The magazine, the bagging of powder... the start it is and the start is always... always the... the place to... *to begin*; indeed, it is! Very good, Pascoe. Jelbert is to serve in the forward magazine.' A final nod and a smile of encouragement to Jago Jelbert, and Pat moved on, returning to his quarterdeck, the youngster bemused but only dimly suspecting what the conversation was really about.

Time passed slowly by as *Surprise* made long tacks, the remainder of the afternoon slipping away with no vessels sighted, nothing at all attracting the attention of the alert lookouts atop the crosstrees. The ambience throughout the ship, of customary routine, of procedural quietude, seemed wholly incongruous to Pat as he paced his quarterdeck, hardly a minute spent in the cabin save for taking the swiftest and smallest portion of his reheated and late dinner, only half of it eaten in great haste, much to Murphy's evident disgust as the steward gathered up the uneaten food and dishes. An all-consuming eagerness to stay on deck had overtaken Pat, to the exclusion of all else, so much so that the apprehension rising within him was such that he felt gripped by a severe tension, reducing him to an almost complete immobility as he fiercely held on to the stern rail. His disquiet was so debilitating that eventually he leaned over the side to throw up his ill-digested dinner, the vile taste of acid lingering until he drank from the water butt near the wheel. He swept the seas himself in every direction with his glass with an anxious eye and great frequency, only the odd word exchanged occasionally with Duncan, with Prosser, with an attentive Simon, and with a curious Marston. All of them hovered close by his elbow as the hours drearily passed, until Pat wondered what the significance of their proximity might be. He pondered over the possible reasons for their close attendance: had his private uncertainty become general knowledge aboard the barky? He was sure that Simon would most certainly never have remarked upon it to anyone.

His musings were arrested as Dalby rang three bells of the first dog watch; there was not much more daylight left to them, and *Surprise* had made only a bare few miles off the east coast of Cephalonia on a long northerly tack. He looked round from where he stood near the helm; the sun hung prominently lower in the sky off the larboard quarter, seemingly hovering as if suspended just above the southern tip of Cephalonia. It was still a very long way to Messalonghi at this rate, he thought, and arrival after midnight was much more likely than his previously calculated time of dusk. Time there to offload supplies before the bright exposure that daylight would bring was certainly sure to be much less than he had planned and hoped for.

For a few minutes of diversion, every once in a while, he allowed himself the luxury of admiring his refitted ship, her spanking new sails hanging taut from their replaced yards, the canvas not yet bleached or aged by the sun in the least. He could still smell the pine resin which waxed the new rigging, not yet fully dried out in the greater heat of the Mediterranean, and from the deck the strikingly pungent aroma of the tar, which soaked the fresh laid oakum between the deck planks, rose to tickle his nostrils. His ship surely was in very fine fettle, and he hoped with all his heart that she would long stay that way.

'Well, coffee's up!' declared Murphy, appearing on the quarterdeck. Pat, wholly engrossed in his uncomfortable thoughts and trying to determine at what time *Surprise* might yet reach the islands off Messalonghi, simply waved him away without a word spoken.

Four bells rang out as Pat was still standing at the stern rail, the low sun throwing a lingering and radiant yellow glow from behind Cephalonia for its final few minutes of reassuring presence. He watched with a rare fascination as the orb dipped below the distant horizon, far beyond the island, to leave a splendid afterglow. He stared down at the eight ship's boats in tow within the broad, white, curved wake as *Surprise* gently came round in another of her tacks to the east, the weak wind falling away to little more than the feeblest of breeze, every shade of red radiating in the skies astern in a splendid panorama of colours even as the air temperature was falling noticeably in just a few minutes. For the first time in the day he sensed the feeling of being hungry; his stomach's rejection of his dinner, no doubt, being the cause. He nodded to Pickering, on watch, murmured to the lieutenant that no lights were to be displayed; he emphasised *none at all*, and he slowly paced towards and down the steps, entering the coach, the air within much cooler than on the deck, the cabin dimly lit by a solitary lamp.

'Well, is 'ee ready for supper?' asked Murphy in a most offhand tone of voice, Pat taking only mild exception. The steward swiftly stepped aside before Pat could remonstrate with him as Simon and Duncan unexpectedly entered the cabin from the coach after a perfunctory knock on the door.

'What, pray tell, has Wilkins prepared?' asked a tired Pat of Murphy, his words spoken without the slightest degree of anticipation in his voice even as his eyes, sore after an exposed day in the wind, drifted with repeated flickering of his eyelids to look to his unannounced visitors.

'Well, he has fresh-baked Greek bread...' Murphy's attention too wandered towards Simon and Duncan; people generally did not burst uninvited into the cabin, and his own curiosity was piqued.

'That is splendid, no doubt, but man does not live by his daily bread alone,' declared a hungry Pat, in a sarcastic voice, 'I read that somewhere in the Bible...' Murphy muttered something scarcely audible, wholly unintelligible but seeming decidedly rude under his breath. 'What did you say, Murphy?' asked Pat in irritated voice.

'Well, never a word, sorr!' came the untruthful reply with feigned indignance.

'That is very good,' Pat glared at his steward, 'Doubtless you are minded that it is better to keep your mouth shut and appear insolent than to open it and remove all doubt!' The first stirrings of hunger registering, Pat spoke up loudly, 'Now, I am amazing short set. What is coming with the bread?'

''tis a brace of roast chickens... all be cooking right proper... sorr... roasting,' mumbled a scowling Murphy in the most affronted tone of voice.

'That will serve admirably,' barked Pat, pleased, 'and there will be plenty enough for my two friends here.' He looked to Simon and Duncan with a smile, 'You do care to join me, gentlemen?' He did not wait for any answer but turned again to his steward, 'Please to bring two bottles of red wine, Murphy. I find I am in the way for a generous tint; that uncommonly good Portuguese will serve very well. And... *Murphy*... shake a leg! You may care to run!'

'Yes sorr!' The steward frowned with a look that he wished might kill, and he left in exceptional haste, darting a quizzical glance to the visitors in passing.

'Naturally,' declared Pat with a first hint of a smile, the irritation of the minor altercation with his steward diminishing as the pleasure of supper with his two closest friends settled upon him, his mood lifting with a small frisson of anticipation, 'I am always delighted when you both attend my table... as you well know... but - *tell* - is there some particular occasion today to which I owe the great honour, eh?'

'Aye... that is to say... *nae*,' declared Duncan, 'The pleasure is all mine... and Simon's, no doubt. It is the rare event when we have found time, the three of us, to take a wee morsel of supper together... and with Simon and I both going ashore we... we...'

'We determined to seize the moment, to beg your hospitality,' interjected Simon. 'It is in our thinking to enjoy a precious hour or two together before we return to... to the possible fray, when such an opportunity conceivably might be denied to us for some considerable time... until our... *our undertaking* is completed.'

Pat was cheered as recollections of enjoyable past meals with his great friends settled upon him, the reassuring thought so much in contrast to his uncomfortable apprehensions of all day and much before that, 'That is a first class notion, so it is. Please, do take a seat. We have plentiful time before we properly begin this... *this caper*. Mr Prosser is minded that... with the dying of the wind at sunset... we will barely shift for the next few hours and, I dare say, we will not make Vasiladi until well after midnight. He expects something of a northerly breeze to blow in a few hours time... which we may profit by... but until then we are in the doldrums. Ah, here is Murphy with the wine.'

The first bottle was entirely poured by the steward into three large glass tumblers when Duncan spoke up, 'Murphy, I didnae get even a wee scrap for dinner and I am fair clemmed, mortal hungry... horses ain't in it. Would ye care to bring the bread directly? I can wait for the blessed chicken - if it will be cooking for some time. Thankee.'

Murphy nodded, hastening away before Pat might inflict his sharp tongue upon him again. He returned within three minutes, a noticeable degree of trepidation upon him, bearing the smallest loaf ever to grace the cabin upon the breadboard. Six keen eyes fastened upon it, all weighing up how it might go round three hungry men, all wondering whether there might be more forthcoming. 'Murphy,' declared Pat eventually, the steward sensing the unspoken degree of disappointment about the table, 'Ain't you heard that old saying... that famous ancient proverb?' Nothing offered in reply other than a frown, and Pat resumed, *'Two breads are better than one!'* With that he burst into laughter, which his friends were pleased to see. Duncan followed with gusto, Simon smiling, while Murphy merely scowled. Pat slapped his thigh, 'Two breads are better than one! Hah! Hah! What do you say to that, Murphy, eh?'

'Well, sorr,' a disgruntled Murphy was tired of being the butt of Pat's acerbic condemnation, Pat's wit being only slightly less excoriating, 'I might say something like the old saying from home... from Galway... You will know it, sorr... *May the most you wish for be the least you get!*' With that said he could not refrain from his own loud guffaw. The briefest moment of thought and Duncan followed with his own uproarious great laugh, and he clapped his hands in delight; even Simon laughed out loud.

Pat stared for only a half-second longer before laughing himself, 'Hah! Hah! Very good, Murphy... something from home - and that is ever a blessing - very good indeed. Now, cut along to the galley and...' to Murphy's rapidly disappearing form, the steward already at the door, '... do count your chickens before they are despatched! Hah! Hah! All at the table burst into fresh laughter once more, a very audible but indecipherable curse heard from Murphy in the coach. 'AND MURPHY,' Pat shouted in full voice before the cabin door might swing shut, 'DO REMEMBER, THERE'S NO REST FOR THE WICKED! Hah! Hah!'

The first bottle of wine having been swiftly consumed, a reflective silence settled upon the table as the three friends waited for Murphy's return. 'Have you spoken to Simon about our trip to London and thence to France?' asked Duncan to spark some conversation.

'Eh? France?' Pat looked up, 'No, no... the less said of that the better. The First Lord himself was minded that the fewer folk with the least notion of what purpose it served was... was, well, you follow the general notion.'

'You have crossed to France?' Simon spoke with a degree of incredulity.

'Oh, it was akin to our proving voyage for the new cutter. I had intended to go to Ireland... you will collect our conversation in Falmouth... to sail to far County Galway, to Connemara. I had hoped to see Sinéad... after such a long time... but that, I regret to say, was not to be. But, Simon, you have not spoken of your own stay at home... in Tobermory... We - *Duncan and I* - are with child to hear of it... the outcome of your intentions... that is to say with the good lady there... in your house... Mrs MacDougall... *Flora*.'

'Flora and her bairns are all well, thank you,' and no more did Simon appear to wish to say on the subject.

Pat blinked his sore eyes again, decided not to press his question, his eyes shifting to his other friend, 'How is your own delightful Kathleen, Duncan?'

'The winter in Lewis has not been kind to her...' Duncan frowned and sighed, 'She is suffering once more from the consumption; only a trifle, and it is - *thankfully* - the mildest form... a gentle coughing and the like. She does not care to dwell upon it in her letters, and so I am greatly in fear that she may be understating her suffering. When we return I must away at all speed for the Isles.'

'You will allow me to accompany you,' said Simon, his firm statement no question.

'You will *both* allow me to accompany you,' pronounced Pat; 'and we will make great haste aboard *Mathew Jelbert*. After all, she is my cutter!'

'Pat, I have not found a moment to speak of the conversation I had with my friend Peddler,' Simon spoke up in louder voice. 'In Tobermory it was; he vouched for his associate, Perkis, in the matter of your considerations... the possible sale of some of your shares in your gold mine. I have known that man, Peddler, since we both went about the village without shoes as children, and I am minded that a deal of reliance may be placed upon his word... on his honesty.'

'It pleases me to hear it, it does, but I have already written to Perkis accepting his offer. I am now a minority owner in the mine, and I must place my trust in Peddler's integrity to continue to hold his twenty percent... so that Perkis... who I confess I do not greatly care for... does not become the majority shareholder to the ... the *possible exclusion* in future of my own interest. We will see what eventuates, no doubt. I will say that I had not, at the time of departing Falmouth, received the promised one thousand pounds from Perkis, and how that will be paid is something of a mystery for... in the days before we sailed to France... my own bank went bust, and that after my visit to it some few weeks beforehand when I was assured all was well! Would you believe it? *My bank is bust!* Duncan, what of your own bank, tell? Are your own precious funds safe?'

'Aye, my funds are safe, for sure. They are in a tin box under the bed in my croft!' Duncan laughed out loud. 'Such little funds as I possess that is!' He laughed again. 'I have never had any truck with banks, none, and it seems as if I was in the right of things there.'

'No doubt of that,' murmured Simon; the recollection of his own bank, the Plymouth Dock Bank, closing its doors on the first day of October with the consequent loss of all his small savings was a bitter memory. 'There is never a day in recent weeks when I do not curse my bank and its owners, for my very home is in doubt as a consequence; the roof is leaking, and the landlord is minded to evict Flora and the bairns so that he might sell the house. It is a great worry for her... *and for me*, I confess.'

'When we return to Falmouth and I am, at last, in possession of the promised funds from Perkis... all will be resolved to her and your satisfaction, I promise you,' declared Pat with conviction.

'How is your beloved Flora?' asked Duncan, staring at Simon with a look that intimated he would brook no evasion, 'Your departure from home... back to... *to hell*; how did that sit with her?'

'It did not sit well in the least,' murmured Simon.

Pat interjected, seizing the moment, 'You have not spoken of how... how well your... *your proposal* was received, Simon. Take note, I do not care to pry.'

'Well, 'ere be the fowl!' cried Murphy, bursting into the cabin, the so welcome sight of the roasted chickens accompanied by the most wonderful aroma. All thoughts in three minds switched in an instant to the food, three mouths salivating. All debate ceased as the meal was enjoyed, savoured. Only minor exchanges were offered over the table as the birds were devoured, the most generous dispensation of two further bottles of red wine accompanying the three friends' pleasure.

At midnight, an unsettled Pat, who could not sleep, a myriad concerns and the most unpleasant of recollections weighing heavily upon him, finished the cold remnants of Murphy's coffee, put on his old sea coat, and stepped out and up to his quarterdeck where he shivered as he looked all about him. The quarter moon, very prominent in the cloudless night, illuminated a calm sea. The feeble wind had nothing of strength about it, there was no great pressure acting upon the sails, not the least tension in the braces, and the barky was scarcely moving. Prosser's prediction had plainly not come true, at least not yet. Pat could hear the customary gentle swinging and creaking of wooden blocks aloft. He noted absently the vaguely discernible slap of water washing along the hull side and he heard the sharp crack as the canvas of the mizzen slapped occasionally as the wind rose and fell back, and from the helm came the murmurings of a half-dozen men conversing in low voice. He estimated his ship was making no more than four or perhaps five knots at best. It was proving to be the slowest of passages. He gazed aloft where the partial moon provided just sufficient light in the clear skies to dispel absolute darkness, and high above his head a great host of stars sparkled in a brilliant and infinite panorama. Pat sighed, his longstanding unhappiness returning even as he sensed the prevailing air of tranquillity and the perception of calm about the quarterdeck and at the helm. Such, he reminded himself with another sigh, was deceptively transient, could not last long, for in the morning *Surprise's* presence would surely come to the attention of the Turks on the hills above Messalonghi, even if the barky was not observed from Cape Pappas on the southern shores of the Gulf of Patras. Quite how much time he would have to offload his stores before the inevitable Turk interference began could not be known. It had taken the best part of a week to stow the cargo in the hold - so great a volume and weight that the ship was, at the very least, a foot deeper in the water than was usual, and more likely nearly two feet. He stepped over to the side and peered down. Only the sparkling ripples of the white wake and the closely-towed boats were clearly visible astern in the weak moonlight, in which he could just about make out a distant *Mathew Jelbert*. His thoughts drifting to a contemplation of the prospects of fighting his ship, he had to consciously put out of his mind the uncomfortable realisation of what might eventuate were he to open her lee gunports in any sea with anything of a strong gale blowing whilst not only the cargo of relief supplies but the great burden of all the water casks too remained aboard, and he sighed yet again.

'A penny for your thoughts, sir,' the softly spoken voice of Abel Jason, appearing at the rail, broke into Pat's concentration.

He turned to face the man whom he had increasingly grown to consider and appreciate as something of a confidant. Jason was a man of generally scientific leanings in his thinking in all respects. His late in life interest in astronomy had been found whilst aboard the barky, and that was an enduring, mutual fascination. Indeed, it was the basis of company which usually developed into dialogue in quiet, private moments; it was also the foundation of cordial exchanges which oft sparked opinions of the frankest nature on many a subject. 'Oh, good evening, Mr Jason. I was pondering over the desirability of returning to Cephalonia, to the Argostoli harbour.'

'Returning to Cephalonia?' Jason's question was murmured in gentle voice.

'Indeed, to await another day, with swifter winds for our arrival near Messalonghi... That is to say, so that we might be assured of reaching that place during darkness.'

'We will not?'

'No, I regret to say. It seems likely we will fetch up there just before the dawn.'

'Is that so critical, sir, may I ask?'

'There is, as is plain, no longer any prospect of an arrival - as I had originally planned - shortly after the dusk, which would have been the better to gain the greatest number of hours in that place before any conceivable detection by the Turk. It will take many an hour to unload our cargo, perhaps several days, the shallow waters of the lagoons and the distance to the beaches being so; and that is time the Turk will not likely permit us to enjoy.'

'And what - pray forgive my curiosity, sir - have you decided?'

'Eh? Oh, I have cast aside the notion of turning around... for doubtless every day is precious to the besieged defenders of the town... Every hour will make a difference to them, bereft as they reportedly are of powder, food and medical supplies. No, when the Turks do appear, we will shift the barky away as quickly as can be... all the way back to the waters of the Ionians if necessary, where she can gain safety in protected territory. I venture the Ottomans would not dare follow her there for fear of an international incident.'

'If my memory serves me, sir, the Turk possesses a considerable fleet in these waters...'

'Quite so.'

'... and hence our presence is one which likely will rapidly be challenged with wholly insurmountable force, or am I much astray?'

'Indeed, you touch upon the great dilemma: how to unload all of the stores within the hold, the powder most particularly... and the great weight of water within the casks upon the deck before... before we might be interrupted, for - *until that happens, I speak of the unloading* - we plainly cannot fight the ship; no, for sure we cannot be in contemplation of that.'

'When we are discovered... and after we have fled, will I presume that it might represent a considerable difficulty for us to return, the Turk being alerted to our presence?'

Pat could not contain a sigh, 'Mr Jason... *Abel*... if any resolution does come to your mind, I beg you will tell me of it.'

'I do beg your pardon, sir; I was, perhaps, a trifle adrift there... thinking aloud.'

'No matter, that question has been sitting heavy with me for some time, and I have yet to find the slightest thought which will answer.' A minute passed in silence and Pat added, 'We may place our hopes in fog, for... were we to be blessed by such... then conceivably... perhaps... well, you will grasp the general notion...'

'Is that likely, sir, fog?'

'No.'

Chapter Seven

Friday 3rd February 1826 07:30 Surprise off Vasiladi

The first indications of the imminent dawn were visible in the far south-east sky, the speckled but absolute blackness in the starry Heavens gradually ceding to grey in the direction of a distant Patras as the navigator in Pat absent-mindedly calculated a near exact east-south-east bearing for the anticipated rising sun. He knew that the port, the base for the Turk fleet which blockaded Messalonghi from resupply, was less than five leagues away; and with the *grego* north-east wind it would be nothing more than two hours steady sailing for the Ottomans, once alerted to *Surprise's* presence three miles south of Vasiladi. The island was the fortified guardian of the channel from the outlying islands of the lagoon to Messalonghi. *Surprise* was anchored in seven fathom water, the nearest deepwater anchorage to the town. It pained him that he could take the frigate no closer to Messalonghi because of the shallows of the lagoons all around it, up to five miles in breadth from the beach to the outlying islands which stretched for ten miles and more along the coast. Throughout the shallows the water was, in more peaceful times, traversed by a host of fishermen in canoes, only a few channels offering passage to any vessel even only slightly larger. He took a deep breath; the rank, corrosive and pungent reek of seaweed was heavy in the air, filling his nostrils and corroborating his leanings towards caution. He shivered in the enduring chill of the morning as he felt the tension rising again within him, gripping both his anxiety-filled mind and his weary body. He stood, motionless, staring, as the eastern sky continued to lighten, the weak grey tint over the far south side of the Gulf of Patras showing the first glimmers of pale yellow colour, the seascape beneath it still a perfect black. Tired, for he had enjoyed little sleep, he stared intently through his telescope as, incrementally, the low sun prepared to show more of itself, ever brighter skies developing until the vibrant orb in its entirety peeped above the mountains of the Morea, when Pat lowered his glass, his thinking awhirl with many and varied trepidations. In the corner of his mind the vaguely audible background activity about the ship only dimly registered. Above the slop of gentle waves sloshing alongside the length of the anchored hull he could hear his crew pulling the eight ship's boats forward to the frigate's beam, four on each side. *Mathew Jelbert* was tied alongside a little further forward, and the frigate's yards were swung round to prevent any contact with the cutter's mast. A preoccupied Pat heard only vaguely Duncan Macleod's sharp voice on the periphery of his own attention, his First's orders barked to the men waiting to begin offloading the water butts. A loud cacophony of exclamations soon followed as they struggled with the heavy weights, a barrage of vile curses and rude shouts erupting from the unhappy men aboard the boats as they were threatened with capsize by too rapid a lowering of the barrels, casks, kegs and butts. The least carelessness was sure to precipitate swift disaster.

'Mr Codrington,' declared Pat, finally collapsing his telescope, 'You are to double the men atop the crosstrees...'

'Double the...' Codrington's query, his astonishment audible in his voice, was cut off by Pat's uncompromisingly bleak glare.

'... and if there is any sighting of even the smallest vessel - *any vessel at all* - then I am to hear of it without a moment lost.'

'Aye aye, sir; double the men at the crosstrees,' Codrington acknowledged in admonished voice and tried to conceal his concern for his captain, Pat not looking well. Such a precaution had never before been ordered in all his time at sea, and the men at the crosstrees would be mightily put out if they were minded to think that they could not be trusted to stay alert.

'Mr Timmins,' Pat turned and spoke to the master gunner, standing nearby, 'Please to ask Dr Ferguson, Mr Marston and Mr Jason to attend the cabin *directly*.' Pat's sharp voice left not the slightest latitude for interpretation of his express timetable.

'D'reckly it is, sir,' the gunner swallowed, nodded and hastened away, his captain's agitation and discomfort plain to see in his glaring countenance.

Pat, his mind in a turmoil of calculations, all relating to the unloading of the relief supplies, slowly stepped down to the gun deck and walked into his cabin, feeling as if he was bearing all the ills of the world upon his weary shoulders. He sat at his table, his chin cupped in his hands, and sighed as he endeavoured to think hard about how many journeys his men might make, would require in the boats. How long would their rowing to Messalonghi town take? How long might it be to unload everything in the hold? All his calculations came to the one conclusion he did not much care for: it would all take too long by far. No, the Turk fleet would certainly appear before he could complete his task. What to do? He wracked his brain relentlessly without success, no more positive idea coming to mind other than that the barky would be obliged to leave before any Turk squadron could fall upon her.

'Well, does 'ee care for breakfast, sorr?' Murphy enquired with his head around the door.

'Perhaps later...' Pat waved his arm in irritation. 'I am awaiting Doctor Ferguson.' He belatedly added to his sharp dismissal, at last deigning to look up, 'Thankee.'

'Doctor Ferguson is in the hold, looking to the stores.'

A few minutes passed until Simon appeared with Marston and Jason. 'Gentlemen, good morning to you; please be seated.' Pat spoke in as steady a voice as he could manage whilst striving for the overtly calm demeanour which he did not feel in the slightest, 'I am looking to the day before us... and I am minded that once you go ashore... *once you go ashore...* it likely will be for something of an uncertain duration.' His visitors simply staring at him, his discomfort of mind plain to see, Pat elaborated, 'The Turk will surely appear at some time later this day, he will not tolerate an unknown frigate standing off Messalonghi town; 'tis sure he will send a squadron - *at least a squadron* - to investigate. If the wind picks up...' Pat paused for an instant to study the faces before him; all seemed nonplussed but curious, '... *if the wind picks up...* then I am minded we will see the Turk at noon or thereabouts.'

Three faces now looked extremely concerned. 'Sir,' a frowning Marston interrupted, 'What will you do?'

'What will I do?' cried Pat in feigned astonishment, 'There is only one thing I can do, Mr Marston, just the one... and that is to bear away at best speed... leaving you here until such time as the barky may safely return. There is no sense... none at all... in fighting the ship; no, that won't do. We will be away as if the very Devil himself is at our heels.' Pat sighed, 'I trust that you all understand that?'

Three heads nodded with noticeable reluctance. 'Then it is of the utmost importance,' declared Simon, 'that medical supplies are unloaded at the earliest moment, for without them we can do little and likely nothing in that place.'

'Very well,' said Pat, thinking aloud, 'After the first journey with only water butts aboard all the boats... only water... they will take medical supplies, powder, shot and more water. The cutter cannot go to the town because of the shallow depth of the lagoons and so will also convey water butts to where they may be offloaded at Vasiladi island. Perhaps in doing so, unloading there, we will remove the butts from the barky a deal faster... and we shall see what reports come back with the boats from Messalonghi so that we may determine what they will carry next. Murphy! Murphy there!' The steward appeared immediately. 'Please to ask Mr Macleod, Mr Codrington and Mr Pickering to attend directly... and Captain Zouvelekis.'

'Well, they be here, sorr, awaiting your say so.' Murphy held the cabin door open and the officers stepped in, all in a state of more than a little curiosity, the surgeons having been summoned before them.

'Good morning to you... and please be seated.' Pat pressed on immediately, his own anxiety not allowing the slightest interruption, even for the customary cordialities. 'Here is my thinking, gentlemen,' he declared, 'It is three miles - a long way to row - to the town beach, and we will be sore pressed for time, no doubt; but thankfully we are blessed with cold weather for the oarsmen. I am of the opinion that six good men per boat... leaving plentiful space for the supplies... will likely take at least an hour... with the weight so in the boats, and if we think of one hour and a half more... or even a trifle longer... before they get back... then no doubt they will be doing very well indeed. On their return the men will be rested and the crews will be changed for the next despatch. If we are able to make *three trips* before we must depart... that is to say... *on the Turk's arrival*... then that will likely be as much as can be managed today... indeed, I am minded that such thinking may be optimistic.'

'We have nearly finished loading all the boats and the cutter with water butts from the gun deck, sir,' declared Duncan, adding with something of an inflection of disappointment in his voice, 'but there be plenty more left to go.'

'Very good. We may consider that the cutter will be faster in returning from Vasiladi... if, that is, we see anything of the *grego*... Mr Pickering, you will command the shore party. You will take with you a half-dozen good men to begin the unloading of the boats... and they - *with you* - will remain on the beach until we are finished in this place. We may hope that you find a goodly number of Greeks keen to help. I am of the opinion that those half-dozen of our men must stand close by our surgeons at all times. Every man going ashore... *every one*... is to take a cutlass and a brace of pistols. Mind, there is no guarantee we will be here to take you off.'

'Aye aye, sir.'

'Mr Codrington, the lagoon is shallow water... For the most part 'tis no deeper than half a fathom... *a mere yard and no more*, and so we may consider that if any boat were to overturn then no man will likely be drowned. For that reason, you may endeavour to overload the boats...'

Codrington stared: this was unexpected. Pickering too looked doubtful, his murmured comment heard by all present, 'I have no aspirations of living forever, I know I will not succeed.'

Pat softened, 'Very well, just a trifle of overburden, Mr Codrington... allowing the smallest of freeboard.'

'Aye aye, sir.'

'When the Turk appears, the barky *must* depart, and I am concerned that we may not have the time to take any of the boats in tow, depending on where they are... If that is the case... that is to say... if it becomes necessary to take off our shipmates... *I am thinking of a breach of the walls or suchlike, the Turks breaking in to the town...*' The three principal shipmates in question - Pat was staring at them as if in unspoken challenge of their intentions - all looked exceedingly uncomfortable with such a prospect, but none spoke up. Pat resumed, 'To take off our shipmates when the Turk has arrived in this place... the cutter - *Mr Macleod* - must be as close as possible. For that purpose, the nearest water of sufficient depth is here...' Pat put his finger on the chart, '... to the west of Prokopanistos island, where you will find one and a half fathoms... Be sure to have a man attending the lead line at all times.'

Duncan, increasingly anxious himself, interjected with some concern, 'The cutter draws eight feet, sir; we will surely need a pilot to navigate any closer inshore if we go the smallest way within the channel towards Vasiladi.'

Pat spoke for the first time to the Greek, 'Captain Zouvelekis, will you be so good as go ashore in the first boat and look to find a pilot in Messalonghi town?'

'Of course, sir... but I am mindful that there is no water deep enough for the cutter closer to the town than Vasiladi.'

'No doubt, hence *Mathew Jelbert* will hold off to the south of Vasiladi - *in the deeper water* - to await you and the pilot.' Pat pressed on without pause, 'If *Surprise* is driven away, as I expect will be the case at any time after noon, then we will endeavour to return at nightfall, if not tonight then tomorrow, to resume delivery of supplies with the boats. Am I plain?' With nods all round Pat brought his briefing to a conclusion, 'Very well, let us set to and shift as fast as fast can be. Good luck to you all... *shipmates.*'

All Pat's visitors hastened out, the cabin becoming quiet and deserted save for a thoughtful Pat, who was plunged back into his anxious deliberations. Murphy remained too, hovering at the door and staring at his captain. 'Well, will 'ee take breakfast now, sorr? Wilkins has made a burgoo fit for a fine Galway man... with plentiful milk from the goat... and the coffee is still a'warming on the stove.'

'Thank you, Murphy,' declared Pat with a sigh. Consciously striving to allow his inner tension to deflate, he spoke in more kindly voice, 'You have my best thanks... from one Galway man to another fine Galway man.' Murphy displayed a rare, toothless smile and an emphatic nod before he hastened away.

The brightening morning air was cold but this was no saviour of the oarsmen who had completed a taxing half-hour with a mile of strenuous rowing. The men were hard pressed and labouring with the heavy burden of their load, but no respite was offered or requested. The weak wavelets of the lagoon, little more than ripples, were increasingly coming aboard, the heavily-laden boats so low in the water. Pickering was cursing and his passengers, Simon and Marston, bailing as best they could with what little was at hand, two tin mugs; largely unsuccessfully. The inch of water in the bottom was inexorably rising to two, and yet they were no more than halfway to the beach.

'I am cold in the extreme,' declared Simon turning his head towards Pickering, sitting in the stern, 'and the damnable wet is coming in.' The lieutenant affected not to hear.

'Perhaps, colleague, we should have remained aboard the cutter, awaiting the pilot?' said Marston with customary restraint.

'With the benefit of that admirable perspective, hindsight, I am inclined to agree.'

'Your concern for the townsfolk of Messalonghi is admirable,' Lieutenant Pickering relented his silence, 'but I doubt they will thank you if you do not arrive.'

'Mr Pickering, that is a quote worthy of your captain himself,' cried Simon, flexing and shifting his sodden feet about vigorously, as if such motion might restore some degree of feeling, 'Perhaps you have been spending too long in the cabin.'

'One... Two... Pull!' a momentary pause for a second, 'One... Two... Pull!' Pickering reiterated his shouted encouragement, the discernible but so slight slowing of the oarsmen reinvigorated, the lieutenant casting his gaze all around to gauge the progress of the other seven boats, all close, four abeam and three astern, every man on their thwarts visibly to his eye sweating profusely. He waved his arm in onward encouragement, no replies forthcoming, every man fixated on pulling hard, paying not the least attention to anything else. 'Keep going, lads!' he shouted to no one in particular.

An anxious half-hour passed aboard *Mathew Jelbert,* the leadsman sounding every minute without pause, until one and a half fathoms was reported in a voice audibly filled with concern, whereupon Duncan declined to venture further. The cutter, her sails slack and flapping in the feeble wind, was swiftly anchored. Motionless, she waited in the waters a half-mile south of Vasiladi and just three cables east of the islet of Komma. Standing atop the blockhouse on the tiny outcrop of Vasiladi, which commanded the approach through a narrow channel to Messalonghi, Greek soldiers watched events. A canoe was eventually launched which was paddled by four men until it came alongside the cutter. A waved arm from Duncan and they climbed the rope net and up to the deck. It was most fortunate that Abel Jason still remained aboard for no one else could understand a word of the animated visitors, all of them self-evidently delighted to see anyone who was not an Ottoman subject. They stepped forward as one to shake hands with Duncan and Jason.

'Sir, declared Jason, 'Allow me to introduce Captain Giachomouzzi, in command of the island; he is an Italian artilleryman... possessing thirty years service, and he is here to aid the Greeks as a volunteer.'

Duncan brightened, much pleased to find a professional military man, 'Captain Giacho... Gia... I am pleased to make your acquaintance.'

'Gentlemen!' Jason seized the visitors attention. He indicated Duncan, 'Captain Macleod is here with the frigate you see anchored out there.' Jason pointed, 'Look to the south-east of Komma. She bears water, food, medicines and munitions for the garrison of Messalonghi.'

This was most effusively well-received, the excited Greeks all speaking at once, until a tired Duncan clapped his hands demonstratively. 'I dinnae care to hear three gabbling as one,' he cried; 'Jason, please to ask these gentlemen... Captain Gia...'

'Giachomouzzi, sir; at your service,' declared the Italian pleasantly.

'Thank you, sir... Jason... ask Captain Giachomouzzi... if they would care to show us the channel to approach the town.'

After a brief exchange amongst the Greeks, Jason spoke up, 'They ask the draught of this vessel, sir.'

The three Greeks all looked on with doubtful faces as Duncan replied, 'Eight feet, perhaps near nine with the present heavy load of water.' The prevalent doubt also overtook Duncan as he surveyed his guests; the Greeks had become silent and were shaking their heads. 'Well, will you ask their reply?' Duncan muttered to Jason.

A hasty conference concluded and Giachomouzzi, for the Greeks, conversed briefly with Jason, a few minutes passing before his report, 'Sir, they say we will not make Messalonghi without grounding, for this vessel is drawing more water than the channel will allow. Indeed, nowhere within the lagoon is there any place with depth enough for this vessel; even on the outer sides of the islands the water is greatly shallow. They ask if you saw the charred remains of the burned-out corvette near the island of Prokopanistos, to the south-west, as you approached. It is a Turk vessel which ran aground a week ago, and it was burned by the fireship of Politis, three hundred men of its crew killed or drowned when it exploded.'

'Damn!' Duncan's fatigue showed plain in his exasperation.

'They have made one suggestion, sir, if you care to hear it.'

'Please...'

'The island garrison of some three score men is without water. If our cargo - *the water* - were offloaded here... our vessel would be much relieved from her present burden, then it is conceivable that we might - *might* - venture just a little closer with this vessel to the town... and then we must go ashore in our boat. Perhaps, in doing so, Captain Zouvelekis may espy our approach and send out his pilot. Captain Giachomouzzi will ask his man, Georgas here, to accompany us; whilst he is no navigator, he is familiar with the channel, being a fisherman and acquainted with the lagoons.'

'Very well,' Duncan sighed. 'In the circumstances that seems an admirable notion. Let us go on deck and put matters in hand. Gentlemen, might I offer you some refreshment? Coffee perhaps... or wine?'

The beach was near at last as the oarsmen, all tiring, breathed sighs of relief. Everyone aboard all eight boats cursed cold, wet feet, their toes long insensitive to the slightest feeling; and then came the crunch of keels on sandy gravel as they finally made landfall, the Surprises gladly leaving their oars to pull the boats further up the shingle, a large gathering of Greeks waiting all about them. Captain Zouvelekis announced their purpose to the crowd, explaining that the distant frigate was the selfsame one which had brought Byron himself ashore some three years previously and which had now returned bearing relief supplies. It was the most welcome of news, that was plain to see in the strained faces of the citizens of the besieged town. Simon studied them carefully, noting the thin, gaunt bodies of most of the people present, some of them almost skeletal, visibly fragile in their poise, their movements measured, careful and slow; plainly the want of food was taking its toll, the deprivation visibly debilitating them, their malnourishment so clear to his practised eye. As the water and a modest first quantity of medical supplies began to be unloaded from the boats he stood back to take stock of the immediate surroundings; a degree of damage to the town's buildings nearby was evident and the intermittent sound of artillery fire reached his ears; nothing which might be termed a bombardment, more of a nuisance. His own nerves steadied, perhaps the situation was not so acutely dangerous as he had feared. He gazed to the north and east, to the low hills surrounding the town, upon which the Turk besiegers were encamped; he stared with a rush of melancholic reflection at the memorable house, a few yards away, where Lord Byron had died, the recollection of those despairing final hours still so vivid in his memory. He had strived to persuade the attendant doctors to remove the leeches, to halt the blood-letting, but to no avail, and the cherished friend of poor Greece had slipped away before his own eyes. It seemed even more evident today, to his thinking, that it had been a great catastrophe, nothing less, for the cause of Hellenic freedom. 'Captain Zouvelekis,' Simon forced himself to break away from memories, from melancholia, and to seize the present, to begin, to organise his medical contribution, 'Will you kindly determine if Marston and I may establish our presence within that house?' He pointed to Byron's house, 'The one over there.' Without waiting for any answer, he called to Pickering,

'Mr Pickering, the men are to shift the water and medical supplies, such that they are, into that house... *that one.*' For some inexplicable reason, not clear even to himself, he had decided that to work within Byron's own house, to deliver succour to the sick and wounded in that very place, would be something of a small personal tribute to his Lordship, one which might serve as the tiniest recompense for his personal inability to save him, a distressing failure which still sat ill on his mind two years after the event, and that thought cheered him just a little.

'Aye aye, sir,' Pickering nodded, no urging necessary, the men already unloading the boats, every one keen to return to the ship, to familiar territory, to the warmth of the galley stove, to dry feet and hot burgoo.

Noon; Pat took the sighting in a crystal blue sky, bereft of the slightest cloud; thankfully there was also little evidence of wind, for which he praised all the saints to high heaven, no prospects for a swift arrival by the Turks. He paced the deck in anxiety, all the time casting his eyes to the horizon in every direction, searching for the boats, looking up to his men at the crosstrees, fretting. All the lookouts had grasped his uncertainty from their shipmates as they changed in rotation, the afternoon watch climbing up the ratlines with the fullest understanding of his concerns. The return of only the second trip of the boats was keenly awaited, the turnaround and loading of fresh stores taking far longer than anticipated. The returnees had described the pitiful state of many sick and wounded people flocking to the beach, to Byron's house, a multitude seeking Simon's attentions. His reported demand, most insistently stated, for further and urgent medical materials to be sent from the ship had overridden all earlier intentions to carry more food and water.

Four bells rang out from Clumsy Dalby at his self-appointed station, followed by his shout of 'TURN THE GLASS!' He was a big man and incredibly strong, although not someone that even his friends would call overly intelligent. Nevertheless, in his own way, he had served his shipmates well, his personal efforts actually saving Simon's life when the surgeon had been marooned on the island of Kasos as the shore party fled in haste from Turk beserkers. The invaders had burned the village where the small shore party had sought refuge after Simon had sprained his ankle on a trip to the interior in study of the local bird life. Dalby had also saved his captain's life in the hurricane of November 1824 when *Surprise*, severely damaged and sinking, was within the Western Approaches of the Channel after she had nearly completely crossed the great Bay of Biscay; Pat had almost been swept overboard in the ferocity of the wind and the great wave of water washing over the quarterdeck, Dalby pulling him back from the rail just before he went over the side. For all those reasons, Pat and all his officers indulged Dalby's efforts to attend the quarterdeck, or as close as he could be when on watch, for the big man was always endeavouring to present himself as a vital member of the crew. Despite all his intellectual limitations, Dalby himself dimly perceived that he was far from the perfectly trained and much experienced veteran which was Pat's only selection criteria whenever fresh crew were sought in Falmouth before the barky departed the town. It was therefore with immense personal satisfaction to Dalby that he was customarily greeted as he took his station near the bell, being the standby or reserve were any of the quarterdeck carronade crews to lose a man in action or a helmsman to be struck down. Even Pat himself might sometimes offer a greeting when his contemplative pacing took him forward to the waist rail and Dalby's station at the bell. There was none such today, Pat's mental focus on all events which might affect his ship being absolute, everything else excluded; even his sole officer remaining on duty, Codrington, was ignored as he stepped up to the quarterdeck. Pat turned about to retrace his steps towards the stern rail, his glass in hand, his mind locked in deep thought.

'Well, would 'ee care for dinner, sorr,' Murphy piped up from the steps; 'Wilkins has cooked a sea pie... 'tis right hot.'

'Eh?' Pat turned about, 'Dinner? No, no thankee, Murphy; perhaps when the boats are returned.' The steward nodded and returned below, and a silent Pat resumed his pacing.

'AHOY THE DECK!' came the excited shout from the lookout at the main crosstree, hailing down in full voice; 'VESSELS! A SCORE... SOUTH-WEST!'

A startled Pat swept the horizon with his telescope, his heart racing, his thoughts accelerating to instant anxiety and a furious tempo. Turks approaching from the south-west presented a far greater and unexpected danger, for they barred *Surprise's* flight to the west, to more expansive waters; perhaps they had slipped out from Patras with the express intention of blocking any escape to safe Ionian jurisdiction. Nothing being visible from the deck he started for the ratlines himself, climbing swiftly to join the lookouts who shifted aside as he hauled himself on to the platform. 'Where away?' came his breathless enquiry.

'Over there, sir,' Trewin pointed.

Pat stared through his glass; the distant sails, barely pinpricks above the horizon, were ten miles off or even more, but the wind offered nothing of help for their approach; it remained weak, a gentle breeze, no more than that. His heart rate subsided to something more near normal; it would be many an hour, likely in darkness, before those vessels might near the barky, and this would offer *Surprise* a better opportunity to steal away without hindrance, to hide in the night. Thankfully, he reminded himself, it was also the final few days of the waning moon, and that too would be helpful to make an escape with much less chance of detection. With a nod to the lookouts, Pat climbed off the platform and made his descent to the deck, anxious faces all around staring at him. 'Mr Codrington,' said Pat in measured voice to his lieutenant whilst striving to present an image of calm, one that he did not feel in the least, 'I believe I will go below and take my dinner...' He stopped, looked to an anxious Codrington, and added as if akin to an afterthought, 'I venture you too may be hungry. Have you dined yet?'

'No sir.'

'Would you care to join me? I collect Murphy mentioned that Wilkins has cooked one of his admirable sea pies.'

'With pleasure, sir.'

'Mr Prosser, please to inform me when our boats are returned.'

The master, aware of the many anxious faces all about the wheel, every man's stare switching from Pat to himself, replied in calm voice, as steady as ever he had managed, 'Aye aye, sir.'

At the cabin table Murphy poured a red wine of Cephalonia, set the table, and hastened away to fetch the food. Codrington tried to make his scrutiny of his captain as unobtrusive as he could, venturing brief glances over the top of his wine glass as he sipped, most parsimoniously whilst waiting patiently for Pat to speak to him, as was the Royal Navy custom.

'Mr Codrington,' Pat spoke up eventually, 'I venture you have the air of a man much pre-occupied... oppressed by some matter or other... or am I much astray?'

'My thoughts, sir, had settled upon those ships... Turks, would they be?'

'Oh... those...' Pat smiled encouragingly, 'They are too far away to determine, I regret to say; but, with the wind so, we will pay them no mind for the moment. When our lads return in the boats... when they are back, that will be the occasion to consider our position, and perhaps we may then discern their flag.'

'Very good, sir.'

'For now, let us not dwell on this Greek venture,' said Pat, striving for a voice which might convey an absence of concern, an absence which he did not feel in the least, 'For the next half-hour we are not on duty, and let us not stand upon strict convention, eh? What do you say?'

Codrington stared, a few seconds passing as he hastily gathered his thoughts; eventually he smiled, 'By all means, sir.'

'How are you faring? I have never spoken with you... or with Mr Macleod for that matter, of one matter of which I have heard little or nothing... the sinking of *Eleanor*. You were there... a damnably black day, no doubt. I am sure it sits ill on your mind. If it is not disagreeable to you, perhaps you might tell me of the disaster, the sinking... Do you care to speak of such dreadful events which you experienced yourself?'

'It surely was terrifying, sir...' Codrington sighed, 'It is so, even now, thinking of it... and Mr Macleod himself has never spoken of it with me... We thought... we were sure... that he had drowned... He was nearly carried away... inside the cabin as she went down; he was looking for some damn - *excuse me, sir* - document. Mason hauled him up no more than a minute before she sank and...' Codrington halted, could say nothing for a few moments, Pat hearing the waver plain in his voice, '... and... and we were sure he was a dead man... He... he retched up a gallon of water before taking the smallest breath into his lungs... and then he coughed for an age...'

Codrington plainly in difficulties with his painful recollection, Pat chose to change the subject, 'I beg your pardon, 'tis plainly a matter best left for another day. Will we speak of families, of home, eh... 'tis a warmer subject.' No response forthcoming from his lieutenant, Pat continued, 'William...' the word was spoken in friendly voice, Pat looking closely at Codrington, 'You will forgive me, no doubt, if I remark upon the absence of any letters ever coming aboard the barky for you... for yourself... I do not care to pry... no... but I have oft wondered why... why that should be.' A pause, still nothing from the lieutenant, and Pat tried again, 'You have never spoken of your family... save once I collect your mother was mentioned. Forgive me if I do not care to dwell on our present circumstances in this place... if I much prefer to talk of other things... at least until after dinner.'

'My mother is well, sir; she lives in London... south of the river... in Lambeth Marsh. She attends... at the Palace.' A nod and a smile from Pat, and Codrington resumed, 'As for my father, why, he was a sugar cane plantation manager. He is buried in the West Indies, in Jamaica.'

'I am sorry to hear it. And where do you belong, William? Excuse me, I am near lapsing into the Gaelic tongue, at least the turn of phrase; that is to say, where are you from?'

'I was born in Jamaica in July of the year 'eighty-eight, but left the island when I reached ten years old; the year 'ninety-eight it was...'

'A good year that was,' Pat beamed, 'Why I was but a ship's boy... thirteen years old... It was my first year at sea. I well collect when Boney's navy was drubbed by Nelson at the Nile. I was, myself, in Pompey, but there was a mighty celebration when the news came home.'

'Lord Nelson was my great hero, sir, as a boy.' Codrington smiled before pausing for reflection. 'My mother decided to return to London. She never greatly cared for the Indies after my father died... The damnable - *excuse me, sir* - the yellow jack it was...'

'Yes, the damnable curse it is... 'tis the most dreadful affliction... as Doctor Ferguson has oft remarked,' said Pat with heartfelt emphasis.

'... and so we took the packet to Falmouth. It was my first sight of the town, and thence we took the mail coach to London.'

'Please to explain how you came to join the navy.'

'I believe that my mother - *she never explained it to me* - had some small influence in society... in certain circles, a great house in Gloucestershire was mentioned. I do not recall the name, I was fifteen and it didn't signify. I was sent to Pompey in the spring of the year 'three... as a midshipman... to *HMS Starling* it was; she was there for refitting after a great storm off Yarmouth, her canvas much damaged. My mother explained that it had been the wish of my great-great-grandfather... that his son should become a navy man, but that did not eventuate... and so my place had been found, a gesture of benevolence made; by whom I know not... *never did*... save that I always believed it to be by some distant cousin, unknown to me... but my mother has always declined to say more.'

'Do go on,' declared a fascinated Pat.

'I collect that journey - *to Pompey* - by coach most clearly even to this day... It was an adventure for a lad... the arrival within the great harbour... so many ships; why, I had never before seen the like.'

'It is the most splendid anchorage, no doubt... a particularly grand sight when the fleet is in port.'

'I can still see - *even today* - the six dour men in the captain's barge - well, it was scarcely more than a dinghy - fetching me from the quay, my mother waving as the boat was rowed away... I collect my own hesitation about waving... six seamen all looking to me with the most severe faces... and then - *my mother still distant and waving* - I climbed aboard the great ship, for so it seemed at the time... aboard *HMS Starling*.'

Murphy brought in the sea pie, delightful aromas arising, two servings quickly laid upon the plates, and Pat set to with a relish he had not felt for some time. Codrington, too, ate with evident pleasure, some sense of normality settling upon the two, and Murphy was much pleased to see an indication, albeit a small one, of his captain relaxing.

'Ahhh... I fondly collect her, I do, yes; *Starling*, a fine vessel she was,' declared Pat in warm voice, looking up. 'A gun-brig; indeed, for a short while she was my first command, all those years ago... in the summer of the year 'three... and in Pompey too. It was but a temporary appointment, a most brief one whilst she awaited her new captain... before she shifted to the Downs, George Skottowe taking over command. I was the youngest lieutenant, but it felt like I was an admiral, no less. Duncan Macleod was with me... even in those early days... and Brannan Barton the cox'n, bless him; he saved my life, boarding *El Valiente*. I have never forgotten him, and his twin brother is the spitting image of him. Forgive me, I digress... memories, William... How precious they are, eh? Please to continue, you came aboard...'

'I did... I stared all about me, greatly affrighted, every face so unfamiliar, a score and more of the hands all looking at me, the newcomer, but after a minute no man paid me any mind... until - James Mower it was - took me in hand with a friendly greeting and showed me all about the great ship... as I thought it to be.'

'Yes, yes, I do collect you coming aboard, William, now that you describe it, I do; I can still see that shining face, the wonderment upon it that never left for at least a week. Ain't that amazing? Happy days, eh?' Pat finished his wine, nodded to an attendant Murphy who cleared the table. 'How was life as a youngster, growing up in the Indies on a plantation?'

'Oh, when you are born there all seems as it should be. There were not many white folk and near none of my age... no children in our household to play with... and precious few people to talk to. As I got older I looked with increasing interest at the slaves, blacks all, many of them from Africa, and I spent many an hour considering their lot, but not a word could I follow of their talk... and so I spoke with the mulattos... asking of them, of their thoughts...' Codrington halted, unsure if his captain's interest extended to hearing about his childhood.

'Please, continue,' prompted Pat, fascinated and enjoying the small relief from his anxieties; 'The mulattos...'

'Mixed race peoples, as is obvious to me now... and generally they were the servants within the house.' Codrington hesitated, 'I was a young boy when once I heard my father say to my mother that his own grandfather had been a mulatto. Not that I had the least notion then of what that signified.' Codrington finished his own wine; he seemed to find purpose and release in telling his story, one which had never been heard before aboard the barky. 'For many years I believed they were folk from another of the Indies' islands... their skin colour... neither black nor white. Only years later did I discover the true meaning of the word... and the setback that such was deemed to be for anyone living in high London society.'

'Indeed.'

'Well, the boats be approaching, sorr,' declared Murphy, putting his head round the door.

'Let us go up, William,' murmured Pat, returning instantly to his alert state of mind.

'Thank you for sharing your dinner with me, sir,' declared Codrington with evident sincerity.

'The pleasure was all mine, I do assure you. We will look forward to speaking further when we have departed this place.' They hastened from the cabin.

The returning boats pulled alongside, and four dozen men clambered up the nets and collapsed in exhaustion, consuming great draughts of water as they sat on the gun deck, slumped with their backs to the guns. Already more men hastened to shift the stores brought up from below to the open gunports for offloading to the boats. 'Well done, lads!' Pat's voice boomed out, 'How is it ashore? Rest, I beg you will not stand.'

'A right chaos, sir,' declared a fatigued Penhaligon, his breathing still deep and fast as he looked up. 'D'reckly we landed we were surrounded by folk... *hundreds of 'em*... milling all about us, every one of 'em looking for food, for clean water... Only with Mr Pickering and his men could we hold 'em off, and so we shifted everything into the house on the beach, Doctor Ferguson directing us where to stow it, Nance and Kelynack barring the door to the crowd outside, for all were clamouring right loud to get in.'

Dalby rang one bell of the first dog watch as Pat looked down to his exhausted men. 'So, it is truly a desperate situation... in the town?'

'It surely is, sir,' Penhaligon's face left no room for doubt.

'Very well; Mr Codrington, please to load the boats as quickly as can be, we will send them again directly. Mr Prosser, fresh hands to row, the strongest lads we have to go aboard. It will be dark when they arrive at the beach... We will show two lights at the maintop to aid their return.'

Another half-hour passed in loading until the sun was low, visibly sinking fast, when the heavily-laden boats departed, forty-eight strong men pulling hard on the oars. Pat stood on his quarterdeck, watching their swift progress until, the sun having entirely disappeared below the south-west horizon, his distant men and boats faded into the soft light of the gloaming. Absolute darkness soon thereafter settled upon the ship, and all conversations about the decks fell away to muted whispers.

His thoughts still pressing hard upon him, Pat paced up and down the quarterdeck, which was lit by a solitary Argand lamp hanging low from the main yard and swaying gently in the weak gusts. He offered a nod to the men attending the helm and the bell as he passed by, time after time until, tiring of the monotony, he descended the steps and walked the entire length of the gun deck, brief acknowledgments made to many greetings offered by his men in passing. He climbed up to the foc'sle and turned about, slowly ambling back along the ship's port side to the quarterdeck. His mind was filled with conjecture and a returning sense of foreboding. He wondered from what direction the wind might be blowing in the morning. Where would that sizeable squadron which had been sighted earlier be at dawn? Having no answers, he returned to the cabin in a mood of biting anxiety, grave uncertainty and much doubt. He sat in his chair and hauled off his boots, his feet hot, swollen and uncomfortable. He pondered ringing the bell to summon his steward, a momentary dream of drinking a cold glass of ale an impossible delight, but he decided against calling for Murphy, opting instead for a few more minutes of solitude, of reflection and a renewed analysis - however bleak - of the situation; what might he conclude before his supper? Were those ships sighted earlier Turks? Would more Turks, if indeed more remained anchored at Patras, also come out, and when might that be? His thoughts drifted to those of the Surprises who were absent, to Duncan Macleod and Simon Ferguson, his most precious of friends.

A very few minutes passed before Murphy appeared, unbidden and bearing a tray with a bottle of sherry and a small bowl: the walnuts had been found. 'Thankee, Murphy,' Pat offered a weak smile.

'Well, sorr, will solomongundy serve for supper? 'tis fresh made today.'

'Indeed, I rather think it will,' declared Pat, an inkling, no more, dawning upon him that his servants, Murphy and his personal cook, were both looking out for his interests, even endeavouring to shore up his morale. Was his tense state of mind so obvious? Did his anxieties show so plain? 'Please to pass my compliments to Wilkins... and you both have my best thanks.'

Darkness had settled upon Messalonghi town, the sporadic Turk shelling falling away to leave a seemingly unnatural silence in great contrast. In Byron's house, Simon Ferguson, with Pickering and the shore party, sat in semi-darkness, the room lit by a smoky oil lamp, all persons present huddled in crowded proximity around a tiny, almost wholly ineffective, wood fire, so little fuel being available. The chilly and draughty room was filled with great bundles of provisions delivered by the boats, all wrapped in hessian sacks. The mood of all was muted, stark, the realisation of the truly desperate state of Messalonghi plain to see in the faces of every man present; a great army besieged a town protected only by earth ramparts. Although it was defended by courageous and determined Greek rebels, they possessed few guns and little powder.

The continuing and sometimes even cordial exchanges between the enemies across the lines had revealed that Ibrahim awaited the arrival of more and heavier guns from the north, from that Ottoman province of Ionnina where the tyrannical rebel, Ali Pasha, had been defeated and murdered by his vengeful captors.

All this and more had been recounted to the Surprises in the few hours that they had been ashore, and consequently all vestiges of hope for the town and any residual optimism about its survival had been brutally extinguished; it seemed as if it was simply a case of waiting for the end, in whatever form it might come. Ibrahim, to his credit, had offered terms; indeed, they were generous ones by any measure, but they had been refused.

Simon reflected on that, his mind a turmoil of indecision: why was it legitimate for the leaders of the Greek combatants to put principle before practicality, to choose death rather than life for all the defenceless inhabitants of the town? Every woman and child would be condemned to slavery in some other, more distant, region of the Ottoman empire; that is unless they were killed outright when the town eventually fell, for such an ending of resistance seemed inevitable; the onslaught, when it came, would certainly result in the sack and burn of many of the houses, and surely the slaughter of all the elders. He sighed with a feeling of deep despair and stared, unseeing and without the least appetite, at his unpalatable supper ration of three dry ship's biscuits.

In the lagoon, a quarter-mile south of the island outpost of Vasiladi, Duncan Macleod cursed his bad luck, for *Mathew Jelbert* had long since grounded; despite the guidance of Georgas, the cutter was firmly stuck hard. Nance had volunteered to go over the side into the cold chill, only to find the depth was an inadequate six feet of water, the cutter requiring eight; he declared such as he jumped up above the water surface to find air in great gasps. The cutter, at least to Nance's cursory inspection, appeared to be undamaged, but her keel was firmly embedded in the unyielding grasp of mud. Long wispy stalks of seagrass proliferated across much of the seabed in clumps, being the apparent binding agent of its unyielding solidity despite the generally sandy nature of it. Nance was hauled back aboard, shivering and grateful for the proffered rum tot.

'We will await the morning and pray for wind,' declared Duncan in morose tone. 'It may be that a strong gust of the *grego* will push her out.' Blank stares were the only response. He tried again, 'There is no doubt that our lads will come out to help us in the boats; they will tow us off.' This, at least, produced hopeful nods. 'For now,' Duncan resumed, 'a double rum ration will do all that is required.' This, at least, was exceedingly well received, the smiles general, the nods of agreement greatly more emphatic.

Saturday 4th February 1826   07:30   Surprise   off Vasiladi

Pat had been pacing his quarterdeck for two hours before the dawn, his sleepless night had delivered no rest for his tired mind. He could not shake the pressing question: where would those ships sighted yesterday be this morning? He felt the freshening wind on his face, cold and a north-easterly; the *grego* was blowing. He stared all about him as the brightening morning light overtook the all-encompassing cloak of darkness, the weak twilight swiftly transitory, when the sky was revealed to be once more bereft of all cloud; it was a day for sailing ships. He gazed up to his men scrambling up the ratlines to the crosstrees; the air was clear, the light strong; they would surely soon see the lie of the land.

'DECK THERE! SHIPS!' The shout came like a dagger into Pat's heart; he felt like it had skipped a beat, or even two. His stomach convulsed and his breathing seemed to pause before resuming in short, shallow gasps. Stuffing his glass into his belt, he raced for the side and climbed the ratlines, buffeted all the time by the wind whipping through the rigging, the clewed-up sails swinging in their bundles about the yards. Finally, he climbed up and on to the maintop crosstree, the exertion of his rapid ascent leaving him red in the face, his breathing heavy. 'Whereaway?' was the only word he could manage to croak to the lookout. He followed the pointing arm, hastily extended his telescope, and he stared to the southwest in alarm and apprehension, becoming conscious for the first time of his rapidly pounding heart. A minute passed before his breathing subsided, even as his strength seemed to evaporate, and he leaned back against the mast, feeling physically crushed, an absolute deflation entirely overtaking him as an overwhelming relief flooded his mind, his words escaping in a whisper, 'I venture 'tis the Greeks... the Greeks! Miaoulis is back!'

'Doctor Ferguson,' declared an excited Pickering, shaking Simon from his uncomfortable state of semi-wakefulness. 'There is a crowd of supplicants outside, two score and more in great anxiety. All are begging your attention... and yet more are arriving every minute.'

'Very well,' Simon blinked, stirred and sat up upon his low cot. He gathered his thoughts, hauled himself out and stepped to the water basin; he reminded himself that the water to wash with was saltwater, and so he splashed a very little on his face and blinked again several times since he had no towel with which to wipe himself. Putting on his coat over his clothes, for he had not undressed, the cold so greatly severe, he stumbled down the stairs and into the company of the Surprises clustered around the feeble fire, little more than glowing embers remaining, where Marston was standing ready and awaiting him.

'Sir, do you care for coffee?' enquired Pascoe. 'Murphy has packed a small supply... *a very small supply*... for you alone, so he said.'

'Bless him,' murmured Simon, blinking rapidly to clear eyelids seemingly still crusted over. 'Perhaps he is not going to hell after all, eh? Thank you. Perhaps we may also allow Mr Marston half of a cup?' He gratefully accepted the bitter brew, too long in the embers, but supremely welcome nevertheless. He sipped it slowly, finding a great satisfaction in doing so, before biting into the hard biscuit offered with it and discovering a wild hunger as he did so. 'Pascoe, please to tell Mr Pickering that I will attend the supplicants in a very short time, this coffee requires a few minutes to deliver its recuperative miracles.'

'Very good, sir.'

'Now, where is my medicine bag... ah, here it is. Cusack, kindly clear a space here, near that window, small that it is. I will require a chair and that table... *yes, that one will serve*... and hot water; fetch all such firewood as may be procured... and bring saltwater to boil if there is no fresh. Lose not a moment.'

'Aye aye, sir.'

'Mr Pickering, there you are. This room is to be vacated by all our men... and one only of the sick is to be admitted at all times... save, that is, mothers with children and those too weak to walk. I will begin shortly; Cusack will call for the first patient. In the meantime, kindly send someone to enquire what medical resource... doctors, surgeons and the like... may be here in the town. It is conceivable that such scarce resources as we possess may be more greatly needed elsewhere... Oh, please to look for what may be found in the line of another lamp, it is something of a tribulation to work in the darkness.'

'Yes, sir,' Pickering hastened away to find Zouvelekis.

'Mr Codrington, the boats are to go immediately, lose not a moment!' declared Pat as his feet reached the deck. 'The squadron in sight is the Greeks. They are tacking into this wind from six miles off, and I doubt they will reach us before noon or thereabouts.'

The waiting boat crews, apprehensive and keen to start, grasped Pat's urgency and began climbing down into the boats tied alongside, every one of them already loaded overnight with abundant sacks of flour, boxes of medicines and dressings, powder, muskets and shot, flagons of vinegar and plentiful biscuit. As the men clambered into the boats to sit upon the thwarts the freeboard instantly diminished by a frightening few inches. Every man was extremely aware that the sea state of the morning, even within the relative sanctuary of the near and visible lagoons, was visibly rougher than the previous day, the wind evidently strengthening, and the surface ripples of yesterday were risen to minor wavelets. Would they make the beach or might sinking be more likely? They did not know. They clung to the slim comfort of the stated shallow depth of the lagoon, for most of them could not swim. Another minute passed with vigorous waving from the men thronging all along the side of the frigate, and the boats pulled away, the oarsmen striving for best speed even as they stared anxiously at the minor bow wave, white water sparkling along the sides, frequent splashes coming aboard. They were all swiftly soaked as they sat and pulled in cold discomfort, few words offered, every man mindful that if the Greeks were coming, and so very slowly, then the Turks too would surely be inclined to depart Patras, and, with the strengthening wind from the north-east, they must certainly arrive quickly. There could be no doubt they would be here before the Greeks, when *Surprise* would be alone, without assistance; and one frigate must flee before an entire Turk squadron. Pull! Pull! was the common thought. Minds raced: get back to the barky as fast as ever could be!

'There go our lads in the boats,' declared Duncan, staring from the deck of *Mathew Jelbert*. 'They will surely call upon us as they pull back for the barky after their cargoes have been delivered to the town.'

'How long might that be, sir?' asked Jason, uncomfortable in the cold and much concerned about their stuck predicament.

'Oh, an hour and a half to reach the beach, I doubt it will be longer, and another hour to reach us; mind, the wind is picking up and 'tis a north-easterly. I fancy we will try and shift her with all her canvas braced to catch it.' Duncan looked to the apprehensive onlookers, 'Lads, let us see what can be done.'

A half-hour later, with not an inch of movement gained, all aboard the cutter accepted the futility of their efforts, a deep sense of frustration descending upon them, poisonous stares offered towards Georgas. The hapless Greek had been unable to convey the shifting nature of the channel and its varying depths to his silent accusers in his native tongue. Englishmen! Had his friends not explained to them that the cutter drew too much water to be sure of closing on the town?

Jason spoke up again, 'I wonder where the promised pilot is that Zouvelekis was to send to assist us?' Duncan shrugged, his patience long shot and his temper frayed to breaking.

Simon stared in deep dismay at the horrific display of the burned and putrefying fingers of the Greek fighter, the merest sniff of the air had delivered the confirmation of what he knew on sight was the prognosis. A sickly, sweet odour was emanating from the hands: gangrene had set in, and the fingers would have to come off. He explained this to Zouvelekis, attending as interpreter. The patient nodded, said nothing; of course, he already knew, in his heart and mind, that this must happen. Simon considered further, searching for some more positive outcome, but concluding without the least doubt that better it was done immediately, before the further spread of decay reached the remainder of the patient's hands; even without his fingers it was better than possessing mere stumps at the wrist, and perhaps he might save the inner part of the thumbs. The Greek had been burned by a premature explosion of powder in a gun, Zouvelekis explained, the untrained crew failing to wet the swab before loading the shot, the fiery discharge occurring as he had struggled to bring the shot to the mouth of the barrel.

'Captain Zouvelekis, please to explain that I possess no anaesthetic... for there is no laudanum arrived yet from our ship that I have found...' Simon could not refrain from a shudder, '... but the patient may drink this half-pint of rum.'

The Greek, in great tension, accepted his miserable lot with stoic fortitude, offering a nod to Simon and biting hard upon his teeth. Whilst the rum was being consumed, the patient drinking as Marston held the glass, Simon prepared the stick to tie between the patient's lips to ensure the unfortunate would not bite off his tongue, talking to the Greek in encouraging fashion through Zouvelekis's translation as he gave the rum a little time to take its modest effect. He scrutinised the burnt fingers closely, the bone visible in several of them as the blackened shreds of rotten flesh peeled away to the least touch; the man must be in considerable agony, and why he was not constantly screaming in pain was entirely beyond belief and Simon's long experience. As he considered this, Simon's stomach turned over with the brutal recollection of past occasions at his shipboard table, of hours when the stream of casualties was never ending, or seemed so. Sixty more sick and injured waited patiently outside, and he had not yet begun the day. For how long could he continue before his mind shrieked 'Enough!'? For how many hours could he persevere before his hands began to shake - a danger to his patients - and before his energy was all gone. He briefly recalled and forced himself to dismiss from his thoughts a memory of similar circumstances as *Surprise* had fought to defend the island of Samos; treating the unceasing burden of wounded had inflicted a brief breakdown upon him, and he had fled to the quarterdeck, Pat's words calming his distress and Murphy calling him back below. He swallowed hard, strived to conceal his burning anxieties from his patient with the slightest of smiles, and he began gently to cut.

Aboard *Surprise* Pat had returned to the crosstree atop the mainmast. He watched the progress of the boats, so very slow they seemed to his anxious mind. As he turned about towards the approaching Greeks, his eye fastened on the sight of *Mathew Jelbert*, her sails straining but the cutter motionless. Her sails were slackened after a very few minutes to spare the canvas, even as he watched, for plainly - he realised - she was stuck fast. Doubtless the boat crews must see that as they passed by and, when they returned, they would help free the cutter. He looked again to the distant Greek vessels, now perhaps four miles away, and he prayed they would arrive before any curious Turks turned up. With his mind filled with apprehension he climbed down and entered the cabin, Murphy following him in within moments and bearing the coffee.

'Murphy, kindly ask Mr Codrington to attend directly.'

The steward set down his tray and hastened away.

'Thank God and Saint Patrick for small mercies,' declared Pat to himself as he poured. What to do other than wait? Wait! How hard it was to accept. He came back to the only conclusion, *wait*, uncomfortable as it was. 'Mr Codrington,' Pat looked up to greet his lieutenant, 'I am minded to contemplate how many more boat deliveries are needed; would you kindly go below... to the hold... Take two good men, and please to count our progress; how much remains aboard? How much has already gone aboard the boats? This is the fourth shipment. Excuse me, would you care to share this coffee?'

'Most generous of you, sir; I will be exceedingly pleased to take a cup.'

'Here, do be seated. Have you eaten breakfast?'

'Nothing at all, sir.'

'Murphy! Murphy there! Bring burgoo for Mr Codrington and I, and another pot of coffee; thankee.'

'The morning is warming, sir, and the wind freshening with it. The men have remarked it, most significantly those hands at the crosstrees.'

'Indeed, I was there myself but minutes ago; doubtless it favours the Turk - if he comes out of Patras. I venture his vessels will make seven or eight knots, and likely more if the wind is stronger in the afternoon, *the early afternoon...* as we have come to expect.'

'Aye, sir; the men are much mindful of that, the prospect is much talked about; I hear little of anything else as I pass about the decks.'

The Greek patient screamed as Simon began, the first finger swiftly amputated, the agonising shrieks persisting despite the bound stick in his mouth; but then, fortunately, he passed out; his own exhaustion, his physical weakness, the acute pain and the consequent shock had bestowed blessed insensibility. Simon doubted it was the rum, for that rarely delivered unconsciousness except to those who were already too weak even to drink it. Simon doggedly pressed on, containing his own distress which had returned with a vengeance; he blinked away the moisture in his eyes, once more the beginnings of tears, and he resumed the cutting away of dead tissue about the lower thumb, cleaning the stump, minutes passing as he amputated more fingers, always looking to find the foundation of healthy tissue, to save what he could. Ten minutes more of careful working, his mind seized by the absolute grip of concentration, unwavering determination holding his body rigid as he leaned over the patient until, his whole body soaked with sweat, he stepped back, a flood tide of weariness coming upon him, his energy all gone and his legs beginning to shake. He mopped his brow, his shirt collar soaked with his sweat. 'That is that,' his few words were spoken to Marston in a whisper. He washed the blood from his hands in the saltwater bowl and took a deep draught of the lukewarm coffee, boiled but better than nothing.

'Be assured that you did admirably well for the patient,' declared Marston emphatically, his first words for some time. 'I believe we may have hopes for his thumbs, God willing.'

Simon blinked and swallowed hard; perhaps there really were moments when only God could do more, he thought, for he could not. Zouvelekis with Cusack and Pascoe shifted the man to the chair.

The eight boats, their cargoes offloaded at the beach, had returned and were nearing *Mathew Jelbert*, the cutter's crew all waving to their oncoming shipmates. A half hour more and the boats came alongside the cutter, the weary oarsmen grateful for a moment of rest, for the late morning sun was warm despite the wind, ever stronger as noon approached. 'Lads,' shouted an exasperated Duncan, 'pull round to the stern and affix these lines to your boats!'

None of the boatmen had any notion of why no pilot had been sent out from the town, other than to say that there was seemingly no organisation on the shore, where all was chaotic, and perhaps the word had gone out but had been forgotten. The ropes were tied, the few men of *Mathew Jelbert* exchanging with the wearier members of the boat crews prior to the attempted tow and recovery of the cutter.

'Ready lads? Pull!' shouted Duncan, 'Pull!' Nothing moved, the boats remained in situ, the tow ropes stretched, the cutter failed to budge an inch, the oarsmen tired and the spirits of everyone dropped; eventually, a frustrated Duncan called a halt, 'Rest, lads; take a minute or two, rest.'

The next patient entered, aided by a companion, his face a picture of stark apprehension and anxious hope. He could barely walk, hardly shift at all; that was patently obvious as he struggled with the few steps from the door with the aid of a stick, with his friend's assistance, and plainly he was in extreme pain. Simon nodded with what, he hoped, looked like encouragement, even as he stared in preliminary inspection; doubtless it was a wound of some form, but where? He spoke in measured voice, indicating the table and, although the patient could not understand his words, the meaning was plain. Cusack and Pascoe assisted the man to undress until he lay naked from the waist down under Simon's scrutiny. The surgeon stared at the now obvious wound; the hip joint was smashed, so greatly damaged that Simon marvelled that the man could move a single step. Marston blanched, for the sight before his eyes looked catastrophic. There was a protrusion where none should be and a hollow where the bone should reside. The wound was swollen to ghastly proportions, and Simon marvelled that the man had not already lost the leg and died from infection. Cusack passed the obligatory half-pint of rum as Zouvelekis translated Simon's questions, 'When did this wound occur and does the patient have any notion of what happened?'

'It was the morning before yesterday, sir; the casualty believed that he had been struck by a spent ball of grapeshot, ricocheting off a stout timber barrier on the defence line.'

'Perhaps its velocity and power to destroy was nearly completely dissipated in striking the wood first?' declared Simon, 'I confess I am much surprised that infection has not set in already, all these hours on and festering in two day's of heat; indeed, the man is exceedingly fortunate that it has not.'

Zouvelekis continued, 'The patient tells me that he believes the lead shot remains inside his hip...'

Marston interjected, 'We may see plainly that it has smashed away much of the bone at the joint.'

Simon took a deep breath, strived for calm, for a measured response even as his stomach turned over again, a flush of acid bile rising within his throat. 'At least we can be grateful that the wound is entirely below the major organs, for I could offer no positive prognosis for the patient in these conditions had such as the bowel suffered damage.' He considered taking a draught of the rum himself, for a second only, and he began to probe gently with his index finger about the swollen wound, Marston staring as he held the patient's hand and whispered words of comfort in his ear; not that the Greek, in his excruciating agony, could understand them.

'Captain Zouvelekis,' Simon looked up from his scrutiny, 'please to explain that when I commence surgery upon such an extreme wound as... *as this one is*, I cannot vouch that the leg will be saved. It is entirely possible... indeed, it is more likely than not... *more likely*... that the leg will be lost, and the patient is to acknowledge that he understands that.'

The emphatic nodding of the patient left no one in any doubt that his pain was intolerable, that anything was preferable to his present catastrophic injury, and he did not give any mind about the loss of the leg, but he begged the surgeon to begin, his words a struggle, his agonies evident.

'I am minded that the grape has broken through the bone and is likely lodged between the shattered femoral head and the socket, the ligament and articular cartilage being much damaged,' murmured Simon to Marston. 'If we are to remove the invader then... *then*...' his words tailed off, for no positive prognosis for recovery could he find.

'We will endeavour to remove the greatest source of his pain, colleague,' declared Marston, 'before we begin cleaning the wound, and after that our patient, God bless him, will be in our Lord's hands.'

Simon nodded, but said nothing; he did not entirely share the chaplain's total faith, albeit he had infinite respect for it. Together, it was true, they had, in past times, performed at least some miracles of surgery; but here, in this stinking hole of comprehensive inadequacy, in this festering place of putrefaction, without medicines, all the surgeon's customary necessities wholly lacking, his own confidence was fragile and his hopes so much diminished that his thoughts filled once more with feelings of bleak despair.

Dalby rang eight bells of the forenoon watch and called 'Turn the glass!' Pat began going through the motions of taking the noon sighting, not the least enthusiasm for a pointless ritual, *Surprise* lying at the same mooring as the previous day; but it filled his preoccupied mind, and so he did it anyway. He had been studying through his telescope the efforts of his men to extricate *Mathew Jelbert* from her grounding, and all attempts were seemingly unsuccessful, and so he pondered what more might be done. Eventually he determined that he would send out the boats wholly empty of stores next time, and perhaps fresh men and more of them on the thwarts would do the trick; at least he hoped so. Perhaps too the cutter might be aided by the increasingly strong wind. Despite that, the oncoming Greek squadron had gained another two miles and they were now making short boards within the narrowing approaches to Messalonghi, and they stood just three miles off *Surprise's* anchorage near Vasiladi. He turned about to study them from the quarterdeck. Perhaps, he surmised, they were keen to stay as close as could be to the outlying islands and not to stray further south where Turk eyes to the south-east might sooner espy them. Two hours more and then, Pat thought, perhaps the Greeks might be near, in hailing distance.

Another hour passed in languorous anxiety, Pat watching every development through his glass, until the returned boats pulled alongside, exhausted men clambering up the netting to enter the gun deck via the open gun ports. Cardew reported to Pat in breathless voice, 'Beg pardon, sir, Mr Macleod's compliments... and will 'ee send the boats with fresh hands to help him get her off... the cutter... she is stuck fast... and mighty hard we have tried to pull her away.'

'Yes, of course.' Pat looked to the bosun, 'Mr Sampays, please to accompany four score of men in the boats, the strongest we possess. Take more lines and the kedge anchor, which may best serve; you may need to haul her off from her deck.'

'Aye aye, sir,' the bosun hastened to do so. Ten more minutes and the eight boats, each with ten men, pulled away, the cutter aground a quarter mile south of Vasiladi with the best part of half an hour's rowing to reach her. It was shaping up to be a memorable day, thought Pat, a chilling wash of foreboding coursing throughout his mind; what was yet to come? He felt sure the day had not run its course.

Simon stared closely at the crushed outer part of the hip socket. Sure enough the grape ball had broken off fragments of bone, but not so much as the surgeon had earlier feared might be the case. An exploratory incision was made and the skin peeled back. The blood flow was much more meagre than he had expected. 'Perhaps there may yet be some small hope for this man,' he declared eventually with the tiniest fillip for his own despairing mind.

'The artery appears to be undamaged, colleague,' Marston pronounced.

'As is to be expected, else I am minded that the leg would have been lost before ever the patient entered this room,' murmured Simon, mostly for his own benefit, for he had not the least wish to be even slightly critical of his friend. 'I am thinking - *with a degree of trepidation, I do confess* - that resection may be feasible; doubtless the leg will ever offer a deal of discomfort to our patient, but an amputation... at the hip...' A deep sigh, and Simon stared at Marston, 'An amputation here offers but small prospect of survival... I believe that in such a case we might likely contemplate the inevitable gangrene and ultimately death. What do you say?'

Marston looked into his friend's eyes; it was a mutual exchange of hesitation, of trepidation. He swallowed, for his own capabilities in no way approached those of Simon's. He nodded, 'I am sure you are in the right of it, there is no doubt at all...not the least... a... a resection is the only hope for our man.'

Zouvelekis said nothing to the injured patient; indeed, he did not greatly follow the whispered exchanges between the surgeons. He was much distressed by the scene before him and strived to content himself with spoken efforts to sustain the patient, urged to do so by Simon, endeavouring to prevent shock overtaking him whilst hoping that he might drift off to a more comfortable unconsciousness before the saw bit into the bone.

'Of inflammation there is plenty, but thankfully there appears to be no infection, at least not yet,' murmured Simon, 'He is the luckiest man of this vile war. Pascoe, is there a mouthful of that coffee left, I have the thirst of the world?'

'Precious little, sir; here it is. Will I make a fresh brew?'

'No, there is no time for that; will you kindly pass the smaller saw... not that one; yes, that one.' Simon drained the dregs of the coffee remnants, bitter and infused with the grounds; he spat into the bloody bucket and returned to the table. 'We must act like lightning, Marston; we are afforded only a very few minutes and no more, else our man will be lost to shock. We must endeavour to complete the cleanest of procedures, with nothing left behind of the ball, else we will surely lose him to infection later. Are you ready?' A silent Marston swallowed hard and nodded. 'Very well,' whispered Simon, 'Let us begin.'

At the beleaguered cutter, Sampays, much welcomed by all, decided immediately to use the kedge anchor, for he too had studied the unfruitful struggles to get her off through his own glass from aboard the frigate. The additional ropes were passed over to the weary and frustrated men of *Mathew Jelbert* and the kedge anchor was dropped. Two men, selected as competent swimmers, dived to ascertain it was successfully biting into the mud and sand of the seabed. A score of fresh men stood ready to haul on the ropes aboard the cutter and sixty more remained in the boats, ready to pull hard on their oars. 'Very well!' the bosun's voice boomed out, 'Stand ready! Ready?' A chorus of 'AYE' from eighty men. 'Heave away, lads! HEAVE... HEAVE! AGAIN, HEAVE!' Two minutes with the sinews of every man straining on their oars and ropes, the lines stretching, but no movement of the cutter, and 'REST!' cried Sampays.

'Brace the yard, hands to the sails!' shouted Duncan in desperation, hoping that this might make all the difference. The sails, slack, flapped wildly in the much-increased wind, until the gaff was braced, the lines of the foresails all pulled tight, every stitch of canvas coming under strain, when the cutter leaned hard to leeward on her larboard side but did not shift in the least.

A dismayed Duncan nodded to Sampays, and the bosun called again for another great effort, 'READY! ONE, TWO, THREE, HEAVE!' Muscles strained until sinews were at tearing point, the lines flexed bar tight once more, and Sampays kept up his shouted encouragement, 'ONE! HEAVE! TWO! HEAVE! THREE! HEAVE!'

Jason, standing well forward and out of the way, marvelled at the incredible determination of eighty men pulling so hard. He felt a near indiscernible movement, a tiny jolt, and almost imperceptibly the cutter shifted a mere inch; one more tremendous heave and she visibly slid a little more. Encouraged, the tiring men renewed their efforts and pulled again, a significant movement resulting at last, and more, until - after a final huge heave by the hands - she slipped astern and floated free. All tension in the lines was gone and the cutter was drifting as, her rudder swiftly pulled hard over, her sails pushed her round in a turn until her bow faced south, towards deeper water.

A jubilant sensation of accomplishment coursed through everyone in a flood tide and a loud chorus of joyful shouts erupted from all aboard in wild, exuberant cries of triumph.

On the deck of a distant *Surprise*, an anxious Pat watched the success of the recovery with a great feeling of relief. At long last the cutter was free, and perhaps she could now serve her intended purpose, although he had already decided that she could not be sent again any nearer to the town. Another half-hour passed before the boats finally returned to the barky, bringing Sampays and the many men of *Surprise* back. The boats were promptly loaded with more stores and sent once more on their way, Pat and all the Surprises settling back to wait. The afternoon advancing, it would be two hours for the oarsmen to reach the beach and, unladen when returning, a further hour and a half until they could regain the ship. 'I will be in my cabin, Mr Mower, should anything arise,' Pat declared, and retired to write his log, inevitably emerging after an hour and in a fierce mood of unsettled anxiety to pace his quarterdeck again. His thoughts were racing with considerations of adverse potential developments; the Turks must by now have been alerted to their presence, so where were they? When might they arrive? He refused Murphy's invitation to take his dinner and paced, another hour in deep thought, up and down, forwards to the rail and aft to the stern, unable to set aside his rising apprehension.

Yet another half-hour passed by, and then came the call Pat had been dreading, 'DECK AHOY!' The lookout shouted down in a voice which could not conceal the tone of panic, 'EAST! EAST! THE TURKS ARE A'COMING!'

Pat's worst fears were fuelled to new heights in an instant, a great surge of tremulation wrenching hard on his very substance, a physical tremor flexing within his chest, his mind racing in the most unpleasant few seconds to a fleeting panic, subsiding only slightly and very slowly as he turned to look to the east, a tumultuous weight of consternation pressing hard upon him, an overwhelming and brutal anxiety rushing all through his mind and body in a chilling realisation of the imminent peril.

Chapter Eight

Saturday 4th February 1826   16:00   Surprise   off Vasiladi

Perched on the main crosstree, Pat stared at the distant ships through his telescope, counting at least a score. 'They are Turks,' he declared to the lookout, 'The Greeks possess nothing of the like of those frigates.' Hastily he climbed down to the deck, an anxious gathering awaiting his words. 'Gentlemen, the wind so greatly increased, I believe we are afforded one and a half hours, no more, before the Turk squadron is here and all about us, and that will be a half-hour before sunset. In such an event we would have to fight for at least an hour until the end of the dusk light. That is a desperate prospect, and it is not in my contemplation to do so.' Pat stared at his senior lieutenant, 'Mr Codrington, prepare to get underway. All hands on deck, to the capstan and cables directly.' He turned to the bosun, 'Mr Sampays, all guns are to be run out, a plentiful supply of powder and shot to be at hand for every one.' Codrington stared; Sampays nodded. No words were uttered as the bleak realisation registered that the firing of the great guns, with its attendant death and destruction, loomed very large before them. 'Mr Mower, signal the approach of the Turks to *Mathew Jelbert*. Macleod is to take the cutter to safety in our wake. I regret that our boats must await his return, I cannot countenance him waiting for them.'

'Yes, sir.'

'Dalby,' said Pat, 'Please to find Mr Timmins.'

'Aye aye, sir.' Ten minutes passed and Clumsy Dalby returned to the quarterdeck. He touched his forelock and reported, 'The gunner has gone ashore, sir. He went in the last boat; he was minded to see what might be done to help the town's gunners. It was reported by Tregenza that they possess but four dozen of poor iron guns... some only four-pounders and, plainly, they are no match for the Turk batteries. Yet more Turk guns and of heavier calibres are a'coming... be expected, so he says.'

Pat frowned, said nothing; Timmins going ashore was certainly not what he would have authorised had he been apprised of it before the gunner departed; presumably Timmins had known that. What was discipline aboard his ship coming to? It seemed to be melting by the day. Dalby spoke up again in low voice, recognising Pat's dismay, 'Sir,' Pat nodded, 'The gunner carried with him half a dozen of the explosive shells he has been making since we left Falmouth.'

'I see,' Pat spoke in a tone of rising and deep dissatisfaction. 'Do we still possess any of them aboard ship, tell?'

'Yes, sir; six more are in the for'ard magazine.'

'Six? Only six?'

'Aye, sir.'

'Very well, Dalby. Let us pray we have no occasion to call for them... and let us get out of this place.'

Simon, in the dim light within the room, mopped his brow, moist in the foetid air; he wiped his bloody hands on his apron, sighed the deepest sigh of relief and stepped back from his table. 'I venture we may hold some small hope that he might survive,' he murmured to no one in particular. An exceedingly difficult amputation of a leg above the knee, the patient's leg macerated into a pulped, fleshy mess and his thigh shattered by a grapeshot strike, the operation had exercised Simon's skills to the utmost for fifteen enervated minutes of absolute concentration. 'Perhaps another pot of coffee would be timely now,' he declared to Pascoe, in attendance. He looked all about the makeshift operating room, his spirits sinking immediately as he stared at the small number of distressed supplicants admitted to await his urgent attentions, sounds of discomfort, of pain, audible from them. 'Marston, we are sore pressed for time... Would you be so kind as to call the next patient?'

'Of course, but before I do, before we are engaged once more, may I congratulate you on saving the life of that last unfortunate. I had, myself, believed that there was no prospect for him at all, his wound being so severe. Your work, dear colleague, was exemplary... it was the very finest of surgical endeavours.'

'One man, he was but one man,' Simon sighed, fatigue and despond weighing heavy on his mind, for the operation had been difficult beyond his expectations, '... and it was but a modicum of success amidst the dying of hundreds of others in this vile place.' He spat into the bloody bucket, 'What does my work, the paltry endeavours of a single man, count for in this bloody conflagration, eh?'

Marston, much taken aback, stared at his friend, 'My dear Ferguson... forgive me, but it may serve us well if I speak of the teachings of those faithful of another persuasion... sadly none of such ilk live in this place any longer. I speak of the Koran. I no longer recall the verse, but the words and their significance I have carried with me since ever the first time I read them.'

'I beg your pardon... for my own ungracious words. Please go on,' whispered Simon, mollified and a little embarrassed.

'Whoever saves a life, it shall be as if he had saved the lives of all mankind.'

'That is... is the most noble sentiment,' Simon nodded, blinking away the tears forming within his sore eyes, 'Indeed it is splendid... and I thank you for it. I thank you for the reminder... of what we are doing here, I do; I am exceedingly grateful to you, I am so. Thank you, Marston.'

'I will call for the next patient,' said the chaplain quietly.

'Pascoe,' Simon sighed, 'would there be a piece of biscuit for a hungry man?'

The next unfortunate, plainly in considerable discomfort and so weak as to be utterly incapable of responding to any summons, was carried in by his comrades and lifted on to the table where he lay back in absolute exhaustion, his face contorted with pain, his breathing shallow. Simon stared, aghast and in considerable dismay, in instant recognition of the catastrophic wounds to both the legs. He blanched and momentarily turned away to conceal his horror, a surge of acid bile rising and lingering within his throat and mouth. Not that the patient was in any state to discern the least of Simon's feelings of dismay, as he hovered on the edge of unconsciousness. 'Both legs must come off,' Simon whispered to Marston; 'Look, there is the first evidence of gangrene... *there*...' The surgeon's finger hovered above the open and suppurating bloody gashes below both the smashed knees, '... and here on the other leg. Do you smell it?' He wrinkled his face as if in disgust with the putrid, sickly-sweet stench.

'I do,' Marston frowned; 'Thankfully it seems that it is only the beginnings of that vile affliction, and perhaps we may have some small hope of saving the life if not the legs.'

For a welcome second Simon marvelled at his friend's resolution and positivity, and in that moment he wished that he possessed a little more of it himself. He nodded, the tiniest of smiles offered to Marston, and he leaned over the casualty in closer examination, his own determination to strive to do more for his patient, to work on a little longer into the dusk, to go on for as long as the light allowed, all rekindled. Perhaps he might yet be able to look to the next one or two unfortunates after the present one, for his own resolve to do so was, he found, a little enhanced. It was just a trifle, but it was significant; it was enough. He looked up momentarily to the attentive chaplain, engrossed in his own scrutiny of the damaged legs, and he whispered, 'Michael... *Michael there*,' adding as Marston looked across the table towards him, 'You will allow me to say that I am the most fortunate man in the world... to have you here at my side... as my helper and... *and as my friend.*'

'The barky's lookout has sighted the Turks, as we feared,' Duncan, aboard the cutter, spoke in a steadfast voice despite his own rising concerns.

'She is hauling up her anchors, sir,' declared Mason to Duncan, 'She is readying to leave.'

'What of the boats?' asked Jason in hesitant anxiety, 'They are not in sight.'

'No, I doubt they have yet made the beach, but we cannot wait for them here. If *Surprise* is departing then we may believe that the Turks will be little more than an hour away and, if we stay, we will be visible to them, and they can reach us at this end of the deepwater channel. We cannot go closer to the town or even the island of Vasiladi for fear of grounding again, and so the boats must remain on the beach. We have no choice but to follow the ship until we are further west, when we will sail as close inshore to the island of Prokopanistos as we can. There is a plentiful number of sandbanks all about it, and so the Turk is unlikely to follow us. You will doubtless collect the burned corvette which is grounded there. No, the men in the boats will remain in the town, ready to take off Doctor Ferguson and all our other shipmates when necessary, and there they must await our return.'

Ten minutes passed and the cutter hauled off to the west in the strengthening wind, towards deeper water, every man aboard staring towards the town, looking at the beach, as if willing prayers and good fortune to the men left behind, and silently praying that Ibrahim's onslaught upon the town might yet be some time off.

The sun noticeably sinking ever lower in its descent through the western sky, *Surprise* picked up speed rapidly with the *grego* wind on her starboard quarter, the islands of Saint Sostis, Komma and Schinias all left behind as she remained outwith the outlying islands of the lagoons, approaching Prokopanistos on the starboard bow. To Pat's mind it was an ignoble retreat, an abandonment of those of his crew who remained behind in the town of Messalonghi, but he had always realised that no alternative would be open to him. The approaching enemy squadron was so greatly more powerful than his solitary frigate; indeed, the powerful Turk frigates would rapidly pulverise the barky to abject destruction if ever the great guns were brought to battle. No, retreat was the sole option, and he had forewarned the shore party that such was the case. Nevertheless, judging by the disconsolate faces that thronged the quarterdeck and the sides, there was a pronounced feeling of unhappiness throughout the ship. He stared aft through his glass, distant sails brought sharply into focus; he sighed again despite the conclusion being plain: there really was no choice. He stared down into the white wake creaming behind the ship as *Surprise* sailed on, faster, swiftly gaining the more open waters to the west, her clean hull a blessing and not the least weed hindrance to her. All her new canvas was a joy to behold to the many experienced eyes studying her progress. Pat stepped to the side rail and stared over towards a distant *Mathew Jelbert*. The cutter was close in to the nearest island. Good, he thought, she could not be followed by the Turks in those shallow waters. He paced aft to stand near the stern rail again and looked through his glass once more; the approaching squadron was a magnificent sight to the eyes of a professional mariner; in fact, it could hardly be described as anything less than an entire fleet. The sailor in him studied it for an hour. Thankfully, the Turks were not gaining the least ground, and the barky was safe. Safe! Pat revelled in the word; he muttered it under his breath and he rejoiced in the thought; indeed, he privately thanked Saint Patrick and all the Saints in the heavens. He did not care to leave his quarterdeck for even a minute of the remaining hour, the final one of the afternoon, and he continuously monitored the pursuers. *Surprise* was faster, and only their distant mastheads were now visible from deck. His attention frequently drifted forwards to where he could make out the distant brigs of the Greek squadrons. They too appeared to be departing, for not even Miaoulis could make any effective stand against this Turk host, so many of them and so powerful. Massive loss would be assured for the Greeks, and for no sure gain.

'Where are we bound, sir?' Codrington broke into Pat's thoughts.

'South-west... staying with the wind, even if we are to return to Cephalonia where the Turk will not follow.'

'What of the cutter... and... and the men left ashore?'

'Mr Macleod must, as is plain to see, stay as close as close can be to the barky as we both flee. He will return when the time is right... to await the boats in the vicinity of Vasiladi. There is nowhere closer to the town with sufficient depth of water to take the cutter closer in.'

'But what if Ibrahim launches his attack upon the town and breaches the walls? What of our shipmates then?'

'I understand that there is a channel deep enough for the boats alone in those most northerly waters of the lagoon where the Greeks still occupy that small town on the islet there... Anataliko it is. Miaoulis has managed to haul supplies in there in the past aboard his boats, whence they are carried to the town by the smallest of fishing vessels... canoes and the like. The townsfolk use flat-bottomed boats in the lagoons. I collect they resemble those Baltic vessels which are termed *praams*. Our lads must escape that way.'

The final minutes of daylight through the small window facing the beach were afforded to an exhausted Simon and Marston as they brought to a close their endeavours for the final patient of the day. A seemingly straightforward cleansing and sewing up of a sword slash across the chest below the lungs, brutal slash though it was, had gone very well; the detritus of clothing embedded within the cut had been successfully cleaned away, the deeper red flesh all exposed to careful scrutiny, but then had come the unexpected and horrifying great gush of arterial blood. Perhaps it had been the lifting of the Greek fighter to the table, a greater flexing of chest muscle resulting in too great a strain upon a damaged and fragile artery. That would never be known. Despite greatly rapid efforts to fold back more skin, to swiftly probe deeper into the wound, to search for the severed vessel, all despairing efforts were fruitless; two panic-stricken minutes of both surgeons' frantic explorations and then, the patient grunting with pain and discomfort, his body becoming ever colder to the surgeon's touch, the heart stopped, the shallow breathing ceased and the patient expired before their wildly blinking, sore red eyes. A crushing sense of futility, of despair, had descended upon them both. Even Marston was visibly set back to such a degree that Simon had never seen before. The surgeon set down his knife and, unthinkingly, wiped away the blood from his hands, his wrists and his forearms, even as it dripped from the table. The deceased unfortunate was carried away as the surgeons stood in abject exhaustion and a degree of shock, oblivious to everything. Two minutes more passed in silence while the sad realisation finally sank in and registered within their minds, their manic thoughts slowing to a numbed insensibility, when both gratefully accepted the small tot of rum proffered by a much dismayed Jim Pascoe.

The inevitable sunset was upon them, a giant and radiant orange orb in the distance on the frigate's larboard bow. Wispy streaks of low cloud reflected brightly on their undersides as the sun began to dip in red farewell into the water, its afterglow perpetuated above the horizon as if it were reluctant to cede to the coming night. To all aboard the barky it was most welcome, pure and simple; the Turk was renowned for being averse to fighting at night and, in any event, the pursuing fleet never looked remotely like catching the fast-fleeing frigate. The Greek vessels, ever more indistinct and distant in the dim twilight, were finally lost to sight, when the lookouts called out that the Turks were turning about. *Surprise* was all alone once more on the grey expanse of rippling sea, all her canvas aloft but under not the least strain for the wind had dropped away to its customary dusk breeze, darkness merely minutes away. Pat gratefully embraced the mental relief and the release of his enduring nervous tension even as his mind cast about for the return solution. Perhaps the new morning and the visibility afforded by daylight would facilitate his decision; until then he determined that *Surprise* would hold her station in the open waters between the mainland and Cephalonia, and in the night until the dawn light of a new day she would simply make long boards, out and back, to no progress at all in any direction, at least until he could see some prospect of a safe return to Messalonghi.

'Mr Codrington!' a tired Pat called out to his lieutenant at the waist rail, 'We will spill our wind, at least for a few hours... and wait for the cutter, and then we will hold our station, here twixt the mainland and Cephalonia.' He explained his thinking to Codrington and Mower, Prosser attending from the helm, all of whom he could see were mightily relieved to be far from the daunting Turk host, perhaps even more so than he was himself, if that was possible. 'Mr Codrington,' declared Pat, 'draw and house the guns, if you please. Thankfully it seems we will have no need of them this night... and perhaps we may sleep tight in our cots? It is not too much to ask, is it, for an honest man?'

'I am wholly of your way of thinking, sir,' replied Codrington with discernible emphasis, Mower murmuring quiet words of accord.

Pat nodded to them both, left his lieutenants on watch, and went below in the feeble, residual dusk light to enter his cabin. A ravenous hunger overtook him, together with another emerging feeling, an awareness of the necessity for a return to some semblance of the most modest normality and routine, the craving for which seized all his thoughts as he lay down on his cot, intending a momentary respite before taking a morsel of supper.

He was fully clothed and too tired even to remove his boots, all thoughts of food wholly forgotten in the single minute before he fell fast asleep. Murphy entered, saw his captain lying prone, unmoving, and he left the cabin with the quietest ever closing of the door.

Saturday 18th February 1826   13:00   *Messalonghi*

'Marston, will you look about you,' declared Simon with a great deal of relief in his voice. 'I do believe we have but three remaining patients, none of whom might be considered to be afflicted with such as the more serious wounds we have dealt with these past days; certainly, none are life-threatening.'

'I congratulate you, colleague, for your commendable endeavours in this place.' Marston smiled with a radiance of infinite benevolence, 'Will I say, you have brought considerable relief to two hundred unfortunate souls and more, these two weeks gone. I am sure no surgeon ever had to bear such a heavy load. I am in awe of your fortitude and dedication, I am so.'

'Please, you are very good and I am most sensible of your appreciation, but let us speak no more of such things, for you have *yourself* rendered the greatest service to these people... rarely leaving my side whilst I have attended their afflictions, and you have oft ministered to their distress *long into the night hours*... with comforting words for many of those poor souls.'

'Oh, it was no more than any other man of God would have done,' mumbled Marston, pleased and relieved to discern the tiny uplift in his friend's spirits.

'Sirs,' Pascoe interjected, 'Begging your pardon, Captain Zouvelekis asks your attention for a minute.'

'Very well, please to send him in,' said Simon.

'Doctor Ferguson, Father Michael,' Zouvelekis spoke in deferential tone, 'We have received reports from the township of Anatoliko, which is an island a few miles to the north. A little grain and other supplies are reaching Messalonghi from that place; they are brought from Porto Sollo on Zante, and taken by small boats for some miles through a narrow creek which has its mouth at the coast near the isle of Petala. These provisions are then carried overland to Anatoliko, whence they can be fetched in canoes and brought through the reeds of the lagoons to Messalonghi. Some of these stores - *so it is reported* - are from your gallant ship, from *Surprise*. She is standing off, anchored, in the deeper water between Petala and Makri, whilst her accompanying cutter takes her stores to the mouth of the creek and the Zantiot boatmen waiting there.'

'I am greatly pleased to hear it, Captain Zouvelekis,' declared Simon in bright voice, for there had been no news of his ship and cherished friends for many days, '... and would there be any other news from that estimable vessel, tell?'

'I regret I have nothing more to report, sir, save that a bombardment has begun from two Turk batteries, one of each firing upon our defences on the Klisova and Skylla islets in the lagoons. I hesitate to add to your burden, but I venture your services may be called upon once again very shortly.'

'Perhaps we should be grateful on this occasion that we have only Scylla and no Charybdis?' murmured Simon, a sinking feeling returning.

'Eh? No Charybdis?' Marston stared at his friend.

'Oh, pay that no mind, colleague. Now, will we look to our last patients, to clear this place before unfortunates afresh come anew. Pascoe, bear a hand there; bring the first man to the table, if you will. Thank you.'

Saturday 18th Feb. 1826 13:00   HMS Surprise   off Petala

'Mr Codrington,' asked Pat, feeling a deal less strained after fully two undisturbed weeks at anchor, 'How are we faring in the unloading of the last stores for Messalonghi, pray tell? Do you have a fair notion of the time it may take us to deliver what little surely remains to the beach?'

'The slow progress is due to the Greeks, sir. There is nothing more we can do; there are but few Zantiots who will venture with loaded boats into the creek; and none will brave the lagoon beyond Anatoliko; they are ever in fear of being discovered by the Turk.'

'No doubt.'

'Mr Macleod is minded to take the next load at first light.'

'But surely there can be but precious little left below?'

'Indeed, sir, the hold is much vacated,' replied Codrington, nodding. 'Mr Macleod's cutter is about to tie alongside, sir, and a deal more of powder has been fetched up to the deck for loading. It will be stored aboard *Mathew Jelbert* before the end of the afternoon watch. I am minded to spend some time below to collect together what few kegs of powder and sacks of biscuit remain when Mr Mower comes on watch at eight bells. There is a scattering of this and that, here and there... in the hold, atop the sail loft and on the orlop.'

'Be so good as to do that, and perhaps you will report your findings at the end of the last dog watch?'

'Yes sir.'

'Please to ask Mr Macleod's attendance in the cabin when *Mathew Jelbert* ties alongside.'

'Of course, sir.'

An hour passed with Pat sipping coffee in the cabin, until Murphy arrived, 'Well, Mr Macleod is back, sorr, climbing aboard now.'

'Very good, will you look to Wilkins and the dinner for us both? A roast fowl did you say? Ah, Duncan, there you are! Come in, do sit down,' Pat was pleased to see his friend. 'Here, allow me to pour you a glass of this fine sherry... the coffee is cold. How goes the deliveries, tell? I have asked Codrington to look to find out what remains below.'

'Thank ye kindly,' said Duncan, drinking the proffered sherry in one, 'I have the thirst of a shipwrecked mariner! May I look to another drop?'

'Of course, here, take the bottle... please.'

'I venture there is one more load for the cutter in the morning... That will be the two score of powder kegs on deck, and precious little will then remain aboard the barky.' Duncan spoke with a degree of relish, of anticipation, in his voice. 'Aye, one more load - *after the powder* - and we can be away from this place... to fetch our lads... and Simon... from the town.' Pat simply stared, nodding; was such a prospect really so close before them? That done, their shipmates recovered, and they could depart for England, to leave Hell behind them.

Saturday 18th Feb. 1826 16:00 *Messalonghi*

Simon and Marston walked along the shore of the lagoon at a short distance from Byron's house, their adopted hospital. The last of their afternoon's three patients had been treated and dressed, when a driving urge for open space and fresh air necessitated their perambulation, an escape from the stinking claustrophobia of the dark, crowded room which was filled with the murmurings of those patients incapable of being moved. A dozen were still there, all enduring pain in loud discomfort, nothing left to the surgeons of the tiny supply of laudanum to help them. In the background came the sound of the sporadic artillery fire, very infrequent and tailing off to a close as the day neared its end. The higher crack of desultory small arms fire from the town walls also faded away. Messalonghi could at least enjoy a long winter night of respite before the dawn brought its unwelcome resumption of danger and acute fear.

The two friends strolled on, acknowledging a wave from an occasional Greek standing guard over women washing clothing in the lagoon waters, others wading to gather what few shellfish they might find before blackness enveloped them, the sun's fading radiance hanging very low in the south-west sky. They paused, staring to the north-west, near the shore. 'There!' Simon cried out, pointing to the sharp silhouettes on the water, 'I do believe that several small boats are approaching.'

'Indeed, there are six of them, colleague,' declared Marston, '... scarcely larger than canoes, and with two men to each.'

A small crowd of Greeks gathered at the shore as the canoes came close, an excitable gabble of loud voices rising as they finally grounded in the sand, two dozen men wading out to help the boatmen pull what were obviously heavily-laden canoes ashore. Simon and Marston halted, both listening as best they could to the fast exchanges but understanding near nothing. In that moment Zouvelekis appeared, stepping up quickly from behind them. 'What are these boatmen about, Captain Zouvelekis?' asked Simon.

'They are bringing powder and foodstuffs from Anatoliko, travelling in the dusk light when the Turk may not easily observe their passage through the lagoon; indeed, they are concealed within the reeds save for the final quarter-mile to the beach. It is the town's only supply since Miaoulis was driven away... precious little that it is.'

'From Anatoliko?' Simon continued with a rising degree of interest, excitement even, 'Did you not say that *Surprise* herself is providing some of these resources... to that place? Will you speak with the boatmen... ask if they have news of our vessel?'

'I will, sir.' Zouvelekis waded into the throng, all busily engaged in assessing the food quantities, dividing it into a hundred and more rations for distribution throughout the town, less interest displayed in the powder which was rapidly diminishing as others carried away the small kegs. After five minutes of anxiety for the surgeons, the Greek returned, 'Doctor Ferguson, Father Michael, these men are not the Zantiots who collect the stores at the creek from your vessel's cutter. They are men of Anatoliko who bring on the supplies when they arrive at that place, the men of Zante resting there before they return to the creek... to the sea shore there to fetch more.'

'But what of our ship? What of our shipmates?' Simon interrupted.

'All is well with them,' Zouvelekis smiled, 'They are at anchor there. These men report that there is but little further to fetch from your vessel, nearly all has been disembarked, and when the canoes return once more then all may be finished.'

Simon stared, said nothing as he digested the welcome news; it was Marston who spoke up, 'I venture that is exceedingly good to hear, Captain Zouvelekis. And how long, pray tell, will it be before these men return bearing that final load?'

'They will return to Anatoliko during this evening, in a few hours time and after they have rested. The Zantiots too will depart from Anatoliko before the dawn, seeking to gain the creek in darkness before they are seen by the Turk patrols. It will be two more days perhaps... when the men of Anatoliko will be here once more.'

'Then please be so kind as to ask if they will convey a letter to *Surprise*, if you will,' declared Simon. 'Come, Marston, we must away at all speed to Byron's house. I must write my note.'

Sunday 19th Feb. 1826 08:00   HMS Surprise   off Petala

Pat stood on his quarterdeck, wrapped in his sea coat against the cold wind whilst gazing at a distant *Mathew Jelbert* disappearing through the Petala Channel, the cutter having departed a half-hour previously with the last of the kegs of gunpowder for the mainland creek. She was making frequent short boards into the channel, the easterly wind blowing strong. Pat estimated it at twenty knots. He sipped from his large coffee flask, enjoying the tiny sliver of normality, such as it was. To his mind the strong, bitter brew was a reminder of another life, that one before the seemingly permanent tension, stress and anxiety with which he felt he was living.

'Good morning, sir,' Codrington broke into his thoughts.

'Good morning to you, Mr Codrington,' said Pat pleasantly, 'and for sure it is a fine one. The sun is shining, and we will pay no mind to the strength of a cold wind. It greatly pleases me to say the powder is all gone at last with Mr Macleod. I have never had a better morning in all my time in Greek waters. That said, I also confess I much yearn these days to return to that blessed place, sweet Connemara.'

'Yes sir... indeed,' Codrington hesitated, 'I regret that my search of the ship took a deal longer than I believed it would, much of the Greek provisions being loaded and stored in haste amongst our own comestibles at the Yard... a deal of shifting needed to find some of it.'

'Oh, no matter, and what remains below, pray tell?'

'There is a score of biscuit sacks, two dozen of corn and nine chests of medicines. I believe that is all.'

'Very good, the cutter can carry all of that in her final load when she returns. Would you care to join me for breakfast?'

'Indeed I would, sir; thank you kindly.'

Sunday 19th Feb. 1826 09:30   Mathew Jelbert   at the creek

'Well, here we are and no Greek men nor any boats to greet us! Where are they?' exclaimed Duncan with a degree of vexation, the cutter approaching as near the shore as she could go, the water shallowing. 'Let go the anchor and we will go ashore in the yawl. Every man is to take a pistol and cutlass.' After five minutes of rowing through the shallows, the yawl grounded on the bleak, muddy shingle at the mouth of the creek. Duncan and his three companions hauled the small boat further up the soft sludge which was the beach, securing it with a line around a large rock. 'Lads,' declared an increasingly apprehensive Duncan after an uneasy two minutes staring about them in silence, not a sound to be heard except for the wind rustling through the reeds, 'Have a care, we will all split up and walk a mile in every direction. Let any man who finds a Greek ask his presence here at the yawl, and we will see if we can gain any notion of where the Zantiots might be. Be sure to be back here before noon for I am minded that this is no longer a greatly safe place for us.' Doubtful faces and nods all round, the four men set off over the boggy terrain, diverging as they gradually gained ground.

Sunday 19th Feb. 1826 11:30 HMS Surprise　　　　　*off Petala*

'Beg pardon, sorr, a cry from the watchman,' Murphy burst into the cabin without even his customary tap on the door. That he was in a state of anxiety was plain for Pat to see. The steward's voice confirmed his excitement, 'Ships! Ships be sighted!'

Pat leaped up in haste from his chair, which fell backwards to the deck; he moved as fast as he decently could without running, although his urgency was plain to behold. He hurled himself up the steps to his quarterdeck and looked up to the main crosstree, shouting loudly, 'WHERE AWAY?'

'SOUTH! A DOZEN OF SHIPS! SOUTH!' the lookout's reply was charged with anxiety.

'Mr Codrington, all hands on deck, prepare to sail!' With that, Pat started up the ratlines clutching his glass.

'Dalby, ring the bell,' bawled the lieutenant, 'All hands, all hands!' A clamorous cacophony followed immediately, Dalby applying himself with extreme vigour and determination. The loud peals of the bell resonated with brutal, alarming clarity throughout the ship.

Atop the crosstree after exerting himself frenetically for two minutes, Pat stared south at the masts of a number of ships. A very short time passed before they were revealed as frigates: it could only be the Turks. The Turks, with six vessels, were eight miles away, perhaps nine; just three leagues at most. They had come out from behind the island of Oxia, else the watchman would have sighted them sooner; they were likely sailing out from their fleet base of Patras. Perhaps news of *Surprise's* presence had reached them there, for she had been anchored for two weeks as her supplies were gradually unloaded into the few Zantiot small boats attending the creek. His mind raced to compute the time it would take the Turk ships to reach *Surprise*: they could probably make six knots on a beam wind, perhaps one or two more, hence they might reach the barky in as little as an hour. Just one hour! Pat's mind raced. The wind was a strong easterly, beneficial to the barky's escape to the open waters to the west, towards the Ionians, and Pat doubted that the Turk vessels would catch his ship when she was out there. His breathing accelerated and he could feel his rapid heart rate. *Surprise* needed most of half an hour to haul up and stow her anchors, but she had just one hour; no more could he count on in which to do so, and then she must flee as fast as she could sail. Pat calmed, he told himself that in such time the barky could surely shake off the most eager pursuer, being so fleet of foot, her hull all cleaned of weed. But only if - his thoughts raced again - *only if* he abandoned the cutter, left *Mathew Jelbert* behind, left his friend Duncan Macleod, Barton and his men to an uncertain fate. Without a doubt, an exceedingly dangerous time was approaching for those of his men nearer the shore.

His anxieties roared away once again as he, very slowly, climbed down to the deck. What to do? Brutal reality registered as he realised that the imminent danger left him not the least choice: *Surprise* must depart at all speed, leaving *Mathew Jelbert's* men to fend for themselves. What would they do? What could they do? At least the cutter was an exceptional sailer and would undoubtedly leave any pursuer in her wake. That was sure, but it depended on Macleod being aware of the Turks, and Macleod could neither see *Surprise* nor the Turks from the other side of Petala island. The land to the south would obscure all view of danger approaching until it was too late for the cutter's men. Pat's heart sank even as he declared the only remedy he could think of, 'Mr Mower, draw the shot from the carronades and fire them all. Mr Macleod must be alerted to the danger.'

'Aye aye sir.' Mower hastened to gather the carronade gunners.

Sunday 19th Feb. 1826 11:30   Mathew Jelbert   at the creek

The four men had returned, mystified, to gather at the yawl. The absence of the customary reception of Zantiot boatmen remained a riddle. Even though *Surprise's* supplies were not the sole provisions coming ashore at the creek's mouth, more were being brought directly from Zante, from the island's tiny beach of Porto Sollo. Yet there was no sign of anyone having been present at the creek. All prior evidence of the activity of many days gone by had been washed away. 'Lads,' declared Duncan, 'I venture we will go back to the cutter; 'tis a puzzle for sure, but no notion of what has happened will we find here today...' He hesitated, a movement in the corner of his eye catching his attention. From behind a huge boulder appeared a solitary, dishevelled figure, plastered from head to foot in mud and crawling on hands and knees towards the Surprises. The man paused, raised an arm in supplication, but plainly could go no further, collapsing face down.

Duncan and his men raced to the exhausted man, gently turning his body and lifting him out of the mud. 'Water, quickly! Your flask!' cried Duncan to Denzel. The life-giving liquid was gulped gratefully, the mud-caked man drinking and swallowing eagerly until none remained. He sat, coughing, for a further minute, for no words could he find. He blinked, finally wiped his eyes with a weary hand to shift much of the spatter of earth and sand speckling his face and irritating his vision, but he could offer no words at all in his absolute physical devastation. Indeed, his eyes seemed wild and unfocused, and nothing of what was said to him appeared to be heard, for there was no reaction at all, none.

'Denzel, Nance, lift him up. We will take him with us,' declared Duncan, 'Perhaps Mr Jason may glean from him what has happened here. Come, lads, back to the boat and the cutter; we will rejoin the barky.'

In that instant all heads turned as the sound of the explosions from *Surprise's* carronades roared across the water. The frigate was not visible, anchored as she was behind the island of Petala, but the message was plain: danger, act in the utmost haste! 'Quickly, lads; we must away at all speed!' Duncan shouted, 'Come on, let's go! Have a care for that man, Denzel.'

The Greek was set down by the yawl and the four men began to struggle to haul it out into deeper water. Afloat at last, Denzel and Nance returned to pick up the Greek, passing him with the utmost care to Duncan and Penberthy who set him astride the midships thwart, holding him sitting upright in his exhaustion and incapacity. After five minutes of furious rowing, the yawl came alongside the cutter. The exhausted Greek was passed up to waiting hands who hauled him up and aboard, the four men of the landing party swiftly following. The waiting men of *Mathew Jelbert* were already anxious to go, the boom was immediately hauled tight, and the sail and the jib filled instantly, hauling the cutter away. 'South! South!' shouted Duncan, who would have no truck with thoughts of the shallower waters of any passage bearing north, although that was conceivably the safest direction. The cutter swiftly gained speed, the easterly propelling her to eight and quickly to nine knots, as gauged by Duncan's eye, no thought for any other practical measurement in their haste.

Sunday 19th Feb. 1826 12:00   HMS Surprise   off Petala

Noon had arrived, when *Surpris*e'*s* anchors had been hauled up and her cables stowed in record speed. Her men were all mindful of the oncoming great danger. Indeed, *Surprise* had been underway for a mere ten minutes and in that time the approaching Turk squadron had left Oxia in their wake and was already in the channel between Makri and the mainland. With a start Pat concluded that the Turks must be sailing at almost eight knots. That was fast indeed! The barky was bearing west, for the safety of Ionian waters, but her speed was slow and only gradually rising as her straining sails hauled her eleven hundred tons through the water from standstill. Pat, with Codrington and

Mower, stared towards the Turk squadron. 'I venture they are five miles off,' he declared at last with some small degree of satisfaction, for that was well beyond the range of even the heaviest calibre guns. Yet *Surprise* was still achingly snail-like in her progress and still far from gaining her best speed. Pat gauged that she was making a mere three knots, maybe four at best. If the Turks were sailing at eight or perhaps even nine knots, then in a mere thirty minutes they would be chasing from within a mile off. No, that could not be, Pat reassured himself: in fifteen or twenty more minutes the barky would be racing at eight knots, the *grego* blowing from near astern, all her canvas aloft and all her yards braced tight to catch the wind. She would then be two further miles to the west. Pat looked up, gazed at the sails and saw immediately that they were under a tremendous load, the hull exhibiting the smallest of lean to leeward, and astern there was the reassuring wash of the white wake, but it was much more muted than when she was at her best speed. Perhaps, he considered, he had one more shot in the locker. 'Mr Codrington,' he called out, 'perhaps we will fetch out the yards for her studding sails...' A minute passed and Pat changed his mind. He reassured himself that *Surprise* would soon show her pursuers a clean pair of heels, even without the extra sails, for they would take a long time to hoist up, to attach them and to boom them out, and then there was the task of hauling up the canvas. No, that would all take far too long. Indeed, it would call for an hour which they did not have. However, at best speed and with her present sails, the barky could surely haul away; yes, he felt sure she would, although it would be a mighty close-run thing. 'Belay that,' he murmured to Codrington eventually.

'There is *Mathew Jelbert*, sir!' cried Mower, pointing, alarm in his demeanour, 'She is coming out... into the channel... Look there! I see her... out from behind Petala!'

'Yes, and thankfully Mr Macleod may now espy the Turks,' said Pat, his voice an audible meld of relief and apprehension.

All eyes on the quarterdeck near the helm turned to gaze aft, the cutter appearing a mile astern. Plainly she, at least, was already sailing at her best speed, well heeled to leeward and turning to race away on a much more northerly course.

Another shout came down from the watchman, 'FOUR OF THE TURKS HAVE TURNED WEST! WEST!'

'The Turk admiral is hedging his bets... the pack are on the fox's trail,' declared Pat, 'Half of the hounds are chasing from astern, in case we bear north, and the others are striving to cut us off if we hold our course for Ithaca. Which should it be, Mr Codrington?'

The lieutenant swallowed hard, 'I am sure you will decide for the best, sir.'

Pat managed a momentary smile, 'I venture our safety lies in Cephalonia, in Argostoli for sure, for the Turk will never follow us there. To the north lies only the long chase and... and the vagaries of the weather, such as it may become. I fancy we will hold to our north-west bearing.'

'A most sound assessment, sir,' declared Codrington, smiling at last.

Fifteen more minutes and *Surprise's* speed was approaching her best, yet those pursuing two Turk frigates and two corvettes which had not turned west, all sailing on a broad reach, had closed the separation to only a mile and a half. The wind on their starboard quarter was certainly helping them more than it was assisting *Surprise*, running before it, the wind force acting at her stern and the foremast sails shielded by the main. 'Bring her round half a point to starboard,' said Pat in calm voice to Barton.

The helmsmen acted instantly and the frigate gracefully began to swing round in a gentle arc, her hull leaning over a little more. Perceptibly she gained speed, making another knot within ten minutes, and her heel accentuated until she was leaning, Pat estimated, by twenty degrees, leaving every man on deck holding fast to something secure. Within five more minutes he was pleased to see her gain another half-knot, the Turk pursuers visibly no longer closing; *Surprise* was holding her lead at about a mile and a quarter. Pat began to relax just a little, for he could see *Mathew Jelbert* two miles off *Surprise's* starboard beam, plainly excelling herself in her own progress, despite the heavy load of powder he presumed she must still be carrying. He wondered whether Duncan might, or even had already, jettisoned it overboard, for it was a huge potential hazard were that Turk corvette which had maintained a more northerly course in pursuit of the cutter to close up to within range of her guns. Pat, watching, did not think the corvette would ever catch *Mathew Jelbert*, for the cutter was flying, surpassing the barky's progress, albeit being far to starboard. As the minutes passed by, Pat felt a huge release, a massive relief, as the obvious danger to his distant friends aboard the cutter was no nearer and surely receding just a little as time went by. As for *Surprise's* own pursuers, the barky was holding her own, just; indeed, Pat had a brief flash of an old feeling, one he had not felt for a very long time, a momentary surge of exhilaration. It did not last, and he returned to studying every single aspect of the chase in infinite detail. He looked at his sails, at the barky's course and towards the chasing three vessels of the Turk squadron close astern; he stared back to *Mathew Jelbert*, at the distant corvette pursuing the cutter and back to his sails once again. The nearest Turk had gained just a fraction more on the barky and was no more than a mile astern, but there she stayed, no longer gaining as both ships were running at their best speed.

As Dalby rang two bells of the afternoon watch the nearest pursuer crossed *Surprise's* wake and fired her larboard broadside. It was a futile gesture, no more, for she was still at the most extreme range for her guns, no shot reaching the barky. Pat stared out to the starboard beam; he studied the four Turk vessels which had turned to the west before gaining the island of Makri. It had cost them a mile as their speed had dropped, as *Surprise* had found with the wind astern. Pat was thankful, but he worried that the separation was simply the distance off the beam of his ship, for the Turks were astern by precious little. It was those ships which might yet present the greatest danger as the separation diminished since all vessels were on converging courses; unless, as he realised, *Surprise* was forced north and away from her intended Ionian sanctuary which was Cephalonia. The next one, Corfu, was a long way away, a considerable distance in which to endure a chase, and that was a thought Pat did not greatly relish.

One hour passed in absolute concentration, Pat being disturbed only by Dalby's loud ringing of four bells of the afternoon watch. *Surprise* continued to hold her own, the island of Atokos left astern on the starboard quarter, the nearest Turk doggedly following at a mile astern and just passing the island. To larboard the lead ship of that group of four was merely one mile on *Surprise's* larboard quarter, laterally closing the separation and getting dangerously close to where her guns might venture long range firing. Pat studied all the Turk frigates, calculating the convergence of courses to his intended point, north of Ithaca, where he intended *Surprise* would make her turn to the south. Plainly the Turk admiral was determined to continue the chase, but what would bring about his decision to give up? Surely the Turks could see that their quarry was holding her own, except for the mutual convergence towards the forward confluence of their courses. Indeed, *Surprise* appeared to be just a trifle faster, perhaps only by half a knot, for Pat could see that all the pursuing ships had become strung out in two long lines, the fastest frigate of each of the two groups ahead of the pack, the slowest trailing the leader by a mile or more. In the far distance, three miles off the starboard bow, *Mathew Jelbert* had passed by *Surprise*, yet the corvette astern of her was, surprisingly, still following, albeit at an increasing distance, visibly nearer four miles as the corvette emerged from behind Atokos island. That was something of a revelation; perhaps she was newly built, her hull also clean of weed? Perhaps she was copper-bottomed? That particular ship-refitting process was becoming general, Pat mused, and it must also be so within the Ottoman fleet's shipyards within the Golden Horn.

As Dalby rang five bells, Arkoudi island was on the starboard beam and Ithaca very close on the port beam; the cutter was now a league ahead, fine on the starboard bow and streaking away to safety, no Turk vessel able to catch her. However, *Surprise's* larboard pursuer had converged significantly closer, was a mere half-mile on the larboard quarter and certainly much nearer to gaining a firing position. The nearest Turk frigate directly astern of *Surprise* was still little more than a mile in the barky's wake. To an increased extent, Pat was discomfited by seeds of concern taking root in his thoughts: the north cape of Ithaca was directly ahead, one mile fine on the bow. *Surprise* was slowly being pinched between that one of her pursuers so close on her larboard quarter and that one astern and a little off to starboard. With a churning wrench of nausea in his stomach and anxiety in his mind, he realised that he was facing the chase scenario of his oft-recurring nightmare, except that *Surprise* was not fleeing the Bay of Navarino, and nor was his ship badly damaged. Worse, perhaps, was the awareness in his thoughts that there were still four hours to sunset and yet another half-hour of twilight after that, and he knew that as the afternoon developed the likelihood increased of the wind dropping. Although he doubted it would cease entirely, there remained the real prospect of all ships becoming almost becalmed, perhaps simply drifting. What would that mean for the barky? By any reckoning, *Surprise* was already sailing within the boundary limits of Ionian waters, was within the Protectorate, but who was there to exert such jurisdiction? Without any English-flagged vessel present, what was there to deter the Turk admiral from firing upon *Surprise* when - as seemed likely - she found herself within range of Turk guns? Pat concluded that it was exceedingly unlikely that such a determined adversary as the Turk admiral had shown himself to be would be put off in the slightest by such flimsy protections as a notional line on a chart; no, he would do all he could to continue the pursuit, even to the extent of his men hauling his leading frigate by rowing from their boats were the wind to fall away. That would be something of a first, thought Pat, a chase of a frigate by a frigate, and all progress made by rowing. He could not quite bring himself to believe an unlikely engagement such as that might eventuate; no, certainly not, it was a flight of fancy. But was the wind dropping just a little?

BOOM! BOOM! The Turk to larboard was firing her chasers. 'Barton! Stand by!' shouted Pat, Ithaca's north cape on the larboard beam; 'Hard over to larboard! Follow the sun!' Already the brightly burning yellow orb was well past its noon zenith and had long started its descent through the sky. Indeed, it was now visibly falling towards the south-west horizon. Pat stared astern in bleak assessment. The proximity to the rocks of the Ithaca shore had at least slowed that Turk to larboard, the hostile frigate spilling its wind, falling back in the chase; she was beginning to turn cautiously towards the north, away from the Ithaca coast, her captain being plainly mindful of avoiding any collision with the leading frigate of his compatriots in the other group astern of *Surprise*. A little of wind shelter was created by *Surprise*'s turn, shifting into the lee of Ithaca's white-streaked cliffs, and the barky slowed perceptibly, perhaps a knot or two lost. The closest Turk pursuer rounded the cape as Pat stared through his glass. She was merely a quarter mile astern, yet the pursuing frigate did not turn at all, holding to her north-westerly course. Pat wondered why, for the Turk represented the only danger to *Surprise*, all other enemy vessels were effectively left too far astern. As he gazed, puzzled, he saw the puffs of smoke erupt from her larboard battery, the boom of the guns immediately following. At two cables distance it was no great threat unless an exceptional shot was to be greatly successful, perhaps breaking a yard or suchlike. Pat breathed a huge sigh of relief. He realised that it was more akin to a farewell from the Turk than any tangible danger. It was certainly a gesture of futility, and the Turk gunners were true to form: no shot came close. The barky sailed on, south-west bound; her safety was assured, and Pat's tension slowly eased away to something more near his normal anxiety, the Turks having finally given up the chase. Perhaps it really was the influence of Ionian waters? Perhaps the Turk admiral had concluded that he could not catch the barky? Pat drew no conclusions from his speculations, save that the relief he felt was palpable, for himself and the men all about him. Racing anxieties were slowing, pounding hearts were returning to a steady beat, and his shipmates all about the quarterdeck exchanged cautious smiles. He reflected on the situation; he knew from experience that it was of the order of twelve leagues to the customary sanctuary of Argostoli, the surrogate home for *Surprise* and her men, but she could not reach there with what little remained of daylight. Nevertheless, he determined that was where she was bound, for he did not care to turn about with so many Turk warships at sea in the barky's wake; no, Argostoli would serve his purpose, an undisputed safe haven, until he could see the lie of the land in the broad daylight of the morrow.

Surprise gracefully sailed on, the wind dropping as Pat had expected, the frigate slowing, and from Dalby came the reassuringly familiar ring of four bells to herald the end of the first dog watch. The coast of Cephalonia was on the larboard beam as the sun finally disappeared into the distant waters to starboard. Its radiant sunset with lingering orange afterlight seemed a fitting farewell to the most manic day the Surprises had experienced for a long time. Pat reckoned that *Mathew Jelbert* would be ahead by many a mile, the cutter having demonstrated her superior speed; and that, thankfully, was one less worry. The grog was issued, the tempo throughout the ship relaxed further and, on his quarterdeck, Pat remained standing at the rail throughout the spectacular twilight, staring silently, unmoving and entirely consumed by the profound feeling of relief that was washing all through him. Yet still he afforded frequent glances astern to confirm that there really were no longer any Turk ships in pursuit. Another twenty minutes slipping by, he focused again on the welcome vacuity of the placid, grey sea astern, only a white wake visible in the darkness, and he sighed a heartfelt sigh of relief: the barky's escape had been a mighty close-run thing, closer even than he had suspected it would be. He felt the trembling of his arms and legs, sensed the continuing slow release of tension affecting him, even as he realised that his oft-recurring, black nightmare had not come about; and he silently thanked Saint Patrick and all the saints, even finding a brief, wan smile as Murphy, bearing the brandy flask, approached to ask his wishes.

Monday 20th Feb. 1826   12:00   Argostoli

Mathew Jelbert was tied alongside the quay and *Surprise* rocked at double anchor in gentle fashion in the harbour. In the cabin Pat sat with Duncan enjoying coffee. 'So you did not offload your cargo... none of it?' asked Pat, basking in rare and glorious relaxation.

'Never a one of the kegs, no; there was not a single man to pass them to... not a soul to be seen in the time we were ashore,' Duncan replied, 'until that poor fellow was espied, crawling out of the mud.'

'This Greek that you found, what was he about?'

'He is a Zantiot... Kladis, one of the men who we expected to see on the shore.'

'What did... did *Kladis* have to say for himself, tell?'

'With his fellow islanders, they had made their way from the sea... They had rowed their boats along the length of the creek towards Anatoliko, all filled with flour and powder, and they were waiting at the customary place where the men of Anatoliki always came out to meet them so as to receive the supplies, to take them on.'

An attentive Murphy refilled the coffee cups. 'Do go on,' prompted Pat.

'In that moment they were challenged by Albanian irregulars in the service of Ibrahim. Having no arms save a few pistols, they surrendered... all except Kladis who - *not the least hesitation* - dived into the creek, where he rolled about in the mud, burying himself within it... all but his head... and that he smeared with mud so as to hide from the Albanians.'

Pat stared in bleak apprehension, a rising trepidation filling his mind, 'The Zantiots were all apprehended and the supplies lost, was that the case?'

'Worse, I regret to say: the Albanians hanged every one of the Zantiots. Kladis did not dare move even as his friends and relatives were strung up from olive trees and died before his eyes.'

A loud gasp issued from Murphy, and Pat sensed the returning flood of his own discomforting anxiety, 'Dear God! Barbarians they are! Such vile people! Damn their souls in hell!' He could find no words for another minute, simply sitting in silent angst as he visualised the horrific end to the Zantiot efforts to help their fellow Greeks. A distressed Murphy hastened to the cabin door, muttering oaths and expletives as soon as he was in the coach.

'What to do now?' murmured Duncan in gentle query, 'The cutter still carries two score kegs of powder and... and Simon is still in Messalonghi...'

'Yes, 'tis our lads in that place I am greatly fretting about...' Pat was thinking aloud, '... for, I dare say, that Turk admiral will likely keep his ships at sea and remain on guard to close the blockade.' A deep sigh, 'I... I dare not take the barky within his sight... eight vessels in his squadron. No, we must await Miaoulis and the Hydriots. Perhaps, were we to sail alongside them... we might succeed in gaining Vasiladi once more and... and we can take off Simon and the others.'

'And what of the powder - *two tons of it* - aboard the cutter?'

Pat scratched his chin, a thoughtful pause before he looked up, 'Why, I venture she may gain Vasiladi in darkness... being so fleet of foot - *as we have seen*. Her escape to the west is assured if... if the Turks are not best placed to block her leaving so close to the lagoons... and, were she to offload the powder to the boats... then she can remain as our scout in that place. Yes, the cutter can report when it is safe for *Surprise*... when she can venture closer without encountering the Turks. *Mathew Jelbert* will tell me when the barky can close on Vasiladi, when the Turks are no longer holding station near that island, when, perhaps, they have returned to Patras. That, Duncan... *old friend*... must be our plan, for we have no other.'

'Then I will tell my lads standing ready aboard the cutter, we will depart this night.'

'No,' declared Pat emphatically, 'You must not. The moon is waxing gibbous, and in two days it will be full and bright. That is not greatly helpful to us, for the moon will light the cutter's approach for every Turk observer. No, I am minded that you must await the old moon before sailing.'

'But Pat,' Duncan protested with vehement anxiety, 'that is two weeks away... two weeks more for Simon and our men... in that wretched town!'

Pat sighed and looked up to his friend, his eventual reply filled with weary resignation, 'It is better to be a coward for a minute than dead for the rest of your life.' A silent Duncan stared as Pat resumed, an unmistakeable and steely determination firming in his voice, 'There are no reports of any imminent dangers to Messalonghi... and we must not risk the capture of the cutter, for that is the sure end for our shipmates ashore. No, we will look to the weather... We will pray for cloud... as the moon, at the least, leaves its waning crescent; and perhaps we will be favoured by dense, low cloud. Heavy rainfall or indeed fog would also be a blessing; well, we can but hope.'

'So be it,' Duncan sighed, 'We will await the dark of the moon as our aid.' He did not add his unspoken thought: and pray that all remains well with our shipmates who remain marooned.

Friday 24th Feb. 1826   07:30   *Messalonghi*

In the subdued light of dawn, Simon and his fellow Surprises sat in an ambience of deep gloom around the small fire within Byron's former house. Its proximity to the waterside periphery of the town, near the lagoon shore, afforded it some small measure of protection from the artillery barrage which had opened at daybreak, concentrated upon the centre of the town and its outer earth walls with their defences atop. The booming repetition of the thunderous sound of great guns firing had heralded the commencement of Ibrahim's much awaited and rekindled bombardment after the long pause of several months. Simon's surgical precision of mind, whilst he drank his weak coffee, was engaged in counting a consistency of eight explosions every five minutes, a deepening sense of despond settling upon him as his thoughts drifted, between explosions, to the imminent prospect of newly wounded people sure to be arriving as the day went on. Scouts from the outlying Greek positions had reported the movement of guns during the night as preparations for the onslaught had taken place, the defenders presuming that the anticipated guns, brought from distant Ianinna, had arrived at long last. Thankfully, no fresh casualties had, as yet, been brought to the makeshift hospital, and Simon's attention remained with those patients already treated and, for the most part, in various stages of recuperation.

'You have received no reply to your letter, dear colleague?' asked Marston of Simon, the merest hint of despond in his voice.

Simon sighed, 'I have not, it pains me to say. It is but a few days and we may hope that there is yet time to hear from our friends.'

'Captain Zouvelekis,' Marston looked with a degree of anxiety to the Greek officer, 'Would there be any news of *HMS*

Surprise... or indeed of the cutter, *Mathew Jelbert*? Anything at all... the slightest thing?'

In the background the artillery fire persisted unceasingly. The sound of falling mortar and shell fire shrilling through the air was audible even within the house, the resulting explosions much more so and the crash of falling masonry following more often than not. 'I greatly regret, Father Michael, that there is none.' The Greek strived to avoid voicing his own prognosis, for it was pessimistic in the extreme, 'I am sorry.'

Chapter Nine

Monday 27th Feb. 1826   02:00   Messalonghi

'Wake up, colleague, wake up!' A much-concerned Marston vigorously shook Simon as he lay in his cold bed. The fire had long been reduced to smouldering embers and there was a bleak chill in the room.

'Is there some emergency, tell?' demanded a bleary-eyed Simon, 'I trust there is the most pressing necessity to awaken a tired man?'

'I can hear firing! Listen, it is not the bombardment we have become accustomed to these three days gone. I venture it is small arms fire, a great deal of it.'

'I cannot conceive of the small arms firing being anything but an assault upon the walls,' declared Pickering with a worrying aura of certainty, 'for that is the general purpose of every bombardment, a precursor to the inevitable attack... and the heavy guns have ceased fire during this past hour.'

'Where is Zouvelekis?' asked Simon in curt demeanour, awakening from his torpor, an utter exhaustion having descended upon him following his surgical treatment of a hundred and more casualties in the recent three days.

'He left the house... as soon as the bombardment ceased... to investigate,' said Marston, yawning. 'I confess I have, myself, been unable to sleep since we retired after supper.'

'You refer to the crumbling pieces of broken biscuit we were afforded, no doubt?' said Simon acerbically, for he was not in a sociable frame of mind; his eyes were sore, his back ached after hours leaning over his table, and his thirst was extreme. 'Is there a precious drop of water to spare?'

'Here, take this,' Marston proffered the flask of bitter red wine. 'I regret that for water we possess only salt.'

'Pascoe,' Simon called out towards the silent men huddled within blankets in the corner, half-awakened and reluctant to stir. 'Be a good fellow and see what can be done with the fire. I am minded that we will surely be called upon to treat the wounded we must expect in the coming hours, and warmth is of immeasurable benevolence to all suffering blood loss and shock. Look about for what fuel may be found - *anything at all that will serve* - and please to coax this fire so that there is at least the smallest of flame... *bigger is better.*'

'Very good, sir,' Pascoe, Cusack and Kelynack struggled to their feet.

'Marston, what do we have left of our medicines?' asked Simon, looking towards his table.

'Precious little, I regret to say. There is nothing remaining of the laudanum, perhaps five gallons of vinegar, a plentiful stock of bandage - *thankfully* - and a sufficiency of thread; I believe that is all we possess... save for a small measure of soap at hand.'

'And four gallons of rum,' added Kelynack dolefully from where he crouched over the smouldering embers, searching for a flame as he turned them with a tiny stick.

'Very well, then we must manage with that. Cusack, will you look to the table? A saltwater wash with a trifle of soap is greatly desirable, for the cleansing after the final operation of yesterday, a most bloody one after the amputation, was not quite - *to my way of thinking* - the diligent task we must endeavour to adhere to. Indeed, the bloody bucket too has yet to be emptied and cleansed. I saw that when I picked up a gangrenous toe from under the table, my suppertime biscuit seemingly with an odour even worse than usual.' Simon grimaced, 'That was, of course, the malodorous toe... and perhaps the bucket with the hand and foot remaining within it.'

'Sir!' Pascoe rushed back in. 'The Turks are assaulting the defences; they have captured an outpost on the earth berm and a deal of firing continues all along the wall. Wounded are being carried this way, a dozen or more be coming.'

'Oh dear,' Simon sighed; 'Will you kindly endeavour to assist Kelynack to bring the fire to life in what little time we possess... Perhaps a trifle more of kindling might be found?'

'D'reckly, sir,' Pascoe hastened out again.

'Cusack, the table... quickly now. Marston, please to empty the bucket. I will scrub my hands and look to the candles... more will surely be needed... I believe there is no oil left for the lamp.'

Five minutes passed with the room filling with smoke as Kelynack endeavoured to coax the fire's charred brush fragments to a burning flame, more smoke than fire, when the momentary beating of hands on the door preceded it crashing open with a hefty kick. Pascoe had returned and accompanied the first casualty who was being rushed in by two of his comrades, the wounded man semi-conscious and groaning in pain, with blood all about his chest clothing.

'Pascoe, please to leave the door open!' shouted Simon, dismayed and coughing, 'and bring this unfortunate over here to the table! Here, here, lay him down... gently there, have a care!' He stared at the face of the man before him. It was contorted in pain. He looked in momentary assessment at his chest before beginning to cut away the sodden clothing. At least his breathing thus far seemed to be steady. Three thick layers of clothing, the outer a dense wool weave to hold the winter cold at bay, were swiftly cut and teased away from the chest flesh, and the wound location was exposed. There was an entry by a projectile into the right breast, a ripped and bleeding hole before their eyes.

'Marston, the forceps,' Simon peered closely at the wound. 'Kindly pour a trifle of rum over the forceps... and the wound. I will endeavour to remove the detritus embedded within it. Look to the vinegar, and will you attend to the cleaning about the wound as I progress? Thank you. Pascoe... Pascoe!'

'Sir?'

'Do we know anything, the slightest thing, about this man... how he was wounded?'

Pascoe looked up from the fire, 'Captain Zouvelekis believed it was a musket ball, sir; one fired from amidst the Egyptians as they were driven back from the wall.'

'A musket ball, eh...' Simon leaned over and put his ear to the patient's face, '... and yet his breathing is not greatly disturbed... but the wound is to his chest... It is something of a puzzle... I would have expected a deal more blood loss... and surely this would lead to breathing difficulties. The patient would also customarily be in some degree of shock, yet - *we must be grateful* - all of that is plainly not so...' Simon's murmurs were audible to Marston and Cusack, both in close attendance and holding candles to illuminate the table and the patient. 'I believe we may entertain the hope that the ball has not, thankfully, penetrated the lung but is lodged within the *pectoralis major*, but I must guard against an excess of optimism, eh? We know that only too well... Mind you, even were it to have penetrated further and torn the *pectoralis minor...* well, that would be no disaster; indeed, I venture we might count it a blessing. What do you say, Marston?'

'I place my hopes,' murmured the chaplain, '... esteemed colleague, in your considerable skill... and in our Lord's benevolence... for we are ever in his gaze.'

'Why, I venture our Lord has been exceptionally benevolent in this instance... to this unfortunate soul... for I am minded that there is no damage to his lung. Yes, the ball is in there... but it is somewhere within the muscular tissue... yes... I have no doubt that is where it is lodged. It would seem that it is not a life-threatening wound after all... I venture the man is in no great danger...'

'Thank God,' whispered Marston, already in dread of a return to a close proximity to blood, gore and death, the immediate prospects of such so very real before his eyes. 'Thank God,' he repeated, taking a deep breath of relief.

'... save for the infernal infection which may yet blight his prospects. Come, let us look to a trifle more of cleaning of the wound, and then I will apply a dressing. I am minded, in this instance, that we will do nothing yet which might aggravate the injury... to further disturb the tissue with any greatly invasive and immediate procedure. We will allow the fellow to recuperate for a few hours at least, and see how well he recovers his strength and fortitude... whilst we look to other unfortunates in the most dire straits.'

'To what reason may we ascribe this fellow's good fortune?'

'Perhaps it was a spent ball, its passage resisted by his thick clothing? There is a deal of fibrous material come out from the lesion.' Simon stepped back to study his patient, 'This is a stout fellow, I make no doubt... muscular indeed.'

'He is a gun loader, sir,' cried Pascoe, still attending the fire, 'So says Captain Zouvelekis.'

Thursday 2nd March 1826 03:00 *Messalonghi lagoons*

Aboard *Mathew Jelbert* all persons aboard stared into the darkness as the vessel slowly approached the islet of Vasiladi from the south, every man harbouring grave apprehensions about returning to the location where the cutter had previously grounded. Their concerns were ameliorated only slightly by the presence of Kladis, the rescued survivor from the creek. Although he was a Zantiot, he professed an extensive knowledge of the lagoons and shallows, being a frequent fisherman within them; indeed, without his guidance, an anxious Duncan doubted whether the cutter would have successfully navigated around the Saint Sostis islet and made the northbound turn to find the only channel of approach towards Vasiladi with water of sufficient depth to avoid grounding again.

On deck near the helm an acutely tense Duncan held his breath, the pervasive anxiety he felt within gripping him with an extreme tension, the likes of which he could only recall when thinking back to his escape from the island of Sphacteria, which had been frightening in the extreme. He had been pursued by invading Turk soldiers as he had raced across the rough terrain whilst coaxing an exhausted Prince Mavrocordato to safety and flight aboard *Aris*. She had been the sole remaining Greek brig still waiting in the great bay of Navarino for island survivors, their own captain most particularly. Tragically, that Greek unfortunate had not made it to the waterside before being shot down and killed. Duncan shuddered at the recollection, his thoughts returning to the present, to the perilous and virtually blind approach to Vasiladi in the darkness.

A quarter of a mile short of the island, the thin crescent of a moon peeked out from behind the cloud to provide at least a sense of where the cutter lay, relevant to Vasiladi and the town. Duncan ordered the anchor dropped. 'Mr Reeve, I am going ashore in the yawl to Messalonghi, to see what is happening with our shipmates in that place. I am leaving you with Killigrew and Davey. If we are not returned by the dawn then stand ready to depart in haste to the west if any Turk sail are sighted. Pay no mind to us, for we cannot lose the cutter and all our boats, for such is the end of all prospects for the rescue of our friends.'

The cutter's yawl was boarded and its sail hoisted, but to little effect in the weak gusts of the breeze blowing off the sea. Undaunted, Mason, Nance, Denzel and Penberthy pulled hard on the oars, towing one empty boat. The island of Vasiladi was quickly passed by when Kladis directed an immediate turn to the north-east, towards the very few lights visible in the distance. Within a few more minutes, and the wind strengthening, Kladis indicated a course change directly to the north, Jason translating for Duncan at the tiller and looking on with an unwavering expression of angst and concern. Another mile of determined rowing, aided by the improved wind, and Kladis emphasised with rapid gesticulations the necessity for another turn; Duncan resumed a north-easterly course.

'At least we are blessed with a south-westerly, something of the *maestro* is with us,' murmured Duncan to Jason, his first words for some time, 'and plentiful cloud to hide us from any observer.'

'I was of the belief at dinner that we were not departing Argostoli for some days to come,' declared Jason, 'and here we are, the town so close.'

'Aye, and I didnae think O'Connor would agree to our leaving, save that the cloud was so dense,' Duncan nodded, 'I have fretted all this past week to leave the quay... I have so.'

A few words from Kladis and Jason spoke again, 'One mile more, that is all that remains for us to reach the shore... the water is already shallowing a great deal.'

Duncan swallowed, 'We must be away from this place before the dawn. I dinnae care to be the target for Turk gunners in the full light of day.'

'It is half past four already...' Jason's voice tailed off.

'Aye, we have but two hours before the twilight begins... and the dawn proper will be upon us a few minutes after seven o'clock. We have precious little time to gain the beach and find our shipmates.'

Thursday 2nd March 1826   04:30   Messalonghi

'Marston, I swear this is too much of a tribulation!' Simon was not pleased. 'There is not the merest glimmer of daylight in that window. Why, tell, have you awakened me at this ungodly hour - *excuse me* - and when is a man to gain a necessary respite, to enjoy an hour of well-deserved sleep? Is there some emergency?'

'We have visitors! Rouse yourself, dear colleague, as swiftly as can be, for time is short,' cried Marston.

'Visitors? And what hour is it, pray tell?'

'Half past four.'

'Eh? Did you say half past four? Half past four! And who is it that dares to presume upon our goodwill at this hour?'

'Why, Mr Macleod has arrived.'

Simon blinked, paused as if to digest the incredible words, 'What? Duncan Macleod, the man himself, is come here?'

'Simon!' a loud shout from near the remnants of the fire and Duncan came forward to grasp his friend's hand. 'Give you joy of our reunion, old friend!'

'Duncan!' Simon stared as if in disbelief. 'I am at a stand; I would never have expected you for the world. What... what are you minded to do here... in this festering pit of despair?'

'I am come to begin taking you and our shipmates away, away and back to the barky. Our cutter, *Mathew Jelbert*, awaits as close as can be at Vasiladi... but hurry, we have precious little time before the dawn. I beg you will make haste.'

Simon's face fell, 'I regret to say that I am unable to leave at present, I have a deal of patients I am caring for... men with the most serious of wounds... and they will remain in need of my attentions for some time, for without such care as I am able to afford them they have but little prospect of surviving... in this vile place...'

Duncan's heart sank for he had not anticipated Simon's response. 'Can you vouch that your presence here will save them?' he asked eventually. 'Can you be sure of that?'

'That is far from certain, for we have no medicines... and such food as we possess is scarcely worth the eating.'

'Then, old friend, that is more the reason that we must take them with us, but without the least delay; we have but an hour or two before the light of dawn and then the Turk will surely begin firing upon us. How many patients do you care for?'

Simon paused, his thoughts racing, a desperate conflict within his mind; to go, to leave was the answer to his prayers of many a night, but critically wounded patients would undoubtedly die if abandoned without the least care remaining for them. 'I... I am minded that there is a score at least that look to my help, perhaps two dozen.'

'Then we shall endeavour to carry them all to the cutter and away,' declared Duncan emphatically. 'Hurry now, there is not a minute to be lost. We have the yawl and one more boat with us. We cannot carry all your patients this first time, but we have seven more boats at the cutter to fetch back. I believe we might look to take a dozen patients with us now.'

Simon blinked as if signalling that his racing mind had accepted the proposal, the blessed salvation; he nodded and he shouted in full voice, 'Pascoe, Cusack! We are leaving! We are leaving! Wake these men, gather helpers from all about. Quickly now! Find some willing fellows to assist us to the shore, to move our patients. Lose not a moment!'

The candlelit room was swiftly filled with a score of Greeks, coming in from those buildings remaining habitable about Byron's house. Young, strong men moved willingly and with evident enthusiasm, despite the hour and the cold, to move their crippled compatriots to the shore line, the first few of the wounded patients soon arriving at the water's edge. The towed boat was filled first with the eight fittest, those who were capable of sitting on the thwarts, and five Surprises of Pickering's shore party pulled off quickly, rowing hard for the cutter. The men of the yawl, still resting, awaited the further unfortunates who were making their way as fast as they could from the makeshift hospital, assisted in most cases by Greeks and more men of *Surprise*.

Duncan, extremely anxious, stood and gazed into the eastern sky for an excruciating thirty minutes as four more of the weakest patients arrived and were assisted into the yawl. His mind a whirl of anxieties, he looked with rising concern into the blackness of the night, discerning a slight and unwelcome aura of lightening sky between the low clouds to the east, the moon once more wholly obscured. His heart rate accelerated: the morning twilight would soon be upon them. He stared all about him until his eyes fastened upon another half-dozen wounded men arriving. He knew that two score more remained within Byron's house and its environs, and his spirits sank. Thirty minutes was all they assuredly would be afforded before the full light of morning when some keen Turk gun commander might conceivably open fire upon the returned boats. The waiting men would all be visible as they waited upon the beach, they would be vulnerable and unprotected. What to do?

Inside the makeshift hospital, Simon moved about his patients with Marston, both men assessing who must be moved by stretcher and who might be assisted to walk. He spoke to each man who was capable of listening as he slowly passed from one to the next, albeit none of them could understand him. However, he was gratified by the looks of appreciation as each man grasped his purpose, and that was something of a help for his own resolution, for he knew in his heart that when he left this place, this sanctuary for those in the most dire need, no one would be here to replace him. That sat most uncomfortably upon his mind, yet neither could he refuse to leave, for he also understood that the opportunity to rejoin his shipmates was limited in the extreme; there might never be another chance to do so, and he rationalised that he must go, although he could not shake off a lingering feeling of guilt. As he looked at the final man, a patient recovering from a severe leg wound, he heard the sound of small arms firing. It was something of a surprise, gunfire starting before the dawn proper. However, the first signs of twilight were visible in the eastern sky and the full sunrise would not be long in coming. Most strange was that the sounds seemed to be coming from the south, not from the hills all about the town to the north and east; for the firing he had become accustomed to was always from those directions, all about the defensive earthworks and walls. How could that be?

Captain Zouvelekis appeared at that moment, his face one of extreme consternation, 'Doctor Ferguson, Father Michael, you cannot move these men.' He pointed to the wounded.

'I beg your pardon?' Marston was the first to speak, for Simon was dumbfounded.

Duncan hurried through the door, greatly alarmed, 'Captain Zouvelekis, do you have any knowledge of the firing... to the south?'

The Greek was perturbed himself, as all could see; 'There are reports coming in that the Turks have moved their flat-bottomed boats, at least thirty of them, all with musketeers aboard, about the islands of Klisova and Vasiladi, and skirmishing has begun. It is plain that Ibrahim seeks to sever all sea communications with Messalonghi.'

Duncan gasped, 'Then our way out of this place is likely blocked, for Vasiladi is near astride the only channel!'

'I regret that is so...' declared Zouvelekis, his face exhibiting dismay and despond, '... and if Ibrahim succeeds in capturing the two islands, Vasiladi particularly, then there will no longer be the smallest prospect of relief for the town by sea.'

'What of our cutter, anchored to the south of Vasiladi?' asked Duncan anxiously.

'I venture she must surely have departed... in all haste to the west,' said Zouvelekis, 'and has probably taken your boat and the first of the wounded with her.'

Simon and Marston stared, digesting the implications for several minutes before Simon spoke, 'What of your boat still here, Duncan... and my patients we have already shifted aboard? What to do? You remarked that the Turks might fire on her at sunrise. Is that the likely case, Captain Zouvelekis?'

'Yes,' the Greek looked utterly crestfallen, 'It will be too dangerous to remain where she is... much too dangerous; she must shift... *and quickly*. Dawn will soon be upon us.'

'Pascoe,' cried Duncan, 'Hurry, fetch Kladis!'

More and brighter glimmers of the dawn sunlight were already visible in a lightening sky as Pascoe and the Zantiot guide returned. Zouvelekis spoke hastily to Kladis in their native tongue, only Marston following a little of the substance of it. A few minutes later Zouvelekis explained, 'Captain Macleod, Kladis believes that, with any passage south blocked by the Turk skirmish line of small praams - they carry a small gun and are firing upon Vasiladi - there is a chance... *a chance*, no more, that passage might be found to the northwest. However, Kladis is mindful that your vessel draws more water than the small flat-bottom boats he has used when fishing the lagoons... and that is the difficulty.'

'Plainly we have not the least choice in the matter,' declared Duncan, already in dread of running aground once more, 'and we are already beyond the hour when we should have departed. We must go now, without the least delay.' Duncan turned to Simon and Marston, 'There is no sense in carrying any patients about the lagoon with nae prospect of medical care, for the yawl will soon be a target for any enterprising gunner; those men aboard must disembark, and these remaining men here...,' he pointed to the patients, '... must stay until we can return in darkness.'

'Then I must stay,' exclaimed Simon, 'for they will remain in need of care for some considerable time to come.'

'I am also remaining here,' declared Marston in a voice that would brook no disagreement.

'Very well,' Duncan bowed to the inevitable, no time to argue the contrary, 'Gentlemen... I regret that I have not the least choice but to haul away, off this beach and far beyond the range of Turk guns... and so allow me to bid you farewell; I will endeavour to return as soon as darkness is upon us.'

'Take care, Duncan,' said Simon in an air of bleak resignation.

'God speed,' murmured Marston.

Duncan halted at the door and turned about, 'Where is Mr Timmins? I havnae seen him... nor Green.'

'They are assisting the Greek gunners...' said Pickering, '... training volunteers somewhere about the defences; they shift about from day to day.' Duncan, his anxiety building, nodded and hastened away.

The four patients in the yawl were swiftly brought ashore and, with all those waiting on the beach, were assisted by their Greek compatriots to return to Byron's house. Duncan sat at the helm, Kladis at the prow, as Penberthy, Denzel, Nance and Mason pulled as strenuously as they could on the oars, bearing for the far lagoon waters to the north-west. After ten minutes of the most strenuous rowing, the yawl had hauled out of range of any Turk batteries about the town. They set up the sail and, with the south-west wind on her beam, the yawl quickly gained speed towards the north-west. Kladis remained perched on the bow, staring down into the channel waters to gauge the depth as best as he could see in the brightening beginnings of the dawn light. Duncan hid his apprehension and anxiety as the sky became increasingly illuminated by a dramatic dawn. The cloud undersides to the east above the town were all lit up with a bright wash of red, stark to see and seemingly, in that moment, prophetic, for the Turk guns besieging the town opened their firing. The booming resonances carried across the water to reach the worried men aboard the yawl, all of them fearing for their shipmates left behind in Byron's house, so vulnerable and seemingly abandoned, for that is how it had seemed in the desperate moment of their flight.

Friday 3rd March 1826   16:00   Surprise   off Oxia island

The day was fast fading as the frigate rocked gently at anchor between Oxia and the Scrofes sandbanks. 'How are you faring yourself, Mr Codrington?' asked Pat, approaching his lieutenant who was leaning on the rail, clutching a telescope and staring to the south-east.

'I confess that this waiting, with so many of our shipmates away, does not sit well with me, sir.'

'Nor with myself, far from it; a damnably uncomfortable feeling it is.'

'When will they return, sir?'

'I am minded that we will see them on the morrow, perhaps at the end of the day...' A hesitant note, 'Unless, that is, the Turks arrive to stand off Vasiladi.'

'And if they do?'

'Well, Macleod will doubtless shift only in the night hours and we must wait. It will serve no purpose were the barky to approach, save to alert the Turk...' Pat scowled, '... when he will doubtless come out from Patras. No, here we will wait.'

Saturday 4th March 1826   16:00   Anatoliko island

'I begin to wonder, is there any way for us to leave this place through the infernal shallows?' declared an exasperated Duncan.

'At least we were fortunate to escape the Messalonghi shore and the Turk guns,' said Jason, striving for something of minor consolation in the general despond aboard the yawl.

'Yes... after taking two days to do so and grounding five times... in the damn mud of this never-ending sea of reeds... for 'tis nae place for a seaman and a proper boat, that's sure.'

'Without Kladis we would never have reached here, I have no doubt of that.'

'Aye, that's the case, but can he get us out? He is ashore presently, gone to speak with the local fishermen; he has memories of a deeper channel, near the shoreline on the west side of the lagoon, but he isnae sure if it has become silted since he was last here, fishing. The mud, as he remarked, is shifting with the wash of the waves such that there is never any constant channel from month to month.'

'Let us hope that such as the western channel will be our best prospect for leaving this place; indeed, I pray that it is, but what of our shipmates... what of Ferguson and Marston... and the others in Messalonghi? How will that serve us to take them off?'

'Once we are able to gain the deeper water to the south, beyond the island of Dolmas, then we may use that same channel which we used to flee the beach, the one that Kladis is familiar with, to return to the town. We will ferry our shipmates and the wounded to Vasiladi and await the return of *Mathew Jelbert* to the island to take them off. I am minded that is our plan. We will close on the town's beach only in darkness. I venture we must make our way out of here, through the reeds and shallows, in the morning to be sure to gain the deeper lagoon waters... and then we will turn about at dusk.'

'But if the cutter is not returned or the Turk is still about Vasiladi... we have just our one boat. What are we to do?'

'If we cannot find *Mathew Jelbert*... with all our other boats... then here in Anatoliko is the only place to evacuate to... a few men at a time.' Duncan's hesitant voice could not conceal his own doubts, 'From here, our lads being armed, we may venture to send a party over the land to the west and so to the creek near Petala where we may hope to find the barky near that place.'

Sunday 5th March 1826 07:00 South-east of Oxia island

Pat stared into the emerging dawn sun, another red sky directly before the bow of *Surprise* as she moved slowly east, not the slightest of heel, the south-westerly breeze so feeble. Everyone aboard was attentive, alert and apprehensive; all wondered when and where the barky would sight *Mathew Jelbert.* Would the cutter be lying on the approach to Vasiladi and, if so, would the Turk fleet, lying at Patras, become alerted to their presence and chase out from that harbour? Pat did not know but, without the expected return of the cutter within a very few days, as he had discussed with Macleod in Argostoli and with Codrington whilst at anchor at Oxia, he had reluctantly discarded his plan to await his shipmates' return and had determined to investigate, at least as best he could.

'Will we close on Vasiladi, sir?' asked Mower, the two men standing near the helm.

'I confess I am in two minds there,' Pat frowned, 'I do not care to provoke the Turk fleet to come out from Patras if we are sighted, for such might well make worse the prospects for Macleod getting away with our people.'

'Indeed,' murmured Mower, hesitating to say more.

'On the other hand, doubtless the cutter would welcome sight of the barky, for she may be hiding behind one of the outlying islands from any Turk vessels. Wherever she may be it is a damn difficult place in which to navigate... for we possess no chart for the shallows.' Pat sighed, 'I hope that Greek fellow - *Kladis, was it?* - is worth his salt. He says he is greatly familiar with the lagoons... their shallows so difficult for any passage, as Macleod has already found out.' Another minute passing in reflection and he added, 'I venture we are making no better than three knots... If the wind does not drop then we will sight Vasiladi by noon, when we might hope that the situation will become clearer.'

Sunday 5th March 1826 14:00 the north lagoon

'Stuck again!' shouted Duncan, frustrated as the cutter shuddered and grounded to a halt once more, 'Damn this marsh to hell!'

'We have left Dolmas and much of the mudbank behind us,' Jason spoke in quieter voice, 'and that surely is good progress, is it not? Why, Kladis is minded that we are nearing deeper water... a cable or two more - *so he says* - and we shall gain the passage he is searching for.'

Duncan's exasperation being somewhat mollified by Jason's voice, he spoke in calmer tone, 'There is something to be grateful for in shifting at the pace of the slowest snail... and the gentlest of grounding.' He growled with seething discontent, 'We may hope she is not stuck fast. Lads! Lads, into the water, and I will cast the line once more. Let us see what can be done to haul her off whilst we yet have light enough to save our day.'

Four weary men climbed overboard to see if the yawl could be hauled off into the marginally deeper water in which she would float free. They waited patiently whilst Kladis gazed all about him, looking for some feature of significance, the slightest *aide memoire*, to find the channel he recalled fishing several years previously, reeds in abundance and stretching as far as the eye could see monopolising the waterscape. In an air of dismay Kladis climbed down to join those Surprises in the shallow water.

Birds all about the boat called out an avian cacophony: warblers, terns and herons all in abundance. 'Why, I venture Ferguson would greatly enjoy this place,' declared Jason, a black look from Duncan being his only response.

The line secured, Duncan called out, 'PULL! PULL!' But there was no movement; the yawl would not budge. 'WAIT! I will join you in the water.' Duncan climbed down with another scowl at Kladis.

'I will help too!' shouted Jason. Brief, sceptical looks from all aboard the small boat were hastily discarded as he also clambered out, the yawl rocking from side to side.

'On my shout,' declared Duncan, 'One, two, PULL!'

Sun. 5th March 1826 18:30   HMS Surprise   off the Scrofes

'I venture we are here for the night,' declared Pat in weary resignation, the frigate drifting in a near total calm since the wind had fallen away in the mid-morning, all on the quarterdeck listening carefully to glean their captain's intentions. 'At least the Turk cannot come out from Patras, and we must be grateful for that smallest of mercies.' He gazed through his telescope in the last vestiges of daylight, the sun a radiant yellow glow fast falling away to dip into the horizon astern; there was barely a ripple upon the sea surface and no vessels in sight in any direction. A slow hour passed with every Surprise on deck, men thronging the waist, a cluster all peering forward from the foc'sle, a score and more encroaching upon the sacred spaces of the quarterdeck, until the last of the twilight was finally gone. An inky blackness descended upon the scene, not the least glimmer of light from the moon. In better times it might have passed for total tranquillity, for not a sound disturbed the absolute quietude. The canvas hung limp from the yards, the braces were slack, and not the least ripple broke the mirror-like surface of the sea, yet every man was uneasy, unsettled. A deep-seated anxiety was common to all as they wondered what was happening, what might have happened, to their shipmates ashore in the tortured town and aboard the departed cutter.

'Let us hope we may see something more of the wind in the morning, sir,' said Mower, approaching his captain, leaning on the rail in solitary thought.

'Indeed, and it is that time of year when we might expect the *maestro* to begin to blow,' murmured Pat, 'I do so dearly wish for a stiff north-westerly.'

Sun. 5th March 1826   18:30   Askos Island in the lagoon

The weary men aboard the yawl had finally reached the visible edge of the shallows and rushes, and clearer water extended before them, stretching far to the south towards the visible outer islands of Schinias, Komma and Saint Sostis. A despairing Kladis's personal standing with them had been restored even as the light had finally faded away to absolute darkness, his seeming rehabilitation bestowing huge relief upon him. Both Duncan and Jason congratulated him most heartily on having brought the yawl at long last through the bewildering labyrinth of narrow passages between extensive mudbanks and endless reeds. The most careful inspection by a man perpetually wading in the water before the yawl had saved them from further grounding, but it had been slow and exceptionally tedious progress, no more than one knot gained for much of the time, often much less. And on many an occasion a time-consuming halt had been necessitated whilst the way forward had been scrupulously assessed.

'There is not the least light, no moon at all, and no compass do we possess to guide us!' declared Duncan gloomily, great exasperation plain in his voice, 'Hence I do not greatly care to shift further in these waters - *being so shallow* - with nothing to see... and not the least of wind to aid us.'

'You are exceedingly cross-grained today, Mr Macleod,' declared Jason in mild voice.

'Indeed,' Duncan sighed in weary recognition that, perhaps, his demeanour had long verged on intolerant, even rude, 'and you have my apologies... I am sorry. It has been a dire day, and that after two days of hauling out of the mud. Oh for a swift return to the Long Isle - *to Harris and Lewis* - and away from this festering swamp... away from this foul and worthless place.'

'Perhaps we must pause here for the night? Perhaps it is time for a modicum of supper... a biscuit or two, and a glass of something warming? It will lift the heart, cheer the soul... after these past few days, eh? What do you say, Mr Macleod?'

'Abel Jason, did I ever remark that you are a fine fellow... the finest?'

'Not to my best recall.'

'Then you will allow me to say it, I am much pleased to be accompanied by such a grand fellow as yourself, I am so; there, I have said it, and I beg you will remind me if that ever escapes my attention.'

'Thank you, it is most kind of you to say so.'

'There, all is said, and now I think we will look to the grog. Denzel, be a good fellow and cast the anchor. Mr Jason and I are minded we will remain here until we better see the lie of the land, the water depth particularly, in the dawn light.'

Monday 6th March 1826   07:00   Surprise   off the Scrofes

Pat had been standing on his quarterdeck long before the first glimmer of twilight lifted the eastern sky out of absolute darkness. The cloud blanket had separated in the early hours and the celestial panorama in the gaps, which he had long been studying, was fast fading; another emerging red dawn was throwing high that portent which seemed, to the fanciful mind, like a challenge cast down by angry Gods. Perhaps, Pat thought, it was heralding what he feared might prove to be a most daunting day, a number of outcomes all possible, some of them greatly unwelcome. The early morning air was cold and he shivered, feeling the chill of the returned wind, feeble that it was. As he felt his hair flickering about his face, he noted with disappointment that it was still the *grego* from the north-east, which was not greatly favourable, except for the Turks. It was still a weak breeze, so soon after the dawn, but he expected that it would strengthen as the day developed, as was the norm, the customary turn of events. Time passing imperceptibly, Pat stared aft at the gentle white wake; at least, he consoled himself, *Surprise* was shifting again, albeit exceedingly slowly and only by frequent tacking. With short boards she could once more make progress towards Vasiladi, but her pace would undoubtedly remain lamentably ponderous in the weak wind, perhaps two knots at best. 'Mr Mower, Mr Codrington,' he declared at last with a sigh, both his lieutenants appearing at his side to break his train of thought, 'Good morning to you both.'

'Good morning, sir,' Mower replied.

Codrington nodded, his face anxious, 'And what - *I beg to ask* - are your intentions, sir?'

Pat paused as the bell clanged *"ding-ding, ding-ding, ding-ding, ding"* in a louder than usual cacophony, or so it seemed; but, he wondered, perhaps it was simply his nerves being on edge, for he was very self-aware of the return of his anxiety. 'We will see how close we might approach to Vasiladi... and ask if the garrison has any news of the cutter or events in the town, of our lads most particularly.' He turned to stare all about the ship in every direction, the light remaining poor in a sky which was increasingly overcast, the cloud gaps closing. He searched for any sign of even the smallest vessel, but there was nothing to be seen. 'We will press on, Mr Codrington. East it will be, but we will hold as close to the islands as we can.'

'Aye aye, sir.'

Pat descended to the cabin, intent on a hasty breakfast before returning to his quarterdeck but, although Murphy delivered a particularly aromatic burgoo with his coffee, Pat could not eat it. In the meantime, he sipped the coffee, all the while turning over in his mind all conceivable possibilities for the missing cutter and his seemingly marooned men ashore. Murphy returned after twenty minutes to find the cold, congealed porridge, and he gazed intently upon his captain, Pat still engrossed in thought and oblivious to his presence. The steward stared, searching for the appropriate words to break the silence, wracking his brain for anything suitable, but nothing could he find, no word at all would come to mind.

'Murphy?' murmured Pat eventually, looking up to see his fellow countryman looking as despondent as he felt himself.

'Sorr... is there... is... can I get 'ee anything else... sorr?'

'Eh?'

'To eat... or... or would 'ee care for more coffee?'

'Oh... no thankee; no, I am not in the way for eating... I have no appetite, none at all... even coffee holds little appeal, but thankee all the same.'

'Well, I have a right grand bowl of coddle... 'tis warming on the stove... for my own dinner... and there be enough for two... good Irish coddle... and 'tis cooked with barley... enough for two hungry men there is.'

'And would you also have two pints of stout?' Pat smiled.

'No sorr,' Murphy brightened, 'but there is in my dunnage a half bottle of poteen... from my cousin's still... He lives in the Moycullen Bogs and the Excisemen ain't ever found it.'

'Murphy, I will gladly share your coddle later. Thank you kindly.' Pat made a conscious effort to find enthusiasm for his voice; 'It will be the grand treat of the world for dinner today, a memory of home, so it will, but allow me to say that it will have to await a later time in the day... and we may hope that is before the potatoes are ruined...' Pat smiled again, '... and then you and I will take a restorative drop of the poteen... I have no doubt that we will enjoy it together with great pleasure. Thankee again, old shipmate, but now I must go on deck.'

Four bells of the forenoon watch and Pat gazed at the island of Prokopanistos on the larboard bow. The wind had shifted to become more adverse, more easterly, and *Surprise*, on her starboard tack with Barton helming her as close to the wind as she would hold, was beginning to come about, to make her turn to go through the wind. Pat had, thus far, marvelled that the frigate had actually successfully completed her tacks, for the wind remained extremely weak, the ship scarcely moving. He concluded that it was both Barton's supreme skill at the wheel - for he had never encountered a better helmsman with so absolute a feel for the helm and the ship - together with the yards hard braced as far as they might be turned. Indeed, the bosun greatly feared for the truss-ropes and the cat-harpins; he had voiced his alarm aloud that the top-yards might be sprung loose and fall. Yet even with such extremes of bracing, the barky was managing only two knots.

'Would we be better served with longer tacks and the yards released to something more near normal?' Sampays pressed again with no little anxiety enduring in his voice.

'In the customary run of things, to be sure, that would be the case,' declared Pat, 'but the closer we hold to the islands, the less visible we are to any observer in the vicinity of Patras. I am, for sure, clutching at the smallest of straws here... not wishing to alert the Turk to our presence... and striving for an extra half-knot to gain Vasiladi as quickly as can be.' Pat looked up to the tops, listened to the customary creaking of the straining braces holding firm all the yards. It was a much more discordant, louder noise than usual. 'However, I venture we might follow your notion when we turn about.'

The bosun nodded, stared up towards the topyards, concern and reluctant acceptance plain in his face. 'I will climb aloft and see how the cat-harpins are faring,' he declared eventually.

'Very well, Mr Sampays,' Pat nodded, 'Here, take my glass and see what may be espied from the top.' His attention shifting to gaze once more towards Schinias island four miles distant and fine on the larboard bow, Pat computed the remaining passage to Vasiladi. It was a mere eight miles until the barky might make her anchorage once past Saint Sostis island; from there it was just one further mile to Vasiladi, a mile which the barky could not traverse as the water was too shallow, thus the boat would have to serve to gain the island. Yet *Surprise* would require at least another three hours at this exceedingly sedate pace.

Twenty minutes more had passed when an alarmed Sampays climbed down to the deck and hastened to Pat's side near the helm, 'Sir, with the glass, I believe I can see *Mathew Jelbert* off the island of Komma; I venture she is anchored.'

'Anything else?'

'Well sir, it is not sure... but I believe I could glimpse what might be the masts of the Turk fleet... coming out from Patras. Young Pennington, at the main-top, was first to see them and he asked my opinion for they are exceedingly difficult to make out, so distant and the light so poor.'

'Mr Mower,' cried Pat to his lieutenant standing near the bell, 'Please to climb aloft, up on high - *to the cross-trees* - and see what you might discern. We must be sure.'

'Very good, sir.' The young lieutenant hastened off. Another apprehensive twenty more minutes for all on deck and Mower scrambled down, his face exhibiting his anxiety, 'I beg to report 'tis true, sir; the cutter is anchored off Komma and there is a plentiful squadron bearing towards us, sailing out from Patras.'

'Damn!' exclaimed Pat, 'and they are blessed to have the wind with them, such as it is. Two hours longer on this course, and I venture it will be no greater time than that, and we will be amongst them. A curse on this day! That will not do! Mr Sampays, you may loosen the cat-harpins and turn back the yards, for we must turn about; we have no choice.'

The bosun looked relieved, nodded, and hurried away without a word to gather his topmen.

'Standby by to bring her about, Mr Codrington,' declared Pat with weary resignation, the inevitability of a retreat sitting ill with him. 'We will await Mr Sampays... and his efforts with the yards.'

'Hands to the braces!' bawled the lieutenant, a flurry of activity resulting all about the deck and the rigging, even as men aloft fought to loosen the cat-harpins whilst frantic efforts were also underway to pull the yards round to something more closely resembling their customary square rig. In the meantime, *Surprise* had slowed even further and was close to a complete stop.

A languorous hour passed until Turk mastheads were visible even from the deck, when Sampays reported, 'The yards are as well secured as ever, sir... and *Mathew Jelbert* has hauled up her anchor and is bearing towards us.'

'Very good,' declared Pat with relief in his voice, 'Mr Codrington, at least the barky is on her larboard tack... you may bring her round... to the south. Haul her round to starboard.'

'Aye aye, sir; Barton, hard a'starboard!'

At the helm Barton and his men hauled hard on the handles and the frigate answered, albeit it seemed reluctantly. Ten more minutes and *Surprise* had completed half her turn, her bow pointing south and frenzied activity continuing at the braces. The hulls of several Turk vessels were plain to see, a corvette and a frigate in the van, nearly a dozen more following, all their sails braced for the easterly wind and little more than three miles away. Pat, anxiety mixed with relief filling his mind, stared through his glass, 'Half an hour, no more, and they would have been upon us.' *Surprise* slowly gained speed, *Mathew Jelbert* astern and following. After a half-hour the Turk pursuers gave up their slow and half-hearted chase, turning about to tack back towards their fellows, all the ships closing on the tiny islet of Vasiladi and its small band of defenders. As Dalby rang eight bells at noon, Pat paced up and down his quarterdeck, deep in thought and pondering over what on earth he might do next, but not the least idea could he find.

Monday 6th March 1826   12:00   approaching Vasiladi

The yawl passed the island of Schinias, her slow but steady tacking continuing towards Komma. Saint Sostis was a distant mile to starboard and Vasiladi directly ahead, where they would find the channel north to Messalonghi which was well known to Kladis. 'Once we pass by Komma we will make for Vasiladi, go ashore there, and thence await the coming of darkness,' declared Duncan to all sitting close about him on the thwarts. Heads everywhere nodded in understanding, a general sense of relief abounding; they would soon be back with their shipmates ashore, preparing to take them off. No proximate noise of guns firing had been heard during the morning, which at least indicated that the Turk attack of four days earlier upon Vasiladi had ceased.

The tired men rowed on in determined fashion, their resolution firming as the deeper water channel's guardian island loomed large before them; but as their boat, so very low in the water, emerged from behind the rocky shield of Komma, which obstructed their view to the south, the Surprises were horrified to see, further to the south-east, an approaching Turk armada, a dozen ships strong and accompanied by what looked to be five heavy rafts in tow. Already one swiftly-sailing corvette had turned to race west, towards the yawl, perhaps intending to cut off any turn she might make towards the deeper water to the south so as to race away; for the waters immediately to the north side of the outer islands were generally too shallow for any vessel drawing more water than the flat-bottomed boats used by the local fishermen. Duncan realised immediately that the corvette might well be faster than the yawl if the small boat turned about, at least until she regained her best speed; worse, the yawl would be dangerously in range of the Turk's guns, certainly her bow chasers, if she turned away to the south-west, for the Turk would soon be able to open fire and might even bring her broadside to bear. 'On! On to Vasiladi!' he shouted. 'We will gain the shallow channel where the Turk cannot follow us.'

Holding close to the wind, Duncan bit his lip as the yawl made precious headway towards the sanctuary of Vasiladi, just three cables to go to gain the island and safety. He joined his men at the oars and all rowed like men possessed, swift, rhythmical, all their arm and leg muscles bulging, their lungs on fire with fast and frantic breathing, every man feeling near fit to burst. Two cables remaining to go, just a few minutes more, and the corvette opened a distant fire from east of Saint Sostis, a score of splashes rising in the waters all about the yawl, several shots ricocheting to splash twice.

'PULL!' screamed Duncan, 'PULL!' Just one final cable to go to reach the island, and then came disaster, a ricocheting ball flew up and smashed broadside on into the yawl, the boat swiftly breaking apart into bow and stern sections, spilling everyone into the water. Fortunately, no man appeared to be injured as the ball was spent and the boat hull absorbed what was left of its energy in splitting asunder. A few anxious seconds and all emerged coughing and spitting swallowed water. Duncan made a swift head count to confirm all were present. Thankfully all could hold their head above the surface in the shallows, some of them being immersed to waist height, others to their shoulders. 'ON! HURRY! TO THE ISLAND! he shouted, pointing, and the soaked men struggled on through the water. Fifteen minutes later the weary Surprises scrambled ashore on the low outcrop which was Vasiladi island, helpful hands hastening to their aid to pull them up out of the water, flasks of wine offered to cleanse salty palates and a little of precious freshwater in terracotta mugs for sore eyes.

Their breathing rate recovering, the Surprises leaned back in their extreme fatigue to bask in the sun and allow some degree of drying of their clothing, all of them gazing intently at the corvette anchored a half-mile distant, for she could approach no closer. Jason hastened to inspect every man physically in their exhaustion even as Duncan spoke with each in turn, both men relieved that all their shipmates had survived without injury. Much to the surprise of all the yawl survivors, both Timmins and Green were with the Greeks on the island. The gunner explained that he had arrived to train the Greek gunners at the request of Captain Giachomouzzi.

Two more hours passed until the sun was hanging low in the western sky when the remainder of the Turk squadron arrived and anchored, a powerful armada only a mile south of Vasiladi, one which did not bode well in the least for the island's few defenders. The Surprises, their yawl destroyed, water for miles all about them, gazed upon the warships with stark dismay. Duncan observed five rafts with the Turk fleet. They were certainly a most uncomfortable enemy resource, for with them they could go into the shallowest waters such as those all around their island refuge. For how long might his shipmates enjoy its tentative safety? When would the Turks approach to attack them? The spirits of everyone sank to new depths.

Chapter Ten

Thursday 9th March 1826 07:00 Vasiladi island

The sun rose swiftly in the eastern sky over the mainland as the tiny Greek garrison and the Surprises, every man being long awake and gripped by an all-consuming anxiety, stared all about the island in every direction. From the north came the sounds of the incessant bombardment of Messalonghi which had resumed shortly after the dawn and which continued without let up, the distant heavy guns announcing Ibrahim's determined intentions as they boomed out their inexorable barrage. At the rocky water's edge, Duncan, standing with the Greek garrison commander, Spiros Petaloudis, and the Italian artilleryman, Captain Giachomouzzi, stared with trepidation towards the south where, emerging from amidst the large Turk fleet which was anchored little more than a mile away, came the approach of the five large rafts, each one being towed by two small sailing craft.

'I venture I see heavy artillery,' Duncan offered eventually to his companions with something more than an inkling of his despondence plainly discernible in his voice, 'Aye, big guns are aboard those rafts.' After another few seconds staring, a deep sigh was forthcoming, one which he did not trouble to conceal; 'Are you prepared, gentlemen?' he asked with a sinking feeling.

'The closer they come the better,' declared the veteran, Giachomouzzi, striving to lift the glaring dismay on faces all about him. 'I have fourteen guns awaiting any attack.' Duncan blinked but said nothing in reply; indeed, the Italian's words seemed to have fallen generally on stony ground, the glum expressions all around unchanging.

The next few hours passed by in silent wonder and grave apprehension for all the island defenders, every man striving to suppress the unwelcome grip of rising fear whilst enduring the doubt and uncertainty about their immediate prospects. Indeed, all considered that their very survival was unlikely, and Giachomouzzi's confidence, if it was in fact real, was not shared by anyone else. Time moved interminably slowly, the sun rising ever higher as the morning progressed, the towing praams and their raft charges closing on Vasiladi until, the island comfortably within the range of the floating Turk heavy guns, one aboard each of the rafts, the Turk crews anchored in the shallow water somewhere between a quarter and a half mile off.

With weary resignation filling his mind, Duncan studied the rafts with his telescope and, with a rising feeling of gloom, reckoned them to be thirty-six pounders: extremely heavy guns indeed; massively powerful and undoubtedly highly destructive. Giachomouzzi's guns could offer no substantive response to such titans.

Several more hours of preparation passed by with the continuing Turk preparations on the five rafts perfectly visible, four anchor cables tensioned for each one, and the guns were turned to aim at Vasiladi island. A huge volume of powder and shot was very visibly delivered by a myriad small boats until it was plain that firing was imminent. Every defender on the island, every man increasingly affrighted, stared in bleak fascination as the sun reached its zenith. Gradually the air temperature had warmed all through the morning and, as noon passed, the five raft-borne heavy guns appeared to be finally loaded and standing ready to fire, their gunners visibly awaiting the order to do so. At last, with the sun almost an hour into its descent, the signal was given and the Turks began their long-awaited bombardment of the tiny outcrop, the early afternoon start offering them plentiful daylight hours in which to crush the defenders' morale. Flames and smoke erupted from the rafts before the whistle of shot flashing by all about the island signalled the Turk ranging shots, soon followed by the thud and skip of those cannon balls which did not bury themselves into the sandy soil smacking and bouncing across the rocky island landscape.

'Heads down, lads!' shouted Duncan. He and all the Surprises had long reconciled themselves to being impotent targets, although Turk gunners were never reckoned to be greatly proficient; indeed, these particular artillerymen were slow in reloading their large calibre guns and their shots were generally ineffectual, being solid shot and not explosive. The island, low and flat as it was, offered no prominent target for even the most skilful of gunners save for one small stone building, a tiny chapel, being the Greek powder store.

From the two brass eighteen-pounders, the best guns which the Greeks possessed, a few shots were ventured from time to time without success until eventually the Greeks gave up, for the Turk rafts remained out of effective range. The Surprises and the Greeks, in reluctant acknowledgment of having no means of reply, reconciled themselves to huddling down behind the stone outcrops as the hours passed under the continuing barrage, time barely creeping by. Fortunately, the bombardment was without casualties and, as the afternoon neared its end, the sun low in the western sky, the defenders' apprehension eased. They had seen only a few men wounded by flying debris and, ultimately, there settled upon the Greeks and the Surprises a dawning realisation that the Turk would not gain the island solely by their intimidating guns and heavy bombardment. This conclusion was followed by much conjecture, offered by men hiding in hollows and behind rocky outcrops, as to what might ultimately follow the barrage, until - as the early evening arrived - it came as a great relief when the Turk gunners ceased fire. A blessed silence, which seemed utterly incongruous after the loud clamour of the great guns, hung heavily over the still waters of the surrounding lagoon, and soon thereafter the diffuse, yellow light of the sunset settled upon the island. A most subdued and dim dusk swiftly followed, until eventually a chill returned as the last vestiges of twilight faded away, the cold evening air bestowing an enveloping finality to the day as it ceded to an utterly silent darkness, not even the smallest ripple being audible at the shore.

Duncan, nervous about the detached isolation of his shipmates, strived to dampen his own enduring fears as the Surprises coalesced around him in an anxious hubbub of review and speculation. He sought to speak in a measured voice, to project a confidence which he did not feel at all, 'Plainly the Turk is intending to overrun this island... and, whilst I doubt he will succeed - *as we have seen plain today* - by simply firing upon us with his heavy guns, I venture we must expect to see his soldiers on the morrow... Yes, I am minded that we must reckon on an attempt at a landing, and perhaps soon after the dawn light.' He looked to the two men who had landed on the island before them, 'Well, Mr Timmins, how do we stand? I speak of the Greeks and their guns. You have been here for some little time to help them.'

Timmins paused momentarily, looked at his shipmates, their faces frozen in apprehensive stares. 'The Turks may safely disembark from their approaching boats into the water whilst some distance from the island, sir, for the water depth thereabouts is - *as you found to your own salvation* - shallow enough to wade whilst keeping musket powder held high and dry. Sure, when the Turk invaders fall in range of the lighter Greek guns many will be struck down... but the Turks will be able to come at us from all sides... and, I regret to say, we do not have enough men to attend all the guns.'

'How well are the Greek gunners prepared, Mr Timmins? I see they have a dozen iron twelve-pounders as well as the two brass pieces, but for how long will they have powder and shot enough to serve our defence?'

'Oh, there is plenty of both, sir. I have made the acquaintance of young Papalouka, he is the son of Petaloudis and is serving as powder monkey in the magazine over there in that chapel. He showed me the stores.'

'That, at least, is a help... and the gunners?'

'I regret to say that they possess but little skill and experience with their pieces, sir; they are artisan workers... from Messalonghi, and there are so few of them - *a mere thirty-four men* - that it is not nearly enough to serve fourteen guns... whilst with the same hands they must also labour to fetch powder and shot... '

'Oh,' murmured Duncan in low voice, the faces of all present looking glum, 'That does nae bode well.'

'But,' the gunner's face brightened a little, 'there is at least a considerable quantity of grapeshot... since I have been showing them how to make up makeshift munitions using stones gathered on the island... for there is a want of metal for such.'

'That will do grave damage to men in the water,' Duncan grimaced at the horrible thought, 'but I venture that it will not halt determined men coming on from all around the island.'

'No sir,' Timmins could not conceal his deeply pessimistic conclusion, 'I have urged Giachomouzzi to concentrate his few men on serving a lesser number of guns, and thankfully he is in accord. I am afraid, sir, there lies our weakness - *the grave want of men*. There are another twenty-seven Greeks remaining who are not tasked with serving the guns in any way... They have not the least familiarity with them, and they stand ready to fire muskets upon any invaders who near the beach. We must hope that it is not a great multitude of attackers... *when they come*.'

A general sense of despond was exhibited on the faces of all present during the brief glimmers of moonlight between successive drifting clouds. It seemed as if the deep uncertainty was emphasised by the merest gentle zephyr of a breeze which disturbed the eerie silence following Timmins' bleak conclusion, for no questions were offered after his gloomy prognosis and nothing further was said by anyone. The overcast thickened as the Surprises sat in miserable reflection. The moon, increasingly, could only rarely be perceived below the dense cloud which had been blowing in from the western skies during the dusk, and eventually there was no moonlight at all, not the slightest glimmer from the tiniest sliver of the new moon. Neither was even the smallest of fires visible anywhere, near and far, to break the absolute blackness, even in distant Messalonghi town. The hungry group of Surprises, with nothing to eat, sat in the silence of their private thoughts for an hour, no man able to perceive his fellows other than as an indistinct presence. Time passed in discomfort, all increasingly thirsty, the wine all consumed. 'Beg pardon, sir...' All looked to the master gunner as he spoke up in little more than a whisper, 'What will we do, sir... possessing no boats... if the island looks likely to be overwhelmed in the morning? What will we do?'

Thursday 9th March 1826   19:30   Surprise   Oxia Island

'What will we do, sir, on the morrow?' asked Codrington, the heartfelt anxiety in his voice plain to hear. Pat, Mower and Prosser were all standing with him at the taffrail, the hour pregnant with uncertainty, the whole day having been the greatest test of patience. No news had been received from either the shore party or the cutter, for *Mathew Jelbert* had been lost from sight after the barky had fled three days ago, nothing at all having been heard from her since. An uncomfortable, tense apprehension had followed, rising generally throughout the ship as she lay at anchor off the south coast of Oxia, rolling gently on the smallest of swell. The sun's farewell glow, obscured all afternoon behind increasing cloud, had been wholly lost into the distant horizon an hour earlier, but no one of the small gathering cared to shift from the quarterdeck, the merest scrap of a sense of mutual comfort found in their assembly, no man wishing to depart for the prospect of a little more warmth below deck even as the air became increasingly chill in the weak breeze.

'We wait,' said Pat with a sigh, his sharp voice unfamiliar and carrying the angst of an all-consuming sense of frustration and impotence. 'Mr Macleod with *Mathew Jelbert* is tasked to hide from the Turk, and I venture the cutter is likely at anchor to the west of Prokopanistos, from where he waits for his moment to send the boats into the lagoon and so to Messalonghi. We - *I greatly regret* - can do nothing more, *nothing*; the Turk will espy us as soon as we shift closer.' He sighed, 'It sits ill with me... but there is no choice... none at all; we must remain here... and wait for Macleod.'

'For how long, sir? I beg your pardon,' Codrington pressed Pat as Mower and Prosser stared at his obvious discomfort.

Pat choked back his impatient rebuke, offered no reply save an icy stare; in truth he was bereft of the slightest notion. *Surprise* possessed only one boat, the tiniest of such, and plainly she could not enter the shallow lagoon waters herself; neither would it serve the least purpose to excite the interest of the Turk squadron which, Pat presumed, remained anchored in the approach to Vasiladi. He reiterated his gloomy conclusion, 'Gentlemen, only Macleod and the cutter can evacuate our shipmates. We can do nothing... nothing at all, it greatly pains me to say.'

Friday 10th March   1826   10:00   Vasiladi island

'Here comes Johnny Turk, sir!' shouted Denzel to Duncan, frantically waving his arm and pointing to the north, towards the distant salt pans of the far side of the lagoon. All the Surprises were, to a man, extremely hungry. No breakfast was available for nothing at all remained on the island to eat. Indeed, all were also struggling with thirst as the potable water was all but finished. In their discomfort and anxiety, they had waited since the beginnings of twilight with patient resignation for what they all knew was surely coming. A multitude of tired, red eyes stared to follow Denzel's hand. The bloody conflict that would spell the end for the island and its defenders was visibly approaching in the form of the oncoming fleet of forty praams, all bearing for the west side of the island. Duncan, with his glass, counted each one filled with thirty uniformed musketeers: Arabs, recognisably Egyptians in their fez caps, men in Ibrahim's service. At the prow of each of the shallow-draught, barge-like boats was a small gun, perhaps a two-pounder; it was nothing that greatly perturbed any of the island defenders, for they had endured the barrage of much heavier guns during the previous afternoon, but the musketeers, some twelve hundred of them, would swiftly overrun the tiny island if they succeeded in getting close and coming ashore.

'They are coming from the salt flats at Aspri Aliki,' declared Kladis to Duncan; 'Those boats have been laid up there, rotting, since Youssef Pasha ceded command to Ibrahim and departed. The Egyptian has ordered their keels removed in order that they might better traverse the lagoon shallows, and their masts too are gone so that more soldiers can be aboard, men without sailing skills who might simply paddle.'

'How do you know this, pray tell?' asked Duncan, staring at the Greek.

'Oh, everything is known in Messalonghi. The Albanian mercenaries of Ibrahim and his Greek slaves fraternise at night with their Messalonghi relatives who leave the walls, all seeking food; there is a deal of trading going on every night, and no secrets between the two sides.'

The Surprises stared at the approaching armada and wracked their brains: how could they be stopped? Each praam was a tiny target for the Greek guns, exceedingly difficult to hit with solid shot, even at close range; only grape would serve their desperate purpose. They waited patiently as minutes ticked by, every defender staring at the Egyptians' progress in abject fascination, watching, wondering, thinking, worrying. All the time Giachomouzzi, experienced artilleryman that he was, resisted the many loud, persistent and shrieking pleas from his Greek gunners to open fire. At last, when the oncoming praams were no more than two hundred yards away, he finally swung his arm down and screamed 'FIRE!' The two best guns the Greeks possessed, the brass eighteen-pounders, roared loudly and kicked backwards in brutal recoil as they spat orange flame and a shower of grapeshot towards the nearest of the oncoming Egyptians' boats. The brutal hail of metal flensed the first two of them entirely bare of men; two score and more much-lacerated bodies were smashed over the praams' sides into the lagoon, a chorus of shrieks of agony erupting from the grievously wounded men. In their severe difficulties and struggling to rise from the water, many of them utterly incapable of helping themselves to do so, they were drowning despite the shallow depth. Loud shouts of encouragement rose up immediately from the Egyptian officers on the adjacent, unscathed boats, vociferously urging their men on. The men in the boats redoubled their efforts and rowed with furious application.

'FIRE!' the Italian screamed again, and the nearest half-dozen of the twelve-pounders roared in violent response, a multitude more of Egyptians in another four barges smashed and hurled into the water by the furious shower of grapeshot. Yet still the Egyptians doggedly came on, paddling frantically, until six more of their boats were struck in rapid succession by the unwavering hurricane of Greek fire, when many others of the praams began to veer away, diverging to left and right, shifting from the most direct track to the beach. From others the affrighted musketeers abandoned their boats entirely by leaping into the water to seek what refuge it might offer, crouching down so that only their heads were above water, to offer only the smallest target that they might present, no consideration afforded to keeping their musket or powder dry in their frenetic haste. 'ON! ON!' screamed the Egyptian officers, brandishing swords high in threatening fashion behind wavering men in the water.

Hundreds of the musketeers waded on until they were just fifty yards off the shore when the Greek guns fired again. A furious blizzard of stone and metal inflicted the most dreadful losses on the unfortunate Egyptians. Men everywhere fell back, dead and dying, their eyes blinded, their faces ripped and torn away; scores of severely wounded men were unable to stand upright and the water surface swiftly became covered with floating detritus of all kinds.

Duncan stared in abject horror; in his cursory calculation, the blood of three or even four hundred dead, dying and wounded men was staining the immediate lagoon waters red, yet five hundred more still struggled on through the shallows, nearing the shoreline. Increasingly, as they got closer, they were less immersed, the water reaching only to their waists. On they came, with fear, resolution and fortitude, spurred on by their officers, wading interminably slowly but inexorably closer towards the Greek guns whose attendants frantically raced to reload.

A dozen or more of the Egyptians' boats with another three hundred men had shied off to left and right, their frenzied occupants paddling desperately away from the direct line of fire of the Greek gunners. As the Surprises watched, the reloaded Greek guns roared again just as the first of the Egyptians began to wade ashore, a ferocious typhoon of death smashing into the fragile and unprotected soft flesh of exhausted victims, striking down panic-stricken men who were grateful to escape the water, but who, in so doing, were exposing themselves to the most dreadful danger as they scrambled up, unprotected, onto the rocky foreshore. Scores of soaked and bedraggled musketeers were struck down by the final blaze of grapeshot from the Greek guns, and hundreds more of Egyptians went to ground. Yet on the fringes of the arc of fire of the guns a hundred and more musketeers had also gained the shore, and they rushed forward towards the few of their opponents who were the Greek gunners, all of whom turned to stare in wide-eyed horror at the onrushing tide of sure and bloody retribution.

In that instant there was a loud explosion from behind the Greek guns, and four men who were carrying powder charges from the magazine were all thrown to the ground in the blast, all much burned and severely injured. Jason, horrified, hurried towards them, intending to help. Duncan, barely controlling his own rising panic and his mind in a racing frenzy, stared all about him in bleak assessment: two dozen Greeks with muskets had not the least chance of driving off hundreds of bloodthirsty Egyptians, enraged men who had seen waves of their comrades shot down in scores, hordes of their fellows mutilated and dying in the water all about them. Here came hundreds more angry men who would be thirsting for revenge, for Greek blood. The defenders realised in an instant that the game was up, and a most rapid flight was the only choice other than inevitable death, but to where? Water of unknown depth stretched for miles in every direction all around the island; if they did not all die on Egyptian bayonets in the next few frenzied minutes then drowning seemed to be the only other prospect. Duncan looked at his shipmates, all clustered close to his side, unconcealed terror in all their wide eyes.

'BACK! BACK!' screamed a frantic Spiros Petaloudis who was already running. The Greek leader was rushing to see if his son had escaped the detonation of the powder magazine in the tiny chapel. Nine dead bodies lay about the burned ruin, all the powder exploded. At the Greek guns, panicked men dropped ramrods, sponges, powder cartridges and shot, and every man turned and ran in terror and panic. From the ground positions of the few defending Greek musketeers, men scrambled to their feet to follow, seconds only passing before every Greek was running away from the oncoming tidal wave of steel, all desperately hastening to escape the Egyptians and their flashing bayonets.

Duncan rose up from behind the rock which had afforded him shelter, and he shouted to the handful of Surprises, 'UP LADS! UP! AWAY! RUN! RUN!' No encouragement was needed in the least and they ran at full pelt to follow the leading Greeks, Jason being dragged away from his patients by Denzel and Mason, leaving the unfortunate four wounded men abandoned.

One minute of running, two minutes, and the leading Greeks splashed into the water on the south-east side of the island, wading out as fast as they could go. Duncan and the Surprises followed, pushing determinedly against the rising height of the water as they left the warm shallows twenty-five yards behind and pressed on towards the greater depths, past ripples at knee height at fifty yards, on beyond waist depth wavelets, further into deep water at a hundred yards out. A cold wash lapped at violently panting chests, splashing its salt spray against breathless faces gasping for air, their frantic breathing becoming difficult; yet behind them was silence. Seemingly no Egyptian possessed dry powder to fire at them, and none of the exhausted Arab musketeers cared to enter the water again in pursuit; instead, the shattered Egyptians looked to assist and rescue their wounded compatriots still struggling in the water to make land.

Four hundred yards out, Duncan and all the Surprises halted, the water lapping at their chests and shoulders. They gasped for air, their racing breathing slowing to a more normal rhythm, a modicum of relief returning for some. Many others were in difficulties, the shorter men having swallowed much seawater. Jason, in particular, was struggling and required constant assistance. The purser was, relative to his shipmates, an older man of almost sixty years of age. His frantic exertions had taken a severe toll on him, from which he could not immediately recover. He could not speak, and he was supported to keep his head out of the water by Denzel and Mason, both of whom were also visibly tiring with the weight of their burden. 'Here, Nance, to me!' shouted Duncan, 'We will help Mr Jason. Denzel, Mason, rest! Take your ease for a minute or two.'

All the Surprises looked back with a desperate fear of enemy followers, wondering whether those remaining boats which had escaped the Greek firing unscathed might, even now, be coming after them to seek retribution for the huge numbers of Egyptian casualties; for it had been, literally, a bloodbath; the lagoon waters had visibly turned red as men died in hundreds in the shallows. Duncan, still gasping for breath, turned to the accompanying Greek, Kladis, and pointed to the leaders of the exodus, a hundred yards and more in front; alarmingly only the heads of most and the shoulders of a few more were visible. 'Where are these men heading?'

'Tourlida island... it is a mile and a half distant from Vasiladi... perhaps a little further...' The Greek struggled to breathe as he spoke, '... but the water depth will allow of wading to it... on the mud.' Kladis shivered; the insidious chill of the water was beginning to overtake him.

Duncan nodded his understanding, a tiny vestige of hope coming to his mind. 'Keep going, lads!' he shouted to the Surprises waiting all about him, even as he still gasped for air himself. 'On! On! Follow the Greeks!' He pulled a silent and ashen-faced Jason forward with Nance helping, and the trio staggered on, struggling, whilst trying to disregard the increasingly cold sensation beginning to set in, their arms and legs losing warmth and some small degree of feeling.

A few yards further on and the first bodies of drowned Greeks became apparent to the eye, those men who had succumbed to the shock of the cold temperature. They were lifeless and floating, having never had any prospect of help for the long trek across the mud and through the greater depths. Every one of their fellows was already severely burdened in holding himself upright whilst struggling to keep going through the water. Duncan bit his lip and strived to ignore the fears flooding his mind, for all he could see before him was more water, an infinite expanse of it stretching away towards a distant haze of low mountains on the eastern skyline, nothing of a visible sanctuary before him even as he focused once more on those Greeks who were ten, twenty and fifty yards in front of him, just their heads and shoulders protruding above the surface. Was that a low island beyond them? Was that Tourlida? Could they really reach it? The chill was beginning to overtake him and his body shook violently once more. He waved his arm to encourage his men and he staggered on, all words beyond him in the desperate struggle - Nance still helping - to hold Jason's head above the water.

Friday 10th March   1826   17:30   *off Prokopanistos*

As the last hour of the afternoon approached and in the weak light of the low sun, Pat and his four men in *Surprise's* solitary tiny boat hauled alongside *Mathew Jelbert*, still anchored with a view to concealment off the west coast of the outlying island of Prokopanistos. All were hungry and weary after the best part of a day's tacking against a feeble easterly wind, sustained rowing necessary to maintain progress, but they were hauled up the side by welcoming arms and so to the cutter's deck, a fractious Pat invited by Reeve to the cabin.

'I see you have four crew aboard, Mr Reeve, but where is everyone else?' Pat pressed immediately. 'Where is Mr Macleod?' he asked in irritable voice.

'With his men, all departed in the yawl soon after first light on Monday, sir. They were bound for Vasiladi and thence to Messolonghi...'

'On Monday? Monday! But that is four days gone!'

'Yes, sir... to find out the situation within the town, to seek out Doctor Ferguson and Mr Pickering,' replied Reeve as if he could not quite believe himself that so much time had elapsed.

'Four days on... four days! Is there no word at all from them of our shipmates ashore, anything, the least word?'

'No news, nothing at all have we heard...' Reeve was plainly dismayed himself. 'Not a word from anywhere... no note from anyone... have we received. There are no longer any fishermen in these waters to speak with; indeed, even the fish have deserted the lagoon since the bombardment of Messalonghi began...'

'But what of Macleod? What of his intentions? What were his orders for you?'

'Mr Macleod made it plain: we are to await his return... or at least his message... and not to shift from this place unless the Turk comes along. You will see we have no sail aloft, the better to keep out of the attention of any Turk scouts.' An anxious Reeve continued, sensing Pat's tense vexation, 'You have observed that I have but four men after Mr Macleod left with the yawl, and that is barely enough crew to get out of this place if the Turk appears. I also have wounded Greeks below, patients of Dr Ferguson.'

'Very well,' murmured Pat, thinking hard.

'I have not received as much as the briefest note from Mr Pickering or Doctor Ferguson in Messalonghi... which might have given us some notion of what to do... but I suppose they are not aware we are here if... if Macleod has not... has not reached the town.'

'Has anything come to your attention at all?' Pat, mollified by Reeve's explanation for his inactivity with the cutter, continued in milder voice, 'Have you remarked any movement of Turk vessels and the like whilst tied up here... the slightest thing?'

'The bombardment of Messalonghi continues in every daylight hour, there is not the slightest let up... and - *I regret to say* - Vasiladi has fallen today... Hocking and Rowe observed the battle from one of our boats when they rowed to Schinias this morning to investigate the firing. They have returned only a half-hour ago. The way to the town by sea is now barred, save for all but the smallest of boat... and that making passage only at night across the lagoon.'

'That is what I am minded to do,' declared Pat. 'We will try for the town after dusk. There is a quarter of a moon to illuminate our way, and we will hope that - *with this cloud* - this will be insufficient for the Turk to see us making the crossing. It is two and a half leagues... seven and a half miles; I venture that will take three to four hours rowing... *if we hoist no sail.*'

'That is a most admirable notion,' said Reeve, his voice exhibiting his own relief at the prospect of activity. 'I will ask my lads to exchange with yours... fresh strength for the pull.'

'If we are fortunate, we will return before the dawn,' said Pat in grim voice, not caring to offer any thoughts on the alternative.

Friday 10th March   1826   17:30   Tourlida island

'I can go no further,' whispered a visibly spent Jason, his body shaking with tremors that even his two shipmates could feel as they hauled him out of the water and set him down on the stony strand of the tiny island. All the Greeks and the Surprises were soaked, dog-tired and chilled to the bone after three hours of wading, the water on several fearful occasions reaching up to their chins, their heads held high and tilted back to keep mouth and nose clear. Only the absence of any alternative had driven them on, despite their mind-consuming fear of imminent drowning. Their bodies were increasingly numbed, all feeling lost in fingers, hands, arms, legs, feet and toes. A dozen of Greek fishermen who had been watching the attack on Vasiladi all day from their huts at the waterside, attracted by the clamour of shouts from the dozens of refugees nearing the shore, had waded out to help the shattered, stumbling arrivals, men in the final stage of exhaustion. Jason plainly being in worst shape of all, he was carried without ceremony and, at the urging of his shipmates, in rapid haste into one of the huts where he was stripped bare of all his sodden clothing before being rubbed down and wrapped in blankets. A tiny fire was lit to restore some warmth to his unfeeling body, a tot of fiery arak pressed upon his lips, even as his unseeing eyes closed. He had not even the strength to drink it, and he fell asleep immediately on a low cot, a concerned Mason in attendance. All the escapees, Surprises and Greeks, crowded in to three of the primitive abodes to gain a little warmth.

'It is two miles more to Messalonghi,' declared Kladis to the huddled, shivering Surprises. 'There is no food here, even the fishermen are hungry; and they are affrighted that if we stay here then the Turks will sight our gathering in the morning light... and will land men from their ships out there, a mile to the south-west.'

Duncan stared at the Greek with a look of profound dismay; he allowed his eyes to range across the immediate few of his Surprise shipmates, his gaze roving further afield to scrutinise the exhausted men of the escaped Greek garrison. 'Two miles more, you say... That is a greater distance than we have struggled from Vasiladi.' With his voice sinking into audible despond, he offered his reluctant conclusion in a whisper: 'I doubt there is many a man here who will manage such a trial, three hours longer in that cold water, I include myself; certainly, there are men who, I am sure, will not.'

Kladis nodded, his own face registering his sympathy with Duncan's words. He brightened a little as he spoke up, 'It will be less of a tribulation, I do assure you, because it is shallower water... and there are many tiny islets along the way, as you would remark in the light of day. These fishermen of Tourlida have said they will guide us... and it is better to leave in the dark of night and to struggle on... on to Messalonghi... rather than be captured or... *or killed* in the morning light.'

'Aye, I havnae doubt of that,' murmured Duncan, wondering if he himself was equal to the task, for his own strength was gone and he shivered still despite wringing the water from his clothes.

'We must depart after an hour or two of rest...' Kladis persevered, '... after the dying of the sun when the Turks atop those ships will be less likely to see us. I would not care to wait longer in case any might come ashore to search for us, for our escape from Vasiladi will surely have been seen by the Turk admiral. Thankfully, there seems to be enough of the moon to light our way, for the clouds are thinning.'

Duncan simply stared with blank expression, speechless; the prospect of returning to the chill of the water for another two miles of wading was much more than his mind could embrace.

Friday 10th March   1826   19:00   *off Prokopanistos*

The tiny boat, towing six more on three lines, pulled away from the cutter as almost complete darkness succeeded the final weak light of the gloaming, the intimidating blackness of the lagoon only slightly ameliorated by the thin waxing crescent of the new moon. 'Pull, lads!' Pat could not resist the shouted incentive, his concern for his shipmates ashore all-consuming and leaving him in a boiling, insatiable fire of anxiety, far greater than the unrelenting tension he had felt in recent weeks. The day's easterly wind had fallen away to a benevolent flat calm, only the occasional zephyr a brief reminder of it, hence the sail was of no use at all, but the Surprises rowed on determinedly, all persons studiously avoiding the least mention of all potentially calamitous eventualities, their mutual accord for silence broken only by the splash of oars as they pressed on for the first mile, time passing and direction found in Pat's constant study of the bright display of stars. After an hour and a half, all in the boat discerned with dismay the thinnest of layers of water vapour rising from the still waters. Within mere minutes the grey fog began to visibly thicken and the rising murk shrouded any prospect of a more distant view of their destination.

Friday 10th March 1826 19:30 *Tourlida island*

'Jason is in no fit state to return to the water,' declared Duncan as Kladis urged the Surprises to rise up from their exhausted torpor to accompany the departing Greeks. 'I will stay here with him until he gathers his strength.'

'I will stay with 'ee, sir,' declared Denzel.

'As will I,' Mason spoke up.

'Beg pardon, sir,' Nance nodded as he stepped forward from where he had been crouched near the small fire, 'I will be with 'ee and Mr Jason.'

'I am a'staying with 'ee, sir,' said Penberthy.

'Lads,' a greatly humbled Duncan stared at his four shipmates as he struggled for his words, seconds passing before he spoke: 'I thank you all, I do... aye, and with all my heart, but this is nae place to stay, the Turk a mile away and with a plenty of boats and men to search this place in the coming of daylight. I fear he surely will.' There was no reply or movement from anyone and Duncan tried again: 'I beg you will all leave... I ask that you all go with Kladis and the Greeks... Leave, I beg you will... Go to safety in the town.'

Friday 10th March 1826 21:30 *within the lagoon*

The fog had continued to rise off the sea surface as Pat and his four men rowed on. He estimated that they were about a half-mile west of Vasiladi. He had not cared to take a more northerly and evasive course for Messalonghi, conscious of both the uncharted shallows and the shortage of time, and he feared that daylight might find them very visible as they sought to return to *Mathew Jelbert*. In any event it was, in the dense blanket of grey fog which lay all about them, exceedingly difficult, indeed nigh on impossible, to be sure exactly where they were. He hoped that the tangible wind had stayed as the easterly of earlier in the day, weak as it was, for that was a little help in holding to their bearing for the town.

'D'ye hear that, sir?' Hocking ceased rowing, the other three oarsmen likewise, and the boat drifted to a halt, everyone listening and looking all about them.

From the north and east, in the proximate direction of the boat's course, came the murmur of voices, the creak of ship's rigging and the small splash of the slowest wash alongside the hull of a vessel, all being sounds most familiar to the Surprises.

'Quiet, lads,' whispered Pat. A minute passed, Pat staring forwards into the murk, and for a fleeting few seconds he saw three corvettes as indistinct images, which were astride their intended course. He put his finger to his lips, 'Ssshhh... Back-water the oars, gently does it... *not a word...* I am minded that we must have drifted some way south of our bearing; indeed, we must already be in the deepwater channel for the town, that one about Vasiladi; gently now, we must shift away from this place without a sound.'

The small boat reversed course, the men pushing on the oars to back-water. With a deal of difficulty, they hauled on the lines of the boats to pull them aside before they might become entangled. Eventually, stressful minutes passing, their towed charges were once more following, astern of the prow, and the Surprises resumed their silent rowing. Every man strived to avoid making the least splash as the oars entered the water. Ten more minutes and a hundred yards retraced, Pat called a halt to turn the tiny boat about and disentangle the lines of the towed boats.

Friday 10th March 1826   22:00   *Messalonghi*

'A quarter-mile and no further,' declared Kladis, surrounded by the Surprises, the party of Greeks strung out in a long line in front and behind. Jason, wrapped in blankets was carried on the shoulders of four Greeks, the Surprises and others sharing the burden in rotation, for he was too weak to stand. Cold, sodden and plastered with mud from head to toe, the escapees from Vasiladi plodded on.

At least, as Kladis had promised, the second part of their trek had proved to be less debilitating than the first, the seawater generally reaching to chests not chins, and the chain of tiny islets all along the way providing periodic relief from the strength-sapping chill of the water. Notwithstanding this, every man was struggling. They were unaccustomed to such prolonged and extreme immersion in the water, their feet perpetually bogged in the mud, and every step was hard work. No food had they eaten for twenty-four hours, their only refreshment having been a few sips of freshwater and an occasional gulp of a thin red wine. It had left everyone debilitated to the point of collapse. Only the mutual encouragement and assistance of shipmates and friends sustained those men who were close to giving up, who were near to lying down on one or other of the barren, low islets. Rest, precious rest tempted every man for a few seconds in every minute before helping hands, kindly words and sometimes curses restored a modicum of determination to wavering minds. The tired and weary struggled on, lifting legs for just one more footstep, and then another; ever onwards, always close to collapse, often stumbling, nearly falling when close companions always seized arms and offered a tiny gesture of support in their own utter exhaustion.

The town was finally looming before them in the darkness and the leading Greeks staggered ashore on the beach, a dozen of sentries calling out and rushing towards them as Giachomouzzi's shattered men shouted out in reply. The Surprises followed, their wearied bodies from somewhere finding the energy to make a few more steps. Legs, seemingly too heavy to lift for a half-hour or longer, now found rekindled strength to carry the shattered men the final hundred yards to refuge and safety.

'Come on! Keep going!' shouted Duncan, 'On! On to the town, where we will rest; COME ON! Fifty yards more, come on! ON!' The Surprises and Greeks struggled for every weary step, any measurable pace long gone, one small step before another, plodding, their minds tired, their every limb exhausted. The beach was reached at long last and up they struggled, up out of the clawing grip of the mud, up out of the cold, chilling water, up to precious dry land. They shuffled along the strand and so to the makeshift hospital, every man collapsing outside to sit against the wall, their strength utterly finished, all succumbing to their absolute exhaustion.

Attracted by the commotion a large gathering of Greeks had come out from their houses nearby to attend to the exhausted men, more emerging after a few minutes with flasks of water, of wine, and blankets. From out of Byron's house came Pickering, Simon and Marston, the noise from the increasing numbers all about the refugees ever louder.

'Simon!' shouted Duncan weakly from where he sat on the ground. He was completely unrecognisable to his friend in his mud-coated clothing, his face similarly plastered with filth. All the time shivering, he continued to speak with difficulty, striving to order his thoughts, to croak out his words, his mouth and throat severely salt-dried, his voice almost gone. 'Simon, thank God you are here and well. Please, will you look directly to Jason first... over there, within the roll of blankets. I beg you will pay no mind to anyone else before him.'

An astonished Simon nodded, briefly seized and shook his friend's hand vigorously. Without the loss of another instant, he turned about and hastened to the unmoving bundle laid down a few yards away. A momentary glance at an unconscious Jason and he beckoned Kelynack and Pascoe, both closely behind him. 'Quickly, lose not a moment,' exclaimed Simon, 'Mr Jason is to be carried into the house, to my table - and set it close to the fire - *as close as can be* - and hurry!' The two men hastened to oblige.

'Bring these men inside, and fetch water, wine and biscuit for them,' said Pickering to Nance and Cusack, staring at the bedraggled human wrecks which were Denzel, Nance, Mason and Penberthy, all four men slumped on the ground in absolute exhaustion, lying next to Duncan and utterly inattentive. A sitting Kladis, meanwhile, was reciting events to a crouching Zouvelekis who then began organising help for his countrymen, nearly three score of them similarly spent and lying prostrate all about the environs of the house, the Messalonghi defenders helping them with water, wine and fiery, reviving arak.

'Jason, dear friend,' Simon whispered into the ear of his unmoving patient, his breathing exceedingly shallow and slow, 'Please to hear me... You are here with me and inside Byron's house, safe and warming. Your friends are all about you. Rest now, I am attending.' Fretting, he called an anxious Kelynack and Pascoe closer to the table. 'Carefully now, Kelynack, strip these sodden blankets from around Jason and then remove all his wet vestments. You are to wash him with warm water - *warm*! He is to be kept on this table close by the fire until he recovers. Pascoe, fetch more firewood, anything which will burn, the slightest thing; there is precious little flame and scarcely enough heat to interest a moth, and... Pascoe, brook no protests. Without warmth I fear for Jason. Quickly now, lose not a moment.'

'There is the town, I see a glimmer of lights,' declared Pat, the weary oarsmen lifting their heads and pausing momentarily to look round over their shoulders. 'Ten more minutes, lads, just ten minutes more and I venture we will be there... Off we go, PULL!' A renewed effort from the Surprises and the boat started forward once again. Pat stared at the vague outlines of the town under the moonlight, the fog relenting as they closed on the shore. 'Why, I venture we will drink up our grog on the beach!' he declared in loud voice, the chorus of accord shouted with heartfelt feeling and considerable relief.

The slightest twitching of his eyebrows under Simon's concerned gaze and Jason opened his eyes to stare upwards, unmoving, unspeaking, no visible muscular flexing of his face at all. 'Jason, dear friend,' Simon whispered, 'Please to blink your eyes if you can hear me.' However, the eyes closed once more and remained closed, no further indications of movement following, and Simon despaired. He seized Jason's right hand between his own and squeezed it tight, relaxing his grip and repeating the exercise on and on, unceasing for a minute, desperately hoping it would register with his friend.

The boat grounded at last in the shallows just short of the beach, and Pat and his men leaped out to wade ashore, pulling the boat up behind them and hauling on the lines to bring close the six towed boats, a shouted challenge coming out of the darkness. 'FRIENDS! We are FRIENDS! ENGLISH! Englishmen... from *Surprise*,' shouted Pat hastily. A dozen Greeks appeared from the shadows to surround them, a tense two minutes passing as the Messalonghi watch considered the arrivals, and then they relaxed, raised muskets were lowered and beckoning hands summoned the Surprises to follow the Greeks.

Sitting on the floor near the fire, which had been reinforced with dry scrub and kindling, two old chairs broken down and blazing within the flames, Duncan Macleod sat in silence and in absolute exhaustion with his four shipmates from the yawl. They were naked save for the wool blankets wrapped around them. All were sipping a fierce Turkish arak, a little warmth creeping back into their chilled bodies, the sensation of feeling finally restored to numbed fingers and toes. They nibbled gently on ship's biscuits provided by Pascoe, and so very slowly they began to feel alive once more. Marston, who had attended them since their arrival, fussed about them, asking them how they were feeling. Their clothing had been taken away by Nance, washed and wrung out, and all of it now hung astride a line hanging from the beams of the ceiling a little distance from the flames of the fire.

At his crude operating table at the other side of the fire, Simon gauged the temperature of the terracotta hot water bottles placed about Jason's torso; he continued to massage all of his friend's arms and legs in turn, pausing frequently to put his ear to Jason's chest or to take his pulse at the wrist. At least his friend appeared to have reached some degree of stabilisation, for which Simon was profoundly grateful. No further deterioration was discernible and his friend's heartbeat was holding to a regularity, despite his breathing being faint and shallow.

'How is he, colleague?' asked a concerned Marston.

'I have observed him shivering, which is no bad thing,' replied Simon. 'However, he is too weak to take anything in the mouth, I have tried with the last of the warmed coffee. We will try again in another quarter-hour if he shows the least movement, the slightest thing.'

In that moment the door swung open and in stepped Zouvelekis followed by Pat and his men. Eyes everywhere swivelled to stare at the arrivals, a euphoric surge rising in the hearts and minds of the debilitated Surprises and those men long marooned in Messalonghi. Duncan and his men remained too weak to rise from the fireside but managed feeble shouts of greeting, Pat's men engaging with them in a vociferous and excited exchange of stories whilst offering their untouched grog rations to their weak shipmates.

Pat crouched down to speak with Duncan, to hear the few words of his story of escape which was all that he could manage to utter. A weak Duncan concluded his tale and nodded in response to Pat's hand on his shoulder, the beginnings of a sense that all would be well settling in his thoughts, his mind reaching out from the confusing inability to think clearly, a debilitation of which he had only dimly been aware for many hours. As the general furore of sound and the exclamations of relief all around the room ebbed slightly, he strived to speak up again, to make Pat hear his voice over the rekindled, joyful banter filling the room. 'Please to look to Mr Jason, Pat; how is he, tell?'

At the fireside table Simon and Marston resumed their vigil over Jason as Pat approached to speak with the doctors for the first time. The relief in his voice was palpable as he greeted them, 'Simon... Michael Marston... How good it is to see you!'

'Pat! It is good to see you; indeed, it is,' declared Simon, glancing up momentarily, his eyes alternating between Pat and his patient

'How is Jason?'

'I regret that he has yet to recover consciousness after his struggle for several hours in the water...'

'Dear God!' exclaimed Pat. 'Will he?'

'The cold is severely debilitating, not only for the extremities such as fingers and toes, but more seriously for the internal organs most particularly. However, in the past hour he has exhibited trembling, and that is a most welcome indicator of his constitution, for the lack of such bodily response would be a sign that he is most exceedingly weak. I believe we may hold to our hopes that... when he warms further... he will recover.'

'Thank God and Saint Patrick for that! Now, may I beg your attention for just one moment, if you will.'

'Please, go ahead, I am listening.'

'Thank you. It is a great relief to see you both, and then to find Duncan Macleod as well... I cannot say how mightily thankful I am... greatly so... and... may I assist you in any way to prepare for returning with me... to the barky...'

'Nothing would please me more,' murmured Simon before looking up at his dearest friend in all the world. 'However, there are a deal of my patients here to minister to. You may collect that our intended evacuation... some time ago... was halted, Mr Macleod departing... not to say fleeing... the beach in haste.'

'Yes,' Pat hesitated. 'But now, I regret that with the fall of Vasiladi, all seaborne resupply to the town is likely stopped. Certainly, with Turk guns on the island, no captain will hazard his ship so close as to unload cargo... Nor can small boats contemplate the narrow passage through the shallows whilst under fire from the island. The situation is desperate... and evacuation must be carried out without delay... *without the slightest delay*. That, old friend, must be my order... you are to evacuate and without the loss of a moment.'

'That is an admirable notion, I make no doubt,' Simon sighed, 'but first these wounded men, these patients of mine... I will not abandon them to be left here without medical help, never in life; and so, brother, when you have evacuated these men... and only then... *only then* will Marston and I consider boarding your boats. Am I plain?'

'No, that don't answer,' replied Pat, his spirits sinking just a little. He looked all about the dark and dimly lit room, the glow of two lamps failing to illuminate all parts of it, the nearer faces of the recuperating Surprises lit more by the flames of the fire. 'How many patients do you tend to?'

'I venture three dozen are in my care.'

'Three dozen... *three dozen*... and there are also two dozen and more of our shipmates here from the barky...' A few seconds passed, Pat staring at Simon, 'Why, I believe we may get all aboard our boats... yes, we will... *we will!*' Pat turned back towards the fire and clapped his hands several times, the loud babble of multiple conversations falling away, every man brought to silence to listen. 'HEAR ME! Hear me! We are here with seven boats - SEVEN - with which to evacuate all of our shipmates from this place.'

'HUZZAY!' Men everywhere shouted in full voice, and loud whistles and clapping erupted from all around the room, the Greek patients everywhere staring in mystified wonder as general euphoria took hold. The mood in the room was now utterly manic, excited, the cacophony general and only gradually subsiding to expectant quietude as Pat visibly strived to resume. 'Lads! Lads! All of you... bear a hand... with the wounded... help all to the beach and the boats. *Mathew Jelbert* awaits us at Prokopanistos and... and we will get you all - *every man jack of you* - out of here directly...'

'Three cheers for Captain O'Connor!' shouted Pascoe, and the exuberant cheering began.

A joyful minute passed before Pat held his hands and arms up high. 'Thankee lads, and now... back to the barky! All of us, to the boats! Let us away... away to the dear *Surprise*!'

Bargeman	weevil (usually in the bread and biscuit)
Blunties	Old Scots term for stupid fellows
Boggies	Irish country folk
Bombard	Mediterranean two-masted vessel, ketch
Bourlota	an old brig converted to a fireship
Bower	bow anchor
Boxty	traditional Irish potato pancake
Breeks	Scots term for trousers or breeches
Bruloteer	Ship's crew member on a fireship
Bumbo	pirates' drink: rum, water, sugar and nutmeg
Burgoo	oatmeal porridge
Capabarre	misappropriation of (usually government) stores
Captain's Thins	Carr's water crackers, "a refined ship's biscuit"
Caudle	thickened, sweetened alcoholic drink like eggnog
Clegs	Scots term for large, biting flies
Coddle	Irish stew-like dish of bacon, pork sausages and potatoes
Crubeens	boiled pig's feet
Dreich	Old Scots for cold, wet, miserable weather
Drookit	Scots term for drenched
Etesian	strong, dry, summer, Aegean north winds
Felucca	small sailing boat, one or two sails of lateen rig
Fencibles	the Sea Fencibles, a naval 'home guard' militia
Flat	a person interested only in himself
Flux	inflammatory dysentery
Frumenty	a pudding made with boiled wheat, eggs and milk
Gabarre	a sizeable three-masted merchant ship, sometimes armed
Gomerel	a stupid or foolish person
The Groyne	La Coruña in north-west Spain
Hallion	a scoundrel
Hoy	small (e.g. London-Margate passengers) vessel
Jollies	Royal Marines
Kedgeree	a dish of flaked fish, rice and eggs
Kentledge	56lb ingots of pig iron for ship's ballast
Laudanum	a liquid opiate, used for medicinal purposes
Lobscouse	beef stew, north German in origin
Marchpane	marzipan
Marshalsea	19th century London debtors' prison
Mauk	Scottish for maggot
Meltemi	Greek and Turkish name for the Etesian wind
Millers	shipboard rats
Mistico	similar to the Felucca sailing vessel
Nibby	ship's biscuit
Praam	flat bottomed boat, propelled by poles in shallow water
Puling	whining in self pity
Razee	a heavy frigate, formerly a two-deck ship cut down to a single deck
Scrovies	worthless, pressed men
Scampavia	a long, low war galley
Solomongundy	a stew of leftover meats
Snotties	midshipmen
Stingo	strong ale
Treacle-dowdy	a covered pudding of treacle and fruit
Trubs	truffles
Yellow jack	Yellow fever (or flag signifying outbreak)

AFTERWORD - PTSD

If you are a serving military person or a veteran (or a friend or family member of either) who is in difficulty or affected by any form of distress, turmoil or anxiety, don't hesitate to seek help:

in the UK, contact either

SSAFA, the Armed Forces Charity

www.ssafa.org.uk/help-you/veterans

or

Combat Stress for veterans' mental health

www.combatstress.org.uk/helpline

email: helpline@combatstress.org.uk

The free telephone helpline is open 24 hours a day,

365 days a year

0800 138 1619 (veterans and families)

0800 323 4444 (serving personnel and families)

in the US, contact the Department of Veteran's Affairs

The National Centre for PTSD

www.ptsd.va.gov

call 1-800-273-8255

email: ncptsd@va.gov

Elsewhere, search the web and find your country's help providers.

Remember: courteous, caring people are standing by to help. There is nothing to be lost by calling. There is not the least shame in seeking help. There is no need to struggle on alone with PTSD difficulties. **Call.** You are not alone.

Printed in Poland
by Amazon Fulfillment
Poland Sp. z o.o., Wrocław